THE BONES BENEATH

A MILITESS & MAGE NOVEL

MONICA ENDERLE PIERCE

GOLDEN
FLOWER

STORIES THAT STAY WITH YOU

Copyright © 2019 Monica Enderle Pierce
Cover Illustration Copyright © 2019 Qistina Khalidah
Title Page Illustration Copyright © 2016 Qistina Khalidah
Copy Editor: Mel Sanders
Proofreader: Cody Arko-Omori/Fantasy Bookworm Proofreading
Cover Title Design: Scott Pierce
Book/Map Design: Monica Enderle Pierce
Print ISBN-13: 978-1-7342440-1-4

THE BONES BENEATH

GOLDEN FLOWER

STORIES THAT STAY WITH YOU

SEATTLE, WA

MONICAENDERLEPIERCE.COM

For all the couples who hold hands while facing down their demons.

KALIX
NORTHERN WASTES
Kholodson Sea
TELEYANSK
SCHORVALA
Yasan Khot
Chono Khot
Beach Camp
Lake Jera
Garrison
Ballard River
The Thumb
Sorgenes Hav
North Selga River
Floria
Talis
URSINUM
Drevya
The Fist
NALVIKA
Lake Talis
Talis
Khara
Kharaton
The Choker
THE GREAT GREEN OCEAN
AYESTRA
The Silver Sea
Ostendra
Ystwyth
BESERA
South Selga River
Eskis
Gurvan Desert
Fayet
OR-HALEE
Lake Selt
Or-Halee Cid
Vala
Selt
Fayet Desert

ONE

I t was the kind of night when thieves and lovers slipped through open windows, taking what wasn't theirs. The kind of night when kings felt their mortality while plotting assassinations and sorcerers brewed potions and raised the dead. The kind of night when Halina jerked awake, unsure if she'd called out in her sleep, struggling to escape the nightmare that had wrapped her in her worst fears.

She stared into the room's deep shadows, clenching her fists as a chill spread through her and the dream dispelled like smoke on the wind. Awake and unsettled, she turned her head. Gethen slept beside her, his profile lit by the dim glow of the bedchamber's banked fire. Premature silver dusted his black hair at his temples, the flickering firelight making its short strands glint.

He murmured in his sleep, frowned, and turned toward her, shifting the blankets. She snuggled against him, driving away the dream's chill with the surging heat they shared when they touched.

"Why are you awake?" Sleep and concern thickened his voice.

She rested her hand on his chest and asked, "When does a dream become a portent?"

Gethen opened his eyes. "Again?"

She rolled onto her back and ran her hands through her mussed, auburn locks. "If I could recall the details, maybe I could sort it out and make it go away." She sighed. "It leaves me feeling helpless. Like I can't control anything."

"Maybe that's the message."

"Ugh, don't say that. It doesn't help."

He took her right hand and absently rubbed the black band she wore on her ring finger. "Let me put another shadow on you."

With a groan, Halina sat up and faced the hearth. "I don't need protection from a dream that keeps returning because I'm picking it like a scab."

He caressed her back. His hand was warm and soothing through her white nightgown and her head drooped as she reveled in his touch. "The last time you let me protect you, it turned out to be a wise move."

She looked at him. The glowing fire lit his face — strong nose, full lips, chiseled bones. "Protect me from swords and spells, Mage, not my over-active imagination."

"I'm trying to protect you from Waldram and your brother. They won't stay home for long. Soon enough they'll muster a combined army and march south."

"I'm aware of that."

"I just want to keep you safe and alive."

She tweaked his stubbled chin. "You worry too much. Ilker won't move against me on the battlefield."

He ducked his head to kiss the halved pinky and ring finger of her left hand. "He doesn't have to. Ursinum's and Nalvika's armies, along with Quoregna's hedge witches and mages and

Waldram's shrikers will coalesce into a force directed against both of us. You know the odds are not in our favor."

"King Ilker of Ursinum is all talk. He has no love of battle. His world is the comfort of his court and the quiet temple of his One God. He'll balk at the thought of facing me across a muddy, bloody field. You'll see."

Gethen sat up. "You read Vika's message: Nalvika is conscripting peasants. Schorvala's army has closed their borders against invasion. Ursinum's armies will fall under Waldram's sway, Halina. Your lands are already occupied."

"Because they're no longer my lands!" She flopped back onto the pillows, arms crossed, brows furrowed. "Thanks for the reminder."

He brushed her curls away from her face. "The truth is ugly."

"Gethen—" Halina reached up to knock his hand away, but clasped it instead, her grip uneven from her war-stunted fingers. She met his gaze. "There's nothing you or I can do to make it pretty in the middle of the night."

"I'm putting another ambit on you tomorrow before you go to Gwyncardarnlei."

"Will that make you happy?"

"Happier, since you won't let me join you at your mother's castle."

"We've had that argument." She stroked his jaw. "Let's not have it again. Feddie and Elof need your protection here more than I do in Surquay. Gwyncardarnlei is well-protected. I want to see my mother and meet my baby brother before I take on Waldram. I need to know where their support lies — with me or with Ilker."

"Don't make them choose between the countess's daughter and the queen's son."

"Of course I won't. My hope is they'll remain neutral. I don't want Queen Ambrosine and my mother involved in this mess. They're still mourning our father's death at Waldram's hands."

He leaned over and kissed her gently. "You're a determined woman, Lady Rhyshis."

"Yes." She yawned. "A sleepy one too, Lord Rhyshis." She closed her eyes.

His fingers left heat in their wake as he trailed them over her bare shoulders, following the intersecting roadway of silvery scars, the hills and valleys of her bones and muscles. His fingers skipped from freckle to freckle, scar to scar. "I love the terrain of your body," he murmured. "I see history on your skin."

"That tickles." She squirmed. The hollow of his pelvis fit perfectly against the curve of her arse.

"Sorry."

"No, you're not."

There was a smile behind his words as he replied, "You're right, I'm not."

Gethen and Halina sparked power within each other. His first touch had stolen her wits and her breath. Heat and lust had burned through her, mirrored in the intensity of his reaction. And he'd saved her when Waldram had stolen most of her blood magic, nearly ending her life. Using his own sorcery, Gethen had rekindled blood magic's flame in her veins and sent it surging with the power of their shared connection.

Magic linked them, though she didn't understand how.

Blood magic flowed through Halina's veins. It protected her in battle and made her a compelling leader, but she couldn't cast spells or summon shadows the way her husband did. She couldn't understand animals or draw power from their spirits like him. But when Waldram had drained that magic from her, she'd felt her life force dimming with it. The two were intertwined – her blood magic and her soul.

She captured Gethen's fingers and kissed his palm. "You, sir, are nothing but trouble."

"Then we're perfectly matched."

She laughed and turned her head, an unspoken request. He obliged with the kiss she craved then rested his hand on her hip, pulled her back against his front, and sighed contentedly.

Halina inhaled. Her husband smelled of honey, wax, and herbs from time spent brewing potions; like sex, smoke, and mead from their evening together. She closed her eyes again.

Ranith Citadel was quiet in the still summer night and only the distant crash of waves on the Silver Sea's shores gave a voice to the night.

The gentle movement of Gethen's body lulled her as his breathing slowed and deepened. Yet she couldn't sleep. The dream was a reminder that war loomed and she couldn't control her destiny. Or his. No matter how much she kicked and screamed and fought to do so.

Halina was a tool for the gods and her people. She hoped fervently to serve both well, restore peace and sanity to Quoregna, and live a quiet life with Gethen at her side.

Failure was unthinkable.

TWO

"How's this, Master Gethen?"

Gethen took the small jar his young apprentice, Elof, offered him. "This is the healing unguent I asked you to make?" He dipped his little finger into the warm, yellowish salve, wiped it off, and nodded as his skin tingled, cooled, then became numb. He sniffed the jar, wrinkled his nose, and coughed. "Bit heavy on the white rose oil, but the formulation's effective nevertheless. How long does the numbness last?"

"How long?"

Gethen arched a brow at the boy. "You didn't test it?"

Elof screwed up his face and hunched his shoulders, looking like a dog waiting to be kicked. "I forgot," he said in a small voice. He'd gained a little height and heft in the four months since Gethen had found the nine-year-old servant boy hiding with Nalvika's adolescent princess in a hedge witch's hut.

Gethen held up his finger, now deadened from tip to the first joint. "Six hours is ideal. More than that and I'll be teaching you another formulation."

"I'm sorry, master."

"Don't be sorry. Be smart. A healer always tests his formulations on himself before giving them to his patients. Do you want to be a healer or a quack?"

"A healer like my Aunt Lauma. More than anything."

"Then don't skip steps. Did you memorize the incantation I gave you?"

"Yes, Your Lordship."

"Good." Gethen drew a small dagger from his belt. "Prove it." He winked at Princess Federika — who sat on the small sofa beneath the stillroom's only window — and pulled the blade across the meat of his palm. After several months of instruction, Elof was proving a good candidate for taking over Magod's work at Ranith and, eventually, Gethen's own healing arts.

"What are you doing?" the boy asked, eyes wide as blood pooled in Gethen's palm.

"Testing you." He held out his hand. "Heal it." He nodded encouragement as the boy gaped at the cut. "Picture the wound healing in your mind as you employ the incantation."

"I—" Elof hesitated. "Are you sure I can do this?"

"I'm sure." Blood dripped between his fingers onto the hearth as he tipped his hand to avoid staining his sleeve. "Focus on the work. Believe you will heal this cut as you invoke the spell." He met Elof's worried gaze. "I won't let you fail."

The boy nodded and stared at the wound. He frowned, looked up at Gethen, and asked, "May I touch your hand, Your Lordship?"

"If that will help you."

His face a mask of concentration, Elof sandwiched Gethen's palm between his hands, closed his eyes, and spoke the incantation. Green light shimmered around his fingers. Warmth and tingling followed. The boy peered at his work and his voice wavered.

"Focus," Gethen repeated.

Elof nodded and the spell strengthened, the glow brightened, the warmth increased. A tugging sensation pulled at Gethen's skin. Elof opened his eyes and released his master's hand. "Did I do it?" he whispered.

Gethen wiped his palm then showed his hand to his student, a pink, puckered line where the fresh wound had been. "Success."

"I did it?" Elof whooped. "I did it!" Grinning, he turned to the others. "Did you see that, Feddie? I healed Master Gethen's hand."

"Very well done," the young Nalvik princess remarked, trying to sound more mature than her thirteen years as she looked up from her stitching.

Odruna said, "I told you there's magic in you." She lounged on the sofa beside her fellow militess, Marja, honing a dagger's blade, the rings in her black braids clinking when she moved her head.

A brown-skinned, blue-eyed, scarred Schorvalan, Odruna Sklaar was second in command of the Order of the Red Blades — a small force of loyal soldiers and assassins Halina had formed during the War of the Winds. The militesses were at Ranith protecting Princess Federika Janne Boorsook from her insane father, Nalvika's King Waldram. Their keen eyes, sharp blades, and relentless discipline proved why Halina trusted them with the girl's life.

Elof grabbed Gethen's hand and examined his work, turning it this way and that, prodding and stretching the wound.

"It's a bit tender," Gethen remarked dryly, and the boy let go with a hasty apology. "Healing salve?" He nodded toward the little jar of unguent.

"Oh! Right." Elof snatched it from the table and scooped out a generous gob, pausing as Gethen shook his head.

"It takes very little if you've formulated it correctly."

The boy nodded, wiped most on the inner lip of the container, then smeared a thin line along the healed wound. He scurried off to find a length of bandaging for Gethen's hand. After returning and wrapping the wound, he looked around Ranith Citadel's small library. "Feddie, let me cut you."

"What? No!" She glared at him, embroidery needle poised and glinting.

"Come on. It'll only hurt for a minute. I promise I'll heal it really fast."

Odruna and Marja laughed. Gethen shook his head. "This isn't permission to wound people," he said. "Healers *heal*. Remember?"

Elof looked down, chagrinned again. "I'm sorry. I just want to practice."

Feddie sniffed and raised her narrow chin imperiously. "Then practice on yourself."

The boy snatched the dagger off the table and snaked it across his thumb.

Gethen made a disapproving sound, but this new ability entranced Elof.

The Schorvalan militess smirked. "Bet you did the same thing when you learned that spell, Lord Rhyshis."

He returned her gaze but not her amusement. "No. Shadow Mage Shemel did it for me."

Elof looked up after making a second cut across his little finger. "If your master healed your wounds, how did you learn to do it yourself?"

"He didn't heal them," Gethen replied, "he made them. The bloodier my wounds, the brighter his mood."

"Oh." Elof looked down at his wounded hands.

Gethen started to reassure the boy that he wouldn't imitate his dead master when something tugged on his senses. Wordlessly, he turned from the hearth and strode from the library, heading for Ranith Citadel's small bailey.

The wicket door creaked as Odruna followed him outside. "What is it?"

"Someone's at the edge of my ward." He went to the stable and quickly saddled Remig.

"Friend or foe?"

"Both. I recognize Captain Thaksin's unmistakably irritating presence."

Her dark eyes widened. "Were you expecting him?"

"No."

Halina's former captain was a jealous prick who'd never hidden his contempt for Gethen, but he was utterly selfless when it came to Halina's well-being. Gethen loathed and admired the pillock in equal measure.

"Stay with the children." He swung into the saddle and urged Remig to a jog as Odruna opened the bailey gate.

Thick fog shrouded the Silver Sea and stretched inland. An unseasonal brume dampening Gethen's spirits, it clung to Kharayan Tor and curled around the forest's tall trees, making the dense woods seem even more haunted than usual. Not even Ranith Citadel, perched atop the tor, escaped the blanketing mist.

Though Gethen couldn't see farther than Remig's nose, he and the horse knew the path through Kharayan Woods after a lifetime of traversing it. They continued at an easy clip toward the line of black stones that encircled the woods and demarcated the start of Gethen's deadly wards and the end of his hospitality for all but a few. He was the Sun Mage, the Keeper of the Voidline — Herra Tomruma — a necromancer of ill repute earned not by his own actions but by the monstrous practices of his numerous predecessors. Still, a reputation, earned or not, had its advantages for a man who preferred the company of the tor's animals and the bees in his bee yard to the majority of Quoregna's people.

Captain Thaksin was not one of the few Gethen willingly hosted, but the man was undyingly faithful to Halina. So they maintained an uneasy peace. But with her gone to visit her mother in Surquay across the Silver Sea, Gethen couldn't imagine a pleasant reason for Thak's unexpected visit.

The darkness of the foggy woods lightened as the trees thinned near the ward line, and Gethen slowed Remig to a walk. Figures moved beyond the stones, growing distinct as he neared.

"Captain Thaksin," he called. "What brings you to Ranith?"

Tow-headed and bearing a face as weather-beaten and scarred as a carriage wheel, the captain of Kharaton Castle's guard stood just the other side of the invisible ward line.

"You'd know if it wasn't for this damned fog," he replied.

Three soldiers wearing the blue-gray of Besera accompanied Thak. Gethen was startled to spy the four-petaled, golden liminth flower of the Rhysh royal line — his family's insignia — emblazoned on their tabards. His gaze immediately went to the remaining members of their party, three women and a small child. All wore servants' clothes, but the two who stood out to him were a dark-haired, dark-freckled, young woman and the ebon-haired toddler sleeping in her arms.

"Cerys?" Gethen was stunned to find his brother's wife and son on his doorstep. He dropped the ward with a flick of his fingers and a murmured incantation, then gestured for them to join him. "Come across. It's safe."

When all stood within the arms of Kharayan Woods, Gethen raised the ward, gathered the group together, and used a travel incantation to bring them to the citadel's bailey. Besera's queen blanched and staggered as the swirl of amber magic and fog dispelled to reveal Ranith's walls. Gethen steadied her. The soldiers muttered curses and prayers, likely inspired as much by the tower's snarling stone demons and skeletal death's heads as by the sorcery itself.

Prince Gerezel lifted his curly head from his mother's shoulder, gazed around wide-eyed, and said, "More, Unca Geden."

Gethen took his nephew from Queen Cerys. "Later, after you've eaten and slept. There'll be lots of time for magic and tricks." He led the group into the kitchen from the bailey.

Odruna met them there. She bowed to the queen when he introduced them. Her smile for Thaksin was lascivious — they had a pleasurable history — but she kept her hand on her sword's hilt as she took in the sooty and bloody soldiers.

Gethen settled the queen and captain at the citadel's dining table. The two women accompanying the queen were a lady-in-waiting and Gerezel's nursemaid. Elof laid out bread and cheese, sunfruits, and mead. Marja fed the soldiers in the kitchen. Feddie was hiding, as she'd been instructed to do should strangers arrive.

Gethen sat with his nephew on his lap. The boy happily dug into the food. "Has Ystwyth fallen?"

"To Ursinum," Thaksin answered grimly.

Cerys picked at a piece of bread, offering bits to her son but eating little herself. She arranged her rumpled beige skirts around her legs. The hems were muddied and watermarked, stained with blood, ash, and soil. She was a small, elegant woman with dark eyes, a narrow band of brown freckles across her nose and cheeks, and thin Beseran stripes that curved from the nape of her neck, over her collar bones, and below the neckline of her worn gown. She was a great beauty but inexperienced with politics and war.

She wore a brave face, but the tremor in her voice betrayed her as she told their story. "Ursinum's army emerged from the fog five days ago. Besera's troops bravely battled to the death, but the surrounding villages were burning and the attackers had breached the citadel when the king ordered our escape."

Gethen covered her hand with his. "What of my brother?"

Thaksin answered, "King Zelal took the surviving guards into Ystwyth's mountains. He'll ambush Ilker's and Etherias's troops as they march onward. We burned their ships, so retreat means a long slog over burned ground, surrounded by enemies."

"Was Nalvika involved?" Odruna asked.

"They weren't part of the attack," Thaksin replied.

Gethen considered the captain. "How did you come to be Queen Cerys's protector?"

"My men and I tracked a shriker to Ystwyth. We couldn't believe our eyes when Ursinum's forces came ashore and set fire to Besera's fishing villages. We hurried for Ystwyth Citadel to warn King Zelal."

"They saved many lives," Cerys said, offering Thaksin a grateful smile.

"If Zelal received an early warning, how did the citadel and keep fall?" Gethen asked.

"Treachery," she replied. "Someone opened the East Gate from inside the citadel."

Gethen inhaled sharply. "Who?"

"A dead man. His fellow soldiers cut him down, but not before Ursinum forced their way through," Thak explained.

Gethen stood. "I'm going to Ystwyth. If Ilker's forces remain, I'll make sure they never set foot on any ground again."

This wasn't his mandate. As Herra Tomruma his responsibility was to all of Quoregna not one kingdom. He'd be punished by Skiron, the God of Death, for this transgression. But he couldn't stand by and watch his wife's brother destroy his homeland and his own family. Especially since the attack was predicated on lies and manipulation brought about by Gethen's own dead master.

He went to a small room adjacent to the servants' quarters where he stored his travel gear. He took a short, hooded cloak from a peg on the wall and pulled it over his head. But his hands slowed.

Cerys made him think of Halina.

Souls fueled Gethen's necromancy — animal or human — though he gained the greatest power from human vitality. But using human life force quickly grew into a savage addiction. And the greatest source of that power was the rare soul imbued with blood magic, like his wife's.

Gethen missed Halina fiercely. He missed her strength, her wit, and her stubbornness. He missed her beautiful, scarred body.

And he missed the blood magic that flowed through her, inextricably tied to her soul.

Halina's blood magic was spellbinding. And that frightened Gethen. It made him question the nature of his love for her. But he refused to lose his wife to his own necromantic drives. He would sacrifice himself before he'd harm her.

At the sound of boot heels, Gethen turned. Odruna and Thaksin entered the room as he donned his leather brigandine.

"I'll come with you," the Schorvalan Red Blade said.

"No, you have two queens and a crown prince to protect." He glanced at Thaksin and added, "Both of you."

Thak offered his hand to Gethen. "Once again I find I'm grateful to know you, Your Lordship."

"I share that unenviable state," Gethen replied and clasped the man's hand.

Odruna said, "We'll defend them with our lives."

"I know you will." Even as he answered, Gethen's travel incantation swirled around him, tugging at the loose hood of his travel cloak. It shifted his world from the confines of Ranith's small storage room to Ystywyth's great bailey.

He knew Besera's situation was grim even before his feet hit the ground. The spell settled around him in a swirl of red embers and black soot.

THREE

"So Ilker revoked your title," said Queen Ambrosine as she set aside her embroidery and considered Halina from her spot on the silver sofa in Gwyncardarnlei's parlor.

Sunset's amber light slanted through the castle's tall windows and birds squabbled in the garden's trees, battling for the best night roost. Halina squinted against the golden rays and traced the window's diamond lattice. She was a blade in search of a specific throat to cut. A leader in want of an army, a mourner in need of revenge's balm. "And he seized my lands," she elaborated. Behind her Arevik sewed and their mother nursed the infant crown prince.

Surquay's castle stood atop the sharp apex of the Surquay Ridge surrounded by mountain hemlocks and golden chinquapins. The castle's eastside windows normally offered an unobstructed view of the North Selga River, Khara, and the sharp, snow-covered Valmerian Mountains stretching from north to south. Today, however, heavy fog boiled below the ridge, obscuring all but treetops and tall peaks. The tumbling murk imitated Halina's churning emotions and she turned away from the tenebrous view.

Ursinum's dowager queen, Ambrosine watched her husband's daughter, her embroidery forgotten in her lap. "On what grounds?" she asked. Her silver hair sat coiled atop her head in a neat crown, held in place by combs bejeweled with black pearls. She wore gray silk, though the mourning period for Ursinum's murdered king had long passed.

Halina settled on the sofa beside Arevik. She drew her longsword from its scabbard and fished a whetstone from a haversack on the floor. She laid a rag over the skirts of her ivory kirtle and pale-green silk surcoat then began honing the weapon's edge. Its blade sang as she ran the stone down its length. "On the presumption that the Sun Mage's power corrupted my mind, leading me to move against Ursinum's interests."

Small but by no means unimposing, the dowager queen considered Halina with eyes the same dark-green hue and hardness of Teleyansk jade. "So your brother accuses your new husband of controlling you."

If Halina's father had been the Bear King in life, his wife was a viper in high grass waiting to strike anyone who threatened her den. King Vernard had controlled the army and, by all outward appearances, the kingdom. But those in the royal inner circle knew Ambrosine held the king's coffers and, therefore, the Bear's leash. Vernard had done little without his wife's input. Their son, Ilker, the newly crowned king, appeared not to have learned that lesson.

"I have yet to meet the man who can control Halina against her will," Ianthe said, contempt in her melodious voice. She sat to Halina's left, her infant son, Prince Vernard, at her breast. With hair, eyes, and freckles the color of rich earth contrasting with her fair skin, the beauty of King Vernard's consort distracted fools from her intellect. If Ambrosine had controlled the king's purse, the Countess of Surquay had held the man by the bollocks while he lived. She'd given him five children, including Halina and Arevik.

"Ilker shouldn't punish you for what isn't your doing," Arevik remarked, her voice hard.

"True," the queen remarked. "And I bet that stings," she added, her bland expression veiled.

"Yes, as a matter of fact, it does. I fought harder than he did for land and title." Halina paused in sharpening her weapon. "But that's not what nettles me most."

"What then?" her mother asked. The countess brought a lighter touch to Ursinum's court than its queen did, but she was not softer than Ambrosine.

"That my own brother questions my loyalty to Ursinum and our father."

Arevik nodded. "There's not a more faithful servant to this kingdom than the Red Blade, and Ilker knows it."

Ambrosine murmured, "What's gotten into my idiot son's head?"

"Necromancy," Halina replied.

Ambrosine's gaze sharpened. "Your new husband's?"

"No, Waldram's," Arevik answered. Halina and her sister shared their father's red hair and fair skin, but the younger Persinna sister had their mother's ethereal beauty and melodious voice.

Ianthe sucked a hissing breath between her teeth and exchanged a knowing look with the queen. "So Waldram Boorsook inherited his Uncle Shemel's propensities."

Halina said, "He did and received dubious training from that dead shadow mage, unbeknownst to anyone."

"Slippery as slug slime and poisonous as hog's weed, that boy," Ambrosine muttered. "I never liked him." Her gaze passed Halina to land on Arevik. "You believe your sister's story of

Waldram's attack on her in Drevya Linna? You believe he's responsible for King Vernard's death?"

"Absolutely," Ursinum's younger princess replied. "I couldn't testify to what I didn't personally witness, but Halina wouldn't lie about such a thing, no matter how much she — *we* — loathe Waldram."

Ianthe and Ambrosine nodded.

"While I treasure my sister's support, Your Highness, what I really need is you and my mother to believe my accusations against Nalvika's prick."

Ambrosine resumed her embroidery. "Should we not?"

Halina sighed. "So few have, but..." She faltered.

"But what?" Ianthe prompted.

"But I find it hard to believe anyone's sympathy is genuine." She reached for her sister's hand and added, "With the exception of Arevik and her good husband." She resumed honing her sword blade. Light winked on its edge.

Ambrosine replied, "I am not anyone, child, and Ilker was my son before he became my king. I know his limitations."

Ianthe added, "Your reputation as the Red Blade precedes you, daughter, as does Waldram's splenetic history with you."

Halina ducked her head, gratified. "Losing Ilker's support and facing his accusations hurt me more than you know."

Ianthe sighed. She absently fingered the round brooch she always wore. A token of King Vernard's love, it depicted a gold bear with garnet eyes surrounded by ivory nightingales. "Your brother always supported and defended you, especially in conflicts with Waldram. The only explanation for his abandonment is magic and manipulation."

Halina nodded.

Far removed from the royal court at Tatlis and Waldram's fomenting conflict, Gwyncardarnlei sheltered Ianthe and the infant Prince Vernard, providing an opportunity for mother and child to bond. The countess had retreated to her castle after the king's burial, mourning the murder of the only man she'd ever loved. Queen Ambrosine had joined her, reluctant to remain in Tatlis while the peers jockeyed for King Ilker's favor. In the void created by the absence of the queen and the king's consort, King Waldram had asserted influence over Ursinum's new king, much to Halina's detriment.

As servants lit braziers and candles throughout the room, Halina ran a cloth down her sword and considered the blade, inspecting it for corrosion. Seeing none, she slid the weapon into its scabbard and returned the rag and whetstone to her haversack. Her hands ached. She flexed her fingers, then cracked her knuckles. They'd seen a lot of war, her hands; scarred front to back, callused from tip to wrist, halved fingers on the left, black ring on the right. Battle had shaped her hands, just as it had made her body lean and muscular and scarred, and her mind sharper than her sword. In this parlor of noble ladies, Halina stood out. Then again, she'd been the freckled freak in Ursinum's court, ridiculed and shunned until she'd started breaking bones and winning battles.

Perhaps she shouldn't be surprised to find herself dismissed again.

"Waldram created those new scars on your palms?" Ambrosine asked.

Halina looked up, startled from her dark thoughts. She considered the pink puncture scars marring her hands. "Yes, Your Highness. In Drevya Linna."

"To take your blood magic?" Her mother shifted the satiated infant prince to her shoulder and gently patted his back. Halina nodded and the countess said, "Your father had the warrior's magic, as did your grandfather. It skipped Waldram's side of the family."

"Covetous, little prick," Ambrosine remarked. "Waldram

wanted that power and resented its appearance in a bastard of the line."

Halina's mother and the queen had advocated for her many times when her father underestimated her because she was a girl. But Ianthe and Ambrosine always believed in her. "You're the strongest of his children," the queen had told her when she was young and her brothers had left her behind once again while they went off on an adventure, and the king had said that was the way of things when she'd complained.

"Girls belong in the parlor. Boys belong on the battlefield," he'd said.

"Bollocks on that," Halina had told her father and received a sharp slap for mouthing off.

Ambrosine had found her nursing a fat lip. "Your mother and I make the hard decisions," the queen told her that day. "Your father is the voice that pronounces them, but we decide who lives and dies, who's worthy of Ursinum's support and gold, and who belongs in a ditch. One day, King Vernard will recognize his eldest daughter's power. One day you'll wear a crown."

"I don't want a crown, Your Highness. I just want to go on adventures like the boys do."

Ambrosine had gazed at her with intense jade eyes. "You'll have plenty of those too, child."

Halina sighed. The growing conflict with Waldram and Ilker was an adventure she never asked for and didn't want. The price for it kept climbing higher and grinding her down. Her gaze strayed to Prince Vernard's face, slack and angelic in sleep. "No one's safe as long as Waldram wears Nalvika's crown," she said, "especially not Quoregna's children. But few offers of aid have reached me."

Ambrosine sneered. "The peers are cowards." She slid a needle through the black silk handkerchief on her embroidery loom, adding the smallest of five red cubs gazing up at a large, red bear. The kerchief was a gift for the little prince.

"What about Ayestra?" Arevik asked. "Did King Danas agree to provide troops?"

"No. He only offered recognition of my marriage," Halina replied.

"But Danas owes you." Arevik frowned and set aside her sewing. "Ayestra owes you. The four kingdoms owe you!"

"He offered the use of some ships." Halina gently stroked Prince Vernard's wispy amber hair, careful not to wake him. She envied her infant brother's untroubled sleep.

"You need soldiers, not ships," Arevik groused as she returned to her stitches. "A few boats won't stop Waldram."

"I won't look a gift horse in the mouth."

"Not if it's showing you its arse," Ambrosine muttered, and Halina laughed.

Twilight's darkness overtook the world outside the windows. Servants closed the gold velvet curtains and unbanked the fire on the hearth. The countess's butler served mulsum, an aperitif Gethen made from honey, white wine, and water. Halina had brought a case with her knowing it was her mother's favorite.

"How long have you led this torrid affair with the Sun Mage?" Queen Ambrosine leaned forward, scrutinizing Halina, a mischievous glint in her dark-green eyes. "Years, I hope."

Ianthe snickered. Arevik's expression wavered between amused and mortified.

Halina paused mid-sip. "I beg your pardon, Your Highness." She lowered her glass. "Affair?"

Ambrosine drained her drink, dabbed mulsum from her lips, and said, "Don't act shocked, Halina. It's not like you to be demure. It's about damn time that mage descended from Ranith's dark tower to join the rest of Quoregna. He's spent too much time locked away with his potions and powers. Meanwhile the world's gone to shit." She waggled her empty glass and a servant scurried over to refill it. She finished this glass in one long draft, swallowed, and returned her attention to Halina as the servant replenished her aperitif. "Well?"

"We met last fall when His Majesty ordered me to negotiate for Gethen's allegiance against Besera during the salt crisis."

Ianthe said, "Let me guess, Vernard said to bring him Lord Rhyshis's fealty or his head."

"And you got confused about which head he meant," Ambrosine added. Both women laughed and even Arevik giggled.

Halina met the queen's gaze and said, "I decided I liked both."

"Well played, Red Blade," the queen said, her amusement morphing into satisfaction. "Ianthe and I told your father Gethen Rhysh was the man you should marry. The stubborn fool ignored us for years."

"He did," Ianthe agreed. "Dug himself in deeper with every marriage contract he considered for you. We told him the man you'd wed was one more dangerous than you, and only Herra Tomruma qualified."

"That snake Waldram Boorsook certainly did not," the queen added as a gong sounded, calling them to the evening meal. She downed her third drink and strode across the room, her strides rock-steady. Like Halina, Ambrosine was renowned for her capacity to drink soldiers and dignitaries under the table while beating them at bones and loosening their tongues to steal state secrets.

After eating, the women retired to their rooms. Halina had changed into her nightgown when she was summoned to her mother's chambers. Pausing at the bedroom door, she said, "Is everything all right?"

"Of course." Ianthe directed her to the dressing table and

picked up her wooden comb. "It's been a very long time since I last readied you for bed."

Halina sat. "You want to comb my hair?" she asked and worked the braids loose from her wavy auburn hair as her mother nodded.

Ianthe stood behind her, sectioned her hair, and got to work. "Don't you ever comb this nest?"

"You sound like Gethen."

"Wise man. I admire him if he can offer such criticism and keep his bollocks."

People said Halina looked like her mother but with her father's auburn coloring.

She considered Ianthe's delicate, dark features in the looking glass and didn't see the resemblance. Gethen — gods bless him — called her blind. Halina smiled. "He's a good man, better than anyone knows."

"Tell me about him," Ianthe murmured.

"He...he holds space for me." She met her mother's reflected gaze. "Do you know what I mean?" She continued without waiting for an answer. "Gethen saved my life, more than once."

"He's not the first man to do that."

"No, of course not. But he saves me from myself."

Ianthe made a small, knowing noise.

"Gethen accepts me for who I am — scarred and flawed and stubborn. Temperamental. He's never asked me to be someone that I'm not. And...I feel safe being vulnerable with him. He has unimaginable strength, Mother, not because of magic, but because he's known such suffering."

"Has he?"

"Oh, yes. Shemel was cruel to him when he was an apprentice, brutal. And Gethen fears parts of himself. He's humble in ways that he has every reason not to be, but he believes deep down that he's an undeserving monster. Yet nothing could be further from the truth." Halina met her mother's gaze again. "Nothing."

"I remember him as a quiet, thoughtful boy. He was diligent about his position as Besera's crown prince. Zelal has done a fine job for Besera, but many of us were disappointed to see Gethen taken from his throne by Shadow Mage Shemel. Gethen Rhysh would've made a truly great king."

Halina nodded. "I believe that."

They fell into companionable silence, both savoring a rare moment as Ianthe braided Halina's hair. Nightjars and mocking-birds warbled to the moon and the eerie calls of night herons echoed in the distance, rising from their nests among the North Selga's reedy shore.

"I failed the king," Halina said as Ianthe took a hair tie from her.

"How?" the countess asked. "Did you not fight to protect his life?"

Halina looked up. "Of course I did. I fought desperately to save him."

Ianthe rested her hands on her daughter's broad shoulders. "Then you didn't fail your father."

Halina stood and paced away, her white nightgown swirling around her long legs. She stopped at the bassinet where her tiny brother slept, swaddled and warm. "But this was the most important fight of all, and I lost, and our father died. In my own castle. At my own table. At the hands of the men I hired." She sighed. "Because of my failure, this boy will never know his father."

Ianthe came to her side and stroked her hair. "You're not going to win every battle."

"I know, Mother, but I have to try. The gods made me a fighter and I have to do better than I did at Kharaton. For my littlest brother. For all of Quoregna's children."

"And you will." Ianthe smoothed the infant prince's fine auburn hair. "You were born fighting, Halina, screaming bloody murder and waving your fists, already looking for a foe. You shat all over the midwife, took another breath, and started screeching again."

Halina laughed.

"Of all my children," Ianthe continued, "you were the one made for battle. My warrior princess. If anyone can protect our world's littlest ones, it's you." She caught Halina's hand and pulled her away from the sleeping baby and over to a sofa beside the windows. They sat and Ianthe continued. "Halina, you're troubled by the king's death and the loss of your lands and title, Ilker's rejection, and Waldram's attacks. You feel lessened by these things."

Halina stared at her scarred palms. "Waldram came very close to achieving my death."

"It's not the first time you've almost died in battle."

"But this wasn't in battle. This was at dinner in my castle. When I close my eyes I see the king bleeding to death. I hear Arevik screaming. And I'm helpless to stop it." She fisted her hands. "I'm hanging in Drevya Linna again, bleeding out as Waldram crows in triumph and his shrikers fawn at his heels. I'm administering the blessings of the dead to soldiers who were betrayed by men who worked beside them for months, and I'm feeling Waldram's breath on my ear and his body against me. I'm drowning in the oubliette and he's laughing at my terror. I'm the Red Blade of Or-Halee. I was a leader of soldiers, the Margrave of Khara. But all that is meaningless when I can't even protect my father in my own home at my own table."

Ianthe took her hands. "Red Blade. Margrave. Princess. Leader. All of that was stripped away. But none of it determines who you are deep down in your bones, Halina. Titles are meaningless. Actions matter. Intentions matter. Your survival *matters*."

Halina sighed and let her mother draw her down into a hug. She closed her eyes. "You've always made me feel strong."

"Because you are strong, Halina. The strongest of my children."

"Lady Rhyshis!"

Pounding at her chamber door had Halina out of bed, dagger in hand, before her brain registered what her body was doing. Stars still speckled the dark-blue sky and not even the cocks were awake to crow.

"Lady Rhyshis!"

Halina yanked open the door, grabbed the servant by his collar, and dragged him into the room. She stuck her misericord beneath his chin. "This better be urgent."

Eyes wide, the boy swallowed, his throat bobbing beneath the blade's sharp point. "Queen Ambrosine requires your attendance in her chamber."

Halina released him. "Of course. Tell Her Highness I'll come with all haste."

The boy nodded and scuttled from the room. Halina kicked the door closed and cursed herself. Away from Gethen, she didn't sleep soundly and looked for enemies around every corner at all hours of the day and night.

She dressed quickly and reached Ambrosine's apartment in minutes. Her mother was already there and both women looked up from a map of Quoregna as Halina entered the queen's blue-and-gold sitting room.

Ambrosine held out a small parchment. "This message just reached us from Besera, sent by your Captain Thaksin. Ursinum's troops made landfall five days ago, taking advantage of the fog. Ystwyth is burning and the castle is under siege."

Halina stared at the message, blinked, and cursed choice words about her brother and all the idiocy in the world. "That larking arsehole." King Ilker had proven himself a disappointment. "He has shit for brains and less backbone than a donkey's cock."

Queen Ambrosine continued, "King Zelal begs our intervention in the matter."

"I'll go to Ystwyth," Halina said. "Besera aided Khara when my people were starving and our own aid wouldn't arrive for months."

The queen nodded. "Present our commands to your brother. This attack upon our ally is unwarranted and unacceptable. Ursinum must withdraw immediately from Ystwyth."

Arevik entered, cinching her robe around her narrow waist. "What's happened?"

Halina passed her the parchment.

Ianthe said, "I worry about sending you, Halina. This may be a trap to lure you out of hiding."

She nodded. "It may. Which is why I'll return to my husband and request his protection. Gethen won't refuse. This threatens all of Quoregna."

"Blood and bones," Arevik said as she lowered the parchment.

"Zelal may blame you for this attack," Ambrosine warned.

"And he'd be partly right. Which is why I need to put an end to this before the whole world catches fire." Halina considered the unfurled map. "Arevik, evacuate the queen, our mother and brother to Ayestra."

Ambrosine shook her head. "King Waldram's disagreement isn't with Surquay. I'll remain here with Ianthe and the prince. Arevik will return home and carry the news to King Danas. I won't be chased across the four kingdoms by my son's stupidity."

Halina's jaw tightened. "Surquay is Beseran, Your Highness.

There's no guarantee Waldram won't bring war here. And he doesn't respect the women of the Persinna royal line."

"Ilker won't allow harm to come to us," Ianthe said. "Gwyncardarnlei is safe."

Halina knew she couldn't win. "If the fighting nears, please go west. Arevik and Magod will protect you." She glanced at her sister who nodded. "Don't try to reach Tatlis," Halina warned. "Promise me that, both of you. I can't bear to lose another member of my family to Waldram's madness."

"Very well," Ianthe said. "We'll seek shelter in Ayestra, if threatened."

"Don't wait until their forces are upon you. Please."

"We won't, child," Ambrosine replied. "I've no wish to lose my hide, especially to that little prick's blade."

Ianthe touched Halina's elbow. "I'll have my boatswain take you across the Silver Sea to the foot of Kharayan Tor."

"No need. I have other ways of reaching Gethen more quickly." At her mother's puzzled expression, she squeezed the woman's fingers and added, "You forget I married a mage."

Halina returned to her chamber and threw her few belongings into her haversack, slung that over her shoulder, and checked the sword at her hip. She'd been a little annoyed by her husband's insistence on creating another ambit for her protection, but once again she found its existence useful. "I'll never hear the end of it," she muttered. She set her shoulders and exhaled a slow breath, steeling her nerves.

"Ambit, take me to Gethen."

FOUR

"Blood and bones," Gethen whispered as he stared at the blackened remains of his childhood home.

Ystwyth Castle's ramparts had collapsed. The keep's roof had tumbled into the baileys and great hall, smashed the kitchen and obliterated the royal quarters. The gardens were nothing but ash and stumps, befouled fountains with fire-scored statuary, and the old bee tree — where he'd first discovered the magic within himself — was a smoldering lump. Khotyr's marble face and figure were blackened, her flowing gown cracked from the heat. Semele drowned in her fountain's blackened water, her upraised arms broken, her face smashed.

Only Skiron still stood on his perch in the trampled and gutted Temple Courtyard. His arrogant smirk nettled Gethen, as if the God of Death found the whole sad scene amusing. Gethen fought a sudden urge to blast the statue with a mass spell, send it tumbling backward off its pedestal to bash Skiron's marble brains out on the courtyard steps.

The West Tower still stood and he took its stone steps two at once until he reached the top. Thinning fog lingered on the Silver Sea and sat in pockets along the ground. He surveyed

Ystwyth and found only decimation. Village, fields, and granaries — all were ash. A lone piebald cow left a swirling brume in her wake as she wandered through charred fields in search of fodder.

Looking south, Gethen spied more ash and soot, burned forests, gutted buildings, and the glow of fire diffused by fog where Ursinum's army marched and burned as they headed toward Or-Halee's border. The Pandydur Crags towered over Ystwyth, their sides blanketed by fog but still dark green with pines and oaks. That's where Zelal's assassins hid, stalking Ilker's men. He turned north and squinted, frowning. Had the attackers backtracked to strangle Besera's narrow neck? There lay Surquay and the home of Halina's mother.

The shrouding fog revealed nothing.

He descended the steps of Ystwyth's skeletal remains, picked his way through the castle's carcass, and climbed over debris and bones to reach the cow.

"Go northwest," he told her. "You'll find fodder and clean streams there and villagers who'll gladly shelter you in exchange for milk." Stroking her soft, ash-crusted nose, he added, "Avoid the south." She huffed a breath, rubbed her head against his chest, and set off as he directed.

He debated his next move. Follow the cow in hopes of discovering his wife alive or go east in search of Zelal?

Before he could decide, a thread of magic burned up his spine and burst in his chest. His eardrums popped, a brilliant flash of amber lit the fog, and Halina staggered into him, appearing from nothing and cursing up a storm.

"Bollocks and bones!" she snarled, shaking and clinging to him.

He couldn't fault her. She'd traveled by ambit, a brutal way of reaching a destination quickly. The last time he'd experienced it, he'd landed on his arse and nearly pissed his trouzes.

Gethen pulled her tight, not caring that her armor bit into his ribs. "You're safe."

"Of course I am. Ilker wouldn't move against Surquay. He's not that..." She broke off and stared around the remains of Ystwyth Citadel. "Oh, gods, Gethen. I'm too late."

Besera's capital had been an unforgettable city. Known as the Home of the Ancients, Ystwyth was named for the massive granite statues upholding its thick walls and surrounding the castle itself. Warriors of old, their names and deeds long forgotten, they glowered down at all who passed through the citadel's gates and scowled at anyone strolling beneath its ramparts. They brandished swords taller than Ranith, wore pointed helms, and clutched broad shields. Most impressive of all had been the brilliant sheen of their silver armor, shined by an army of caretakers who guarded the Ancients zealously. More than one thief had lost their hands after being caught scraping the silver into their own pockets. Ystywyth's guardians had guardians.

But now the Ancients beheld a ruined city, silver streaking their faces like tarnished tears and hardening into slag heaps at their feet. Heat had cracked and blackened them from head to toe.

Gethen followed Halina's gaze. "Behold your brother's handiwork." Tightness spread through his jaw.

She turned back to him. "What of Zelal, Cerys, and little Gerezel?"

"The queen and prince are at Ranith, secreted away during the fighting by none other than Captain Thaksin."

"And Zelal?"

Gethen jerked his chin at the mountains. "Into the Pandydurs to hunt your brother and Etherias."

"Etherias helped with this? That turd bucket. I'll slit him from bollocks to brain. Not that he has much of either." Her expression fell. "Gethen, I'm sorry."

"This is not your fault."

"Your brother may not see it that way."

"Zelal isn't unreasonable and I'm sure he's aware of the growing conflict between you and Ilker." He touched her cheek and added, "I don't blame you, Halina. And neither should you."

She nodded and kissed him. She wanted to fix this, ease the friction with her brother, and end her second cousin's manipulation, but Halina was just one woman. A powerful one, yes, but there was only so much she could control. King Ilker's stupidity and King Waldram's madness weren't on the list.

Gethen offered her a small scroll. "Thaksin sent this. It's from Vika."

"She's still in Tatlis," she murmured as she read the message. "And many who should be aren't. Vika says the capital is almost devoid of protection. Ilker ordered the entire force to march here and spread out along the Silver Sea's eastern shores. He's threatening Or-Halee with no provocation and—"

"He's left Ursinum vulnerable," Gethen finished for her.

"Tatlis is defended by cripples and children. Her citizens are fleeing south to Vala. Reports put Nalvika on the march, but they're not going southeast."

"They're heading southwest?"

"Toward Tatlis." She looked up, her face stricken. "Waldram will take Urisnum while my idiot brother tears apart our long-standing alliance with Besera and boils his troops in Or-Halee's deserts."

"But Thak told me you have allies in Ursinum. They've armed peasants and set up patrols. They've done what they could to prevent Waldram from taking the kingdom."

She shook her head. "They're a weak front at best. Especially if he sends more shrikers. They won't last against those beasts."

Gethen nodded. "We need to go to Tatlis."

Halina rerolled the message. "Not yet. We need allies. The

troops Ilker sent to Or-Halee will be no threat. Eskis will blockade the South Selga between Emelin and Fayet, forcing my brother's army to traverse the Fayet Desert at mid-summer if he wants to take Or-Halee Cid. But there's no crossing those sands at this time of year. His troops will sit on the edge of the desert for months, watching the heat shimmer, cursing their luck and their king's stupidity."

"Thak said you have allies among Ursinum's lords."

She nodded. "I can always count on Vala and Eskis. Plus Floria, Ansissi, and Valmer in the north; they'll be the first defense against Waldram."

"He mentioned Selt and Ahlas, too."

"They'll back me?" At Gethen's nod, she muttered, "That means they're worried. They're never quick to join a battle."

"And Khara will go wherever you lead. Thak said Eugen was very clear on that."

"Yes." She gave him a pained smile. "Eugen is a good man and he should learn to be more ambitious. He could be margrave, not merely Kharaton's steward."

Gethen matched her smile. "Why do you think he's siding with you?"

She shook her head. "I hear what you're implying, but I don't want the crown. I just want my brother to pull his head out of his arse before he suffocates." She bared her teeth and snarled, "I won't bow to Waldram. Quoregna is *not* an empire. It will *never* be an empire as long as I'm alive."

An arrow flew past and thudded into the heat-blistered wall behind Halina. She raised her shield and intercepted another bolt as Gethen brought up his own defenses, a glowing, red shield of magic, symbols and spells flickering across its snapping surface.

They stood on the edge of Ystwyth's Tylee Forest. Archers and soldiers emerged from the dark woods, soot and blood marring their armor and faces. They bore Besera's colors and a few wore the royal liminth blossom on their tabards.

A man with a shock of black hair slicked into a fin atop his head stepped forward and ordered their deaths. "Thlad noo."

"Na. Veethec chen thlad eich doog?" Gethen told them to wait and asked if they'd really kill their duke.

The man stayed the arrows with a gesture. He stepped closer and peered at Gethen. "You're not my duke," he replied in the common tongue. "You're one of those filthy curse callers with an Ursinian bitch at your heel."

Gethen straightened and stalked across the field, summoning his shadow armor as he advanced and ignoring the arrows loosed by panicked archers, his mass incantation easily turning the bolts aside.

"Bollocks!" Halina drew her sword, keeping her shield up. She didn't benefit from the magic he wielded with the flick of a finger, the twist of his tongue.

To his credit, the Beseran captain held his ground and drew his own sword.

Gethen stopped just beyond arm's reach and said with remarkable calm, "You would be wise to respect my wife. After all, Lady Rhyshis's reputation as the Red Blade of Or-Halee precedes her and I won't stop her if she chooses to remove your tongue."

The man's gaze flicked from him to Halina and back. Behind him mutters rose.

"Is it really Lord Rhyshis?"

"Gods, Herra Tomruma's returned home."

"The Red Blade?"

An older soldier came forward and took a knee. "Forgive our ignorance, Your Lordship. We didn't expect your return, but you're the spitting image of your father, and I recognize the Red Blade."

The captain kept his gaze on Gethen and Halina as he asked the soldier, "You're certain?"

"As certain as I'm Beseran and you're a mongrel." He reached over, grabbed the captain's arm, and tugged. "Pay respects to our lord and lady, you damn fool. He can kill you with a thought and she'll gut you for far lesser offenses."

The man shook off his hand but considered them more carefully. "Prove you're the Duke of Rhyshis."

Gethen bristled. "Prove that you owe me your allegiance?"

Halina stepped forward and touched Gethen's arm. "Captain Thaksin was here," she said, her nearness diffusing the anger coming off her husband in heated waves. "He brought an early warning and King Zelal entrusted Queen Cerys and Prince Gerezel to him. He delivered them safely to Ranith Citadel and sent word to me at Gwyncardarnlei. That's how we learned of this attack. If the king didn't trust us, we still wouldn't know Ystwyth had fallen."

The leader considered her as the older soldier said, "The only way she'd know that is if she's had contact with Captain Thaksin."

"Take us to King Zelal," Gethen ordered. "I came to see my brother."

Finally, the captain nodded. "We'll take you someplace to wait for the king. He'll decide if he wants to trust you or have you executed."

Gethen folded his arms. "Fine."

Halina paced beneath the broken span of an ancient temple's entrance. Pointed arches and sharp spires delineated the crumbling building's outline. The demonic faces, claws, and skeletons carved into its walls marked it unmistakably as a shrine to Skiron. The vines snaking through gaps in its roof and the dirt and bird shit covering the geometric designs across its floor proved how far the God of Death had fallen in Besera. Gethen had spied the circle-and-crescent symbol of the One God marking several sign posts and tree trunks on the path they'd taken to this temple; more proof of Skiron's decline.

Zelal's men had argued about tying them like prisoners, finally settling for leaving four armed soldiers to guard them as the remaining patrol returned to the king's camp. Gethen shook his head as he considered the backs of the young soldiers standing at the entrance. Not even old enough to grow beards, they'd foolishly left Halina armed. Likely they'd survived Ursinum's assault by hiding. He prayed Zelal had more experienced soldiers at his side.

Grit crunched beneath Halina's feet. "Like a caged wolf," he murmured from the shadows.

She glanced at him and kept moving. "Me?"

"You."

"Can you blame me?" She drew her borrowed sword from her scabbard and tested its weight. She didn't much care for it, but said it was better than no sword at all. She'd spent enough time recently staring at the tips of other soldiers' weapons to be grateful for any sharp point in hand. A few practiced swings and she moved through a set of figures, lunging, parrying, and blocking unseen enemies. "Besera needs our help. Tatlis needs our help. My brother...he needs a sharp slap. Yet here we are, cooling our heels while the world burns."

"I understand."

She paused. "You're more patient than I am."

"Not always."

She laughed. "True. You were ready to boil Zelal's men in their own juices."

37

Gethen snorted. She wasn't wrong. His muscles and joints crackled as he rolled the stiffness from his shoulders.

They'd been waiting since the moon was high overhead and now the sky was pink and soft blue, the stars were gone and soon the sun would split the horizon.

Halina's sword whistled through empty space. Her feet scraped the gritty, broken tiles of the temple floor, her shadow grew stronger as the sun rose behind her.

She pivoted suddenly, her blade's point stopping at the chest of a figure standing in the doorway.

"Is that any way to greet a king?" Zelal asked.

Gethen and his younger brother looked much alike, though Zelal's eyes were dark brown, not gray, and his hair lacked the premature silver that Gethen sported at his temples. Both men were long-legged, handsome, and sharp-eyed, with bronze skin and broad shoulders. Both wore weaponry — bloody and beaten plate and mail for Zelal; leather bracers and a studded brigandine over a short hooded travel cloak for Gethen. Both resembled mercenary fighters more than a king and a sorcerer. Both looked feral and dangerous.

Halina sheathed her sword and bowed. "My apologies, Your Majesty."

Gethen stepped from the shadows and greeted his brother in Beseran. "Fee braud."

"Braud." Zelal clapped his older brother on the shoulder. "You look like a vagabond," he continued in Common. "Necromancy hasn't been kind."

Gethen shrugged and muttered, "Necromancy is what it is and power is a curse."

"A truer statement I've rarely heard." Besera's king rubbed his eyes.

"Are you well?"

"That depends. Are my queen and son safe?"

"Safe and well-guarded at Ranith."

Relief washed over Zelal's begrimed face. His shoulders relaxed, his chin lifted, and he exhaled. "Thank you." He clasped Gethen's hand and wrist. "Thank you for sheltering them. I know becoming involved in Besera's troubles violates Skiron's mandate."

Gethen shook his head. "The world's problems are my problems, Zel."

Halina added, "And Besera suffers because of my family's actions. I'll do what I can to correct this injustice."

The king offered her a pained smile. "This isn't your fault, Lady Rhyshis. The Council of Kings allowed Waldram to brood and scheme. We should've kept closer watch on Hjalmer's youngest son. His penchant for battle and lust for power were well known. And, much as it pains me to admit it, we neglected Nalvika's recovery after the war. We should've offered more aid to the people."

"The Boorsooks wouldn't have accepted your help. They're too proud," she replied.

"That may be so, but our inaction permitted Waldram's rage to fester."

Gethen shook his head. "His intentions to conquer Quoregna were fostered by my own master. Shemel trained his nephew in the dark arts unbeknownst to even me. This ambition to rule the four kingdoms isn't Waldram's alone and it isn't new."

Zelal's brows furrowed. "What do you mean?"

Gethen's mouth pressed into a grim line. "Shemel created an ambit with part of his soul and gave it to Waldram before his death. He continues to exist through Nalvika's king. He's guiding Waldram's hand in all this destruction."

"Bones," Zelal muttered. "Can you stop them?"

"I have to. Shemel's continued existence violates the sanctity of the Voidline. That puts his warmongering within my domain. With Shemel's help, Waldram is manipulating the four kingdoms to bring war again."

Zelal asked, "But why?"

"My dead master is a driving force behind this madness, but there's something greater at play here, something I can't put my finger on. I feel certain worse looms on the horizon. Khara's unnatural winter, Waldram's shrikers, and Shemel's emergence tie into some greater calamity unfolding in the shadows."

Halina caught his hand and squeezed his fingers. As Herra Tomruma — the Keeper of the Voidline — Gethen should've known Shemel's evil soul hadn't left the mortal realm. That he'd missed noticing its presence troubled him.

It was Zelal's turn to pace while Halina and Gethen watched and listened. "That explains why King Ilker's lost his mind. He's been compromised by Waldram or Shemel," he glanced at Gethen as he said this, "or whatever sorcery you want to blame."

"I'm sorry for it," Halina replied. "Did you speak with him?" She sat on a wooden bench, eyeing it dubiously as it creaked beneath her arse.

"Briefly. He was beyond reason. He blames Besera for Vernard's murder." He met Gethen's gaze. "He blames you for orchestrating it and claims you've corrupted your wife's mind."

Halina crossed her arms. "Any corruption was purely physical and instigated by me. Ilker's long been a sententious arse with a misguided penchant for controlling his sisters."

Zelal laughed.

"One does not constrain the Red Blade of Or-Halee, whether he's her father, brother, or husband," Gethen remarked, turning to his brother. "Your wife, however, would have me deliver you safely to her side at Ranith."

Zelal grimaced. "Queen Cerys is ignorant of war and a king's duties. My place is here with our people, driving the invading army from Beseran soil. Her responsibility is to protect our line's future by sheltering our son. Unlike Lady Rhyshis, my wife is not a warrior. And she will do as her king and husband bids her, whether she agrees with me or not."

Halina stiffened beside Gethen. Ursinian women and men maintained equal legal and social standing. Beseran women did not enjoy the same privilege. Though he hailed from Ystwyth, Gethen grew up and lived most of his life in Ursinum. He had an Ursinian wife and Ursinian sensibilities when it came to her choices and opinions. Besides, Halina could skin him with a butcher's skill. Her prowess with sword and knife were not exaggerated, nor was her temper.

But, to her credit, she said nothing about Cerys's rights. Instead she said, "We need allies and a plan."

"Would seeing the Red Blade sway enough of Ilker's troops?" Gethen asked.

Halina frowned. "Some. Maybe."

The king shook his head. "Fewer than you hope. Etherias leads and his generals have charge of the infantry."

Halina rolled her eyes. "If ever there was proof that Ilker's mind is compromised, there it is. That nincompoop Etherias doesn't know his arse from his elbow, let alone what to do with an army." She huffed a breath. "But you're right, he's a lickspittle and won't jeopardize the chance he thinks he has for high standing in Ilker's eyes. His ambition is far greater than his abilities. He'll rule the generals with an iron fist and they, in turn, will yoke the troops."

"So our only option is Or-Halee," Gethen said.

"Yes. The desert reduces the threat of a quick attack, but we can warn Arik-bohk and, in so doing, secure an alliance," Halina replied.

Zelal nodded. "All right. We have a plan. The two of you will go to Or-Halee while my forces hunt Ursinum's army, picking off Etherias and his generals and culling the herd."

Gethen said, "And we stop Nalvika from destroying Ursinum, find Waldram, and send Shemel to face Skiron's judgement before the God of Death decides I'm a failure."

"That too, brother."

Halina looked down at her feet then met the king's gaze. "I don't care if you gut Etherias, but try to spare my brother. I know he doesn't deserve leniency, Your Majesty, but as you've said, his mind is not his own. And...I really don't want to wear Ursinum's crown."

"I make no promises," Zelal replied, "but I will show Ilker mercy. He was my friend far longer than my enemy." He turned to Gethen. "Will you go immediately to Or-Halee?"

"Yes, unless?" Gethen said.

"I would beg another favor of you." Zelal pulled a sealed message from his tabard. "Deliver this to Cerys. I'd like her and Gerezel to know I'm alive."

Gethen glanced at Halina. She nodded and he said, "Gladly. We can afford a quiet night before engaging in what promises to be a protracted battle."

"Diolk." Zelal thanked him.

"Kroisol, fee braud," Gethen replied and embraced his brother.

FIVE

"Still mad at me?" Thaksin asked as he came around the curve of the citadel and stopped in the kitchen doorway.

"No." Halina grabbed his bearded chin and tugged. "You've earned my forgiveness, old man." She gently slapped his cheek. She was hanging back while Gethen delivered Zelal's message to Cerys in the great hall.

Thaksin stepped into the room, took a knee, and bowed his head. "My queen," he murmured.

Halina hissed. "No." Her next slap wasn't affectionate. "Get up. You have a king. I won't be pitted against my brother for Ursinum's throne."

He held her gaze as he stood, no apology or uncertainty in his eyes. "I understand your reticence, but you must see that King Ilker's judgment can't be trusted. He's endangered Ursinum and our allies."

"That doesn't mean he can't be made to see reality."

Thaksin scrubbed the back of his skull with his gnarled knuckles. "You're walking into a trap set by Waldram, and your brother is the bait."

"More than likely true, but I'm walking in with my eyes open, my sword in hand, and the Sun Mage at my side."

Marja stood at the kitchen basin peeling sunfruits. "Waldram doesn't think you'll fight Ilker."

"Which proves he doesn't know me and my brother is a moron." Halina took one of the sweet, yellow fruits. "I'll do what I must to protect Quoregna from Waldram. Even if that means killing my fool of a brother on the battlefield. But Ilker will back down. He's never matched me in a fight, fair or unfair."

Princess Federika appeared at the foot of the servants stairs, followed by a bleary-eyed Elof.

"And I won't hold back, brother or not," Halina added. "There are too many innocent lives counting on me to protect them." She beckoned Nalvika's future queen to her side.

"I'm glad you've returned, Lady Rhyshis. Will you stay for long?" Feddie asked.

"No. In the morning Lord Rhyshis and I leave for Or-Halee to negotiate an alliance. We need a large army to stop your father and my brother from creating a second War of the Winds. Odruna and Marja will remain to protect you. Thaksin will protect Queen Cerys and Prince Gerezel. But we'll return as soon as possible."

"Can I go with you?" She met Halina's gaze evenly. "You promised to teach me diplomacy and how to fight."

"And I will when I return. But I won't take you into the heart of a growing conflict, Your Highness."

Elof yawned and scratched his bed-tousled head. "It'll be fine, Feddie. You can help me practice sorcery and I'll help you learn to fight."

"What do you know about fighting?" she asked, looking down her nose at him.

The boy's chin jutted and challenge flashed in his gray eyes. "I know how to punch a fella in the bollocks."

Feddie tittered. "Very well. Just don't punch me."

"You haven't any bollocks," Elof pointed out in all serious-ness. Halina, Marja, and Thaksin laughed.

Halina took a small, leather-bound book off the long kitchen table and gave it to the boy. "Your master wants you to study this. He'll test you when he returns and expects you to read the entire book."

Elof took it, his eyes like saucers. "But I don't read so well, Lady Rhyshis."

"I'll help you," Feddie volunteered.

"Really?"

"Of course. And you can be my court mage."

Halina bit her tongue. That would never happen. The armistice agreement that ended the War of the Winds forbade Nalvika from employing court mages. Another reason Waldram's lies and attacks were so egregious.

"Go on," Marja said, "start your day. Odruna will discipline you if your chores aren't done." She shooed them out the door into the bailey, adding, "Don't give the Schorvalan an excuse to pile on the punishment." The children set out toward the extraction room and the stable, the militess on their heels.

Cerys's voice rose from the modest great hall. "These accommodations are entirely too small. And where are your servants? Gerezel requires a governess. The soldiers lack barracks. They cannot sleep in the tower with us. The kitchen's too tiny to cook a proper meal and there's no parlor."

Away from her husband's authority, the young Beseran queen evidently saw no reason to hide her displeasure from anyone, especially Gethen. Her immaturity showed and it had an ugly face.

Thaksin exchanged an uncomfortable glance with Halina before retreating from the kitchen into the bailey.

"Coward," she mouthed at him. He waved her off. She

snatched a handful of sunfruits from the basket Marja had left on the table and stepped into the archway leading to the great hall. Unseen by Gethen and Cerys, she leaned against the cool white wall, eating to keep her sharp tongue occupied lest she stab Zelal's wife with it.

"I understand this is where you live, Lord Rhyshis," the queen continued, "but you've chosen an ascetic's life." She pressed her hand to her chest and added, "I did not." She gestured around the room, her son sleeping on her shoulder. "Your entire keep is smaller than my apartment!" Cerys stared about Ranith's great hall, an expression frozen somewhere between horror and dismay twisting her lovely face.

Rather than annoyed with his brother's petulant wife, Gethen wore a tolerant smile. "Ranith is small but comfortable and safe." He paused then added, "As long as you don't go above the fourth level."

"Why?" She glanced at the stairwell. "What's there?"

"Ruins. The fifth and sixth floors are open to the elements and tainted with necromantic magic left by one of my less circumspect predecessors. Not even I venture up there, unless absolutely necessary to battle some spirit back into the Void."

"Oh." She abruptly sat on a chair before the blazing hearth. Gerezel slumbered, his mouth open, eyes closed, face sweet.

"And don't leave the tor," Gethen continued. "In fact, I recommend you remain within the grounds of the citadel. The tor is warded with deadly magic and Kharayan Woods belongs to the wolves."

"Wolves?" she squeaked.

"I'll tell them you're my guests, but they're not domesticated pets. Nor would I want you to encounter a wraith." He scowled, and so did Halina, remembering as he continued. "The last time a stray wraith escaped my control, it nearly killed my wife."

Cerys stared at him, her brown eyes as wide as a startled doe's.

Gerezel stirred in his mother's arms, stretched, and murmured. She automatically shifted the child and gently shushed him.

Gethen's tone softened. "This is the safest place you can be, Your Highness. The tor's populace consists mostly of blackthorn deer, songbirds, coneys, and squirrels. The wolves won't trouble you, I'll make certain of that. Ranith Citadel is a haven and its sorcery is tightly controlled. You and the crown prince will be quite safe under my roof."

She nodded and stroked the sleeping toddler's back, considering Gethen. "Why aren't you with my husband, fighting for Besera, Lord Rhyshis? You're still a subject of the kingdom, a duke. You should be acting as a guide to the people in this trying time. You're obligated to support your king and rally the people against Ursinum. If you won't fight for your king, then you don't deserve to call yourself Beseran, let alone Duke of Rhysis, in absentia or not."

Annoyed by her ignorance, Halina popped another sunfruit in her mouth and bit back a sharp retort. Clearly Cerys knew very little about Gethen and even less about magic and the role of the Sun Mage in Quoregnan affairs.

"Were it true that a king was my lord, you would be correct in accusing me of dereliction of my duties," he said, his voice admirably calm. "But Zelal isn't my lord, nor is Ilker, Danas, nor any other mortal king. I serve one master and protect one people: Skiron and all Quoregnans. I don't intervene on behalf of one kingdom or individual."

"But you're protecting Princess Federika from her insane father. You fought to save your Ursinian wife on multiple occasions, and you're by her side in this fight against Nalvika and her own kingdom. You're a hypocrite, Lord Rhyshis. Or just selfish."

Halina bit her tongue.

Gethen drew a long, slow breath. "It seems you're misinformed about the nature of my service to Quoregna, Your Highness. I protect and accompany Halina because King Waldram seeks to steal the blood magic coursing through her veins. Should he attain it, he will become a more powerful sorcerer than I am. He will give Shemel the strength to take possession of his body. My former master, in turn, will destroy me. In my absence, Shemel will rend the Voidline, harness the souls dwelling in the Void for his own purposes, and enslave every mortal in Quoregna. I protect Halina to protect all of us. I would do that even if she was my mortal enemy rather than my greatest love. I protect Halina because it is my duty to do so."

"But—"

"But although I cannot side with Besera at the expense of Ursinum, I can help ease a growing threat of war. King Ilker punishes Besera based on lies, but his actions don't threaten the security of the Void. I cannot move directly against him or I risk the ire of my master, Skiron."

"But King Waldram isn't a sorcerer," the queen insisted. "I don't know who perpetuated that lie, but I've known him for several years and I've never seen any evidence of his alleged magical powers."

Halina shoved two sunfruits in her mouth. Besera's queen was maddeningly ignorant.

"That's unsurprising," Gethen replied, his composure a balm to Halina's growing ire. "My wife has known her second cousin for twenty-nine years and only discovered his necromantic abilities a few months ago when he used them to nearly kill her." Gethen smiled at Cerys, a wolfish, predatory, and not-at-all soothing expression as he added, "Necromancers are a secretive few, not warmly welcomed by polite society, Your Highness.

Even if Waldram's intentions were benign, it behooves him to hide his powers. Magery was made illegal in the Nalvik court by the terms of the armistice the Council of Kings signed to end the War of the Winds, as you surely must know."

Cerys frowned but held her tongue. Gerezel fussed and she stood, stroking the child's back and rocking him. She looked around Ranith's simple hall. "I suppose it's a cozy enough prison."

Gethen offered her a pained smile. "Certainly better than Ystwyth's ashes, Your Highness. Or a funeral pyre."

She faced him. "I don't mean to be ungrateful for your efforts. I just—" She sighed and sat again. "I just don't like being dismissed like useless scraps tossed on the kitchen midden."

Halina entered the great hall. "You're not useless, Your Highness. You're protecting Besera's future. What's more important than that?"

"Assuring there's a Besera for him to rule," Cerys replied.

"Leave that to the soldiers," Halina said.

"That!" The queen jabbed her finger at Halina. "That's what insults me. The implication that I'm incapable of defending my kingdom because I'm a woman. I can ride just as well as you. I can carry a sword."

Gethen raised his hand to his temple. "Didn't you see the fighting as you fled Ystwyth? Ursinum's army is not a trifle."

Halina strode across the room and held up her hands. "Don't romanticize war because you don't understand what really happens on the battlefield. This is only a glimpse at what war looks like. These scars and wounds are the reality of battle. Soldiers sacrifice their skin, their bones, their limbs and lives. You don't understand what battle does to a body."

Cerys stared at Halina's halved fingers, the silvery scars crisscrossing her knuckles and wrists.

"I bear scars that would turn your guts," Halina continued. "I've made and received wounds that still give me nightmares. War is brutal, Cerys, a nightmare that lingers long after the fighting has ended. You're not a soldier, no. That's not the role of women in Besera. But you have something I sacrificed when I went to war." She touched Gerezel's black curls then pressed her hand to her own scarred womb. "I'll never bear a child. A sword took that from me, a sword wielded by one of Nalvika's captains during the War of the Winds." She smiled, a bitter, vicious expression and added, "But he'll never produce offspring either. I made sure of that."

Cerys looked down at her son. "I was a girl during the War of the Winds. My family sheltered me far away from the fighting. But," she raised her gaze to meet Halina's, "I want to do my part to protect my home now that I'm Besera's queen."

"You are," Halina said, some of her voice's edge softening. "Wars are won on many fronts, Your Highness, not just the battlefield. Besera's soldiers will fight even harder, knowing their queen and crown prince were driven from their home by an enemy bent on their capture."

Cerys nodded and kissed Gerezel's upturned face.

Gethen bowed. "Excuse me now, Your Highness. I must find Kharayan's wolves."

The young queen nodded. Halina watched him leave then turned to her. "I hope Your Highness will learn to spend more time thinking and observing before she finds fault with her host. Queens can't afford to estrange allies, especially when their safety is guaranteed only by the good graces of those they're grumbling about."

The queen's eyes widened. "You dare speak to me so harshly?"

"Yes. By your own admission you're ignorant of the politics at play here. Nalvika seeks the destruction of anyone standing in their way. If you think Waldram will hesitate to murder you and your son, you're more foolish than you appear. Ystwyth is ashes. There's nothing left of your citadel and city. You're young and ill informed, and I regret that no one's educated you on the reality of this situation, so that task falls to me, Your Highness. I order soldiers to their deaths. The battlefield doesn't allow for minced words or nice manners, so I'll be blunt. Stay behind Ranith's walls and you and your son may yet survive Waldram's attacks. And have enough brains to recognize that your brother-in-law doesn't have to bother with you and his nephew. He chose to aid Besera. He's no more beholden to the country of his birth than he is to any other kingdom in Quoregna. The deaths of one foolish queen and her little boy are as insignificant as a grain of sand on a beach to a man who's responsible for every soul, living and dead, in the mortal realm and the Void."

"But I'm his queen," she snapped.

"No, you're a child." Halina left her sputtering as she strode down the hall leading to the basilica. She paused and turned back to see the indignant girl standing, son on her hip. "Tomorrow I leave for Or-Halee to marshal allies to Besera's cause. Gethen will come with me."

"And leave us?" Cerys said, her eyes wide.

"Yes. Stay put if you wish to stay alive."

Gethen crouched in the cemetery behind the basilica. Black Duesh and white Gwyn sprawled before him. The fog had lifted and the wolves lolled in a pool of sunshine. Contentment softened their master's expression as he rubbed their bellies.

"They've gotten big," Halina remarked. A large pile of bricks sat beside the wall. She climbed it, her arms wide for balance. "What're these for?" she asked as she reached the top.

"A kiln."

"You already have one."

"It's not large enough." He ran his hands through the wolves' summer-short fur, his eyes and expression peaceful. The animals stretched and sighed. Gethen murmured something in a language Halina didn't understand.

"Don't let Cerys's ignorance annoy you," she said.

He slowly raised his gaze to meet hers. "I'm accustomed to that." He smirked and added, "It troubles you more. You can't help but defend me."

She jumped off the bricks, landing in a crouch and a clank of plate and mail. "You're right. It does. And I'm supposed to protect you, remember, Sun Mage?"

He stood, topping her by only a few inches, and gently tugged one of her loose braids. "You had that agreement with the Shadow Mage." He tickled the tip of her nose with her hair and added, "I can protect myself."

She wrinkled her nose in response. "Let's not talk about who protects whom." She'd needed his protection from Waldram and it irked her still, not because she was annoyed by Gethen's help, but that she'd been trapped in a compromised position that had cost her father's life and almost her own. Halina circled the subject back to Cerys. "I had words with our young guest."

"Which I'm sure she didn't appreciate, not that you mind her irritation."

She brushed her palms on her trouzes then slipped her hands around his waist and pulled their hips together. "I never let royal opinion stop me."

"You never let much of anything stop you."

She shrugged. "I'll stop when I'm dead."

His brow furrowed. He captured her arms and gave her a

little shake. "Don't say that." His hands came up to cradle her face. "Don't make light of it." He searched her eyes, his own gray gaze intense. "The thought of losing you—" He kissed her, pulled back, and added, "That hurts me more than you'll ever know."

Halina bit her lip. "I'm sorry," she whispered. She hated seeing him so vulnerable, but her near-death had rattled him. It had rattled both of them. Waldram's hidden sorcery was powerful and deranged, made more dangerous by blood magic stolen from Halina.

Gethen had fought shrikers and used human souls to win the battle with Waldram, paying a price Halina didn't fully understand. He was still paying it. He didn't discuss it, but she felt how it troubled him and dictated his actions and decisions. Some nights he trembled in his sleep, curling into a ball and moaning as if in agony until she reached for him. He'd quiet then, as his sorcery burrowed beneath her skin and nestled behind her breastbone, beating like a second heart.

Gethen pulled her into his arms and held her close. Halina sighed. "I take your strength for granted," she murmured. "I shouldn't."

He kissed her temple. "It's my own fault and I wouldn't have it any other way. I want you to give me your woes, Halina. Never forget I'm here for you."

She pulled back to meet his gray gaze. "Don't forget *I'm* here for *you*. Whatever this thing is that's weighing you down, know you can share it with me, Gethen. I've seen worse." He pulled away, but she snagged his collar. "Don't shut me out."

He swallowed and shook his head. "You don't know what you're asking."

"You're right. I don't. Because you're not sharing. But I do know whatever this monster is, it's growing inside you and you don't know how to slay it. Or you do and you fear that you can't."

His jaw set. His brow set. His gaze hardened. "Halina, stop."

The sepulchral tone in his voice hinted at a danger far worse than anything she could imagine. But she forged on anyway. "I love you, necromancer or not, and I won't be pushed away by the darkness dwelling within you. Whatever it is, we'll face it together."

Gethen looked past her toward the Silver Sea and the smoke-shrouded mountains of Besera on the far eastern shore. "Maybe," he murmured. His gaze returned to pin her, a dark hunger there that he rarely showed her. He pulled back, escaping this time. "Not today. Not until we've stopped Waldram and destroyed Shemel." He turned and added, as if an afterthought, "Then maybe you can help me."

She nodded. His expression ran through anger, regret, fear, and settled into neutrality. He peered at her from the corner of his eye. "I won't refuse your touch, wife." He reached for her hand.

Halina grasped his fingers and pressed against him, rubbing her cheek against his arm, the muscles hard beneath his tunic. "I won't turn away yours either, husband." She tilted her head back and reveled in the hunger of his kiss. Gethen was a deeply complicated man, dark and dangerous and fiercely loyal. She never tired of his affection or his intelligence. She hushed the voice in the back of her mind that warned of danger. The Sun Mage was the most dangerous man she'd ever encountered. It was what made him so compelling. Like the wolves he adored, Gethen Rhysh was an untamed creature, an indescribably spellbinding man who could turn against her if pushed too hard.

But Halina had survived countless battles following her instincts. She trusted her husband — dangerous as he was — as much as she trusted her sword. Gethen would never attack her. Never.

She slipped her arm through his and tugged him toward the

open basilica. "Come, mage, let's leave the petulant queen to sulk while we enjoy each other. Tomorrow we travel to Or-Halee and meet another king."

"Are you optimistic for an alliance?"

"Always," she said, neither sounding nor feeling it.

SIX

"Have you ever visited Kasr Bez-Gecidi?" Halina asked.

Gethen stretched and yawned. "Once or twice when I was still the crown prince. I don't remember much of the castle except its enormous, white gates." He pulled her closer, rubbed his stubbled jaw against her shoulder and inhaled. She smelled like sweat and sex and him. She smelled perfect.

Halina squirmed. "Nowhere else in Quoregna will you find the like."

Gethen nipped her shoulder to make her writhe again. There was nothing better than a naked militess squirming against him. "Are we talking about a foreign castle or my beautiful wife?" he murmured. "Because the latter is infinitely more interesting than the former."

Halina slapped his hands away playfully and slipped from their bed. "Get up, lazy mage. We have business with the ruler of the desert."

Gethen watched her dress. "Just for once, I'd like to lay in bed all day with my naked wife. Is that too much to ask?"

"With war dogging our heels? Yes." She threw his clothes at his face. "Out of bed. I need you to work your magic."

He smirked. "I thought I did last night. All night."

Halina buckled her sword belt around her hips. "You did and I have no complaints, except about your morning idleness."

He sighed and climbed out of bed. There was no stalling his wife when she had a goal in mind. The woman was relentless. "You need to describe the castle to me. I haven't enough clarity from my fuzzy memories to take us there," he said as he cinched his belt.

"Kasr Bez-Gecidi's gates are as tall as Ranith and as white as snow. Gold glitters atop its great dome and its four minarets."

As she spoke, Gethen summoned another travel incantation to take them to Or-Halee Cid — the seat of Or-Halee's power — and its resplendent castle, Kasr Bez-Gecidi. He reached for her hand, twining his fingers with hers.

"The city is dry and dusty at this time of year, coated in a fine layer of crystalline grit. It's midday and the overhead sun sets the grit aglow so that the air shimmers. All the buildings are white, but the people wear bright colors. That's why Or-Halee Cid is called the Jewel of the Sun." She laughed and added, "Too bad it doesn't smell as pretty as it looks. The heat is oppressive, like standing inside one of Amma Xana's bread ovens, and the thousands of people and animals packed inside the city's walls make the stink unbearable."

Sorcery twisted around them, mimicking the wavering desert heat. Sweat trickled down Gethen's temple and between his shoulder blades.

"The sound is a constant rumble of humanity competing with the crashing waves of the Silver Sea meeting the Southern Green Ocean. Reed flutes, drums, and bells hold a rhythm all day and night as Semele's priestesses dance and sing to their goddess, calling worshipers into the temples."

Now the incantation took up the sounds of the desert city and Ranith Citadel disappeared as Gethen droned the words that would transport Halina and him across the Silver Sea's wide expanse to Semele's sacred city. The oppressive heat told him they'd arrived. The stench and noise Halina had promised followed and Gethen's eyes watered. He squinted at the towering gates before him and glanced at Halina as she cursed.

"Why're they closed?" she muttered.

Gethen craned his neck to see the top of the gateway but no handles or locks were visible.

The gates were blinding white and covered in carvings of flowers, birds, and beasts.

The voices and music were more mournful than he'd expected. He looked around. Instead of a rainbow of jeweled hues, the city bled. Walls were draped in red. People wore the color from head to toe. The streets were strewn with red flower petals. "Maybe they're closed for the festival," he said and gestured around.

"Festival?" Halina looked away from the closed gates. Her eyes widened. Her expression fell. "Gods."

"What?"

"The city's in mourning."

"For Vernard?" It seemed unlikely, no matter how tightly allied the two kingdoms might be.

"No." She sniffed the air like a hound scenting prey. "For itself. It stinks of fear." She turned back to the gateway, drew a misericord from her belt, and pounded its hilt on the gate. "Death or invasion are the only reasons to close the gates during the day." Her pounding echoed into the vast, domed fortress before them.

Gethen frowned. A gathering crowd gawked at them. "Halina, we've been noticed."

She glanced over her shoulder then returned her attention to the gate and continued pounding. "So?"

He peered up to the ramparts. Soldiers had noticed the growing crowd. They pointed downward at the woman pounding on their entrance. "The kasr's soldiers have spied us too."

"Good. Then they can get their arses down here and open the gates."

Arrows were aimed, aligned with the gazes, nocked and taut while Or-Halee's captains considered the red-haired woman hammering on their front door.

"We may die very soon, skewered by a lot of sharp pointy things," he said.

A clunk came from the other side of the gateway. "Finally," Halina said and sheathed the dagger as a tiny window slid aside to reveal a pair of dark-brown eyes.

"Who are you?" a man with a high, thin voice asked in the common tongue.

"Halina Persinna Rhyshis, Duchess of Rhyshis in absentia and militess of the Order of the Red Blade. With me is Gethen Rhysh, Sun Mage and Duke of Rhyshis in absentia. We require an audience with Arik-bohk."

The little door slid shut with a clunk. A louder clank followed, then squealing as a wicket door swung inward to admit them. The larger gates remained firmly closed and locked.

Gethen and Halina stepped inside the fortress of Or-Halee's bohks — its kings — and faced a phalanx of heavily armed guards brandishing curved sabres.

Unperturbed, Halina pressed her hands together in the traditional greeting to the vizier and the armed men. "I thank you for opening your doors to us."

Gethen mirrored and echoed her. It was the traditional greeting any visitor offered their host in Or-Halee.

The man returned the gesture and bowed low, acknowledging their royal status. But the soldiers didn't, nor did they sheath their weapons.

The vizier led them into a small antechamber. "Wait here, please." He disappeared back into the fortress's maze. Four soldiers took up positions blocking the doorway. Two young servants clad in red entered with platters of summer dates and pitchers of koumiss. Halina reached for a glass. Gethen hesitated.

She glanced at him. "Drink and eat. It's not poisoned. The Or-Haleeans never poison the first meal they offer you." She raised the glass to her lips and drank deeply.

"That's reassuring," Gethen muttered and helped himself to several red dates. They were a fruit he'd always enjoyed as a boy, but seldom tasted as a man. Ursinum's markets rarely offered them.

Servants brought cleaning cloths for their hands and replenished the drinks and dates while Halina and Gethen waited. Wailing drifted through the open windows. The desert heat was milder here. Fountains burbled somewhere within the confines of the fortress's gardens. Wide corridors and open pergolas directed the ocean breeze through the fortress.

Halina went to the windows and closed her eyes to the glare of the sun off the water. The breeze lifted wisps of her hair around her face in a gentle dance.

The door opened and the vizier re-entered. "Come with me, please." He gestured for them to follow. Behind him, the guards remained watchful and wary, their weapons still in hand.

Gethen and Halina trailed the slight man through sparkling silver hallways and beneath soaring ceilings. They passed through white marble courtyards with mirrored pools, homes to long-necked water birds and rainbow-hued fish. Windows high above revealed wispy clouds in an azure sky.

They passed beneath a golden archway and into the private apartments of Or-Halee's royal family. Halina was one of the privileged few foreigners to have slept in a bed beneath this part of the kasr's vast roof. At seventeen, she'd convalesced beneath the watchful eye of Arik-bohk's personal healer. More soaring hallways, more silver and gems, more gold leaf and carved wood and marble. Finally they stopped before an elaborately carved wooden door, decorated with a drape of red silk.

"You're familiar with Semele's temple?" the vizier asked and when Halina and Gethen nodded, he opened the door and ushered them inside.

Preceding Gethen into the tiny temple, Halina got halfway down the aisle toward the altar when she suddenly stopped, reached back, and clutched his hand. A small strangled sound came from her.

Gethen looked past her to the altar. Seven small coffins rested there, draped in red and surrounded by lit candles. Reflecting the flickering flames were seven tiny Or-Haleean winged diadems, the symbol of the kingdom's ruling family. They rested upon the coffins as befit the children of a king. Behind them was an adult-sized casket, a larger diadem atop it, jewels glittering in the candlelight.

With a tremulous breath, Halina composed herself and continued forward to stop before the ring of lit candles. She pressed her hand to her throat, her face a mask of bereavement. Her other hand still clutching Gethen's, she whispered their names, reading them off the inscriptions upon the diadems.

"Fazil and Fatima, Rafiq, Inbar, Nakia, Zara, and little Walid." Her gaze went to the large coffin and she slowly shook her head. "Niesha-bohkina. Oh, Arik." Her voice caught on the king's name. She looked back at the vizier. "How did they die?"

"Fear." The reply came from the corner of the temple, a

familiar voice, a stooped figure. "Except the queen. She died fighting the shrikers that took her children."

Halina turned. "Amma?"

"Shrikers?" Gethen couldn't believe his ears. "In Or-Halee?" He turned on the vizier and snarled, "Why didn't anyone send word? When did this happen?"

"Last night," Amma Xana replied. "The bohk is hunting the murderous beasts as we speak."

Behind them, the guards had entered the temple. More than four now stood between them and the door. Gethen's mood darkened as he considered all the unsheathed blades. Their mission to bring allies was looking like a trap and the jaws were rapidly closing.

Halina said, "This is a bittersweet reunion." She went to the elderly woman's seat and kissed Amma Xana's hands.

"It is." The old woman squinted up at Gethen as he joined them. "I see you've kept the Sun Mage at your side. Baichu will be glad."

"Must she be so nosy about my business?" Halina muttered.

Amma Xana's youngest adult daughter, Baichu had been Halina's friend for a decade. She relished love and rumors, and secrets — especially the salacious kind.

Laughing, Amma Xana slapped Halina's arm. "You know that girl cares about everyone's affairs." She sobered, a shift as sudden as the desert's winds, and she pulled Halina close. "Be careful, child," she murmured, her voice so low Gethen almost missed the warning.

Halina nodded and said loudly enough to carry to the vizier's ears, "I know, Amma. I can't believe shrikers have crossed into Arik's lands. I came here seeking an alliance but, instead, find only sadness." She bowed her head, resting her cheek on Amma Xana's shoulder.

The old woman turned her head to murmur in Halina's ear. "Suspicion plagues Gethen."

He asked, "Where's Appa Unegan?"

"With Arik-bohk," Amma replied. "The old fool fancies himself a monster slayer." She shook her head and muttered, "Will get himself killed."

Gethen grimaced. "I should join them. I have a regrettable amount of experience slaughtering Skiron's dogs."

Amma nodded. "So I've heard and so I told him and Arik. They didn't want to wait for aid."

"Understandable," Halina said. "Thaksin hunted them across Khara for months. For every one you destroy, two more seem to appear." Her gaze moved past Gethen and hardened when she considered the growing number of guards in the temple. She turned back to Amma Xana. "But I'm pleased to see you've recovered from the battle we fought together."

"Fought? Ha! I ran while you and your mage destroyed the Rime Witch's servants. I'm not fool enough to take on a more powerful enemy. Sometimes you have to let a foe have a small victory."

"So you can live to fight another day," Gethen murmured.

Amma Xana tapped her nose. "Exactly." She waved her hand at the coffins. "There lie the only witnesses to the arrival of the shrikers." She poked Gethen's leg with her toe. "Perhaps you can find Niesha in the Void, Sun Mage, and provide evidence of who summoned the beasts."

"We already know the answer," Halina said.

Amma squinted at her and Gethen. "I said you need proof, child, not conviction." She hoisted herself up from the bench and gestured for Halina to follow. "The Sun Mage has many enemies and detractors."

Gethen said, "And their numbers grow hourly."

The soldiers stepped past the vizier, their weapons pointed

at Gethen. Their captain said, "You'll come with us, Sun Mage. By order of Arik-bohk you are to be retained for questioning in the deaths of Or-Halee's bohkina and her children."

Halina's hands became fists, but Gethen and Amma Xana restrained her.

"I'll do as the bohk asks," he said, "and trust he's a reasonable man."

"He's lost his children and his wife," Halina replied. "I wouldn't be reasonable given those circumstances."

"You're not Arik-bohk," Gethen said and kissed her forehead.

"Ha! A truer statement I haven't heard today," Amma said. She hooked her arm through Halina's and pulled her back as the soldiers moved to take Gethen into custody. "We will speak with the bohk on your husband's behalf. Or-Halee's king respects you, Red Blade, and me. We will help him see reason."

Gethen sat in a circle of dim light, sun pushing its way through many feet of stone to reach his small, dark cell. If he stood, he'd strike his head on the stone ceiling. The room was only large enough to permit him three steps in any direction and its meager furnishings were a pile of rags and a bucket. So he sat, and he waited. After six days, he was far from hopeless, but he'd like a bath and a soft bed. He'd befriended mice, a golden desert asp, several scorpions, and the bats that came and went through the hole in the ceiling.

Halina visited daily, sitting outside the iron-lattice door and snarling at the guards when they tried to make her leave before she was good and ready. It amused him to hear her cowing the soldiers.

Last night she'd considered him through the iron bars, her

blue eyes lost to the prison's darkness. "Do you leave when the guards aren't watching?"

He'd reached through the bars and stroked her cheek. "If I did, I'd smell sweeter."

Wrinkling her nose, she'd turned her head and kissed his fingers. "They must realize they can't really keep you imprisoned. Arik knows that."

He'd shrugged. "I agreed to imprisonment until the king returns, so here I sit."

"While Nalvika marches toward Tatlis, Besera burns, and more shrikers pour over the border."

"Yes. But Besera and Ursinum will fight back, and the bohk is hunting the shrikers." He'd pulled her fingers through the grate and kissed them. "You and I must be patient."

She'd stroked his lips. "Patience is not my strength, you know that."

But this morning she hadn't come to Gethen's cell. He hoped that meant Arik-bohk had returned. He glanced at the scorpion resting on his shoulder, warming herself and the hundred minuscule offspring clinging to her back. "Morning sun is comforting, eh?" he asked. She twitched her tail which Gethen took as agreement. He closed his eyes and let the sun rejuvenate him, like it did the scorpion and her young.

Footsteps echoed down the stone hallways, growing louder as they approached. Not Halina's footfalls, these were soldiers; he knew from their heavy shuffling gait. They reached his iron door. A key rattled in the lock. The lock clunked. The door creaked open.

"Arik-bohk will see you now."

Gethen lowered his chin and opened his eyes. He lifted the scorpion off his shoulder and held her to the sunny opening. "Climb up and find a rock to hide beneath before the bats awaken," he told her. She slipped off his fingers and scuttled toward freedom and the bright morning sun. He stepped from the cell and straightened, groaning as his muscles and joints stretched. "I want a bath and clean clothing before I meet with the bohk."

One of the guards shoved him. "You'll stay filthy and stinking, mage." The man's companion laughed and stuck his sword in Gethen's face.

Gethen's vast patience was the only reason the men kept their eyes, but the ropey shadows that whipped forth to wrap around their necks, wrists, and ankles, and the dagger-sharp shadows that suddenly hovered before their faces showed how thin that patience had become.

"Don't murder your hosts," Amma Xana said from the stairs at the end of the hall.

Gethen sniffed, and a flick of his fingers turned the shadowy weapons to nothing. "Someone should teach them better manners."

"Quite so." She turned and started up the stairs. "A bath and clothes have been arranged. Your wife disapproves of your current state." Her nose wrinkled and she added, "So do I."

He was left alone to bathe in Halina's chamber. Presumably she was with the king, so he made quick work of the filth covering him, changed into the dark-red trouzes and tunic laid across the bed, and was just buckling his belt when a knock announced a visitor. "Come," he said.

Halina entered, relief and wariness playing across her face. Someone had given her a red court gown and braided gold into her hair. Diamonds flashed at her throat and around her wrists.

"You look regal," he said.

She considered him from head to toe. "You look less feral, though Amma told me you threatened the guards."

"I don't respond well to intimidation."

She scowled. "You shouldn't have to."

He shrugged. "What's the king's mood?"

"He's in mourning, but Arik is a reasonable man even so. He'll listen to you. Tell him the facts as you know them. I've already shared my story. They'll match because they're the truth."

Gethen nodded. "You're rattled."

She folded her arms and her expression darkened. "I didn't think Waldram had the power to summon so many shrikers. I think he's gaining strength and..."

"And what?"

She met his gaze. "Adherents. Amma thinks his power is coming from other mages."

Gethen puffed out his cheeks and blew a slow breath. "That's unfortunate."

"I don't understand why they would follow him."

"If they're Nalviks, he likely promised to restore their position in the kingdom. He's offering respect and a chance to come home."

"You mean lies."

"Of course." He tucked a stray lock of auburn hair behind her right ear. "He did gain a lot of power from you and he has Shemel's guidance. It makes his lies potent. Nalvika's mages and witches were punished for the actions of a few. They crave legitimacy."

She kissed him, then took his arm and led him toward the door. "First we convince a king that you're the good man I say you are."

"Ah, but I have you blinded and fooled, remember?"

She shot him a humorless look. Halina's temper was as thin as his patience. It became more brittle as six guards took up positions around them. They descended two floors, passed through a massive courtyard and a glittering throne room, the gold thrones draped in red mourning cloth. A door behind the thrones led to a small meeting room. It held an oval table around which sat six advisors, men and women who served their bohk faithfully.

Before they entered the room, Gethen was shackled. Halina protested, but he shook his head and murmured, "Let them if it makes the king's advisors feel safer."

Arik-bohk was a plain man with heavily muscled arms, white hair and beard, and thick salt-and-pepper eyebrows. Only the dark circles beneath his eyes revealed the sorrows so recently visited upon his family and Or-Halee's citizens. When he spoke, his voice was resonant and commanding without being strident. He met Gethen's gaze evenly with his own dark eyes and listened patiently as his advisors spoke. Amma Xana sat to his left, representing Gurvan-Sum and the Dargani desert tribes. To his right sat Jevon, his second-in-command and leader of Or-Halee's legendary cavalry.

The king gestured to an empty seat opposite him. "Please sit, Lady Rhyshis." There was no chair for Gethen.

"No thank you, Your Majesty. I'll stand with my husband."

Arik-bohk studied Gethen for a long moment. His gaze drifted to the shackles and his brow rose. "Jevon, do you think the Sun Mage could be stopped by those fetters your soldiers have clapped around his wrists and ankles?"

The hawk-nosed commander wore a perpetual scowl. "I hope they would slow him down should he choose to become combative."

Amma snorted. The king's gaze shifted to the little witch beside him. "You have an opinion, Amma Xana?"

"A good leader knows his enemies from his allies," she replied.

Jevon nodded. "He also knows their strengths and weaknesses."

"Then you're not much of a leader, Jevon," Halina said.

Arik-bohk laughed. Amma cackled. Jevon's frown deepened.

Gethen suppressed a smirk and the other advisors shifted uncomfortably, unsure how to react.

The king smiled broadly at Halina. "I've missed that sharp tongue, Red Blade, but I don't think Jevon has. Then again, he coveted it for many years and now sees it'll never cross his lips."

Halina replied, "Perhaps your commander's jealousy blinds him to reality, Arik."

Arik nodded. "Perhaps." He leaned forward, his arms resting on the table before him, hands loosely clasped. "A good leader doesn't let his own pain influence his decisions. Don't you agree, Lord Rhyshis?"

"I do. That was my first and last lesson every day when I was Besera's crown prince."

"Yet, you're protecting the Red Blade."

"To protect Quoregna."

"And what if protecting Quoregna means letting her die? Can you do it?"

Gethen returned the king's steady regard. It was a question he'd avoided since the day he'd realized he loved Halina. "I'll do everything in my power to avoid that situation."

A faint smile crossed Arik-bohk's lips. "So will I, Sun Mage. But sometimes we must make the most painful decisions, the ones that place others in harm's way."

"True. And that's when it's good to have wise voices around you."

"And the wisdom to listen to all of them."

Gethen lifted his chin. "What are the wise voices telling you about me, Your Majesty?"

This time Arik-bohk's smile was small and weary. "Many different things. The ones I find most interesting are the ones that dissent, the ones I'm discouraged from appraising."

"I'm surprised you hear any of those."

"One or two."

"Halina?"

The king nodded. "Amma Xana thinks highly of you, as well, even though your presence in Gurvan-Sum nearly ended her life. She was honest in her assessment."

"No surprise," Gethen said.

"Not in her honesty, no. But I hadn't expected her to be so vehement about your innocence. It's unusual for her to challenge my decisions with such absolute conviction. She's generally more circumspect than passionate. It was good to be pushed by her." He cocked his head toward the diminutive woman and added, "Though I don't think my other advisors appreciated it. She made me scrutinize my suppositions about you."

Gethen wondered if that was good or bad.

Jevon spoke again, his voice even but his sentiments unflinching. "Your Majesty, we cannot trust Besera or this necromancer. He claims to come in peace but all accounts place him or Besera's agents at the scene of deaths and attacks. Who else could summon and control Skiron's dogs, but the god's own servant?"

The king nodded to another of his advisors, a black-skinned woman with a scar cleaving her face from forehead to upper lip. "What do you have to say, Fanlei?" She'd stood a white wooden marker on the table before her, a request to speak.

"We received word from our garrison at Besalee." She held up a small scroll. "A large contingent of Ursinum's army is marching toward our border, just as Lady Rhyshis warned. And third-hand reports place more of their soldiers on Ystywyth's doorstep."

A wave of indignation circled the table.

Amma Xana managed to look equally horrified and vali-dated as she looked from Halina to Gethen.

"Hmmm." Arik leaned back and stared at a spot in the center

of the table. He seemed unaffected by the proclamations rising around him:

"We'll drive them back to Tatlis!"

"Let them try to cross the desert. If the heat doesn't get them, the snakes and the Dargani will."

"I agree. Let them face the desert folk. They know what to do with invaders."

Beside Gethen, Halina remained quiet and watchful, her gaze pinned to Or-Halee's king. His was the only voice that mattered here.

The bohk raised his hand. The room fell silent and he turned his attention back to Jevon. "What news of the shrikers?"

The man's full lips disappeared into his mustache as he pressed them into an angry line. "Two more villages report attacks, Osh and Aksu."

"That far into our lands?" The king looked up from beneath his shaggy brows. He slowly shook his head as he took in the room of advisors, his gaze finally resting on Gethen and Halina. "How do we stop them, Sun Mage?"

"Remove their heads, burn their bodies," he replied. "Send Dargani sun sorcerers to fight them. But nothing will slow their numbers until their source is cut off."

"Their source." Arik-bohk held Gethen's gaze, challenge in his dark eyes. "You stand by your claim that King Waldram of Nalvika is their creator?"

"Yes."

Halina said, "As do I. He's the instigator of all the war and madness spreading across Quoregna."

"Why?" the bohk asked.

Her head tilted. "Why is he doing this or why do I accuse him?"

"Both," Amma Xana answered for the king, following the thread of truth.

"He believes he's righting wrongs Quorgena has perpetrated against Nalvika's people since the armistice was signed to end the War of the Winds."

"Wrongs?" one of the advisors barked. "He's insane."

"Yes, he is," Gethen said. "Driven mad by necromantic magic he's ill-trained to wield." He didn't mention Shemel. That was a harder truth to sell.

"And I accuse him because I witnessed him summoning the shrikers," Halina continued. "I bear new scars from his attempt to steal the blood magic from my veins and kill me."

The bohk said, "But Lady Vala accused Lord Rhyshis and Besera of plotting to murder you and your father."

"My sister didn't accuse him. She repeated the lies she was told. That's the truth as she heard it. But it is not the truth."

"How can we know?" Arik-bohk asked.

"We can remove the Sun Mage's head," Jevon said matter-of-factly.

Gethen snorted. "That is one method." Halina looked aghast at him, clearly mortified by his amusement. "Not one that I endorse, of course," he added.

"Nor do I," she said. Turning back to Jevon, she added, "Especially since you'd be killing an innocent man."

"Hmmm." Arik-bohk studied them. He turned to Amma. "Will the Dargani send their mages to fight the beasts?"

She nodded. "They already ride south and east to intercept the monsters." The king turned away, but she continued speaking. "There is a way to confirm the Sun Mage's claims of innocence, Your Majesty."

"Oh?"

"Exposure." Amusement glinted in the devious, old woman's eyes as she explained, "Shrikers won't attack the one who controls them."

SEVEN

They rode east, a parade of soldiers swathed in red following a king in mourning. On the first night, the soldiers sat around a blazing fire, drinking koumiss and taking bets on how long Gethen would last either against a shriker or against their swords.

"He created the beasts," one said. "Keep your weapons in hand."

Another added, "This may be a trap to kill us all. Did you think of that?"

The soldier to his right lowered her drink and said, "A trap set by Amma Xana? You saying that 'cause she's Dargani?"

"That's not what I meant." He looked down. "He fooled her too." Belligerent again, he added, "He's powerful enough to lure the Red Blade into his arms."

The group hooted and taunted him about lusting for Halina. When he didn't deny it they laughed louder, jostling him and tousling his hair.

She watched and listened from the shadows, judging their mood as the drink loosened their tongues.

"Learning anything new?" Gethen stood behind her, his

hands on her waist, his breath tickling her ear. She'd demanded they remove his shackles over Jevon's objections.

"No."

"Do you miss that camaraderie?"

She thought for a moment. Did she? "Maybe a little." She stroked his jaw, her gaze still on the group around the fire. "Drinking too much and telling lies for laughs was fun, but on the way to a battle fear sat with us around the campfire, and on the way home death was our companion." She tickled his chin. "I traded all that for something better and I feel no regret."

He pulled her against him and murmured, "You might be a fool."

Her fingers drifted up into his thick, dark hair. "I might be." She relaxed into him. "But maybe that's part of who I am now."

"A fool?"

"Why not?" She turned in his arms. "What if we just run away from all this? Let the world burn while we hide in a hole somewhere?"

"That's an interesting dream, but—"

"Just a dream and not one without consequences." She sighed and held him, pressing her lips to his neck, feeling the steady rhythm of his pulse beneath her lips. "I'll protect you from the shrikers."

"Always my protector?"

"Always," she whispered, and he tightened his arms around her.

"Don't worry, Militess, I can handle a few undead dogs."

"A few."

"You think Arik-bohk plans to throw me into a pit of them?"

She laughed. "Probably not. That's something I'd do. He's much more civilized."

"Beastly woman." Gethen cupped her face, tilted her head, and kissed her slowly, his lips caressing hers, his mouth opening, tongue sweeping her lower lip. They broke the kiss and held each other.

Halina wasn't happy with Amma Xana's suggestion, though she could see the brilliance of it. The risks were high and they could be handing Waldram exactly what he wanted — Gethen's death.

As if reading her mind, he said, "If this gives Quoregna the proof it needs to show I'm not responsible for these beasts, I'm willing to face a horde of them."

"One will do. Let's hope for just one, all right?"

"Very well."

She yawned and sank into his arms. "We should sleep."

Gethen nodded. "Jevon said it's another day's hard ride to the latest village reporting shriker sightings."

"We both need to be ready to fight." She yawned again and he did too.

He steered her toward their small tent. "Agreed. I'm as tired as you sound. The bohk's prison guards made no attempt at providing a comfortable bed."

"You have complaints?"

"Many. The service was dismal."

On their third day riding east, they came to a decimated village that sat at the mouth of a narrow canyon. The few surviving villagers claimed several shrikers had attacked from a cave within the ravine, dragging adult victims into its darkness.

They found the place, confirmed when the horses shied from the narrow opening into the gulch.

Halina sniffed the air. "Putrid things," she muttered.

"It only gets worse." Gethen dismounted mirroring her frown. "Several shrikers? Is that three or four or more? It's best to know exactly how many you're dealing with before facing these things."

"Three," one of the old men replied, but two others contradicted him, claiming there were four.

Gethen cursed beneath his breath then cocked a grin at Arik. "Care to join the fun, Your Majesty?"

The king shook his head. "Kind of you to invite me, mage, but this fight is yours alone."

"Not alone." Halina dismounted and handed her horse's reins to one of the nearby soldiers. Gethen cursed even more, but she raised a finger to him. "I missed out on the fun last time. I owe these cunny whores and their maker, King Jigglestick. You will not deny me my revenge."

He bared his teeth at her, but it was a battle he'd never win. "Fine. But you'll follow my lead because I'm the one with experience fighting these things."

"Agreed."

"I don't think this is wise, Halina," Arik-bohk rumbled as he dismounted his horse.

She snapped, "Too late for wisdom, Your Majesty, three days too late." She unsheathed her sword and joined Gethen at the mouth of the canyon. They stood above and opposite the ground-level cave, a black gash in the yellow hillside.

"This is a terrible location for a shriker fight," he muttered.

"But a good spot to trap them. We can block the canyon's mouth and shoot them as they emerge from the cave."

"Arrows are useless."

"Not if they're on fire."

He nodded, acceding the point. "Roasted shriker is not a pleasant smell."

Her nose wrinkled. "Neither is fresh shriker." Her gaze roamed the rocks. There were few hiding places beyond the cave. If the beasts were inside, they'd have to come straight at Gethen and her. "How do we do this?"

"With a lot of fire and a silencing spell. It'll be fast and vicious. Don't let them get a hold of you. They like to shake their prey." He summoned shadows from the curved hillsides and the cave itself. They flowed like smoke, unnatural and eerie, as they pulled away from the darkness and encircled him, taking the shape of dark, iridescent armor. It solidified upon him, moving with his muscles, rippling and shifting like a creature with a mind of its own.

"I'd very much like some of that armor, Sun Mage," Halina said, running her hand over his vambrace. It was cold and strangely changeable, hardening beneath her touch then softening as if determining she wasn't a threat. "It's like it has a mind of its own," she murmured, enthralled.

"It does." He glanced away from the cave. "It's an ambit." She drew her hand back, suddenly wary of the power coursing through the armor. "Still want some?" he asked, sounding bemused.

"Yes." She met his gaze. "If it would obey me."

A piercing shriek echoed from the cave mouth. Halina clapped her hands over her ears. Behind them, the horses squealed and lunged.

"Hold the monstrosities here," Arik ordered his men. They dismounted and locked their shields to block the opening. "We cannot let them pass."

Gethen started a susurrus incantation as a shriker appeared at the cave opening.

The enormous dead dog glowed from within, a sallow light visible through its parchment flesh — the incantations Waldram had carved into its bones to quicken his undead servant. It lunged from the cave and slunk into the sun revealing raw, jagged bones knotted together with gray ligaments, yellowed skin, and mangy patches of brown fur. Its rotting teeth were visible in its exposed skull and its eyes oozed pus.

Gethen launched a fiery spell at the beast. It screamed and maggoty spittle flew from its jaws as it lunged at the scribed wall of flames. Halina winced as its shrieks were echoed by others from within the cave. Gethen sent out a spell to silence their hair-raising cries.

She stood at his side cursing up a storm as the shriker prowled before them, its tail lashing the air and its claws gouging the baked-clay ground.

Gethen said, "I wish you were Thaksin right now."

"Why?"

"Because I'm still irritated with that pillock and I'd rather see him torn apart by these things than you." He summoned a long-sword from the shadows. "Get ready. I'm lowering the spell."

"Bollocks." She raised her sword and braced.

He dropped the mage fire and moved left as she went right.

The shriker sprang at the chance to kill, following Gethen as the source of its frustration. That was its last mistake. Halina cleaved its head from its neck, a clean, powerful slice.

"You sure about that?" she asked.

Gethen shrugged as she returned to his side and another shriker emerged from the darkness. "Maybe." The monster charged. He raised his hand and scribed an amber spell in midair, a round, sorcerous shield to protect Halina and him. It flashed and squealed as it deflected the beast.

She timed her next blow to catch the creature as it tried to recover from crashing against the spell. Slipping beneath the shield, she slashed upward, removing its jaw and half its snout. The shriker shook its broken face, confused by the sudden loss of its teeth. It lunged again. Halina rolled clear. Gethen slammed his sword through its skull, pinning the monster to the ground.

His wife followed through with another blow, severing a second shriker head.

Two more beasts charged toward them from the cave. "How many of these damn things are there?" she snarled and pivoted away. The air rippled around her as one of them just missed her hip with its claws.

Gethen set it ablaze and snarled a mass incantation that threw the fourth shriker back against the mountainside. He held it in place, his hand up, a string of spells coming from him in a monotone litany of destruction. The creature writhed. Its bones cracked. The glow inside it flickered, dimmed, extinguished.

Halina's attention returned to the flaming beast. It prowled and shrieked, its piercing cry still silenced. The stench coming from its burning flesh made her gorge rise. It stumbled and fell, rose, and staggered toward Gethen, still determined to destroy its attacker. The heat coming off it kept Halina at bay. It lunged toward him.

"Look out!"

He diverted his powerful incantation to it, hurling the creature down the rocky slope they'd climbed. It came to rest at the bottom and its corpse jerked and twitched, setting the stubby brush around it ablaze.

Halina wiped sweat from her forehead and turned toward Gethen, but movement caught her eye. She jerked him sideways and tried to jump clear but couldn't avoid a collision with a fifth shriker.

More than once in her life, Halina Persinna had been trampled by a warhorse.

This was worse.

Horses didn't have claws, and they didn't smell like death.

She hit the ground and tucked her chin to her chest, covering her head and neck with her arms. Weight smashed her into the rocky soil. She gasped as her ribs cracked. Claws punctured her leather brigandine, slashed her shoulder and back. Searing pain shot through her face.

The ground shook and furnace heat blasted her then was gone, taking the shriker's weight with it. She slowly uncurled and opened her eyes in time to see her husband eviscerate the monstrosity with his sword. He'd pinned it with a mass incantation, hacked its head off, and now slammed his longsword through its spine. He left the weapon impaled in the beast, rocking to and fro as he ran to her.

"Semele's blood," he cursed and lifted her into his arms. Her face hurt worse than anything. Maybe her jaw was broken. "Don't speak," he said. "Its claw tore your cheek open. I need to get the poison out and close the wound." He climbed the hillside.

Amma Xana met them halfway. Arik was with her, and more soldiers followed.

"Are you sure all the beasts are gone?" the bohk asked.

Gethen bared his teeth in a feral, humorless smile. "No, but if more emerge, *you* deal with them. I've proven my innocence." He continued past them toward the ravine's mouth. "Amma, fetch my haversack and someone erect a tent," he snapped over his shoulder.

Once the shelter was up, Gethen cleaned and stitched Halina's face and the punctures on the rest of her body while she swallowed colorful curses. He made her drink something foul and smeared something stinking all over her wounds. At least she hadn't lost any teeth this time.

He dressed her in one of his tunics and sat on the edge of her cot, gently brushing her hair back from her battered face. "Your ribs are bruised, but I didn't feel any breaks." Her left eye was swelling shut. She touched it. "Your eye is fine. And there's no sign your organs are bleeding. All things to be thankful for."

She huffed and rolled her good eye then tapped her teeth and mumbled, "Nah brkn."

"Not broken? Your teeth?" She nodded. "Another good thing," he agreed and brushed his lips across her forehead. "No more speaking. The swelling will worsen before it improves."

Amma Xana poked her head into the tent. "How's our warrior princess?"

"Amma, I respect you, but I do not think this is a good time for you to be speaking to me." Gethen was like an angry wolf, his voice a low warning growl.

"Direct your anger toward the right target, Sun Mage," she snapped.

"In this, I will direct my anger at you, old woman. You knew Halina couldn't stand by and watch me fight."

"I knew it was the only way to prove your innocence."

"And nearly got my wife killed!"

Appa Unegan slipped into the tent, his hands raised as if to ward off an attack. "Peace, Gethen of Ranith," the old man murmured.

Halina caught her husband's hand and tugged to get his attention. He looked down at her and she shook her head, mumbling, "Please dnt," from the side of her mouth.

Gethen exhaled. "I will be calm, for you," he told her.

Arik-bohk entered the small tent. Jevon and four soldiers came with him, presumably to keep the king safe from Gethen's boiling anger. Halina would've laughed at the pointlessness of that if she could. The wound followed the hollow of her cheek down to split the corner of her upper lip and it would leave an ugly scar.

Arik started to speak, but she raised her hands and gestured for parchment, ink, and a quill.

Are you satisfied? she wrote.

"With your wounds? No. With Gethen Rhysh's claims of innocence? Yes."

Good. That's what matters.

Arik shook his head. "Your well-being matters, Red Blade. More than you know."

She ignored that. It was a pointless platitude she'd heard too often. *Do we have an alliance?*

"Yes. Once Or-Halee is rid of this plague of shrikers, we'll drive Ursinum from our border and send food and medical supplies to Ystwyth. But I cannot send soldiers."

Gethen shot a black look at the bohk. "What about Nalvika?"

Halina wrote: *Waldram?*

"You've proven the Sun Mage didn't summon the shrikers. That's not the same as proving King Waldram did. And it doesn't prove he's controlling King Ilker." Arik-bohk shook his head. "I cannot involve my people in your family's dispute, Halina. And I will not charge headlong into a second War of the Winds."

Nalvika's marching on Tatlis. This she underlined.

"I sent a bird to confirm that threat. The message I received from Tatlis said all is well. It seems you've been misinformed on that count."

She snapped the quill and sat up, swaying a little until Gethen steadied her.

"That's your final decision, Your Majesty?" he asked.

"I'm sorry to disappoint you, Lord Rhyshis, Lady Rhyshis, but, yes, that's my final decision. Unless you can offer irrefutable proof that King Waldram is using necromancy to create shrikers and manipulate King Ilker, I cannot endanger my people in these disagreements. If Ursinum and Besera wish to bring their dispute before the Council of Kings, I will listen and mediate, of course."

Halina closed her eyes and drew a deep breath, wincing as pain shot through her bruised ribs. Aid wouldn't come from Or-

Halee. Arik-bohk was too circumspect to rush into war. She respected him for that, even though he was making a terrible mistake.

Before they left, Appa Unegan and Amma Xana promised to speak with Mahish, the leader of the Dargani, about an alliance. "I can't make any promises," Appa said. "Their loyalty is to Arik-bohk first."

Halina nodded and wrote: *Thank you for trying.*

Gethen remained silent. His forgiveness wouldn't come soon or easily. But she thought it would eventually arrive.

They returned to Ranith and after four days of recuperating, Halina was weary of the mixture of pity and horror Cerys wore every time they spoke. But Besera's young queen demonstrated more patience as Gethen recounted their time in Or-Halee, reserving her opinions on the outcome.

"I thought you'd be angry, Your Highness," he remarked.

"Because Arik-bohk is addressing his people's needs before Besera's?" She passed her sleeping son to his nursemaid. "No, I can't fault him for that, especially knowing how much he's lost and seeing the damage those beasts can inflict." She glanced at Halina and quickly away. "I must be patient and trust my husband and my countrymen to turn back this invasion."

Halina nodded and thought, *Cerys might make a decent queen yet.*

Her wound's swelling was gone, thanks to her husband's foul brews, and the pain had eased from fiery to dull. The punctures she'd garnered on her back, shoulders, and chest were healing well. "I'm the most interesting palette," she remarked as she surveyed her battered body in Gethen's looking glass. Her speech was back to normal, though she sometimes dribbled mead down her chin if she wasn't careful.

He looked up from a book, something about ancient weaponry written in an arcane language. "A painted lady," he remarked.

"Good thing I'm not Ursinum's ruler. They'd call me the Queen of Scars."

"And I'd have to snarl all day to prove my ferocity."

She laughed and pulled a wine-dark kirtle over her head, careful not to snag her stitches. She joined him on the couch. A map of Quoregna was unfurled on the low table before it. She leaned over and traced a line northeast from Ayestra to the Northern Wastes.

"To Teleyansk?" Gethen asked.

"Yes. We'll forge an alliance with Emperor Lokshin, trading his army for Nalvik steel. We'll split our forces. Half will go west to take Nalvika then south toward Tatlis. The remaining forces will free Besera and cross the Silver Sea. We'll trap Waldram in Ursinum between the united armies. By the time my brother and that idiot cousin realize what's happening, we'll be standing in their tents."

Gethen considered the map. "This could work."

She sniffed. "It could."

EIGHT

Three weeks had passed since Besera came under siege. Halina and Gethen had returned to Ayestra and, true to his word, King Danas provided a single ship and crew. She thanked him politely for the paltry aid, reserving her curses for later that night.

The *Banriona* was provisioned and they would set sail the next day in hopes of finally securing the army Halina so desperately needed.

Not a moment too soon for Gethen. Ayestra offered the tempting power of too many innocent souls. He'd avoided them by hiding in the quarters he shared with his wife or attending her sister, Arevik, whose constitution was taxed by the summer heat.

On their last day in Essendra, Halina was killing time by dueling with the soldiers who would accompany her and Gethen to Teleyansk.

Gethen watched her from a shadowy archway as she pushed her limits against militairs who wouldn't gut her, but who made her work hard for victory. She rolled her shoulders as she walked Essen Citadel's dusty practice ring. She licked sweat from her upper lip and spat. "Damn dust." Midday heat shimmered from the ground. "I'm sweating like a roast pig." She wiped her face with a rag, careful around the lingering shriker wound.

"I feel like one," one of the gathered soldiers agreed.

"You look like one," another man said and the group laughed.

Halina was testing the mettle of the troops who'd back her during the voyage to Teleyansk. And she was showing them her worth, proving she was as strong as ever, new scars be damned.

She squinted at the cloudless Ayestran sky. "I've got one more round in me, you dunderheads. Who's last?"

"I am." Gethen pushed away from the white stone wall and stepped into the sunlight.

Spying him, the militairs hooted and clapped, excited to see the Red Blade and her battle mage face off.

She stopped circling, tilted her head, and turned her squint on him. "To what do I owe this rare honor?"

"Curiosity, dear wife." He entered the arena, summoning his shadow armor and longsword to surprised murmurs from the onlookers. He moved around her, stretching his arms and shoulders, getting in a few practice swings with the blade.

"Hmm." She wiped sweat from her brow and nodded. "I'll go easy on you, husband."

Gethen stopped and raised his sword to a mid-level guard position. "Please don't."

Halina smiled and cocked her head at the soldiers. "He likes it when I'm rough." They laughed and called encouragement to both her and Gethen as she saluted him with her sword.

Husband and wife circled and tested, the ring of their weapons resounding off the bailey's stone walls. Though sweaty, Halina wasn't spent and she parried his strikes with ease.

"You're a bit rusty, Lord Rhyshis," she commented after landing a score on his right thigh.

Gethen inclined his head. "Swordplay isn't my first line of defense, Lady Rhyshis."

"Clearly." She lunged in to close with him, a blow he narrowly evaded. The soldiers clapped and offered Gethen advice:

"Run, mage!"

"Now we know who's got the bigger sword!"

"Might want to employ some of that famous magic, if you plan to survive Her Ladyship's steel."

Gethen spied the speaker of that last comment and flashed a wolfish grin at the woman.

A narrow band of shadow whipped out and caught Halina's left ankle. She widened her stance and fought its pull. The crowd booed, but she shook her head. "No-no," she said. "I didn't restrict his weapons." Battling magic was an ongoing challenge. "I'll pit all of you against the Sun Mage's sorcery. You need to learn how to beat a mage."

Her sword passed harmlessly through the shadow and, in response, it tightened and Gethen yanked her foot out from beneath her. He lunged forward, but she'd anticipated his move and swept her sword back low, aiming for his feet. Gethen jumped, narrowly escaping, but his shadowy grip failed. Halina was up and after him with a series of lunges and thrusts that had her husband on the defense until another shadow captured her sword arm and yanked her off her feet. She landed on her back with a rattle of plate and mail. Gethen's blade tapped her chest. She raised her hand, one finger up.

"Point given," she said as he pulled her to her feet. "That's why we want him on our side."

Gethen said nothing as he watched and tested.

Halina asked, "What's your game, Mage?"

He just smiled. She paused and her expression said he'd pay for every bruise that night.

They circled, lunged, parried more, but now cautious, Halina watched his hands and avoided the bailey's gloomy corners.

With his next attack, the shadows wrapped her in a dark miasma, blinding her to his movements. Her soldiers protested.

Halina shouted, "Quiet!" but not quickly enough and she responded to the whisper of Gethen's feet too late, unable to avoid the touch of his sword against her throat.

The darkness lifted. He stood behind her, his lips so close to her ear that she shivered against him when he said, "Point."

But he'd forgotten that Halina didn't obey rules. She pivoted, caught his arm and shoulder, and threw him arse over elbows to the ground. Landing astride her husband, her misericord at his throat, Halina said, "Given and taken."

She was off him and circling as he nodded and smirked. "I see it's time to push harder, Militess," he said as he stood.

Halina gave her husband a lascivious smile and replied, "Later, Mage."

The onlookers roared.

She squinted, clearly trying to understand what he aimed to accomplish. Pushing her harder with sorcery was dangerous. She wouldn't injure him deliberately, but Halina had a temper and she couldn't always snuff its lit fuse.

She didn't give him time to ponder the wisdom of his plan. She came at him, dodged his parry, and disarmed him with a powerful sweep of her sword. His weapon clattered across the stones outside the practice ring, making the soldiers hop and dodge. But Gethen wasn't about to lose that easily. He summoned shadows to capture her arms and waist, swept out his arm, and threw her across the arena. She hit the stone wall hard enough to knock the breath from her. Halina shook her head and cursed a fine selection of inappropriate words.

Gethen called upon his sun sorcery and heat replaced the cold of the shadows. Sweat trickled down his wife's temples and beaded her upper lip. The heat was oppressive. The ring shimmered with it. A guttural sound escaped her, an animal growl that should've sent him scuttling for safety.

"Fight back!" Gethen commanded as he retrieved his sword. "Make me stop, Halina." The soldiers were shouting at him, demanding he release her. He kept them at bay with a fiery shield spell. Their anger was palpable, a rising rage that further fueled the confrontation. Gethen didn't doubt his wife was seeing red.

She closed her eyes and strained against the pressure of the sun. He was putting its weight on her, forcing the air from her lungs with its mass. She bared her teeth. Her hands were trembling, her sword's tip rattling against the paving stones.

"Come on! Fight it!" Gethen ranged back and forth in front of her, a feral wolf, his teeth bared. "Stop being weak!"

Her gaze pinned him and he knew he'd broken through a barrier. Halina peeled herself from the wall. She pushed back on the sorcery, slowly raised her sword as if cutting through stone, then the control on her rage broke. She cleaved the air, his sorcery, the power holding her bound to the wall and slammed her sword's blade into his, again and again until, with a resounding ring, the blade of his bastard sword snapped and the shadow-bound weapon disintegrated.

"Hold!" Gethen said and raised his hands to her, palms out.

No sound came but Halina's breathing and the call of sea crows above Essendra Bay.

She wanted to kill him. And she didn't. Confusion and an almost blinding rage consumed her. Gethen saw it in her eyes. She pivoted away from him, stomped across the arena, and hacked at one of the straw-filled practice dummies. She lopped off its head, gutted and sliced it apart. Then, still filled with rage, she roared and threw her longsword across the arena. Militairs ducked and gawked as she stormed across the bailey and into the castle, shoving servants aside.

Gethen was right behind her, dispelling his armor and dodging the chaos in her wake.

Two servants were in their apartment when she kicked open the bedchamber door. "Get out!" she shouted as the door slammed into the wall and bounced back. They scurried past her and Gethen, who strode calmly behind her.

Halina rounded on him. "Get this armor off. I can't breathe in it. Off-off, get it off!" She was shaking, barely in control of herself. "What did you do to me?" she snarled.

"Pushed you past your limits." Gethen pulled at the leather buckles and ties. "I had to."

When he lifted the chainmail shirt over her head, she staggered against him. The padded gambeson followed and she cried out with relief as cool air caressed her skin. He steered her toward the bathing room. "You need water."

"I need to stab you!"

"Water first." He backed her to the washstand, grabbed its full ewer, and emptied it over her head.

Halina gasped as the cold water cooled her fire. "Bollocks!" She gripped the edge of the stand and blinked water from her eyes. "What did you do to me?" she repeated, calmer. "The last time I lost control in battle was the day my brother Halion was killed."

"When you were named the Red Blade?" She nodded and he said, "I was proving a theory."

"What theory? That you're a fen-sucking mongrel whom I should've killed when I had the chance?"

He laughed and pushed wet hair back from her face. "No. That your blood magic will enable mage armor."

She gaped. "You mean like the armor you wear?"

"Yes, but strengthened by blood rather than shadows." He found a towel for her.

Halina rubbed the water from her hair. "But I'm not a necromancer. You said the armor is an ambit. Wouldn't I have to summon and command it?"

"Yes and no. Summoning is simple. If it wasn't, Waldram wouldn't be the threat he is. But sustaining the armor on your body requires a framework of magic for the ambit to hook into."

"I don't follow."

He thought for a moment. "It's like your own armor. Each piece connects in a specific way to its neighbor to create a defensive structure around your body, and your arming jacket supports all of it. Right?"

"Obviously."

"Magic is an armor ambit's equivalent of your arming jacket."

She nodded, understanding dawning in her eyes. "I see. So without magic, the ambit can't maintain its armor shape?"

"Precisely. Mage armor works somewhat like the ambit you used in Drevya Linna and Tatlis. I'll create the armor ambit, tying it to your soul and limiting its independence. You'll summon it when you need it, dispel it when you don't."

"It can't be that easy."

He laughed. "It's not, at least not at first. Eventually it'll become second nature. You might even learn to utilize it as a full set of weapons."

Her gaze sharpened at that. "Like daggers and ropes the way you do?"

"Possibly."

She pursed her lips. "Won't people think I'm a battle mage?"

"Some already do, Red Blade."

"Oh." She chewed her lip. "But why did you push me so hard?"

"To see if your blood magic empowers you to fight."

"All right. Why?"

"Because you'll protect your armor as much as it'll protect you. It's a living thing."

She frowned. "I don't understand."

How could he put it simply? "Armor ambits abandon cowards."

Understanding dawned on her face. "So it'll only protect me if I have the strength and will to use it?"

"Yes, and the fundamental structure in place to maintain it, which is where your blood magic comes in."

She followed him as he went to the small table beside the windows where the light was best. He'd already unpacked his haversack and set out a spread of ingredients and containers, a mortar and pestle, and a small cauldron.

"You expected your theory to be correct, I see."

He looked up at her from beneath his brows. "When am I ever wrong?"

"I can recall a time or two." She shivered and pulled her wet tunic over her head.

"I'm trying to concentrate," he muttered, suddenly distracted.

"And I'm trying to get dry." She waggled her fingers at the crowded table. "Control your lust and do your mage thing." She pulled a kirtle and surcoat from a trunk by the bed then stripped off the rest of her wet and sweaty clothes. Gethen watched her, entranced by his wife's trim, scarred body. He shook himself and refocused. "Dress in trouzes and tunic."

"Why?"

"That's what you wear under armor." He dropped a chunk of

silvery antimony into the cauldron then carried the vessel to the hearth and nestled it into the coals. He heaped wood and kindling around the black pot and set it ablaze with blue-white mage fire.

Halina dressed, poured a glass of mead from the decanter beside the bed, and slumped on the couch, watching him work. "Your armor ambit dwells in your shadow?" she asked and he nodded. "I always thought you drew the shadows to you."

"Not quite. When I summon the ambit it draws forth the shadows, weaving them into its armored form, powered by my soul. It protects me to protect itself. If I die, it'll cease to exist."

She yawned. "Will this take long?" The room was warm and the blazing fire was heating it even more.

"A few hours." He ground ingredients in the mortar, adding them one at a time — black salt, niter, and pyrolusite. "Changing the antimony is a slow process."

She stretched out on the couch and closed her eyes. "Wake me when you need me."

Gethen let her sleep. He'd pushed her hard in the practice ring and restoring her energy was necessary before he finished the armor ambit. She'd need focus and strength to learn how to wield it. He ground the last few ingredients until he had a light-gray powder. To this he added clarified water and five drops of yellow liquid brimstone. He checked the antimony, then sat before the hearth and focused on heating the cauldron evenly. He stripped off his tunic, mopping sweat from his face with it as another hour passed.

"Gods, it's hot in here," Halina murmured as she sat up and stretched.

"It takes a lot of heat to transform antimony into a liquid." He checked it again and, satisfied, snuffed the fire and lifted the cauldron out of the smoldering coals and onto the hearth. He fetched the mortar and carefully added its contents to the liquified antimony. Thick, white smoke rose like a spirit over the vessel as the ingredients bubbled and hissed.

Halina poured another glass of mead for herself and brought him one, too. She returned to the couch, tucked her legs beneath her, and watched him work. As the smoke eased, Gethen poured the cauldron's mixture into an open copper pot. He crooked his finger at her. "Now you're needed."

She stood, stretched, wiped her sleeve over her face. "Can we open the windows to let in a breeze?"

He did and cool air flowed through the room. "You know how this goes. Turn so your shadow stretches across the floor." She did, her eyes closed to the bright sunlight pouring through the open windows while he shoved a chair aside and rolled up a rug so that nothing obscured her shadow. He crouched at its edge, slid his fingers just above the floor, and murmured an incantation as he scooped his hand through the shadow, closing his fingers into a fist, and pulling his hand back into the light.

Halina shivered.

"Come." He returned to the small pot, held his fist above it, and droned another incantation. Amber light glowed between his closed fingers but disappeared when he opened his hand. The black shadow had transformed into something both liquid and vaporous. It pooled in his palm and turned back on itself when he tipped his hand, refusing to fall into the pot until he blew it off.

"Did you add your soul to this one too?" she asked.

"No. I don't want it confused about whom it protects." He stirred the cooling mixture with a copper stick then reached for her hand. "You know what I need next, and this requires more than just a few drops." He traded the stick for a small dagger.

"As long as you leave me with some." She placed her hand in his.

"I said *more* not *all*." He held her hand over a dram cup and she hissed as he sliced her pinky from tip to base, not deeply but a wound that would bleed freely. After filling a quarter of the cup, he released her hand, emptied the cup into the pot, and added more water to the mixture. He stirred it ceaselessly and droned his incantation while Halina pressed a rag to her hand. Finally, satisfied with its consistency and color, Gethen strained the mixture through a cloth. Nodding at her hand, he asked, "Has the bleeding stopped?"

She peeled back the rag. "Not quite. Why?"

"There can't be any free-flowing blood when I perform this last step."

"Because?"

"It's blood armor. The ambit will take its shape from shadows, draw power from your soul, and use blood to reinforce its form while in battle."

"My blood?"

"Your enemies' blood."

Her brows rose. "That's terrifying."

"For them, yes."

"So why does it matter if I'm bleeding now?"

"Because it's attracted to blood, even its master's. I don't want it to consume you and itself."

"Oh."

"Let me see your wound." She offered her hand and he murmured a healing incantation to speed its closure.

She squinted at her finger when he was finished. "I didn't know you could heal open wounds that easily. Why didn't you do that to my face?" She touched her wounded cheek.

"That wound was poisoned and needed to drain." He led her to the window and repositioned her so that her shadow stretched across the floor. While speaking another incantation he slowly poured the liquid, outlining her shadow. It spread and filled the shade, becoming part of the darkness and momentarily tinting it crimson before darkening to black.

Halina stared at her shadow. She looked up at him. "Now what?"

"Now you learn how to summon it."

"It'll immediately form armor around me?"

He nodded. "At first, you may need to speak the summoning aloud, but soon thinking it will be enough and, eventually, just the desire will draw up your ambit."

She faced him. "All right. Teach me."

"Gveed, enaith, a cysgud, amdivin vi ad vy engilenion."

"That's an old tongue. What does it mean?"

"It's the root language of modern Beseran. It means, 'Blood, soul, and shadow, protect me from my enemies.'"

She closed her eyes. "Repeat it a few times?" He did and she mouthed the words as he spoke them. Finally, she nodded. "All right. Let me try." Gethen stepped back as Halina spoke the incantation. "Gveed, enaith, a cysgud, amdivin vi ad vy engilenion." She gasped and her eyes widened as the shadows swirled and undulated around her, drawn from beneath the bed, the corners of the room, and the places behind the couch. It snaked around her, forming the same living armor Gethen wore into battle, but deep crimson in color. Her sol avuus symbol skittered across its surface. She stared down at it, her arms held away from her body, awe in her expression. When the armor finally solidified upon her, she murmured, "Khotyr, take me." She met his gaze. "It's...it...makes me feel protected...and powerful."

He nodded, a slow smile spreading across his face. "It's comforting, eh?"

"Lighter and warmer than I expected." She rapped her gauntleted knuckles against her breastplate. It rang like plate armor. "Sorcery beyond my imagination," she murmured.

Gethen laughed. "You've seen me draw up mine often enough."

"Yes, but I never thought I'd ever wear some. It's astonishing." Her smile was bright and beautiful, made lopsided by her scar yet no less charming to him, and he matched it with his own.

"You need to perfect dispelling it too."

Halina strode around the chamber, reaching and moving, getting accustomed to the feel and movement of the armor. "What's the incantation?"

"Esbryd, euk meyun tehveuk. Which means, 'Ambit, go in peace.'" She had him repeat it several times then used it herself.

After the armor had dissolved back into the shadows, she looked bereft. She gave him a sidelong glance and summoned the armor again, laughing like a child receiving sweets on Semele's Day. Gethen shook his head and dropped to the couch. He wouldn't deny her the excitement of discovering the armor's power. She found joy in it that he'd forgotten. As a boy, he'd first created and summoned his own armor out of a desperate need for protection against Shemel. Now he could delight in her pleasure.

He yawned. The fight and the spell casting had drained him. He'd used a lot of energy creating the armor and the magic that normally buzzed through him had quieted to a slow thrum.

Halina dispelled the armor and sat opposite him gazing out the window at the deep, blue bay. Her brow furrowed, mouth pinched as all her delight evaporated.

"What's wrong?" he asked.

"Ha! Where do I start?"

"With the truth."

She sighed. "Thaksin called me queen." She slowly shook her head. "People get killed for that kind of thing. Armies assassinate their leaders. Siblings poison each other. I've never sought the crown." She straightened. "Never. Ilker's the rightful king. He's Ambrosine's only living child. I'm the bastard and I was lucky to have Khara. I know that." She looked at him. "I never wanted more than that."

He beckoned her to join him and took her left hand when she did. He kissed her stunted fingers. "You have to decide who you are, Halina." She opened her mouth to speak, but he continued. "Yes, you're my wife." He kissed the back of her hand. "And yes you're a duchess, a princess, a former margrave. You're a leader, a soldier, the Red Blade of Or-Halee. The victim of Waldram's ambition. The woman I love." He turned her hand and kissed her palm. "But those are labels other people have assigned to you." He held her gaze again and said, "Who are you when all of it's stripped away? Only you can decide that."

NINE

Halina swayed one direction as her gut went the other. On the Great Green Ocean's high seas, the *Banriona* was a world of constant sound and motion. The ship's towering canvas sails snapped and rattled with the ever-changing winds. Her boards groaned, her stays creaked, her chains clanked with the ceaseless waves. And those waves crashed against her hull, bass and baritone to the gulls' tenor cries.

In contrast, the ship's constant pitch and shift caused Gethen no distress. They'd left Ostendra ten days prior, and he took every opportunity to climb the mainmast and stare across the ocean. He hung over the forecastle rail watching dolphins cavort alongside the ship's prow as she cut through the dark water. He spent hours on deck at night, studying the stars or watching the eerie glow of tiny creatures flashing beneath the waves.

"I believe they're food for other beasts, but I have no idea what makes them glow," he murmured to Halina as he made notes and sketches. "I think it's the same internal fire that glow flies and night moss share."

Refusing to be hampered by her unsettled stomach and

unsteady legs, Halina sparred twice daily with the soldiers who'd come aboard.

Though, on Gethen's advice, she hid her blood armor.

"Let's keep that advantage from our enemies until the last moment," he suggested.

This morning, as the *Banriona* sailed northeast, shadowing the distant line of the Northern Wastes on her portside, Halina stood in the tiny cabin she and Gethen shared, clad in her dark crimson armor. She thought the dispelling incantation, *Esbryd, euk meyun tehveuk*, and the armor flowed away from her to rejoin the shadows.

Gethen lounged on their narrow bed. He'd awakened sullen and hadn't taken his usual climb up the mainmast, choosing instead to glower out their cabin's tiny portal and mutter to himself.

The rhythmic calls of the sailors drifted down from the deck. Halina had watched them tugging the stays in a coordinated dance of strength she admired. It took skill and cooperation to sail a tall ship. "It's like a small army," she'd remarked to the ship's master on their first day out from port. "The ship is your courser and the sea your field."

"Sometimes our foe, too," he'd replied.

Halina shivered and turned to Gethen. "I'm always cold after shedding the ambit. Is that normal?"

He shrugged. "I've never paid attention. I'm usually just relieved to be alive after battle."

She laughed then leaned down to kiss him. "Thank you for creating it."

Despite his mood, he smiled at her touch. "I'm happy you're willing to accept it. I remember a time when you considered the mere suggestion of my help as an insult."

She straightened. "I've learned a bit about my vulnerabilities since then."

"And your strengths?"

"Those too." She carded her fingers through his hair. "I count you among them."

He stood and braced against the ship's sway. "That's flattering," he remarked, his attention straying to the portal.

"And true."

He pulled her against him. "I'm glad you think so."

"It took me a while to figure it out." She studied his profile — strong jaw, sharp cheekbones, heavy brow over intense gray eyes. "You're always here for me." She kissed him gently, wrapping her arms around his waist and softening against him. If she couldn't have the comfort of her blood armor, she'd enjoy the support of its maker instead. He was the better of the two anyway.

He brushed her hair over her shoulders, tenderness replacing some of the severity in his expression. "Thank you for letting me be here for you. You're the only person to ever trust me this way."

"What about Magod and Noni?"

He shook his head. "This is different."

She sobered. "Why don't you trust me to be here for you?"

"What? I trust you." The somber veil dropped over his face again.

"Not with everything. Not with your vulnerabilities." His brow furrowed. He pulled back, but she locked her arms around him. "I know you're hiding something from me, Gethen. Something about necromancy that you think will drive me away if you divulge it."

He turned to stone in her arms. "Some things are best left unknown."

"Why? You know everything about me."

"And you don't want to know everything about me." He escaped her grip. Yanking open their cabin door, he paused and added, "I share what I can, Halina. Trust my decision on what I choose not to divulge."

The door closed. Halina sighed. "Well, you bungled that," she muttered.

As if to mirror her husband's mood, thunder rumbled, distant but distinct. The thud of feet on the deck overhead reminded her how small the ship really was. Doubtless someone had overheard that exchange. Not that it mattered. Spouses argued; everyone knew that. Whatever this secret was, Gethen feared it. Or feared her reaction to it. That felt closer to the truth and it hurt. She loved him. There was nothing he could ever do that would make her love him any less. Enrage her, yes. He'd done that plenty of times. But not jeopardize her love.

Lightning flashed through the portal, followed a breath later by a thunderclap and the hiss of rain on the sea. The sails snapped, stays twanged, and the shouts of the crew took on a strident tone.

Halina lurched through the short passageway to the ladder from the hold. Rain and salt spray smacked her face as she emerged onto the deck. Sailors battened down the hatches. The sails snapped and bellowed.

"Best remain below deck, Your Ladyship," one of the men shouted. "Storm's coming up fast. Don't look like we can outrun her. Will be rough up here."

"It'll be rough down there, too!" She headed toward the forecastle where Gethen stood with the master, both staring at a wall of black clouds and flickering lightning. Staggering across the deck, she reached her husband's side just as he said, "I'll do what I can, but weather work isn't my strong suit."

"Any help will be appreciated by my crew and ship, Your Lordship. That's not a natural storm."

"Definitely not," Gethen agreed. "There's weather magic behind it and more than one mage brewing the mix."

"How can you tell?" Halina asked.

"It's moving faster than the wind," the master replied.

She grunted at that unpleasant revelation. "Waldram's allies are behind it?"

Gethen nodded, glaring at the oncoming storm. He scribed glowing, golden symbols in the air and murmured incantations.

"How could they know where to find us?" she asked.

"I don't know and I can't worry about it now," Gethen snapped. "I'll do what I can to slow the storm."

"What can I do?" she asked.

The master replied, "Go below deck, Your Ladyship."

She ignored him. "Gethen, let me help you."

He reached for her hand, but didn't break his focus. She grabbed hold and winced as heat flared across her palm and a prickling sensation shot up her arm. "Fight my pull. Don't let me take it all," he said through clenched teeth and returned to his incantations.

Halina nodded and concentrated on their bond, steadying him but also trying to stop him from taking too much of her blood magic. They'd never worked this way before. Of course they'd fought the Rime Witch together, but this was more deliberate. And he seemed to fear that he'd drain her. Something he hadn't worried about before. She sensed the strain on him through their bond, knew when he was flagging and let him draw more strength. But his sorcery felt seductive, like the brush of lips on her bare skin. She sank into it and shivered. Her gaze drifted across her husband's broad chest and lingered on the corded muscles of his forearms. Heat filled her and she closed her eyes, lulled by the buzz of magic flowing between them.

"Halina!" Gethen yanked his hand from her grasp. Her eyes snapped open as he snarled, "I told you to fight me!"

She swallowed and nodded. Gripping his arm, she tightened

her hold on their bond and looked around the ship to distract her mind from his magic's allure.

The *Banriona's* shrouds stretched from her decks to the sails, like spiderwebs spun from hemp. Soldiers clambered up them and spread out along the yards, hauling up the sails and securing them as the shrieking winds threatened to tear both sailors and sails from the masts. Shouts were lost to the pounding surf, crackling thunder, howling gale. Rain sheeted across the sea, a charcoal curtain disappearing in the bright white whip of lightning. Thunder cracked on its heels.

Stinging needle raindrops and sleet pelted their skin. Halina blinked salt spray from her eyes, one hand gripping the stays, the other tight on Gethen as the ship pitched and bucked with the storm's growing violence.

The *Banriona's* bow slammed down as each wave broke over it, sending white spray across the decks, knocking sailors off their feet, and swamping everything. The water frothed and flowed across the wood. It broke against the hatches, threatening to flood the Ayestran ship and drag her into the ocean's depths.

Gethen droned on and the storm rolled back upon itself and spread across the sky. But he was losing the battle. Heaving gray-and-white waves had replaced the peaceful sea. Only lightning forking across the clouds' iron bellies and glimpses of blue-green water distinguished the dark sky from the dark sea.

The *Banriona* keeled before a massive wave, her sails almost tipping into the brine. Gethen grabbed the rail and clenched Halina's arm. She clung to the shroud and swallowed a scream. Sailors shouted, catching hold of the stays and shrouds, the masts, rails, each other. Just as quickly, the tall ship righted, pitching to and fro.

In the momentary lapse of Gethen's focus, a flash and a crack split the sky. Lightning struck the mainmast, splintering it from tip to base. Shrapnel flew. Bodies plunged. Sails shredded and stays snapped. Wooden blocks, freed of tension, hurled across the deck like flails, sweeping sailors into the water. Movement flashed at the corner of Halina's vision. Instinct saved her and Gethen from certain death as she jerked to the side, dragging him with her. Even so, a block clubbed his temple and knocked him overboard. Halina held on. They plunged into the raging sea.

Ears ringing and skin prickling from the lightning's power, Halina surfaced. She gasped and coughed and, miraculously, still kept hold of her unconscious husband. She wrapped her arm around his chest and pinned him against her, keeping his head above the waves. Searching the water, she grabbed a splintered wooden yard, stays and sail entangling it, something to keep both of them afloat.

She expected cries of "Man overboard!" but heard only screams and the horrible crack of splintering wood. The *Banriona* had keeled over completely, her masts and sails in the water, sailors and soldiers floundering, sinking, enormous waves pounding the drowning ship and crew.

"No!" Halina shouted. "No! No! No!"

The cries of dying sailors barely rose above the gale winds, the thunder, and the horrible sounds of the ship coming apart.

"You cunny whores!" She cursed the weather witches who'd beset the *Banriona*. "When I find you, I'll split you from arse to eyeballs!"

The former Margrave of Khara, daughter of a dead king, wife of a necromancer, shouted at the iron-gray sky, then choked on the Great Green's cold brine and tightened her death grip on her husband. His blood turned the green water a sickly hue and was a siren's song to the sea's toothy hunters. But their shared heat kept her alive even as sailors and soldiers succumbed to the frigid water all around her and silently sank to dark, unseen graves.

"Khotyr, take me," she cursed. She'd never keep her hold on Gethen and the yard in the heaving waves, but there was rope firmly attached to the wood, so she lashed her unconscious husband to her and her left arm to the log. Wood, bodies, barrels, and all manner of flotsam drifted around her — all that remained of the *Banriona* and her crew. Halina rested her head on the yard, sucked a deep breath, and chose not to cry.

She'd seen worse, but not by much.

King Vernard choking on his own blood in Kharaton's great hall. "That was worse," she told herself.

And her dear older brother Halion being skewered through the skull on the field in Or-Halee. "Worse."

Her eldest brother Tirius's agonizing death after being tarred and set afire. She tightened her grip on Gethen and nodded. "Worse. Much worse."

As quickly as the storm had come upon them, it subsided, its fierce howling replaced by a more rhythmic sound. Halina raised her head. In the distance, waves broke on the Northern Wastes' scrubby shore. The storm had carried the ship much closer to land than she'd realized.

She brushed her lips across her husband's head and started kicking. It would take a few hours, she figured, but land was better than sea any day in Halina's opinion. "Come on, Mage. The gods haven't completely abandoned us yet."

TEN

Gethen opened his eyes to colorless surroundings. He lay in a shallow, milky lake. Above stretched a black, starless sky.

The Void.

"Blood and bones."

If he was here, something had gone very wrong. He sat up and looked around. Nothingness stretched in all directions. "Skiron's blood and bones." He'd only seen this part of the Void twice and he didn't want to meet the one who dwelled here again. Skiron the Destroyer. The God of Death. Gethen's true master.

He raised his hands. Rather than gray, they remained their normal bronze hue. That meant his body hadn't died in the mortal realm. But why had he crossed the Voidline?

What had happened to his wife and the ship? Was Halina safe?

With a small splash, Gethen stood. He squinted in every direction, finally spying a distant...something. Tower? Figure? He wasn't sure, but it was the only feature in an otherwise empty landscape, so he jogged toward it, his feet sending ripples through the white water.

If he was in the Void not of his own volition, and his body wasn't dead, then he'd been brought here by Skiron. He'd face the god, take whatever punishment or commands he was given, and return immediately to aid Halina. To resist was pointless and would only delay their reunion. His wife needed him. The power of Waldram's weather witches made that clear.

And there was the matter of how they'd been tracked. Luck played no part in it, he was sure. Was it treason? Or some other means? He must solve that riddle quickly.

"I'm watching you fail."

The godlike voice came from behind him. Gethen turned. Skiron wore Halina's likeness and a sneer. The god's eyes were white orbs and Gethen's gut clenched at the sight of them in his wife's beautiful face.

"I've only begun to fight," he replied.

"Not an auspicious beginning."

"I'm trying—"

"Not hard enough," Skiron snarled. He cocked a hip, a strangely feminine gesture for the God of Death. Inspecting Halina's fingernails, he added, "The ship sank."

Gethen swallowed fear's acid. "My wife?"

"Alive and keeping you that way too."

The god sniffed, picked her teeth, considered what she'd found and flicked it into the white water. Gethen shook his head, disoriented by Skiron's chosen form. The God of Death valued him no more than what was stuck between her — *his* — teeth. "I'd prefer you use a different appearance," he said.

Skiron lifted Halina's chin, looked down her nose at him, and sniffed again. "I thought this was your favorite skin."

Gethen showed his teeth. "She's not a 'skin.'"

The sneer returned to Skiron's lips. "Oh, I see. You think I'm disrespectful of your mortal lover."

"I think you're disrespectful of all mortals."

Skiron disappeared and, once again, spoke from behind Gethen. "I don't respect that which is made to worship me, mortal. I am Death and your world would not exist if not for me." A cold breath brushed his ear as the god whispered, "Remember that."

Gethen turned to find Skiron now wearing Shemel's visage. "That's not a better choice."

The god laughed and the ground trembled with the sound. Ripples spread out in the white lake, traveling to infinity. "Good. I enjoy watching you suffer, Sun Mage."

Gethen ground his teeth. "Give me guidance. Show me how to stop Waldram from creating shrikers. Tell me what steps to take to defeat Shemel before he crosses permanently into the mortal realm."

"Stop Nalvika's mad king? Defeat your former master?" The god's head tilted. "Why? They're serving their purpose."

Gethen gaped. "What purpose? To create war and bring suffering? They're slaughtering innocent children. Murdering people for pleasure and power. Shemel threatens to escape the Void. Waldram corrupts sorcery. Why allow this to continue?"

"Blind fool!" The god struck Gethen, sending him tumbling arse over elbows through the water. When he stopped somersaulting, Skiron loomed over him, a massive figure of roiling demon faces, claws, and teeth. "Gifted powers you cannot fathom and abilities you fail to utilize. You. Serve. Death." He shrank back down to Shemel's form and his tone was dismissive as he sneered. "You are a disappointment." Skiron stabbed a clawed finger at him. "Bring death, necromancer. Spread fear. Propagate contagion. If you do not, I'll find others who will." With that and a dismissive sniff, the god simply disappeared.

The water around Gethen rose. He stood and looked around, but there was no higher ground. He cursed as the white fluid topped his knees and crept toward his hips. There was nothing pleasant about his master, and he wished fervently to be Semele's or Khotyr's or, better yet, no god's servant. But it hadn't been Gethen's choice from the start and it was unlikely to go his way any time soon.

He slogged through the water toward the distant point. He could just make it out now, a lone, spindly tree. He wouldn't reach it before the water topped his head.

The *Banriona* sank. Gethen shook his head at that news, wondering if it was a lie.

"Did you bring me here just to lie and taunt me?" he wondered aloud, but the god was finished with him and no response came.

Up to his chest now, Gethen swam. The tree loomed, a skeletal hand stretching out over the lake, equally beckoning and threatening. He kept his head above the chalky, tepid water. It matched the liquid that had trapped the Rime Witch so many months ago.

Finally reaching the tree, Gethen clung to its trunk, the water still rising around him. How it could still be rising was immaterial. Skiron was toying with him like a cat playing with its prey. It reminded him of life under Shemel's cruel tutelage.

Gethen clung to the tree's top branches, but something had snagged his foot and the water continued to rise. He sucked a breath, ducked under, and worked in vain to free himself, but the branches had closed around his foot and continued to reach up, encasing his ankle, his calf, his knee. He straightened, tried to reach the surface, but it was beyond him. He panicked. His lungs screamed for air. His brain grew hazy, thoughts disorganized as instinct took over. Gethen pounded on the branch, kicked the tree, tore at the wood, but it slipped through his fingers and wouldn't give. Bubbles escaped him, precious air, fragile life.

His lungs convulsed. His mind raged.

"Gethen."

He opened his eyes.

Halina's face loomed over him. He rolled to his side and vomited water.

She held him while he retched. "You have no idea how heavy you are when you're water-logged."

He tried to reply, but more water came up. He got onto his hands and knees, heaving half the ocean. His head throbbed. His lungs burned. Saltwater stung his nose and eyes. "I'm lighter now," he managed to croak.

When he'd finally run out of seawater to puke, he stood with her help. They were on a stunted, scrubby beach near the outfall of a creek. She led him to fresh water and he drank almost as much as he'd purged. The storm was merely a memory on a now-clear day, though the sun was well past its zenith.

"What happened?" he rasped.

"The foremast stays failed. You were knocked overboard by a block. We're lucky your skull's intact."

"How long was I out?" He winced as his fingers found a gash on his forehead, bandaged with fabric torn from Halina's tunic. He didn't remember being clobbered by the wooden pulley, but a sizable lump attested to the blow.

She squinted at the sun. "About six hours." Her lips pressed into a thin line and her voice was tight as she added, "I was afraid you'd never come back."

He caught her hand and kissed her war-stunted fingers. He touched his head and murmured a healing incantation to close the wound and ease the bruising and swelling. "Skiron wanted to chastise me."

Her eyes widened. "He spoke to you?"

"Unfortunately. Dragged me into the Void."

"He's angry with you?" Her brow furrowed. "That's unfair."

Gethen snorted. "Fair isn't a word I'd use to describe the God of Death."

"I suppose not. He thinks you should've stopped Waldram by now?"

He shook his head and winced as pain shot down the left side of his neck and traveled down his arm. The block had done a fine job as a bludgeon. "Skiron thinks I should mimic Waldram and Shemel."

"What?" She gaped. "Skiron *wants* war? But why?"

Gethen started to shake his head, then remembered the pain. "I'm not exactly sure, except that he's the God of Death."

"What about Semele and Khotyr? They represent life. Surely they can't want this massacre too."

He shrugged, and winced again. "I don't know. I've never heard from the goddesses."

She stared at him then shivered. "This is madness."

"Madness and chaos. And I don't plan to satisfy Skiron any time soon. I didn't choose to be the Sun Mage. That was the gods' doing. I won't bow before their demands."

"Easier said than done, don't you think?"

He grimaced. "My head hurts too much to think right now." He scanned their surroundings. She'd erected a crude shelter from driftwood, a ragged sail, and the wind-blown grasses that dotted the beach. She'd gathered items that looked like debris from the shipwreck — another sail, timber, rope.

Halina asked, "Are you hungry?"

"My gut says no."

"Good because there isn't much to be found."

"If there's seaweed, I'll be fine. Fresh water is a boon. Did you eat?"

She nodded but didn't offer up her menu. That meant it was

an animal of some kind and, knowing he didn't eat meat, she spared him the details, which he appreciated.

She said, "After that clobbering, you shouldn't move around much for a few days. Doubtless you're concussed."

"Doubtless. But we can't remain here long. We've got to figure out where we are and if it's better to forge on to Teleyansk or return to Ayestra."

"We're much closer to Teleyansk. When the stars emerge, we can get our bearing." She yawned. "Meanwhile, I'd like a nap."

He agreed and she helped him into the shelter. She lowered a flap made from sailcloth over the opening and wrapped more canvas around them.

"Why does Skiron want misery?" she murmured, sleep thickening her voice.

Gethen yawned. He wasn't cozy, but he wasn't freezing either. The grasses made a surprisingly comfortable bed and the heat he always shared with Halina warmed both of them. "Turn off your brain, Militess. We have plenty of time to contemplate that unfortunate mystery."

She nodded and her breathing slowed.

Gethen tightened his arms around her. Everything ached, maybe his heart most of all. He had a theory about Skiron's motives, and if he was right, all of Quoregna faced some ugly truths and uglier choices. He set a ward around their camp, the deadliest he could muster, and let sleep claim him.

Gethen awakened to thin morning light and sharp pain from head to foot. Not all of the discomfort could be attributed to the wallop he'd gotten from the *Banriona's* block. His sorcery had been drained by the demands of the storm battle. Skiron's abduction didn't help. He needed a long, peaceful rest or immediate access to souls. Neither was coming.

Halina slept against him, her body gently shifting with her slow breaths. Her presence was enticing, her blood magic humming and readily available. With it he could satisfy his cravings and so much more. But driven by need and desperation, he dared not access it. If he started taking her blood magic now, Gethen wouldn't stop. Like Waldram, he'd steal what wasn't his and gleefully destroy her soul in the process.

He swallowed a curse and tried to rise without waking his wife.

"What's wrong?" she asked, one hand on him, the other on a misericord.

"Just need to piss," he mumbled and crawled from their shelter. He staggered down the beach, dragging in deep cleansing breaths and hoping she didn't follow. His hands shook. His fingers cramped. But even with distance he remained fixated on Halina's blood magic.

"Gods! Enough!" He sat abruptly. His chin on his knees, he stared at the rolling waves and wondered if he could harness the ocean's power somehow. He dug his fingers into the sand and laughed humorlessly. "Shemel was right, you're weak, Gethen Rhysh." If only he was strong enough to take just a little of her magic and stop before draining her. But Gethen didn't trust himself, or her, after what happened between them on the *Banriona*. His obstinate wife was much to willing when he reached for her blood magic.

He sighed. His growing weakness was dangerous.

His fingers found a shell, flat and round with a leaf-like pattern on one side and frilled edges. What creature had called it home? He peered around the desolate beach. "What creatures call this shore home?" Maybe he could find another animal willing to loan him its soul. He snorted. "Little scuttling crabs don't offer much power."

Sea crows soared overhead and blue plovers darted along the water's edge, chasing the waves. They seemed unlikely to give up their freedom to help him. Birds rarely did, he'd discovered long ago.

"Why are you sitting on the beach looking grumpy?" Halina strode toward him, her auburn hair wind-tossed and the wound on her cheek raw and angry.

He faced the sea. He should make her stay away, but he couldn't. He wanted her near. Always. And that was dangerous for both of them. "I'm feeling as desolate at this beach," he said as she reached his side.

Halina squinted at the Great Green Ocean, then toed his hip. "Stop feeling sorry for us and help me gather seaweed. I'll make a briny soup to break your fast." She dropped a makeshift sack at his side and headed up the dune at his back.

Gethen shook his head and stood, brushing sand from his hands and trouzes. Nothing kept her down for long. He gathered a few handfuls of sargassum weed then went looking for his wife. He found her above the dunes picking up driftwood deposited by many storms.

"How do you do that?" he asked.

"What?" She considered a branching piece that resembled a mask, held it up to her face and peered at him through its gaps, a demon of wood and flesh and wild red hair.

"Keep going." He pulled tufts of dried grass from the sandy soil and shoved them into his sack, kindling for the fire. "No matter how bad things get, you keep going. You get angry, but you don't give up."

She bared her teeth, looking even more demonic. "I'm the Bear King's daughter. It's not in my nature to give up." She pointed northeast. "Yasan Khot is that direction. We'll rest, regain our strength for a few days, then start walking." Her expression and voice turned serious and she held his gaze as she added, "Quoregna is counting on us. All those children — Feddie, Elof, Prince Gerezel, Prince Vernard, every child in the four kingdoms — they need us to end Waldram's tyranny." She lowered the driftwood and added it to her collection. "I won't fail them, Gethen. *We* won't."

ELEVEN

Halina thought Gethen looked more himself after two days of rest, though the knot on his head hadn't completely disappeared and the left side of his face and his eye were bruised purple and black.

"So Skiron is a prick," she said as they gathered driftwood and dried grass, a daily task. "Unsurprising."

"Yes, and no, not surprising. Shemel learned everything he knew about cruelty and depravity from our god."

"But why does he want so much suffering? I know he's responsible for shepherding the dead back into living bodies, but why seek so much destruction? Aren't there enough spirits in the Void already? His command insults Semele and Khotyr."

Gethen was long in answering and she turned to look at him. Finally, he yanked a bunch of grass from the sandy soil and said, "I have an uncomfortable theory about that."

Again she waited and again he took a long time to speak.

"The gods need our prayers," he finally said.

"Need?" That seemed a strange choice of words. "They're gods. Why would they need anything from us?"

"Prayers equal faith." He squinted into the afternoon sun,

then closed his eyes. "And without the faith of mortals, do you think the gods can continue to exist?"

Halina stared at him. She'd never contemplated the existence of the gods. They'd always just been there. She'd prayed to them, cursed them, honored and celebrated them. Khotyr, Semele, and Skiron were ever-present entities in the background of her life.

Gethen looked at her. "Why do you believe in them? Why do you think they exist?"

"I—" She frowned and tilted her head. "I never really thought about it."

"Few people do. They just accept the existence of the gods and give them power over their lives." He pulled more grass. "I've often wondered why. And now I'm wondering what would happen if everyone stopped caring." He leaned toward her. "Would the gods disappear?"

She looked around, more than anticipating the sudden appearance of Skiron to strike down her husband. But nothing changed. Wind whipped across the sea, raising whitecaps on emerald waves. Gulls rode the drafts, calling shrill insults to each other. Waves came and went, rhythmic, unchanging. "I don't know. What would happen if they did?"

"That's another good question." He pointed to a dead fish, its carcass dried to a papery flatness by the arid wind. "This fish didn't believe in Khotyr, but it was born. It didn't believe in Semele, but it lived its life doing the things fish do. It didn't worship Skiron, but it still died." He spread his arms. "The whole of the world doesn't pray to the Triumvirate. It doesn't hang bones and baskets and ribbons. It doesn't plead for help when its children sicken or offer praise when its stomach is full or it survives a battle." He dropped his arms. "The world, the animals, the plants come into existence, live, and die without needing the gods." He toed sand over the dead fish and added, "Sometimes I think the Triumvirate's become an excuse."

"For what?"

"Failure. War." He shrugged.

Halina surveyed the barren landscape. "I never considered that." She shoved a piece of silvery driftwood into her carrier. "The people of Teleyansk don't worship our gods. They follow the One God." She'd never thought much about her brother's religion. "Ilker does too, and the Ayestrans. A lot of people in Eskis as well. Nothing bad has resulted from their choice." She hefted the heavy bag farther up her shoulder. "So why would faith matter for the Triumvirate's existence?"

Gethen brushed his hands against his trouzes, leaving sand behind. "During the War of the Winds, Quoregna's people begged and prayed for succor. For many of them, it never came. The gods ignored their desperation. After the war, the One God's temples proliferated. His followers preached about order rather than chaos, peace rather than conflict. That held a lot of appeal to people who'd just survived one of the most brutal wars in Quoregna's history, a war where mages and kings brutalized the masses and pillaged the kingdoms."

She nodded. "That's when Ilker started following that faith. My father didn't think much of his choice, but he also didn't care enough to forbid it. King Vernard couldn't be bothered with gods and worship. He never went to the ceremonies, never prayed. He said prayers were a waste of breath." She laughed. "That was one of the few things we always agreed on. I mostly cursed the gods. But I guess I also assumed Khotyr had strengthened me during my battles. She took my side."

He touched her scarred hand. "If that's so, she didn't do a very good job."

Halina laughed again and said, "Hence the cursing." She sat on a smooth log and dropped the sack at her feet. "So you think the gods noticed the defection from their ranks of believers and they're moving to consolidate their — what? — power?"

"Yes."

"It's not a very good plan. It could just as easily push worshipers into the arms of the One God if they believe the Triumvirate has abandoned them."

"True, except Khotyr and Semele have started visiting their priestesses." He sat beside her. "In Ayestra, I heard rumors of the goddesses' servants having visions of the Mother and the Daughter."

Halina grunted. "I heard that too. I thought it was drivel. But now?" She shook her head. "A two-pronged assault: Skiron promotes war and death while the goddesses promote faith in their existence to reassure the people that they haven't been abandoned. He's driving the people right into Khotyr's and Semele's arms."

"And he expects me to play my part in terrorizing the populace. He's made his disappointment in me abundantly clear."

"Are you in danger?" The thought that Skiron would harm Gethen to get his own way made her see red. And made her feel helpless. How could she protect him against the God of Death?

He smiled thinly. "As long as Skiron has enough faith sustaining his existence, I'll be threatened by his strength. The god can pull me into the Void and punish me there, but he can't touch me here."

"Hmmm. I never thought they'd directly interfere in mortal affairs."

"They don't, except through visions for their worshipers, and my existence, of course." He picked up a pebble and threw it into the waves. "My predecessors did a good job of spreading Skiron's terror."

"But you're a sun mage."

"Yes, one of only two recorded in the the histories. An aberration I think Skiron, like Shemel, considers a mistake."

She took his hand and leaned against his side. "My favorite mistake."

He turned his head and kissed her temple. "And you're my favorite bastard."

"So what do we do about these misbehaving gods?"

"I don't know yet. First we take care of the troubles they've caused for the mortal realm. I think reducing their power is a long-term goal."

She nodded. "We'll have to whittle away their influence. And try not to get killed in the process." She straightened and dug her heel into the sand. "People tend to get violent when you threaten their way of worshiping. My father found that out when he considered banning the One God's temples from Ursinum. It was the one time Ilker threatened him with any real heart. I thought we were facing a fracture within the family." She kicked a stone, sending it tumbling into the breakwater. "It fractured anyway, brought about by Waldram and the gods." The whole situation filled her with bitterness.

Gethen's arm went around her shoulders. "We'll find a way to resolve this and reunite your family."

"We need to save your brother first."

"We need to get out of his arid wasteland first."

Halina straddled the log. "How's your neck?"

"Sore and stiff."

She gestured for him to put down his bag and turn his back to her. She'd been massaging the muscles of his neck and shoulder regularly, trying to get the ligaments to relax after the sudden, vicious clouting they'd received. He sighed under her touch and his gratitude was enough to lift her spirits.

"You know, there's one good side of learning the gods are behind all this," she remarked.

"Oh?"

"It proves my father didn't suddenly become a combative king without reason. He may have been a pillock and an awful father, but he was always a damn fine ruler, worthy of sacrificing my skin and bones for."

"And it proves Ilker's turn against you is definitely not of his doing."

She nodded and murmured, "Also a relief."

Gethen's chin sank to his chest as Halina kneaded his neck and shoulders.

"We need to drive Waldram's forces back to Nalvika," she said. "If King Pudding Prick thinks he can scare me off by murdering the people around me, he's as stupid as I always thought."

Gethen chuckled. "King Pudding Prick? Is that an official title?"

"It should be." She squinted at the sky then surveyed the scrubby, dry land stretching out around them. "Based on the stars' positions last night and the captain's last coordinates, I'd say we're a fortnight from Teleyansk's capital on foot, maybe more."

Gethen stuck a piece of sargassum between his teeth and followed her gaze. "Sounds right." He rolled his shoulders and neck. His ligaments crackled and he sighed gratefully. "Are you sure about going on to Lokshin's fortress? I can easily return us to Ranith or Ostendra or any number of safe, warm places."

"I'm sure. We need allies and I've exhausted all the ones I have in Quoregna. Lokshin is our last hope. I won't let the *Banri-ona's* sinking be for nothing. A lot of good sailors and soldiers drowned." She shuddered. She still heard their screams. Another horror to add to her growing collection. "I'll secure that alliance and bring back an army, Waldram be damned and dead. I won't let him get away with murdering all those people. There will be consequences." She gave him a half-hearted smile and added, "Though I'm not above admitting that if I get truly hungry, I may send you home for supplies. And horses. It's not impossible now that you have a reference point to return to."

"Just say the word and I'll vanish."

Halina rubbed the back of her neck. "Are you up to the task?"

"Yes. Plus, I can pick up unguent and some good mead. To Ranith and back in a few hours with enough supplies and a somewhat decent map to get us the rest of the way to Lokshin's gates in Yasan Khot."

"Good. Because after I raise an army, I intend to stake Waldram's head on the end of my sword and keep it there until all the meat falls off. Then I'll grind his skull into dust and dump it on Ranith's kitchen midden for the pigs to eat."

"Please don't foist that poison on the pigs. They don't deserve such abuse."

"You're right. I'll dump it down the jakes then piss on it for good measure."

He smirked. "I'll take my turn, but I won't be pissing down the hole."

Halina laughed and it felt good. They had little reason for humor, but self-pity wasn't a trait they shared. Gethen and Halina saw a problem and sought a solution. "Very well. When do you leave?"

"Now." He nodded toward their makeshift camp. "Let's take the wood and kindling back to the fire, then we'll both go."

She shook her head. "I'll stay behind." When he opened his mouth to argue, she said, "Look around. This place is almost featureless. This little camp and I are the only anchors you have in a wasteland."

It was true and she knew he knew it. They stood on the edge of the ocean, staring inland at a landscape almost as colorless as the Void. The ground rose gradually from the sparse beach and all was the hue of gruel. The sand, the scrub, the distant sloping plains, all of it the same indistinct shade. The Great Green Ocean was an endless, emerald expanse with ever-changing whitecaps. A few spindly trees jutted from the soil here and there, all looking crooked and indistinguishable. The grasses were stunted by the constant wind and showed no more color than the rest of the land. The Northern Wastes were desolate, dry, and scrubbed clean of distinct features.

"The creek is unique."

"Is it? How do you know?"

Gethen frowned, unable to argue the point. Nothing about the beach stood out enough to anchor him to the location, nothing but their meager camp and Halina.

"Go," she said and set off toward their shelter. "The sooner you leave, the sooner you'll return." She swept her arm out to indicate all the nothingness around them. "Nothing's coming to threaten or rescue me while you're away."

He sighed and followed her. "I hate it when you're right, especially when my instincts say you're wrong."

She looked over her shoulder at him. "I'm taking logic over instincts today."

He dropped his kindling by their shelter and drew her into his arms. Gethen traced the wound on her cheek. "This is infected. It requires better care than I've provided." It was red and raw from the salt and sand. "I'll return as quickly as possible."

"I know you will. And I'll be fine while you're gone."

"I hope you're right."

She kissed him. "Don't be so pessimistic. It's not like you."

He kissed her forehead tenderly, hugged her close, then stepped back and spun a travel incantation to take him back to Ranith Citadel.

Halina watched him go, wearing a mask of confidence that she didn't wholeheartedly feel.

After the glow of Gethen's travel spell faded, the bleakness of the Northern Wastes closed in. "Should've gone with him," she muttered, regretting her decision to stay behind. The barren landscape seemed as close to the Void as she could get without leaving the mortal realm. Having spent time in the colorless land of the dead, she'd rather avoid it and anything like it for as long as possible.

She shook herself and stacked the driftwood. They'd likely remain on the beach for another day, planning their route based on the maps Gethen brought back. The wood and the grass were needed. Even with their shared heat and adequate shelter, the nights were damnably cold. She hoped he brought unguent for her lips. They felt like the dried fish he'd found above the waterline.

After stacking all the wood and separating out the longer, thicker grasses from the short scrub, Halina lined the floor of their small shelter with the heavier ones and tucked the rest in a corner so the wind couldn't steal it. She drank from the creek, the frigid water making her hands sting and her teeth ache. She stank and wanted a bath, but she'd have to be a lot more odorous before she was willing to brave that much cold misery.

The wind whistled past her ears, insistent and annoying. Her remaining companions were the darting plovers and soaring sea crows. The former only wanted each other's company and the latter heckled her. "Rude beasts," she called back. She chewed dried seaweed not enjoying the taste but preferring it to the complaints of an empty gut.

"Fourteen days to Teleyansk," she muttered. How much destruction would happen in Quoregna while they were absent? Besera could fall. Ilker could die and Ursinum would suffer under Waldram's tyranny and spite. Gethen's absence might let

Shemel re-enter the mortal realm and unleash all the demonic souls banished to the Void. "Bollocks."

She squinted at the hazy northern sun. Gethen hadn't been gone two hours. It would be another two or three before he returned, especially if Cerys cornered him. The poor woman was probably riddled with worry and antsy with impatience.

"I can't fault her for that," Halina murmured to the shorebirds. "I'm terrible at being idle too." Snorting at her understatement, she found an angled shell, flat and sharp-edged, and whittled a long piece of driftwood into a spear. She couldn't decide if it was a tool for hunting or a weapon. Tool most likely, in a land with little life and fewer threats. Though there had to be enough food to support all the seabirds. She'd eaten a few small crabs that first day on the beach, while fretting that Gethen would never awaken.

Halina worried her lower lip between her teeth. She didn't like the story he'd told her of Skiron's taunting and cruelty. She shivered, knowing the horror of drowning all too well. "Prick, indeed." If she ever had the chance to confront the God of Death, she'd not hold back. Why should she? At that point, she'd likely be a permanent resident of the Void. If she had to rely on his questionable hospitality, she may as well make it clear where she stood on the relationship. He was setting a shit example for the shadow mages and necromancers. She much preferred her husband's approach to the dark art. Gethen used his deadly magic to destroy those unseen creatures that dwelled in wounds and caused suffering and death. He was a good man. She wouldn't let anyone, not even Skiron, devalue Gethen's humanity. That was a bill of goods she'd bought and sold all her life, until she met the man and saw just how humane he was. That he was handsome and intelligent and willing to push her were boons. Also that he was a damn fine lover. That could not be discounted.

Halina laughed at her own lust. She turned the spear and continued honing the tip, engrossed in the simplicity of the task. She didn't hear the wolves until the seabirds took flight, calling warnings to each other. Her head jerked up. She looked around and spied them. Her breath caught.

Two lean, brown wolves stood a dozen feet from the shelter, their yellow eyes fixed on her. These were not her husband's companions. Duesh and Gwyn were black and white, respectively. These were locals, and she looked like a fine meal.

Halina slowly stood, the spear in hand. "Never run from wolves," she repeated, a childhood lesson. "They live for the chase. Stand your ground. Show no fear."

She planted her feet wide and raised the spear before her, horizontal to the animals. "I don't want to harm you, but I won't go down without a helluva fight, so you better decide if I'm worth the effort."

One of the animals flattened his ears. The other lowered his head and tucked it beneath his companion's chin, a defensive posture.

Halina held her ground. She wouldn't attack or retreat. Maybe Gethen's presence had attracted them. "If you've come to see the Sun Mage, you're welcome to wait as long as you don't try to make a meal of me."

The animals rumbled.

"Bollocks to you, too," she growled back, baring her teeth and bracing for a fight.

TWELVE

"Demon!" Queen Cerys's lady-in-waiting shrieked when Gethen emerged unannounced from Ranith's still-room. If he hadn't been in such a hurry and so foul-tempered, he would've been impressed as the willowy woman jerked a torch from its wall sconce and brandished it like a weapon.

"I'm no demon," he growled and snuffed her threat with a wave of his hand.

She squawked and backed into the wall.

"Is that you, Lord Rhyshis?" the queen called from the stairs above, her voice quivering.

"Yes, Your Highness, flesh and blood and irritation from top to toe."

"I wish you'd announced your arrival," she said.

Gethen swallowed a waspish retort. "I don't make a habit of announcing myself in my own home."

"But your arrival was rather startling," she persisted as she descended the stairs. She peered up at him and her eyes widened. "What happened to your face?"

"A wooden sail block met it abruptly during a storm. I'm told the ship sank, though I was too unconscious to notice at the time. My good wife saved me from drowning."

"Sank?" She looked past him into the stillroom. "Where's Her Ladyship?"

"Back on the beach in the Northern Wastes where she insisted I leave her. An agreement I regret already." He stepped around his brother's wife and continued to the first floor library for a map. He'd already filled his haversack with unguents, herbs, and potions from his stillroom.

"I don't understand." Cerys followed. "I thought your destination was Teleyansk to forge an alliance with Emperor Lokshin."

"It still is. But our ship sank off the southern coast of the Northern Wastes." They entered the library. "I've returned for supplies, a map, and a horse. We'll ride the remaining distance to Yasan Khot." He crossed the library to a shelf filled with scrolls and pulled out a handful of sheets until he found the one he wanted. He shoved it into a leather holder and slung that over his shoulder with his haversack.

"How can I help?"

That question surprised him. He turned and peered down at the young queen. "Food," he finally replied. "Bread, wafers, dried fruit, and hard white cheese. Also several bottles of mead."

Cerys summoned her maid and headed into the kitchen with the woman. Gethen followed, rubbing his chin thoughtfully as he watched the queen and her lady gather supplies. He fetched travel packs for them to fill then crossed the bailey, went through the postern door and into the woods.

"Remig!" he called and followed it with a whistle. "Where are you?" He followed an animal path until he heard a whinny and the crunch of leaves and branches.

Gethen's courser, Pedran, remained in Ostendra and Halina's warhorse, Abelard, was in Tatlis. The only horse in Ranith was his chestnut warhorse, Remig, whom he'd released to roam Kharayan Tor. The horse came through the woods and greeted him with another whinny.

"I'm pleased to see you, too," he said and stroked the gelding's velvet muzzle. The horse looked fit and healthy, if a little feral. "I need your strong back in the Northern Wastes. It won't be a warm adventure and the food won't be as hearty as what you have in the woods, but at least you'll have companionship."

Remig snorted and shook his head. Gethen laughed. "You're right, it's a beggarly trade. Come on, old friend. Halina's waiting on a cold, windy beach in the middle of nowhere. Let's not leave her alone for long."

The horse followed him back to the stable where Odruna and Thaksin waited with the mead Gethen had requested.

"What's this I heard about Halina being stranded in the Northern Wastes?" Thak stood with his feet planted wide, chin lifted, anger flaring his nostrils.

"She insisted. I argued against it. She won the argument." Gethen left Remig grazing in the bailey while he returned to the kitchen for the rest of his supplies.

Thak dogged his steps. "I wouldn't have lost that argument."

Gethen ignored him.

Odruna scoffed. "Don't flatter yourself. You've never won an argument with the Red Blade. None of us have."

"Everything you asked for is packed," Cerys said, "plus spare clothing for you and Lady Rhyshis."

Gethen ducked his head. "That's thoughtful of you, Your Highness, thank you." He hefted the bags but paused before heading back out. "Any news from Zelal?"

She caught her lower lip between her teeth and shook her head. She'd fetched Gerezel from wherever the child had been and now let him teethe on her finger.

Gethen smoothed down the boy's black locks. "I'm sorry. Halina and I will bring help as soon as we can."

Sudden tears shimmered in her eyes. "I know," she whispered.

"Be patient and have faith in your king's strength."

"I will, brother." She rested her hand on his arm. "Safe travels and best of luck with Emperor Lokshin."

Gethen bowed over her hand. "Thank you, Your Highness."

In the bailey, Feddie and Elof loaded Remig's saddlebags, working together in silence while Odruna and Thaksin argued about going with Gethen — not that he'd allow either to leave.

His thoughts were on Halina as he skirted the tower's wall, following the sunshine in search of Ranith's wolves. He'd been gone too long from the beach campsite and cursed himself for not warding it. "That blow addled my brain," he muttered. He spied Duesh and Gwyn lounging in the tall grass beside the basilica's open wall.

"Hai, wolves, come."

They raised their heads, yawned, and rose, trotting over and rubbing their faces against him.

"I'm pleased to see you, too. I hope you're in the mood for adventure. I'm taking you with me to Teleyansk." He drew strength from the animal's souls, pulling enough to feel the warmth of their spirits but not to exhaust them.

Feddie and Elof appeared with Remig in tow. "Unless you wish to join the argument brewing in the bailey," Nalvika's princess said, "you'd better leave soon, Your Lordship."

"You could take us with you," Elof said hopefully.

Gethen shook his head and took the reins from Feddie. "You're still safest here, even if all you hear is quarreling. The wards are strong and your protectors are true and capable."

The children nodded, their faces glum.

To Feddie, Gethen said, "I hope you're practicing your sword work. Halina will test you when she returns."

She nodded. "I am. Odruna and Marja won't let me slack off."

"And I've read almost half your book, Master Gethen," Elof volunteered. "Feddie's a good teacher."

"Excellent," Gethen replied. "Choose a spell and a formula to perfect and demonstrate when I'm home next."

"I will," the boy said, bouncing on his toes and grinning.

With Remig's reins in hand and both wolves pressed against his legs, Gethen spun another travel incantation and fixed in his mind's eye the sight of Halina upon the barren beach, the spindly trees, narrow creek, and makeshift shelter nearby.

His amber magic spun out and away, revealing the Northern Wastes, the shelter, the green water, little creek, and skeletal trees. Gethen cursed long and loud. What he didn't see was the most important thing. He didn't see his wife.

"Halina?" He looked around turning in every direction "Halina!" Gods, where was she? Why had he left her behind? Why had he failed to ward the camp? Why had he failed his wife again?

"I'm here," came the reply.

Why hadn't he looked inside the shelter before assuming the worst?

"Are they still out there?" she asked, shoving aside the ragged bit of sail that hung over the shelter's opening. Her question made him stop second-guessing his instincts. So did the wary look she gave their surroundings, her gaze pausing on Duesh and Gwyn.

He scanned the beach. "Who?"

"Wolves." She crawled from the shelter. "They appeared a few hours ago. We had a face-off for a while, then they laid down and I figured they were more curious than hungry. They never came any closer than the creek, and I got too cold standing out there, so I gave up watching them." She shrugged. "I guess they got tired of watching me, too." She pulled the bags from the saddle, ran her hands down Remig's neck, and scratched Duesh and Gwyn behind their ears.

Gethen immediately set a deadly ward, wide enough to allow the horse to graze. "That'll keep your uninvited guests from skulking into the camp."

She slung the bags to the ground beside their shelter and inspected the contents, taking advantage of the cheese and bread. Her expression brightened when she found the mead, and she took a long swig from one of the bottles.

He knelt in the sand beside her and pulled her against him.

Halina laughed. "You were worried about me?"

"Yes, and feeling foolish for not setting a ward, more foolish for leaving you behind, especially with wolves in the area." He rubbed his jaw and scanned the beach again. Why hadn't he sensed them?

She brushed her fingers over his temple and kissed the corner of his eye where the bruise still showed darkest. "I'm fine and, apparently, rather uninteresting. Or I smell so bad not even wild wolves consider me edible."

He shoved his face into her dirty hair and inhaled deeply. "You smell perfect," he murmured.

Halina pulled back and considered him with a wary gaze. "You must be in love or insane."

"Both." He tilted her head back and captured her lips with his. Halina softened against him. Heat flared between them and he suddenly didn't care if those wolves returned. He'd warded the camp and his wife's body felt good. Magic flowed between them, buzzing like a beehive as his sun magic matched her blood magic.

"Come into the shelter," she whispered against his mouth. Her breath tasted sweet. It hitched as his hands stroked her jaw.

"That's an excellent suggestion," he replied.

Remig grazed and the wolves patrolled, rumbling their suspicions as they scented the unexpected visitors.

That was a mystery Gethen would solve...later. Right now he was only interested in the mysteries of Halina's strong body and very talented tongue.

Inside their shelter, she studied his face, tracing her fingers over his brows and down his cheeks. "If the gods destroyed me right now, I would gladly go into the Void if it meant I could spend eternity with you, Gethen Rhysh." Her gaze rested on his mouth.

He pulled her close, reveling in the smell of her skin and the tickle of her breath on his lips. "Let's hope they don't. The Void's an inhospitable place. I prefer to remain here and alive so I can enjoy the warmth of your body."

Halina pressed her lips to his, a slow, gentle kiss.

But the demands of sorcery couldn't be ignored and, as much as he desired her, Gethen had nothing more to give. She pulled back and he pressed his forehead to hers, fatigue slowing his brain.

"You. Are. Drained," she said and sat up.

He shook his head wearily. "I tapped the wolves' souls."

"I'm not completely unaware of your needs and right now wolf magic isn't one of them." She brushed his hair off his forehead. "You're always caring for me. Now it's my turn." She didn't wait for his response, but tugged off his boots.

Gethen watch with tired amusement. "What is it you think I need, wife?"

The look she gave him made his heart jump and rekindled his desire.

Halina straightened and moved her fingers along the front of

Gethen's brigandine, unhooking its fasteners. With the last one open at his neck, she slipped her hands beneath, pushed it off his shoulders, and tossed it aside. His hooded travel tunic followed, pulled over his head without hesitation. The lighter tunic he wore beneath joined the growing pile of discarded garments. She lay down against him, smiling as his desire for her became unquestionable.

"It seems I've captured your attention," she said.

Gethen's voice was husky as he replied, "I'm fully focused on you, Your Ladyship."

Her throaty laugh was beautiful. He shivered as her fingers skated across his skin following the whorls and curves of his Beseran stripes, leaving a hot trail; the heat they shared whenever they touched.

Her gaze ranged over his chest and up to his lips. "I love the look of you." She pressed her face to his neck, inhaled deeply, then exhaled a hot, trembling breath. "I love the smell of you." Her hands drifted to his waist. She yanked the buckle free from his belt, pulled the ties that held his trouzes in place, and shoved them down around his ankles. Her hands moved south. She gripped him, sliding her fingers over his cock, making him gasp. "Most of all," she murmured, "I love the feel of you." Her mouth found his. Her lips and hands excited him.

Magic stirred behind Gethen's chest, in the place where it always burned, waiting to explode when he needed it most. It had shrunk to a small flame, a warm buzz after the demands of the travel spells. But Halina stoked it into a growing conflagration. He relieved her of her own clothing. Yet she stopped him from taking control and pushed him back. She straddled his lap and eased him into her body.

He groaned. There was nothing as exquisite as the feel of her around him. He loved the animal sounds she made. Tupping her was like fighting her, exciting, visceral, completely engulfing his heart, mind, and body. Nothing existed but Halina and the magic surging between them as she rode him slowly, surely.

She whispered her love for him and encouraged him to take the power of her blood magic and renew his own sorcery's strength.

"Take what you need," she whispered. "Take my strength, my body, my heart. Take me, Gethen."

"You give and give," he said, the words a panted rhythm has she rode him. "How do you know what I need?" His hands in her wild, auburn hair, he captured and held her, staring into her blue eyes, trying to decipher the mystery of how she knew him so completely. "You don't know how deep and desperate that need is."

"Yes, I do," she panted. "I do."

No, she didn't. She couldn't. If she truly knew the monster locked inside him, how close he came to losing control of it every time he drew another soul, she'd leave. If she knew what a nightmare beast he battled at all turns, the horror that Shemel had become and he so desperately struggled to deny, she would kill him. She'd have to.

"I know you, Gethen, and I don't fear you. I want to know everything that dwells inside you." She stared into his eyes. "Trust me. I can help you." She cradled his face between her palms. "Let me help you."

Gethen encased her in his arms, lay back, and rolled, coming up atop her, his cock still buried deep inside her. He started to unleash that control and let the monster have what it wanted so much, the blood magic that flowed through her, the incredible power that kept her alive through the worst battles, compelled soldiers to follow her blindly, drove him to worship her completely. He stroked in and out of her, hard and fast, wanting to feel every inch of her, needing to possess all that she was.

But if he followed that monstrous desire to its natural end, he would consume Halina and destroy her soul, just as Waldram wanted to, the way that Shemel had goaded him to.

"Halina." He strained, grit his teeth and growled deep in his chest, fighting necromancy's burning need. "I can't. I won't." He kissed her fiercely, a bruising, biting kiss that made her whimper.

She gasped as he pulled back. "You can't hurt me," she said and wrapped her arms around him, pinning his hips against her with her long legs. "You won't. I trust you, I know you. You're not Waldram. You're not Shemel. Believe in my strength."

Eyes closed, muscles rigid, he drew a deep breath and pulled the wild madness back from the brink. He forced it down and fettered it. She remained still beneath him, holding her breath too, waiting to see what he would do. He opened his eyes and kissed her gently. He pulled out and rested his forehead against hers, no longer needing to finish what she'd started. "No, Lady Rhyshis, I won't show you that. I can't. It's not your strength I doubt." He gazed into her blue eyes. "It's mine."

"Gethen—"

He silenced her with a kiss. "If you love me, Halina, you'll trust me in this. There are some aspects of my dark magic I never want you to know."

She searched his face then nodded and buried her face against his chest. "I love you," she whispered.

"I know."

"You told me I need to decide who I am." She raised her head and met his gaze again. "So do you."

Gethen sighed and stroked her salt-snarled hair. "I know," he repeated.

THIRTEEN

Halina studied Gethen's profile, a dark line against the dim interior of their driftwood shelter. "Do you know what I consider your finest quality?"

He arched a brow at her and raised his palm, producing a small amber flame from nothing but air and intent.

She shook her head. "No."

He doused the fire then pointedly gazed down at his crotch.

Halina laughed. "No, though it is among your greatest assets."

"What then?"

"Your mastery of the fine art of shutting up." She snuggled against him. "You listen. You let me rant. And you don't judge or try to fix me." She sighed. "I wish other people would learn that skill. It's rarer than you think."

"I don't see anything to fix."

"That's exactly what I mean." She ran the tip of her finger down his profile from forehead to chin. "You let me be me." She paused. "And it doesn't hurt that you're a handsome fellow."

"Am I?"

"Oh, yes." She tugged his beard. "But falsely modest."

Gethen snapped his teeth at her fingers. She laughed and started to sit up when he stiffened and stopped her. He cocked his head, listening. She did too but heard nothing. However, Gethen's ability to sense things she couldn't was not to be underestimated. She waited, breath held, muscles tense.

"We're not alone," he murmured.

"How many?"

"Two at the edge of my ward. More behind them."

"Duesh and Gwyn aren't reacting."

"No. And that's odd." He grabbed his tunic and trouzes as she did the same. "Their souls are...strange."

They emerged into the fading light of day, a red sunset casting a bloody glow across the sand. Gethen's wolves sat beside the opening of the shelter, their eyes keenly focused on two brown wolves at the invisible edge of Gethen's ward. Riders on shaggy horses ranged behind them, two dozen figures standing against the growing darkness of fading day.

"Your visitors from earlier?" Gethen asked.

"Likely, but the riders are new."

The horsemen were armed, but they weren't brandishing their weapons. Halina and Gethen slowly approached the ward line. Duesh and Gwyn joined them. As they neared, silvery magic erupted around the two brown wolves and both creatures transformed into men clad in brown furs.

"Amitat shidet — animal magic," Gethen murmured. "That's ancient sorcery."

"You've seen it before?"

"No, but I knew it was possible. That explains the otherness of their souls."

"Greetings, strangers," one of the shifters said in the common tongue, his voice deep and gravelly.

"You should speak first," Gethen said beneath his breath.

"Why?"

"So they'll know you're a powerful woman with her own voice. Tell them who you are and that we're married."

She nodded. "Greetings. I'm Halina Persinna Rhysh, daughter of King Vernard of Ursinum, Duchess of Rhyshis in absentia. This is my husband, Gethen Rhysh, Duke of Rhyshis in absentia, Son of King Maczen of Besera. We seek an audience with Emperor Lokshin. Our ship was wrecked and we came ashore here three days ago."

"You're far from Yasan Khot," the man replied. He spoke with the rounded accent of the far northern peoples. Though he and his companions were small, they had the same dark, narrow eyes and round faces as Gurvan-Sum's populace, the same straight black hair and small noses.

His companion asked, "How do you have a horse and wolves if your ship sank?" His gaze hadn't left Gethen.

"I brought them," Gethen replied.

"That's why you left your wife alone, mage?"

Gethen smiled. "The Red Blade doesn't require my protection."

"We noticed her fearlessness," the first speaker replied.

The other one asked, "You travel with wolves. Do you practice amitat shidet?"

"No, only sun and shadow magic," Gethen replied. "The wolves are my companions, Duesh and Gwyn."

"So you're a death mage, uhklin id shid?"

Shaking her head, an old woman rode forward on a shaggy, red roan pony. "Ugul-ugul." She dismounted with more ease than Halina would've expected from someone so craggy, and she swatted aside the two shifters. She jabbed a gnarled finger at Gethen and said reverentially, "Ezen ni Kuchin Togoldor."

"Ezen?" the second shifter asked, obviously surprised.

Halina looked at Gethen. "What's she saying?"

"Master of the Void," he replied. Louder he said to the woman, "Ene bol namaig dudsan yoom."

A wide, toothless smile lit her face. "I knew it," she crowed in Common. "Powerful magic. Powerful. I felt it in my bones and in my soul when you came upon our lands." She swatted both shifters again and snapped. "Show some respect. These are important visitors."

Gethen bowed his head to her. "Thank you, Kuchin Shulam." He lowered the ward with a wave of his hand.

She strode across the line and took his hands. "Kenbish. That's my name." She gestured to the two shifter men. "These two fools are my sons, Odgerel and Gansukh. We are honored to host you and the Red Blade of Or-Halee in Chono Khot." She knelt and held her hands out for Duesh and Gwyn to sniff. The wolves did and even rubbed their heads against her arms while she laughed.

Halina started to refuse their hospitality, but Gethen surprised her by accepting. "The honor is ours."

The other riders watched silently as Halina and Gethen gathered their few bags, saddled Remig, and mounted. Odgerel and Gansukh resumed their wolf forms and ran ahead of the party. Kenbish rode beside Gethen, chatting amiably about sorcery and Ranith's wolves. She admired Duesh and Gwyn's loyalty as the animals remained close.

On the other side of Remig, a Chonyn soldier rode on a speckled pony. He peered up at Halina and remarked, "I never knew southern mares were so impressive."

"Remig is a gelding."

"I didn't mean the horse." His smile revealed two broken front teeth and even more cheek.

Bollocks, she thought. This was going to be a long ride.

"Is it true you fight alongside men?" he continued.

"Men and women. I've commanded armies since I was a girl."

"Commanded them," he said, "but not fought beside them."

Halina's chin rose and she looked down her nose at him. "Do you think these scars came from embroidery needles?" She leaned forward and gestured at the angry puckered line marring her face. "A shriker gave me this gift." She bared her teeth and added, "You should see the scar I gave it in return."

He grinned. "I like your stories. Maybe a few are even true." Some of the riders around them laughed.

She shrugged. "Maybe you'll find out when your trouncing becomes part of them."

He continued to ride beside her, studying her from head to toe. "A husband shouldn't leave his wife alone. Maybe he doesn't care about you."

Halina arched a brow at the cheeky pecker. "Why don't you tell him that. See how well he takes your advice."

"Making enemies, Arban?" one of his companions asked.

Arban grinned. "Considering taking a new wife."

Halina rolled her eyes and ignored him after that, deciding small talk with the fool would only get him killed faster and most likely by her.

He nattered on about his prowess hunting, prowess drinking, prowess fighting and tupping and raising goats, and she believed none of it. Instead Halina watched the changing landscape as they left the Great Green Ocean behind and gained low hillocks in its stead. Waving grasses and spiky tussocks appeared among tumbles of rocks haphazardly tossed like the gods had played at bones and abandoned each game to start anew as they formed the landscape.

Their group rode at a steady jog toward distant rolling hills. The sun disappeared and a waxing moon rose, casting silvery light across the cold, dry steppes. The wind came up, whistling in Halina's ears, making her shiver and pull her wool cloak closer. Remig turned his ears back and snorted, champing the bit. Gethen ran a soothing hand along his neck and shoulder. Halina hoped they didn't have much farther to travel.

They didn't. Surmounting the next rise, they came into a wide valley. What appeared to be small hillocks with fires flickering among them resolved into round, wooden structures and tents made of hide.

"Chono Khot," Arban said.

Gethen interpreted, "Wolftown."

Deciding to be civil, Halina asked, "Arban, does everyone here speak the common tongue?"

"Yes. You need to if you want to deal with the markets in Yasan Khot."

As they rode into the village, people emerged from the tents to call greetings and see the strangers. Children stared from behind their parents. Men and women sized up Halina and Gethen, muttering in their native language.

Duesh and Gwyn seemed a particular curiosity for the Chonyn, who showed no fear around the large predators. And both wolves calmly accepted the pets that accompanied that interest.

"Wolf magic, indeed," she murmured to Gethen. He nodded and watched everything and everyone, his gray eyes keen.

Halina figured she'd lose her husband for a few hours as he tested and questioned Kenbish and her sons, curious about their shifting abilities and other examples of their rare form of magic.

They dismounted and Remig was fed and corralled with the Chonyn ponies. Kenbish led Halina and Gethen to a small tent, part of a group encircling a large central lodge. It sat between tents belonging to her sons, a place of honor.

"Thank you for your generosity," Halina said, bowing to the old woman.

Kenbish waved the gratitude away. "Rest while food is prepared. We'll dine well tonight. The Chonyn have never hosted such honored guests."

"We're the ones honored by your hospitality," Gethen replied.

They were left to clean the filth of many days from their skin and change into clean clothing. "Extra clothes! Thank you," Halina said, delighted to find trouzes and a tunic, as well as the luxury of a copper kirtle and emerald surcoat.

"Thank Cerys. It was her idea."

"That was good of her," she murmured.

"Indeed. My brother's young queen surprised me. I thought she was imperious and impetuous, but she seems to be rising to the role of protector."

"This may be the first time she's had any real responsibility resting on her shoulders alone."

"She's led a sheltered life." Gethen stripped his tunic off and dunked his head into the provided water bucket. Halina fetched a cloth and was content to bathe her husband's torso. She followed the whorls of the Beseran stripes that outlined his ribs and muscles, loved how he watched her hands and her face, how his skin heated beneath her touch.

"Too bad there's not more time for leisure on this trip," he murmured and pulled her against him.

She laughed and swatted him playfully. "You'll get me wet."

His wolfish grin made her breath quicken. "Exactly," he growled. But they knew it wasn't a night for lovemaking. He shook himself, dried his skin, and dressed in clean clothes.

After Halina bathed and changed, they joined their hosts in the lodge and were introduced to Chonyn food. There were black-striped pods holding nutty red seeds the size of Halina's thumb, a spicy dish of legumes and vegetables that reminded her of Amma Xana's chingis, slabs of fire-roasted roots with white goat cheese melted and bubbling on top, plus their first Chonyn beverage to finish the meal.

"Gonsu," Odgerel said as he placed a wineskin on the round table before their gathering. "Green milk. It helps with digestion."

"What's in it?" Halina sniffed the pale-green, milky drink and wrinkled her nose at the unmistakable astringency of alcohol. It smelled woody and herbal, not unlike the black-thorn tea Gethen brewed during the darkest months of the year.

"Mare's milk and winter thistle spirits," Arban replied.

"It's best served warm." Kenbish filled small, clay cups and served Halina first. Gethen shook his head, but the old woman poured a cup for him anyway. Halina slid it in front of her and several of the men laughed.

"Did I do something wrong?" she asked.

Arban reached for the cup. "Women can't handle more than one drink."

Halina placed her hand over it. "Is it dangerous for a woman to consume too much?" she asked Kenbish.

The elder glowered at the men. They looked away but not ashamed. "Only if the men around her can't keep their hands to themselves."

Halina smiled. "Then I'm sure I'll enjoy the second cup, since all these men are honorable." That inspired more laughter.

"Indeed," Gethen said and gave Arban a look that promised suffering if the Chonyn man forgot his manners.

"Erool mendee — to your health." Arban raised his cup. So did everyone around the table, Halina included. She sipped the liquor, found it significantly more palatable than Schorvalan soma, and let the rest slide down her throat. It spread a comfort-able fire from her tongue to her gut and she turned the cup over and tapped it on the table with a satisfying rap.

The men hooted and she looked around. They gingerly sipped their drinks.

"I believe you're supposed to savor it," Gethen remarked.

Halina smirked. "I did, like the Ursinian soldier that I am."

One by one, the Chonyn men downed their drinks and upended their cups. "To Ursinum!" each proclaimed as he finished while Halina clapped and laughed.

Arban leered at her. "What about the second drink, soldier?"

She lifted the other cup of gonsu. "Will you join me or am I drinking alone?" She knocked it back and waited to see if it had a compound kick when mixed with the first, but she was far from drunk. The men around the table downed their second draft, not wanting to be outdone by the Red Blade.

"A third!" Arban called. Kenbish frowned. Some of the men laughed and held out their cups, most looked askance at him and left their cups upended.

Halina raised her hands. "I don't want to drink all of Kenbish's supply."

"I brought the gonsu," he snapped. "Would you make me drink alone?"

"I'm sure the others will enjoy a third round with you," she declined gently.

"But you are the guest." His eyes and his tone challenged her. She'd refused his flirtations and now turned aside his dare. If she wasn't careful, he'd twist her rebuffs into insults.

Beside her, Gethen's ire flared. Feeling its heat, Halina rested her hand on his leg. Kenbish's gaze shifted from Arban to her guests, irritation darkening her expression.

Gansukh leaned across the table. "I'll drink with you Arban, so you stop putting your head in the wolf's jaws."

Arban glared at him. "I don't want to drink with a dog. I want to drink with the Red Blade of Or-Halee." Snatching the wineskin from the center of the table, he poured a drink for Halina and another for himself. He put the cup before her and raised his own, his gaze locked on hers. "To your gods."

Another challenge. Would she insult Khotyr, Semele, and Skiron by not meeting it? But he misunderstood where her loyalties lay.

"No." She took the cup and raised it. "To yours." Halina downed the drink and this time didn't turn over her cup. If Arban wanted to look like an arse, she'd give him all the help he deserved.

Chuckling, Gethen gathered a handful of the black-striped pods and relaxed into his seat. He cracked two of them and popped their red seeds into his mouth, watching Arban with a soft smirk.

The Chonyn man considered her and her husband over the narrow rim of his cup before murmuring, "To the gods," and downing his drink. Kenbish refilled Halina's cup and stared pointedly at his. Arban lowered it, the old woman refilled it, and Halina immediately lifted hers in salute.

"To new friendships," she said and downed her fourth cup. She held it out for a refill, never taking her eyes off Arban.

Around the sixth cup of gonsu, the Chonyn men made bets for and against Halina. Around the tenth, Arban lost control of his left eye. It wandered upward into its socket as if afraid to see Halina easily down the next drink and smartly snap her cup back down onto the table for a refill. And with the fourteenth cup, he lost his senses and his seat and made friends with the floor.

Gethen leaned over to consider the unconscious man. "Someone should assure he doesn't inhale his own vomit." The other men, after settling their bets, rolled Arban onto his side.

"It really wasn't a fair contest," Halina lamented.

"No," Gethen replied. "He didn't know you've been drinking soma with the Schorvalan army since you were seventeen."

"Sisteen." She stared down at Arban and muttered, "I hobe I haven't made anenemy." She was a little morose now that she was full of mare's milk and winter thistle spirits.

Kenbish cackled. "I doubt he'll remember this evening, Lady Rhyshis."

"Let alone know why he should be angry with you," Gethen added. He stood. Halina followed and he caught her elbow as she swayed. "You're not unscathed, wife."

"Cerdanly not," Halina replied. "And I need to piss."

All the men gleefully pointed them toward the Chonyn version of the jakes. It was a civilized little tent with separate areas for privacy. A seat over a bucket was far better than squatting drunk over a hole, and Halina appreciated the fresh water waiting to wash her hands.

Gethen intercepted her and kept her on a straight trajectory to their tent. Once inside, he pulled off her boots and loosened her sword belt as Halina tried unsuccessfully to divest him of his clothes.

"What do you think you're doing?" he asked, amused by her fumbling.

"Seducing you?" she replied although she wasn't at all sure that was true. Her mind was muzzy.

Gethen laughed. "You're far too drunk to follow through on such ignoble intentions. I predict sleep will win out the moment you're in that cot."

She considered the fur-heaped bed and couldn't argue, nor could she recall what she'd argue about if the bed didn't look so inviting. "Are you joining me?" she asked as he settled her into the bed and pulled the blankets over her.

"I'm going to ward the tent then speak with Kenbish."

"Whadabout?" She plucked feebly at his sleeve. "Sorcery stuff?"

He kissed her fingers, pausing on the one that bore the

ensorcelled black ring he'd made for her. "Yes, Red Blade, sorcery stuff."

Halina sighed and snuggled into the bedding. "Should I come along?" she mumbled.

"Definitely not." He kissed her and directed Duesh to curl up by the tent's central hearth and guard her. Then Gethen murmured incantations to ward the tent. Halina was barely aware of the door flap settling behind him and Gwyn as they left.

FOURTEEN

Chono Khot rang with song and laughter. Though the sun had set long ago, people still moved about the village, eyeing him as Gethen sought Kenbish and her sons. He had questions, a lot of them.

Gwyn paced at his side, her amber eyes keen in her white face. Her comfort set him at ease. Halina would be safe here; the Chonyn respected the wolves and the wolves protected her.

That calm was hard-won for Gethen. The cravings had returned with the growing weakness of his sorcery. Without enough rest and with so many demands upon his magic, necromancy's appetite for souls was growing within him. Laughter sounded louder. Voices more strident. The pull of so many spirits tortured him and Gethen locked down his unnatural inclinations, unwilling to garner enemies when he and Halina were just building friendships and trust among the Chonyn. Borrowing from the wolves helped, but there was only so much he could take before he endangered their lives too.

He entered the main lodge, a building made of rough-hewn logs, its circular roof held up by massive tent poles. Wolf heads, carved into the tops of the poles, gazed down on the laughter and singing that filled the lodge. Men and women watched him and Gwyn, curiosity behind their dark stares. Some lifted their cups to him, others nodded as he caught their gazes. He nodded back, scanning the crowd.

Gansukh rose from a table at the far end of the lodge and waved. "You're looking for Kenbish, I think," he said as Gethen reached him.

"I am, as well as your brother and you. I have questions."

Gansukh nodded. "I'm sure you do."

He pulled aside a curtain made of hide and led Gethen into private living quarters. Rough-spun, wool rugs softened the hard-packed dirt beneath his feet. Carved chairs and couches held over-stuffed pillows and heavy furs and blankets. A fire crackled in a central fire pit.

Kenbish emerged from behind another heavy skin curtain. "Do the wolves go everywhere with you?" She wore a wool dress and her silver hair hung in a braid down her back.

"They usually remain at Ranith Citadel, but I needed their help with this mission."

"Mission? An interesting choice of words. As if you've been tasked to do this by your wife." She gestured for him to sit. "Or was it your death god?"

"Definitely not Skiron," he replied with a rueful laugh. "He'd rather I cause chaos than prevent it." He sat and stretched his cold feet toward the hearth. Gwyn settled beside him, content to warm herself by the flickering fire.

Kenbish arched a brow at him. "You defy your god?"

"Don't we all?"

She cackled. "So you know about amitat shidet."

"I know wolf magic is forbidden in Teleyansk. I know the Chonyn have fought the government's ban on it for generations."

The old woman stared into the fire. "Lokshin's ancestors

discovered a way to curse ours through bribery. And the Chonyn gradually embraced the One God over the Amitan Sunsun," she looked up, "the animal spirits of our ancestors. Plague came to their herds. Starvation and poverty followed. Teleyansk seized the fertile valleys our people once occupied."

Gansukh added, "The Chonyn and a few other animal tribes were marginalized, our trade restricted, our cultures and native languages outlawed. Fewer and fewer shifters are born. Those who are, hide their magic for fear of being murdered by the government."

Gethen nodded. "I've heard the sad plight of the Chonyn in many places. Anywhere people are supplanted for power, this marginalization occurs."

Odgerel had quietly joined his brother and mother, as had an adolescent girl, Terbish, their foster sister. "Are you here to kill us?" she asked.

"Why would I do that?" he said, surprised.

"Teleyansk has used necromancers against us before," Kenbish replied.

"I don't serve Teleyansk."

Odgerel leaned forward, his black eyes as sharp as a predator's. "You defy your god and our emperor. Who is your master, Sun Mage?"

"I'm my own master. I serve the mortal realm. Kings and commoners are all equal in my eyes."

Kenbish growled, the first sign she too practiced shifting. "You are a liar, mage."

He held the woman's gaze for a long moment. "Why would you make such an accusation?"

"You serve the Red Blade," she snapped.

"I love her. I agree with her. But I don't serve her, nor would she demand my service; Halina's not that foolish."

"And if she asked you to choose her over Quoregna?"

Terbish asked, a surprisingly astute question from someone so young.

"She wouldn't," Gethen replied with a calm certainty he felt about very few things. "That's why I married her."

Kenbish sat back.

Gansukh asked, "If you're not here to kill the last of the shifters, why do you and the Red Blade seek an alliance with the Emperor of Smiles?"

"We seek allies to defeat King Waldram of Nalvika. He's practicing necromancy and seeks to steal and corrupt Halina's blood magic."

Kenbish's gaze sharpened. "The woman is a blood mage?"

Gethen shook his head. "She benefits from blood magic's lethal power but doesn't wield it. It's woven into her soul."

Odgerel muttered, "That explains her reputation."

"It's well and truly earned," Gethen replied. "I don't suggest going against her with a sword."

"Not if her determination in drink is any indication of her prowess in battle," Kenbish said and cackled again. Clearly she'd enjoyed Arban's downfall. She sobered. "So Nalvika's king has discovered his sorcery, has he? The spoiled princeling grew into a rotten king." She spat into the fire. "Do you seek our aid too?"

"Do you offer it?"

"No, we can't join the South's war. It would devastate our people and end your hopes for an alliance with Teleyansk. As it is, I can't predict what Lokshin will do if you request his help."

"You have reason not to trust him. We are not the same in that regard."

"True, but you have no reason to trust him either."

Gethen nodded. The Chonyn didn't have the resources to move against Nalvika, and Teleyansk would never permit it. If Lokshin's government discovered shifters still practicing among the Chonyn, they'd be hunted into extinction. While the emperors were more than willing to use sorcery to win their wars, their distrust of the craft was well known.

A burst of laughter announced the arrival of two children as they charged past the curtain and played dodge around Terbish's chair.

"Hai!" Kenbish snarled and the children stopped, eyes wide. Only then did they seem to notice Gethen and Gwyn.

"Chono!" the girl squealed and threw her arms around the wolf's neck, burying her face in Gwyn's white fur, all fear of the matriarch forgotten.

The wolf's tail thumped the rug and she rolled over and offered her belly for scratching. The girl and the boy obliged.

Kenbish shook her head. "Out with you," she said sounding more amused than annoyed.

"Can't we stay with the wolf?" the boy begged. "We'll be quiet."

"No. Out."

Terbish took their hands. "You should've been asleep hours ago. I'll put you to bed with a story." She led them from the matriarch's private quarters.

Kenbish propped her callused old feet on the edge of the fire pit and studied Gethen. "So you defy your god and kings for this woman?" she asked.

He considered the adolescent girl, the small children, and all the other younglings he'd seen in the village. And his resolve to stop Waldram and Shemel sharpened its focus. "No, I defy them because I won't let Quoregna's children be sacrificed for a madman's ambition or to preserve the gods' existence."

Odgerel cocked his head. "Your gods require sacrifices?"

"They require faith," Gethen replied, "and that comes quickest from people's suffering. I won't be party to making that happen. Better no gods than those who thrive on their followers' misery."

Gansukh slowly nodded. "Your motives are honorable, master mage, but if you seek a force to bring war against kings and gods, won't you be fulfilling your death god's wish for despair anyway?"

"Sadly, yes, in the immediate future. But I mean to free Quoregna's people from the long-term servitude that will come with King Waldram's mad ambitions and Skiron's mere existence."

Kenbish said, "I'd heard the Red Blade was a strong-willed woman, but I never would've believed she'd yoke the four kingdoms' most powerful mage to help her battle the gods. I don't know if that's a war you can win, Sun Mage, but I admire your commitment to a noble cause. I wish you and your wife success. I regret we cannot aid you. It's a worthy war you fight, and I don't say that lightly, Kuchin Togoldor."

He ducked his head. "I'm humbled by your belief, Kuchin Shulam."

"Now," she said, settling a fur over her lap. "What do you wish to know about amitat shidet?"

Gethen smiled. "Everything."

They laughed.

"What fuels your transition? Is an ambit needed to maintain the spell? Can anyone master the ability?"

"What's an ambit?" Gansukh asked.

"A type of wraith," Gethen replied and the three shifters muttered.

Kenbish shook her head. "We use no summoning to become our wolf selves. The ability is min mon chanar."

Odgerel nodded. "Arisanda," he said and translated, "in my skin," when Gethen frowned.

"It's a part of you? You were born this way?"

"Born with the ability to free the wolves that live within us, yes," Kenbish replied.

"Is it a gift from the Amitan Sunsun?" Gethen asked.

"No," she said. "We are the Amitan Sunsun and they are us. They are animals. And we are animals. Long ago, before the gods existed, the spirits walked upon the earth, flew among the clouds, and swam in the waters. The people lived among them. Sometimes the wolves or the bears or the birds, the whales or any other animals wanted to walk on two feet and speak with the people. So their spirits took human form. They became Khun Sunsun. Sometimes they fell in love with humans, they lay together and had children. Those children had both human and animal spirits."

Gethen nodded, fascinated by the story. "Your family comes from such a pairing?"

"Yes," Gansukh said. "We are Sunsi Khun. To become wolves is to become another form of ourselves. I'm Gansukh the man and Gansukh the wolf. I know myself as both."

Gethen considered that. "Then amitat shidet isn't a skill to be learned. It's part of your nature or it's not. Right?" They nodded and he continued. "It's not unlike my sun and shadow magic. I wasn't given the ability to wield magic. It dwells within me," he touched his chest, "and always has. I learned to use it well, to shape and direct it with incantations and sheer will, but it didn't come from the gods."

Kenbish smiled. "Of course not. It is tany mon chanar — in your nature."

"Arisanda," he agreed.

Odgerel grinned. "In your skin."

Gethen considered what they'd explained. "How do you maintain the change? It must demand a great deal of power to transform."

Kenbish shrugged. "It comes from the world around us. The

156

trees and plants, animals. The movement of the wind and water. All of that creates a rhythm, like the beat of my heart, the movement of my lungs and my blood. I feel the world and the life pulsing within and upon it. It is a body and I'm part of it." She looked at her hand. "If I want my fingers to curl, I don't think about it. I just curl them." She made a fist. "Amitat shidet works the same way." She eyed Gethen. "Do you think about a spell before you use it?"

He shook his head. "Not unless it's new to me or I rarely employ it."

She laughed. "That's how I feel when I want to become a hawk."

"You can become other animals?" Gethen was surprised. He thought they were confined to only one form.

"Of course," Kenbish replied. "But I don't like heights."

Gansukh laughed. "And you can't swim, so you never become a fish either."

She eyed him. "Watch your manners or I'll transform into a bear and give you a good thump."

Odgerel explained, "Some forms come more easily. We all donned our wolf skins first. That's our most natural form. But we can become any animal we're familiar with."

"You have a truly fantastic ability," Gethen said. "I regret it's a form of magic closed to me."

"I don't," Gansukh said. "Even in Chono Khot, we know the Sun Mage's awesome power. I would be even more afraid of you, if you mastered amitat shidet."

Gethen smiled ruefully. "Power can be a curse, especially when it causes fear even among your friends."

Kenbish nodded. "And turns people against you with no cause other than their fear."

FIFTEEN

Halina awoke with Gethen against her. His arm lay across her hip, heavy and lax. He breathed evenly, deeper than dreaming. He'd come to their bed late. She brushed her fingers over his hand, but he didn't respond to her touch.

Reluctant to disturb him, she slipped from beneath the bedcovers, shivering in the predawn chill. She jammed her feet into her boots and threw her cloak around her shoulders. The wolves eyed her sleepily. Duesh stretched, yawned, and followed Halina as she left the tent. Surprisingly, it wasn't her stomach but her bladder that inspired this foray into the Northern Wastes' chill. She'd expected a rebellious head and gut after so much gonsu, but her mind was lucid and her stomach's only protest was its emptiness.

Halina didn't miss the pull of the ward Gethen had erected around their tent as she crossed it, nor did she doubt Duesh's company was at her husband's command. The wolves rarely paid her any notice in Ranith. She found the jakes in the muted morning light and took a long piss then went looking for food.

She received an unexpectedly enthusiastic greeting from

Arban as she entered the great lodge. "You must be hungry, Militess," he called and waved her to join him.

He had a spit and a metal griddle set on the fire and the scent of sizzling eggs and gamey meat made her mouth water.

"How's your head?" she asked as he served her.

"Better than ever," he replied and offered her a steaming mug of something herbal and slightly astringent. "Winter thistle milk tea without the alcohol," he explained refilling his own mug and taking a long drink.

Halina raised her mug. "To your continued health."

He grinned. "To new friendships, yeh?"

She laughed and dug into the eggs. The meat was snow hare and delicious. There was also a big pot of pink gruel made from goat milk and the red seeds Gethen had enjoyed the previous night.

"You're not what I expected of a Southern woman," Arban remarked as they ate companionably while awakening villagers drifted into the lodge.

"What did you expect?"

"Soft. Weak. Fearful and fussy. That's what we see of the women from Teleyansk when we go to Yasan Khot for market days."

She shrugged. "There are plenty of those women in the South. And I'm sure there are strong women in Teleyansk."

"The Red Blade's reputation precedes her," Kenbish said as she meandered into the main part of the lodge from behind an animal hide curtain. "You chose not to believe the rumors and stories, Arban."

He nodded. "You taught me a valuable lesson, Lady Rhyshis."

Halina smiled. "And you introduced me to a very fine drink." He and Kenbish laughed, and she added, "Will you share its recipe with my husband? He's a skilled mead maker, and I hope he'll add gonsu to his reserves."

Kenbish nodded. "Consider it done." She sat beside Halina and accepted a heaping bowl of gruel from Arban. An adolescent girl joined them. She was introduced as Terbish, Kenbish's fosterling, and watched Halina with avid curiosity.

"I suppose my husband explained our reason for being stranded on your beach," Halina said.

Kenbish nodded. "And requested our aid."

"Which can't be provided beyond your generous hospitality because of Teleyansk's power."

Kenbish eyed her. "You're an astute woman. Though we want you to succeed, this is not our war. It belongs to you and your gods. To involve the Chonyn would be to expose us to unwanted scrutiny."

"I've been around power and politics my whole life. You don't last long in Tatlis if you don't figure out who has everyone by the bollocks."

Arban and Kenbish laughed. The girl gawked.

Halina considered her. "What do you want to ask me?"

"Your Ladyship?"

"You've been studying me like a hawk watching another predator. I think you're learning, so what more do you want to know?"

"I—" She glanced at Kenbish. The old woman nodded, so Terbish continued. "How did you become a warrior? And why? You're a princess, right?" Her eyes followed Halina's damaged hand, took in her scarred face. "Why go to war?"

"Some people are born to fight." Halina considered her halved fingers. "Queen, princess, pauper — rank doesn't matter. Until it does. I was born into privilege *and* responsibility. The two go hand-in-hand, or they should. Not all nobles fulfill their duty to defend the people relying upon them for protection. I've always taken that responsibility seriously, most of all when I lost my place of privilege."

"What do you mean? You're a duchess."

"I was the Margrave of Khara until my father's death led my brother to the throne. In turn, he was deceived by King Waldram of Nalvika and stripped me of my rank. I'm a duchess in absentia through marriage. But my king hasn't sanctioned my union with the Sun Mage, nor will he until the blinders lift from his eyes."

"How will you do that?" Terbish asked.

"By killing King Waldram."

Kenbish eyed her. "Bold statement."

"I'm sure Gethen told you Waldram is using necromancy and unleashed shrikers to hunt Quoregna's children."

The elder nodded. "He did. But are you the right one to judge and execute him?"

"If not me, who? Our gods stand by and watch the suffering unfold. They encourage Gethen to inflict cruelty and misery. It's only because he's a good man that he doesn't use his power to usurp all the kings and make Quoregna his empire."

Arban grunted at that. "Why doesn't he?"

"Because I have no interest in ruling and even less interest in cruelty," Gethen said as he settled beside Halina. Gwyn was with him. She paced the lodge, sniffing the air, then joined Duesh. "Go hunt," Gethen murmured to the animals. "Not the livestock." Needing no more encouragement, both wolves departed.

The Chonyn watched the animals and the mage.

"Are they your pets, Lord Rhyshis?" Terbish asked.

"No, they're my companions and my aides."

"Your aides?" She looked perplexed. "How?"

"They loan me the power of their souls when my sorcery grows weak."

Silence followed.

Terbish murmured, "That's not natural."

"It is for me and the animals," he replied. "My magic is fueled by souls."

Terbish asked the question everyone wondered when they learned Gethen was a necromancer. "Do you take people's souls, too?"

"Only if I'm very desperate."

"Let's hope you don't become desperate," Arban muttered.

"But I thought your power came from the sun?" Terbish said. "Isn't that why you're called the Sun Mage?"

Gethen shook his head. "I wield sun magic with greater strength and precision than other kinds of sorcery, like mechanical magic or weather work or mind magic, but my sorcery isn't powered by the sun alone."

"Can you shift like Odgerel and Gansukh?"

Gethen's gaze found the brothers across the lodge. "Sadly, no. I would very much like that ability."

Halina said, "You asked about my choice to become a warrior, Terbish. Did I satisfy your curiosity?"

She nodded. "Would you show me how to fight?"

That surprised Halina. "Don't Chonyn women go to war?"

Kenbish shook her head. "The Chonyn don't forbid women to enter battle, but few pursue a warrior's life. It's not easy or comfortable, as you well know, Lady Rhyshis."

"If one of your soldiers will loan me a sword, I'll gladly demonstrate."

More Chonyn had entered the lodge as they'd talked and the enthusiasm for Halina's exhibition became clear with all the swords suddenly proffered. She stood, scanned the weapons, and chose the longest, much to the surprise of the onlookers.

"I fight with a longsword," she explained, testing the heft and balance of the weapon. It was heavier at the hilt than Ursinian swords, and a little shorter, but certainly serviceable.

Arban stood. "I'd consider it a privilege to face you in the ring."

Gethen eyed him and Halina laughed at her husband's dubious expression.

"To three touches," Kenbish declared. "No blood will be drawn."

Halina nodded. "Three touches. No blood." She followed Arban from the lodge, trailed by her husband and the rest of the village.

A square was cleared and marked with logs. Halina paced its edges, stretching her shoulders, arms, and neck, testing the sword and accepting a wooden shield. She considered summoning her blood armor, but a glance at Gethen convinced her otherwise. It was overkill for sparring with Arban. She held her husband's attention, another question behind her gaze. His slow smile showed he knew her mind. He was hers to utilize, a wicked surprise for her sparring partner and audience.

They faced off. Halina saluted Arban with her sword. He danced forward, testing her nerve and revealing his reach. He couldn't overcome his ego; it took over and made him foolish again.

She let him come, easily evading his strike. She caught the hilt of his sword and yanked him off balance, tapping his shoulder with the tip of her own weapon.

"Point," Kenbish announced. The audience cheered.

"Maybe you should let a real warrior fight her, Arban," a large man goaded from the edge of the square.

"Like you?" Halina asked, pointing her sword at the man's chest. She glanced at Arban and winked.

He grinned, clearly pleased to be part of the scheme this time. Offering his sword to the blustery fellow, he said, "Prove yourself against a worthy opponent, Taban."

Jeers and calls rose as the man hesitated.

Halina cradled her sword like a baby and waited for the warrior to choose pride over sense.

Catcalled into submission, the hulk of a man, entered the ring. She sized him up and settled into a deeper stance, a quieter focus. The man knew how to use a sword and shield. He had reach and heft on her, so closing with him was a guaranteed loss. For all her height and skill, Halina had learned at an early age not to close with a larger opponent. Taban's weight was a deadly advantage. But it also could be used against him, if he was inexperienced, which she didn't think he was.

She considered her shield, Taban's beefy arms, and tossed it aside. She gestured to the ax hanging from the belt of one of the other warriors. "May I?"

The man glanced at Kenbish. She nodded. "We didn't restrict weapons."

Halina neatly caught the ax, gave it a few practice swings, and faced her new foe. She ground her heels into the dirt, balanced on the balls of her feet, and watched his shoulders.

He came at her quickly, powerfully, and apparently ignoring the rule against drawing blood as his sword whistled past her skull. She dodged and wove, always moving and unpredictable, like the wind swirling around a mountain of a man. She leaped back as he surged at her, trying to pin her against the onlookers, but she neatly slipped beneath his arm and tapped his arse with her ax.

"One," Kenbish said.

Halina didn't miss the frustration that crossed the man's face or the flare of magic from her husband. She *did* miss Taban's conspirator, who flung a handful of sand at her face as Taban charged her again. She ducked the grit but couldn't evade the bull. A glancing blow off her shoulder knocked her into the crowd.

"One for Taban," Kenbish announced.

Halina shook her head and blinked. She spat sand. But there was no time to regroup as Taban's helper grabbed her sword hilt and tried to pin her in place. She released the weapon and barely slipped her opponent again.

That settles it, she thought. *Two can play dirty.*

"Gethen, if you please," she said.

Two ropes of shadow magic shot forth and ensnared the men. No matter how they fought, they couldn't escape the wraith's hold. Simultaneously, Gethen produced daggered shadows that hovered at their throats.

Halina sauntered across the practice square and tapped Taban's chest with her sword.

"Two out of three," Kenbish said.

The magic dispelled and Halina saluted her opponent. She was leery about his reaction, but he returned the gesture.

"A worthy opponent," he said.

"Worthy, indeed," she replied. "You're strong and devious with an unexpected ally. Some would say we both fought dishonorably."

"There's no honor in death, just maggots," Kenbish said. "We live in a hard land. Only a dead fool fights with honor. The ones who survive use every weapon at their disposal."

"I agree," Halina replied. She found Terbish at the square's edge and asked, "What did you learn?"

The girl's eyes shone. "To use whatever weapon you have to win, and to move like the wind."

Halina thought she'd created a new Chonyn warrior that day. "No one cares about winning or losing when they're on the battlefield," she corrected. "They only think about surviving."

Around the practice square, the warriors nodded. Survival was all that mattered.

Halina sought out the sword's owner, but the man raised his

hands. "Keep it, Red Blade. You'll need it and you wielded it well."

"It's a fine gift." She bowed to him, touching her forehead to the sword's hilt. "I'll use it with and without honor."

The gathered warriors laughed.

Gethen came to her side and the Chonyn eyed him with respect and, Halina thought, a new kind of caution.

"You bring a weapon into battle that we've never seen before," Arban said, nodding at the Sun Mage.

"My husband fights beside me, but he doesn't fight for me." She accepted a braided sword belt from one of the men.

"But you offered aid when she beckoned," Terbish said to Gethen.

"I aid the Red Blade because she's the strongest weapon Quoregna has against King Waldram's madness and the gods' tyranny. I protect her to protect all of us."

Halina and Gethen packed their bags, gratefully accepting food and a wineskin full of gonsu from their hosts.

"Follow the Kherlen River until you reach the Orkhan Cleft. The main road follows the southern split, but at this time of year the northern fork will still be clear of snow and ice. The only hazard to watch for is the Elk People," Taban explained over the map Gethen had brought from Ranith.

"Elk People? They don't sound very dangerous," Halina said as she ran her finger along the route he'd described.

"It's not elk they hunt," Arban said.

"Ah." She straightened, rolled the map, and returned it to its leather sleeve. "We'll keep a sharp eye out."

Gethen tightened Remig's cinch. "Perhaps your reputation will precede you, Red Blade, and they'll avoid us."

"Or your reputation, Sun Mage," she replied. Gethen swung into the saddle and Halina accepted a leg up behind him from Arban. She surveyed the wide valley, its spread of tents, and the grazing goats and ponies. "I'll miss Chono Khot," she said and clasped hands first with Kenbish then Arban, Odgerel, Gansukh, and others. She'd grown fond of the wolf people in her short time with them. She trusted them like she trusted Mahish and the Dargani and the people of Gurvan-Sum. She sobered as her thoughts strayed to Or-Halee and Arik-bohk's distrust. She'd thought that alliance was unshakable.

Gethen clasped their hands too. "Your generous hospitality won't be forgotten," he told Kenbish.

"Safe travels," the old woman replied. "And may your gods find wisdom in your strength."

Remig jogged away from the village and onto the road to Yasan Khot. Duesh and Gwyn loped ahead.

"I just hope this effort bears a fruitful alliance," Halina muttered, mostly to herself, as she pressed against her husband's back and studied distant, snowcapped mountains.

"You're thinking of Arik-bohk."

"His distrust still sticks in my throat."

Gethen's resentment was obvious in his voice. "He didn't trust your judgment and nearly got you killed." His hand found hers at his waist and squeezed, his anger even more obvious than his resentment. "I'll never forgive him for that."

Halina sighed. "I hate that he's made you hate him, that all those sailors died aboard the *Banriona*, that Besera is suffering, Ursinum is vulnerable, and most of all, I hate that children are still dying."

"All those things are symptoms of the disease Waldram is spreading." He frowned at the mountains. "Fomented by Shemel and desired by the gods."

Halina rested her forehead against his back. "How can we

win a war that the gods themselves want?" Her options were dwindling fast.

Gethen's gaze remained on the mountains. Her own desperation was reflected in his eyes. "I don't know," he said. He inhaled, squeezed her hand again, and seemed to find some well of strength deep inside. "I don't know *yet*. But we will, Halina, I promise."

She tightened her arms around him, taking strength from his certainty. "Come on, Mage, let's get to Yasan Khot."

"All right, Militess."

He urged Remig to a gallop. The horse eagerly stretched out and found his stride. The wolves raced beside him. Halina smiled, happy to enjoy the wind in her hair and the man she loved in her arms.

SIXTEEN

"At least the suppuration is running clear now." Gethen cleaned the edges of the scar bisecting Halina's cheek. The malignant wound had reopened, taxed by wind, salt, and too many days without healing unguents.

"Good," she muttered. "I'm tired of feeling like shit."

She'd developed a low, persistent fever the eighth day of their travels and, by the tenth evening, Gethen had insisted they camp for at least another full day while he reopened and drained the wound. "You need rest."

"That's what death is for and this little scratch isn't going to kill me," she snapped.

"It will if you ignore it," he snarled back and spiked her mead with a sleeping draft.

"I've survived much worse, and you know it."

"You survived because you did as your healer instructed." He folded his arms across his chest, fisting his hands to hide their shaking. His power was stretched as thin as early winter ice and he felt just as brittle and treacherous.

She drank the mead and watched him. Pus wept from the middle of the wound. The edges had closed with new pink tissue, but the center wouldn't heal. Gethen dug deep for the power to quell the infection and draw out the shriker's poison, while keeping a ward around them and maintaining his connection to the ward at Ranith. He couldn't risk drawing strength from her blood magic. And he was avoiding taking from the horse and wolves, preferring to keep the animals strong and alert. Instead he coaxed what power he could from the trees and plants around them, but they were stingy sources, keeping their strength close like their roots grasped the ground, unwilling or incapable of sparing much for him in such a harsh environment.

Halina lowered her empty cup and sighed. "You just drugged me." She met his gaze and there was worry in her eyes. "How can I defend us if I'm unconscious?"

He lifted a copper travel pot from their campfire and added a measure of powdered liminth root to the steaming liquid. "I've set a ward. The wolves are patrolling. And I'm not incapable of protecting you." He reached for his haversack.

Quick as an asp, her hand shot out and she caught his wrist. "Do you think I don't notice everything about you?"

She'd surprised him with her speed and he couldn't hide the shaking of his hand as she gripped it.

"This is the thing you don't want me to know, but you can't keep denying it." Her gaze held his, unflinching. "Gethen, I can't help you if you don't share the burden."

He scowled at his unsteady hand. No matter how he willed it, the trembling wouldn't stop. Nor would the itching, like ants scuttling beneath his skin. His need had grown too great, taxed by fatigue and demand, the addiction slowly intensifying ever since King Hjalmer and Queen Ektrina's spirits had sacrificed themselves to empower him. He sighed. "I told you I can't share this."

"Let me help you." She encased his hand in hers.

"No. This is my burden." How could he explain that he'd

battled the urge to rip the spirits from everyone they met in Chono Khot and struggled not to murder the sailors aboard the *Banriona*? That he shook and ached with need like a nocoli addict craving the leaf? After all the brutality Waldram had inflicted upon her to steal her blood magic, she couldn't possibly trust Gethen once she learned her cousin's cravings paled beside the lethality of her husband's addiction.

Her fingers tightened but nothing stopped the tremors now. "Your secret endangers both of us." She searched his face, a desperate plea in her eyes and voice as she whispered, "Please trust me."

He clenched his teeth until they hurt, resolved to keep his secret locked behind them. She didn't understand what she was asking. Silence stretched between them, gaining weight, smothering him like a wet blanket.

Halina's next plea shredded that silence and knifed his resolve like the sharpest blade. "Say something." Her voice caught. "Say you're not giving up on us."

His gaze jerked to her face. "Gods, Halina. No. Why would you think that?"

"I've trusted you with my life, my secrets, my body and soul. Why can't you do the same?"

Gethen swallowed. Her plea was as raw a wound as the one marring her cheek. "If I keep this from you, will I lose your trust? Or will I lose it if I confess?" He hung his head. "It's an impossible choice I don't want to make."

"I love you. That's why I married *you*, not Arik-bohk, not Eamon Danas, nor any of the dozens of men my father promised me to. I knew I was marrying the most dangerous man I'd ever met. A man with secrets and struggles I couldn't comprehend, but also a man who followed me into the Void to save my life, who swallowed his pride to hold space for me. A man who never gives up on me, who sees me in ways I can't, and who doesn't think I'm broken." Her voice and gaze were steady as she added, "There's nothing you can do or say that will make me stop loving you, Gethen Rhysh. Nothing."

He turned away, measuring his addiction against her certainty, and let out a harsh breath. "Before Thaksin gave me his soul's power to save you in Drevya Linna, I'd only subsumed four other souls." He swallowed again, stomaching guilt. "The first was a nocoli addict in Besalee Portcity. Shemel forced me to take that soul and I hated every moment of it even as I thrilled at the power I got from it. The next morning I awakened sick with guilt and swore I'd never consume another." He scowled at the lie that had become. "The second was Shemel's, taken the night I killed him. The third and fourth were King Hjalmer's and Queen Ektrina's in Drevya Linna. They empowered me to avenge their deaths."

He rubbed the back of his neck where an ache had settled. "But the worst was Thaksin's. The power he gave me was spell-binding and painful. It amplified my desire for you like no other soul could." He kept kneading his neck muscles. "I respect and resent him for it still."

Halina's head tilted to the side and her gaze narrowed, but she said nothing so he continued.

"You don't understand," he said. "Nothing compares to a soul's seductive power and the thrill I get from taking it." He looked at her from beneath his brows. "It's better than the best sex we've ever had. Much better, and we've had some incredible sex." His head came up. "Necromancers crave that high. With every soul we take the need grows more insidious. It weakens our resolve, breaks us, turns us into monsters. Murderers. And it's inescapable."

She waited for him to continue, her expression neutral.

"The only thing more compelling for me than souls is your blood magic." Gethen licked his lips. "It's intoxicating, Halina."

He met her gaze head-on. He'd put the truth in her hands and hope she could forgive him. "I never should've permitted you into Ranith, into my life, and into my heart. I should've warned you to stay away, but I needed your help. Then I needed you. Falling in love was a mistake."

Halina blanched. "How can you say that?" The pain in her voiced knifed him.

"Because it's true." He raised his shaking hands. "Because I'm addicted to your blood magic, and that makes me a greater danger to you than Waldram ever was."

She exhaled a slow breath then gripped his chin and forced him to look at her. "You are *nothing* like Waldram." Ferocity had replaced her pain. "You've been chewed up, spat out, shunned and feared, yet you still feel shame when you confess your struggles." Her eyes searched his. "You're not a monster, Gethen, you're just a fool."

He blinked at that, confused. "A fool?"

"Yes, a fool for thinking I didn't know you were addicted to my blood magic. An idiot for thinking I would hate you for it. And a pillock for not discussing this sooner."

He groaned and pulled her against him, burying his face against her neck. He never wanted to let go.

She wrapped her arms around him. "Most of all an arse for not realizing your sorcery has been empowering me in return." He tightened his grip as she murmured, "Waldram stole, Gethen. You borrow, you transform, and you give back so much more than you take. And there's no one I'd rather have at my side in peacetime or war." He was beyond gratified when she added, "Because there's no one I trust more than you."

"I love you," he whispered.

"I know."

The sleeping draft overtook Halina and she curled up on her side, her cheek resting on the poultice he'd fashioned to draw out the rest of the shriker's poison. Gethen spooned around her and covered them both with wool blankets. "Stay close," he called to the wolves and Remig.

As gratified as he was by her acceptance of his addiction, he didn't feel much relief, and sleep was a long time coming. He stared at a sky filled with unfamiliar stars and wondered how an undeserving monster like him had gained the love of such a perfect woman.

He ground his teeth. Waldram, Shemel, and ultimately Skiron would use her love as a weapon against him. Losing her would make him the most dangerous beast ever unleashed on the mortal realm. Shrikers would be like pups compared to the wrath he would unleash if he lost Halina to his foes, and he had the terrible, sinking feeling that Skiron was counting on it.

When he finally drifted to sleep, he dreamed of fire, blood, and misery.

Duesh and Gwyn rumbled, a deep menacing sound that should've warned off anything foolish enough to approach the ward. Whatever was beyond the dim light of their banked camp-fire either had no sense or had ill intentions and too much determination. The wolves' rumbling escalated to snarling.

Gethen shook Halina awake, his hand over her mouth to keep her quiet.

"What is it?" She sounded groggy.

"I'm not sure, but the wolves don't like it."

"Did it try the ward?"

A guttural scream answered her question.

"Tried and failed."

"Bollocks." She struggled to sit up. "You shouldn't've drugged me."

"And you should've done all your healer instructed." He waved at the campfire and drew off the flame, extinguishing its light.

A whistle and a thud made Halina curse. "They have arrows."

"I noticed." Gethen murmured to Remig, "Down. Stay down." The horse lay down, becoming a harder target. "Can you summon your armor?" he asked Halina.

"I would if my mind wasn't so muzzy."

Gethen said the words. "Gveed, enaith, a cysgud, amdivin vi ad vy engilenion."

Halina repeated them and her blood armor formed. She howled gleefully and drew her Chonyn sword. "Come on, Mage, let's rout these turds."

Gethen ran his hands over Remig's neck, drawing the horse's soul into himself, then he summoned his own shadow armor and stood. He launched a fireball into the air. It hovered overhead, revealing a line of scrawny warriors, painted in mud, and riding horned elk. Helm in place, Halina looked like a demon from beyond the Void, a blood wraith, vengeance walking. The Elk People fired more arrows. She batted them aside with her sword, then cackled gleefully when she successfully summoned a shield.

Gethen whispered a spell to the elk, promising them freedom from the spurs and whips of their riders. The animals reared and plunged, unseating some unsuspecting warriors, rolling over a few, distracting all. Halina strode forward, crossing the ward with a flare of red magic. She swung her sword, cleaving heads and limbs, cracking skulls and bones. As she waded into the chaos her armor ambit strengthened its form with the spilled blood of her fallen foes.

Despite the horse's borrowed spirit, Gethen's power flagged. He couldn't face a prolonged fight and more elk riders were charging out of the brush around them. They'd be surrounded unless he did something drastic.

Kenbish had said she empowered her transformation from woman to wolf using the world's inherent force. "It is a body and I'm part of it," Gethen murmured. It was worth a try.

He called, "Halina, fall back to my position." He whispered to the elk: "Run. Save yourselves."

Gethen crouched and pressed his palms to the dirt. He reached deep inside himself and into the world. He pulled up the magic that resided within the soil. "It is a body and I'm part of it," he repeated. He commanded the smallest creatures, the worms, beetles, and things that were too small to see. He drew them to his will and commanded them to alter the earth.

This was an ancient spell, and he wasn't sure it would work until the ground vibrated.

Halina looked at her feet, at him, and retreated from the battle, her armor still drawing blood from the bodies around her as she backed toward the camp. She crossed the ward and Gethen asserted more force.

The vibrations grew into shaking. The elk scattered. The warriors shouted as the earth opened beneath their feet. Men tumbled into the churning maw, their screams choked and silenced by dirt, roots, rocks.

Arriving attackers turned their mounts and fled back to the steppes, leaving elk to snort and prance, some trapped by the half-buried bodies of their dead riders, the warriors' feet ensnared by the rope stirrups hanging from the elks' saddles.

When the temblor stopped, Gethen remained on his knees, head hanging, breathing hard. He hadn't been so utterly spent since the day he'd fallen from Drevya Linna's walls while tracing the shrikers to their source, King Waldram.

Halina cut the elk free from their dead masters. She removed their saddles and bridles and sent the animals into the wild. She dispelled her helmet but not her armor.

Gethen had lost his armor. He lacked the power to maintain its form.

She knelt before him. "Can you ride?" He shook his head. Dispelling her armor then, she pulled his trembling body against hers. "Take what you need," she whispered. "However much to get you on your feet, keep you in the saddle, and maintain us both until we reach Yasan Khot."

Too tired to argue, Gethen extracted a trickle of her power and managed to stop himself from greedily drawing so much more. It was enough to help him move, ride, stay upright and alive as Halina struck their camp, climbed into Remig's saddle, and pulled him up behind her. She set the horse and wolves to an easy jog and they left the Northern Wastes behind, crossing into Teleyansk without fanfare or even a marker to show they'd reached Emperor Lokshin's land.

It was when yellow-clad horsemen intercepted them that Gethen realized they'd reached their next goal. As Halina identified herself and her husband and requested a meeting with Lokshin, he considered each of the soldiers and saw not men, but souls he could exploit. He shook his head and cursed himself. To be so weak and vulnerable at this time in their journey was to invite disaster.

The soldiers escorted them — with drawn swords — into a wide valley and toward the largest citadel Gethen had ever seen.

He sent a silent plea to Skiron. *If you care at all for your servant, grant me the strength to resist temptation in this city of souls.*

Gethen couldn't be sure, but he thought he heard the God of Death's laughter in the distant cries of the street beggars, the moans of the whores, and the mumbling of the addicts filling Yasan Khot's slums and alleys.

SEVENTEEN

The smell met them before they reached Yasan Khot's gates, a dark, sweet scent like flowers and peppers left to dry in the sun. It wafted on a cold, dry breeze and tickled Halina's nose. "What's that?" she asked the soldiers.

"What?"

"That smell."

They laughed. "The City of Bones is known for its wealth and its odor."

"Altan tsetseg," Gethen said and the men stopped laughing. "Golden flower."

"You mean golden spice?" she asked. "I didn't know it smelled so strong."

"It doesn't in the small amounts that come to Ursinum," he replied.

One of the soldiers said, "The first summer harvest just came in."

"I must get some while I'm here. It's useful in medicinal meads and unguents." Gethen gave her a sidelong look and added, "Especially if your wife often requires healing."

She wrinkled her nose at him. "I only tasted it once, but I

liked it very much." She sobered. "Golden flower cakes were served at Tirius's ascension ceremony." Her oldest brother had officially become the crown prince that day, but he never got to wear the crown. Instead, he and their brother Halion died in battle during the War of the Winds. Ilker ascended to the throne after King Vernard's murder. She looked outward and spied a purple streak atop the next rise.

Gethen followed her gaze. "The flower fields?" He pointed and the soldiers nodded.

"But the spice is golden," she said.

"The blossoms are purple. The spice is their yellow stamens, dried and crushed into powder."

As they topped the rise, Halina reined in Remig and stared.

Yasan Khot — the City of Bones — stretched before them, buildings and flowers as far as her eyes could see. Like a blocky quilt, square fields of purple flowers were surrounded by a near-solid wall of tin-roofed huts. Workers came and went, bringing in the harvest, pulling spent blooms, and planting new fields. Children played games in the lanes separating the buildings from the fields and elders tended cooking fires, wove, and repaired equipment. In every direction, the city spread out, each block surrounding a large flower field.

At the city's center rose an enormous, walled compound housing the most radiant citadel Halina had ever seen. Golden tiles shimmered upon its roofs. Golden symbols decorated its purple walls and towering white gates. It sat above the fields and plains, built on a barrow as big as all of Kharaton.

Between the castle and the fields, city buildings squatted, their forges belching smoke as merchants of all trades wove through its spiderweb streets. While the fields and the castle offered straight lines and clear focus, this narrow band of Yasan Khot was chaos, noise, and stench.

The city's southern perimeter ended in a long, low cliff.

Wharves jutted into a wide bay filled with ships of all shapes and sizes. Paneled sails billowed in the wind. Sailors shouted over the waves. And on the wharves, all manner of goods were loaded on and off the ships and boats, fishing nets were repaired, fish were gutted, barrels rumbled, animals protested, soldiers, sailors, and fishermen shouted.

Halina and Gethen followed their escort through the fields and alleys, marveling at the visual feast.

"Do all these people work in the golden flower trade?" she asked as they passed under block after block of dyed yellow and orange silk strands drying on lines stretched across the alleys. They swayed and undulated with the breeze, a serpentine fire winding its way through Yasan Khot's body, leading to the royal compound — the heart and brain of Teleyansk.

"No, this is the Silk Quarter," one of the soldiers replied. "There are many types of work in Yasan Khot. The Royal Forge occupies the eastern quarter and much of Teleyansk's metallurgy takes place there. But we also house our empire's renowned porcelain factories in the north."

"What's in the west?" Gethen asked.

"Our merchants live there." He gestured toward an area of raised houses, obvious wealth in their wide-ranging gardens, blue-dyed roof tiles, and clear-glass windows.

For all its crowding and bustle, the people of Yasan Khot went about their business with little complaint, greeting each other loudly, laughing at shared stories, arguing over prices and products. The women walked and talked, baskets of dried flowers or bundles of silk balanced on their heads. Children dodged in and out of the crowds, laughing, shoving, rough and tumble, unaware that life was anything but an adventure.

Their horses' hooves clip-clopped on the cobblestone avenues, an even jog that sent people dodging. But it was Halina and Gethen with their fair eyes and her flaming hair, their large horse and the two companion wolves trotting beside them that made the citizens stare.

Halina glanced over her shoulder. Behind the two rear guards, a parade of the curious had begun.

They passed beneath a golden gateway, its crossbeam held up by twin statues of the One God, and entered a new ring of the city. Here the cobblestones were whitewashed and led directly to the citadel. The buildings were either open-sided temples with shrines to the One God or small wooden houses. All were painted white. All bore the same golden symbol on their doors and walls — a circle with outward-facing crescents surrounding it to create a scalloped box, the symbol of the One God, a sun surrounded by moons. It represented the heavens and the earth, as well as each of the seasons coming together to form the year.

The crowd stopped outside the gateway and watched as the soldiers halted before a set of tall, white doors set into the citadel's purple walls.

A woman stood before the doors, her hands folded at her waist, her gown made of white silk and embroidered neck-to-hem with purple flowers.

The soldiers dismounted. Halina and Gethen followed suit and Duesh and Gwyn moved to Gethen's side.

The woman glided forward and bowed deeply. "You are most welcome, honored guests. I am Qadan, Third Empress and Second Advisor to His Imperial Highness Lokshin. Who are you and why have you come?"

"I'm Princess Halina Persinna Rhysh, Duchess of Rhyshis in absentia, the Red Blade of Or-Halee. This is my husband, Prince Gethen Rhysh, Duke of Rhyshis in absentia, the Sun Mage. We seek an audience with Emperor Lokshin to discuss a military and trade alliance."

"You are most honored guests, indeed." The woman indicated a nearby hut. "Please accept His Imperial Majesty's hospitality. Bathe, eat, dress in clothing free from the dust of the road." She led them toward the small building. "Recover from your weary journey in the Court of Guests while I bring your presence to our emperor's attention. You will be summoned."

They returned the woman's bow and entered the house. Servants bustled forth to take their bags, their travel cloaks, even their boots.

They tried to lead Halina to a separate bathing room, but Gethen halted them. "I go where my wife goes. You won't separate us."

The servants argued with him, polite and a little anxious. "A clean bath awaits you, too, my lord."

"I don't care. It can cool. I won't leave her side."

Halina swung between amused and exasperated. But when Gethen looked ready to set the servants aflame, she stepped in.

"Enough," she said, her voice firm with the authority of her station. "Do you question your emperor's desires when he expresses them?" They shook their heads and looked down. "I thought not. Yet you question the decisions of the Duke of Rhyshis?"

One said, "We only think of his comfort, Your Ladyship."

His voice stony, Gethen said, "My comfort will be best served without arguments and separation from my wife. Her safety is paramount."

"Do you suspect us of harboring ill will?"

"I assume everyone and everything is a danger," Gethen growled and was echoed by Duesh and Gwyn.

Halina snapped, "Leave us," and turned her back. Lokshin's people fled the bathing chamber without another word.

Gethen watched the wooden door slide shut. "I'm out of practice."

"You mean at being imperious?" He nodded. She shrugged and stripped. "I'm happier when they listen and obey the first time. I don't like using that tone, but their status is beneath us and it's best to remind them from the start."

"You do it well."

"Ha. Ha. You're so amusing."

He looked confused. "Am I? I wasn't trying to be funny."

She shook her head. "Let's hope we get what we came for and get out quickly. Palace walls have ears."

"Eyes too." Arms folded, he leaned back against the tall tub and glared at the door while Halina dunked beneath the warm water, emerged, and scrubbed her scalp and skin. "You don't need to guard me, you know. You can leave a wolf and a ward."

He shook his head.

She stopped scrubbing, realizing he hadn't warded the house. Considering how uneasy he was, it could only be because he couldn't summon the magic to do it. He was too exhausted and using the last of his energy to keep necromancy's cravings at bay. "Oh," she said and rested her face against his broad back. "I'm sorry. I didn't think before I opened my mouth and shoved my foot in it." Gethen squeezed her fingers. He said nothing. He didn't have to. She submerged to rinse away the remainder of the soap then climbed from the tub and toweled off.

The long tunic and trouzes left for her were unlike anything she'd worn before. "I'm not sure I have these ties right," she said as she fumbled to close the silk tunic.

Gethen pushed away from the tub and slid open the door. "What's your name?" he snapped at one of the servants.

"Nadi," she squeaked.

"Come help Her Ladyship dress."

The girl scurried into the room, a mouse beneath a hawk's hungry glare as he towered over her, his flinty eyes unblinking.

Halina considered her imposing husband and the timid girl. "You're scaring all of them, whether you mean to or not."

He turned that glare on her. She shook her finger at him. "Don't scowl at me. Your days of intimidating me are long past."

Gethen sighed, equal parts annoyance and regret replacing his glare. "I'm not trying to intimidate anyone." He looked at her from beneath his dark brows and folded his arms. "But the Court of Guests is no-man's land." He gestured around the bathing room and at the clothing. "We could be stuck here for a very long time, waiting on the whims of the emperor until we realize we'll never be seen at all."

The girl adjusted the tunic ties, wrapped a wide, black sash around Halina's waist, and stepped back.

"Thank you, Nadi," Halina said. "You made that look easy."

The royal-blue tunic came to her knees and split at the sides. It fell over matching trouzes, both pieces decorated with long-necked white birds. The silk was thick and luxurious, but the sleeves didn't even cover her wrists and the matching slippers were too small. She kicked them into a corner and put her travel boots on as the servant girl watched and chewed her lower lip.

To her credit, Nadi recovered her composure enough to ask, "Does Her Ladyship require help with her hair?"

Halina touched the mop of red curls and snarls. "I suppose I do." She saw the look on Gethen's face and said, "After Lord Rhyshis has bathed, you can return and do something with this mess. It needs to dry."

After the door closed behind the girl, Halina said, "I don't like this situation either. It's too vulnerable, but I'm determined to weather the test. Lokshin knows we're here. I'm sure he was informed of our presence the moment we came in sight of the city. If he wants to watch and wait, so be it." She sat on a padded bench and toweled her hair dry. "I may hate the truth of it, but we're the beggars here."

Gethen grunted and sat beside her. "Untenable," he

muttered through clenched teeth. Duesh and Gwyn settled at his feet, watching him.

She lowered the towel and took his hand. The tremors were there and a growing tension that made her jaw ache. "Take what you need from me."

"No more." He shook his head. "It's too dangerous." He pushed her damp hair back from her face. "I'll find another source of strength. And I'll find some patience too." He kissed her temple. "I just hope Teleyansk's emperor doesn't take too long to observe his guests. There are people counting on us and their time is running out."

"I know." She nudged him. "Get clean. Scraping off the crud does wonders for easing the road weariness."

He shrugged. "I'm not weary from travel. Any time alone with you is a blessing."

She smiled and went back to toweling. "You still stink."

He pulled his tunic up and sniffed it. His expression said she was right.

Worry for Ambrosine, Ianthe, and Prince Vernard wormed its way into Halina's thoughts. Had Ilker found his senses? She doubted it. Had Waldram's army reached Tatlis? She prayed not but feared the worst. Were Feddie and Elof safe or had assassins discovered their location? She didn't even want to entertain that possibility.

After Gethen bathed, they ate from a variety of meatless dishes while Nadi braided Halina's hair. She secured the plaits into a crown atop her head with jeweled combs. Whole chickens were provided for the wolves, a gesture that eased some of Gethen's ire.

As they were finishing, Qadan returned. "His Imperial Majesty will see you."

Halina nodded and laid aside her napkin. "Excellent."

"You will be summoned when it is time." She left and Halina scratched her scarred cheek.

"Itchy?"

"Yes, in more ways than one."

"Don't scratch."

She gave him a humorless smile and lowered her hand. "Let's escape this little prison." She shoved back her chair.

He nodded. "I want to check on Remig."

"A good excuse to get outside and explore the compound."

Servants were lighting lanterns in the courtyard when they emerged from the guest hut. Remig occupied a stable behind the guesthouse. He nickered a greeting for Gethen and Halina, and even sniffed at the wolves. He had fresh hay and clean water, plentiful straw to rest on and good shelter. He'd even been curried, and his tack had been cleaned and stored.

"Lokshin's people are thorough," Halina remarked, fingering the horse's well-oiled saddle and bridle. "And they're not keeping Remig from us, so we're not prisoners."

"Yet."

"Thanks for that, Lord Cheerful."

"You're welcome." He tucked her arm through his and led her from the stable into the purple light of dusk. "Let's have a stroll," he murmured. "I want to show you something."

People outside the gateway stared and whispered as Gethen and Halina exited the stable and strolled along the groomed path between other buildings. "What is this place?" she wondered aloud. "The Court of Guests seems defensive, but there's no wall to separate the city from the palace walls." Encircling the imperial grounds and as deep as a city block, the manicured area contained houses, stables, and temples. Yellow-clad guards came and went among the buildings, some leaving the area through the open gateways, others entering the palace grounds through the white gates.

"No need for a wall when you have a ward," Gethen replied and nodded toward a row of golden flowers that stretched between the wooden posts demarcating the space and encircling the entire court compound. "That's not for decoration."

She squinted at the narrow garden and posts. "Are you sure? I didn't feel a ward when we entered."

"It's there. Don't run through it to prove me wrong."

She laughed and slapped his arm. "I'm not that pig-headed. I just didn't know Teleyansk still used mages."

"Oh, yes. The Shin Dynasty was the first ruling family to employ battle mages. There are few sorcerers in Teleyansk now, but they all serve the emperor, whether they want to or not."

"Conscripts?"

He nodded. "Anyone gifted with magic is identified during their youth and taken to the Imperial Magistry for training. They pledge their service to the emperor and empire or they're deemed a threat."

She looked around. "That's why we're delayed? Because Lokshin is deciding if you're a threat?"

"You've noticed our guards?" The same soldiers who'd accompanied them into Yasan Khot had remained in the no man's land between the outer ward and the imperial compound's inner gates. "They're battle mages."

"That explains their light armor and weaponry."

"They're quite deadly, my love. Don't challenge them."

"You don't have to tell me twice. I've seen the devastation a battle mage can do." She squeezed his arm meaningfully. "Are they a threat to you?"

"Until I can strengthen my sorcery, yes."

"Bollocks," she muttered. "Take more of my blood magic."

"No."

"But—"

"No, Militess." He didn't look at her, but the force and finality in his voice was something she hadn't heard since the early days of their relationship, when they were still adversarial.

"You say *I'm* pig-headed," she muttered and stopped walking. "You need power. Why won't you draw on my blood magic like you did after the Elk People attacked?"

He pressed his lips to her ear and whispered, "Because this time, I won't be able to stop." He pulled back and looked down into her eyes.

She saw hunger in his gaze, something feral and barely controlled and...deadly? *Yes, deadly,* she thought.

"Your blood magic is tied to your soul. Right now there are few greater threats to your well-being than my addiction. I will not risk tapping your magic, Halina. I'll find another source for power, even if it means summoning all the rats from the palace to beg for their souls."

She swallowed, searching for something to say. "Well, that would be a great favor to the emperor, I'm sure." She swept her hand from Gethen's head to toe and said, "Your Imperial Highness, may I present the Rat Mage?"

He smiled weakly. "That's one way to gain an alliance."

"Whatever it takes to save Quoregna."

Night swallowed the last of the day's glow. Yellow lantern light spilled across their path as they followed the line of golden flowers, circumnavigating the palace's walled perimeter. There were four white gateways altogether, one facing each cardinal direction, marked with the One God's symbol and guarded by two yellow-clad battle mages. She still couldn't sense the ward, but Gethen wouldn't lie about it. No one stopped their stroll, but the mages watched them, their gazes sharp, weighing and measuring the foreigners.

Back at the guesthouse, a bed awaited them, soft sheets and heavy blankets warmed with coal pans. Sleeping clothes had been provided. And their own travel clothes were clean and folded. No one kept Halina's sword from her. "I'm surprised." She ran her hand over the scarred blade. "They don't see me as a threat."

"Insulted?" Gethen asked.

"Maybe a little." She pushed the blade home in its scabbard and left it beside the bed then slid under the bedding.

He pulled her close. "They underestimate you."

She yawned and murmured, "Wouldn't be the first time."

EIGHTEEN

G ethen opened his eyes. He stood in a milky pond beneath a black sky.

"Again?" Why was he in the Void instead of bed? He turned a circle, expecting to see Skiron. Instead he found an octagonal mausoleum. Made of black marble, its white twin existed on his land in Kharayan Woods. It was the site of several battles with Shemel and with the Rime Witch, the place where Halina had almost died.

The mausoleum's door was open and a slight, dark-haired girl with white, pupil-less eyes sat on the steps, her knees pulled to her chest.

"Yisun?" he asked, watching her with suspicion. The last time he'd encountered the Rime Witch, he and Halina had battled the demonic girl, ultimately entombing her inside the mausoleum beneath a sheet of frozen water and some very powerful wards.

"Guess again," she answered in a booming growl that could only come from Skiron.

"Oh, it's you." Gethen folded his arms. "Have you grown weary of counting souls?"

The God of Death grinned, showing predatory teeth too large for the young Dargani woman's mouth. "I like this fire you've found, Sun Mage. Threatening your woman boils your blood. I'll remember that."

"Get to the point of this meeting. I'm tired and need sleep."

"Is that what's making your hide itch and your muscles twitch?" Skiron sneered, his voice so strange coming from the dead woman's mouth. "I'm not so sure you're correct."

Gethen snarled an unintelligible curse at his master god and turned away. He'd find the Voidline and return to the mortal realm without Skiron's help.

"Don't turn your back on me, maggot!" Gethen was yanked around and thrown facedown in the water. "Did you enjoy drowning so much you'd like to do it again?" Skiron came off the steps. He morphed into a giant of a man, bald and pallid, naked but for red, living curses written and writhing across his skin, hissing and rattling like poisonous snakes. His massive foot came down on Gethen's neck and pressed his face into the pond's spongy muck.

Gethen coughed and struggled.

Skiron laughed. He grabbed Gethen's hair and pulled him up, bending him backwards, his nightmare face inches away, his hot, stinking breath worming up Gethen's nose as surely as the milky water and slime had.

Gethen spat. Gunk and fluid splattered the God of Death. It coated his face, dripped from his chin, and slid down his neck and chest. Skiron only laughed and dropped him.

"Pretend you're strong, if it brings you relief. Your delusions amuse me. But we both know the Red Blade's blood magic is too tempting. And you're too feeble to resist." He strolled around Gethen, climbed the mausoleum steps, and resumed Yisun's form, sitting beneath the portico. "You'll surrender to necromancy's hunger, and glorious slaughter will follow. Quoregna will beg their gods for mercy when the Sun Mage's full power is unleashed against them. You'll have the revenge you seek against Shadow Mage Shemel and that weakling King Waldram, but only after you drain your woman's blood magic and consume her soul."

On his knees, Gethen bared his teeth at his unwanted god. "I. Will. Not."

Skiron laughed. "Why do you think she was created and set on your path? Destruction is your purpose. To be destroyed by you is hers."

Before Gethen could respond, the God of Death waved Yisun's icy fingers dismissively and the Void's colorless landscape disappeared, replaced by the bedchamber in the Yasan Khot guest house.

Halina snuggled against him, her breathing deep and slow. Duesh and Gwyn snored gently from the floor beside the bed. Crickets chirruped outside. An owl hooted from the adjoining stable.

Gethen stared into the unfamiliar room's strange shadows, clenching his fists as fear and frustration spread through him. He turned his head to gaze at his wife's face in the dim glow of the bedchamber's shielded lanterns. Shadows obscured her features and hid the freckles that dusted her nose and cheeks. The curve of the scar left by the shriker's claw taunted him, a reminder of his failure.

Gethen looked at the ceiling. Worsened by Skiron's games, the pain and agitation of need wouldn't let him rest. He itched to draw Halina's blood magic, fixated on her breathing and the surge of power flowing through her even as she slumbered, trusting, loving. Vulnerable only for him because, like a fool, he'd asked her to believe in him. And, like a greater fool, she did.

He covered his face with his hands and swallowed a groan. Skiron was right. He was feeble. He lowered his hands and fisted them so tightly his nails dug bloody crescents into his palms. Unable to sleep and driven mad by his warring desires, he slipped from bed and dressed. He'd put space between himself and Halina, if only for a few moments. He wanted crisp air and the stars in the sky above.

He beckoned the wolves to his side and murmured, "Keep her safe. Let no one enter after I leave."

The animals took up defensive positions, Duesh at the bedside, Gwyn at the door.

Gethen went into the courtyard and around to the stable.

"I'm sorry to disturb you from a well-earned rest," he said to Remig. "I need a little of your strength." He ran his hands over the horse's flanks, drawing silver sparks of energy from Remig's wild spirit. He shook with the effort to not take everything. Remig was willing, as generous with his soul as he was with his wide back.

Gethen left the horse dozing and returned to the narrow foyer of the small guesthouse. There was no movement from the bedroom. His wife slumbered, peaceful and secure, the wolves on guard. He focused his limited energy and warded the house, a deadly trap for anyone foolish enough to enter uninvited.

He left to follow the path of golden flowers, considering the blooms and the faint ward Teleyansk's mages had erected around the palace. Unlike his own wards, this one's power flowed from the golden flowers. Earthy and cool, it snapped with enough power to hold an intruder in place and in pain. He crouched to study the flowers and the ward, fascinated by an unfamiliar use of magic. Lokshin's battle mages watched his every move.

Gethen reached out, hesitated, and caught the attention of a guard. The man quickly averted his gaze and Gethen chuckled. "You don't need to pretend. I know I'm being watched."

The battle mage nodded. "Can you blame our caution?"

"Of course not. I've warded the guesthouse and left the wolves to guard my wife. Suspicion flows both ways."

"So it does." The man pushed away from the shadows. "You're curious about the golden ward or the flowers?"

"Both. I've never known plants to be anything but stingy with their energy."

"Most plants and trees are, but these are unique to our use. We train with them from childhood."

"Are they a different cultivar from the purple ones harvested all around Yasan Khot?"

The man nodded. "They are."

"I've long known their medicinal properties, but this application of sorcery is new to me." He reached out again then looked up. "May I?"

"Of course. The ward keeps intruders out. You're a guest of His Imperial Majesty. He would not begrudge you a flower."

Gethen murmured his thanks as he plucked a yellow bloom and considered it. He studied its many frilled petals and the yellow-orange stamens jutting proudly over its center. He sniffed it then popped it in his mouth. It tasted spicy, sweet, and earthy. His tongue tingled unexpectedly. "Interesting," he murmured as he stood. "I could brew some powerful metheglins with these."

The man smiled. "Perhaps our master physician will discuss his formulations with you, Lord Rhyshis."

Gethen bowed slightly. "I would enjoy that conversation." He turned and strode toward the nearest gateway. "Meanwhile, there's a city to explore."

"You're wandering so late?"

"The best time to learn a place is when it's asleep. Less noise and distraction to get in your way."

The man glanced at several nearby mages.

"You may follow, if you think your emperor wants me so closely watched, but I won't be easy to track." With that, Gethen stepped across the gateway threshold and into a shadow cast by its lanterns.

Shadow travel was bitterly cold, utterly devoid of light, and pulled the breath from his lungs. A directionless spell, it was a leap of faith in his own sorcery. And the knowledge that the distance traveled was limited to a few streets kept Gethen from panicking every time he employed the spell. He emerged in a narrow alley. A pair of cats hissed and spat before their instincts recognized him as a friend.

He crouched and crooned. "Shall I rub your ears?"

The gray tabbies obliged, crooked tails held high and throats buzzing as they twisted in and around him, climbed on his legs and smashed their faces against his scratching fingers. They willingly offered up their souls and Gethen tugged little bits of green spirit magic free, leaving both cats curled up on a wall, safely snoozing as he set off in search of more generous animal allies.

Yasan Khot's night folk crept forth, ghosts and demons watching him with hope and suspicion.

Women whispered of warm beds and illicit pleasures. They reached for him, the tall stranger in their midst, but Gethen avoided their fingers, afraid of the mad cravings they would unleash.

"Morga?"

Gethen hunched his shoulders. The gaunt beggar was filthy and wanted money. The distinctive, astringent sweetness of nocoli wafted off him and his hands shook as he pawed at Gethen's sleeve.

"Morga?"

Shaking his head, Gethen stepped away. The man's desperate spirit lingered, a leash to bind him, temptation slowing him like an anchor. It was Besalee again. It was Shemel laughing and tossing coins at the nocoli addicts, sliding their souls from their skin, slippery as eels, sick as dying dogs. Gethen averted his gaze and yanked his sleeve from the man's tremulous grip. "No money. No," he replied in Common and turned down another alley seeking escape from need and nightmares and memories he could never forget.

"Morga?" The man followed him like his memories did, like Shemel had.

"Ch morga! Ch!" Gethen snarled in Yansk this time and strode faster, his long legs taking him away from temptation. Why had he come into the city? Halina was right. He should've stayed on the royal grounds and called out the rats.

He turned another corner and spied an old dog lounging on the low porch of a dark hut, her muzzle gray and haunches bony. Sitting beside the dog was an elderly woman, her hair as hoary as the dog's, her body as withered. They peered up at him, wisdom in their ancient eyes.

"Looking to make trouble or escape it?" the woman asked, her voice thin and crackly as dried parchment. She patted the step beside her, an invitation to rest.

"Trying to avoid it, Grandmother," he replied and sat on the porch, the dog between them.

The hound raised her head then groaned the way old dogs do and rested her snout between her front paws. Her eyes closed. She sighed. She couldn't be bothered with troubled mages.

"Why did you come here?"

The question surprised him and he squinted at the woman. She squinted back at him, stuck a gnarled golden flower root between her teeth and chewed its end.

"For help," he said.

She cackled. The dog opened a bleary eye at the sound, sighed again, and rolled onto her side. "Why would a powerful mage need help from an old woman and her dog?"

"How do you know I'm a mage?"

The root waggled at him as she spoke. "Everyone knows who you are. Yasan Khot isn't stupid or silent. Rumors got here before you and the Red Blade arrived. We wondered what was taking you so long."

"Huh."

She offered up a dried root and he stuck it between his molars and chewed. It made his mouth tingle like the flower had. His jaw unclenched, his shoulders relaxed. The night brightened.

"It's not my help you need," she muttered and nodded toward the shadows where the addict squatted. "It's his." She dandled the sleeping dog's floppy ear. It twitched beneath her fingers. She peered into the darkness at the broken shadow of a man lurking there. "My son wants to die."

Realizing she meant the addict, Gethen shook his head. "I can't help."

"Yes, you can. You can help each other."

"That's not why I came here."

"Don't you know not to lie to grandmothers?"

"I'm not lying. I came to Teleyansk with my wife to form an alliance with your emperor. We seek his help."

"Feh!" She spat around the root, sending a phlegmy lump into the street. "She came for that. Your problems are different." She stabbed a finger toward her son, who'd slunk from the shadows to cross the street and hover at the end of the porch, need wafting off him like the sweat oozing from his pores. "You need power. He needs to die."

"Morga?" the man whispered, his voice rattling, the sound a snake's tail makes when it's ready to strike.

"He's rotting. Brain's gone. Body needs to follow. Or do you think he should suffer? And me along with him? Do you know what it's like to watch your child die a slow, rotting death?" She chomped the root, made it squeak between her teeth. "You can save us all."

"Save?" Gethen shook his head. The tingling had spread down his spine now. The night seemed as bright as day. "How is killing him saving him?"

"The One God waits," she sang.

The man lunged at Gethen, a dull glint of moonlight on metal the only warning of a blade in his hand.

Instinct produced shadow armor, a vambrace around Gethen's upraised arm. The rusty blade slid off and thudded into a wooden post.

The dog yelped and jerked to her feet, skittering away from the attack.

Gethen's fist snapped out and caught the man's jaw. The crack of bone was unmistakable, but it didn't stop the addict.

Snarling and spitting curses, he slashed at Gethen's chest. Gethen spat the golden flower root in the man's face and evaded the wild attack, pushing him back with a mass spell.

"I don't want to fight you," he said, gaze following the dull blade as it snaked and jabbed, as unpredictable as its wielder.

Sudden weight landed on his back and hands gripped his throat from behind. The old woman had turned on him. "Do it now," she hissed. "Kill him while they take the Red Blade!"

Gethen roared, seized her gray hair, and yanked her over his shoulder. The man lunged forward, but Gethen threw the old woman at him, sending both sprawling.

The tingling had turned to numbing. Gethen's legs felt jellied, all his strength spent in that one effort to defend himself.

The woman hissed as she scrambled to her feet and came at him. Her eyes were wrong now, white orbs and no pupils.

Yisun? Gethen slammed her with a heat spell that set her aflame. She shrieked and twisted, throwing off false flesh to reveal a familiar figure. The Rime Witch, bony fingers tipped with ice, skin cracked and gray, hair a wild mass.

Shocked by the appearance of his old enemy in the mortal realm, Gethen almost missed the man's next attack. Movement at the corner of his eye warned him and he flinched aside but not fast enough as the blade caught his cheek and opened a shallow gash down to his chin.

An incoherent snarl left his lips. Gethen grabbed the addict's wrist when he slashed the knife back. While he kept the heat spell on his demon foe, he lost all inhibition about robbing the man of his existence. He dragged the soul from the man's body, filled himself with its power, and watched the addict die, a crumpled bag of bones falling like a lump of refuse on a narrow, dirt lane.

Empowered by the human soul, Gethen tightened his grip on Yisun, binding her to the Voidline, using his power and the golden flower's essence to wrap a shimmering net around her as she shrieked and struggled. She was far weaker than the last time they'd faced off. Then, she'd been a young woman, a powerful witch who harnessed the weather to torment him and Halina. Now, she'd resorted to tricks to distract him. It had almost worked, but she'd grown desperate and shown her hand. How she'd escaped her prison again, he could easily guess. Skiron had freed her from her icy tomb.

"I spared you once, Witch," Gethen said, his voice filled with the dark, sepulcher power of the Void. "No mercy this time." He grabbed her throat and pulled the soul from her corrupt flesh, taking her power for his own. What remained of Yisun's spirit scattered to the stars, lifting and dispersing like embers from a dying fire as her body collapsed and fragmented in the street, covering the pathetic addict's remains in a fine coating of white ash.

Filled with an immortal power that he never wanted, nearly

insensate with the high of the souls, and driven by the witch's words, Gethen seized the shadows and summoned his armor.

He spied the dog cowering in the hut's darkened doorway and whispered, "Run," before flinging a travel spell around himself and leaving the alley behind.

NINETEEN

Halina awakened to find her husband gone. The wolves lay before the door, their amber eyes watching her. "Gethen?" She listened, then sensed the distinct vibration of his ward. He'd gone out. "Searching for rat souls?" she murmured to Duesh and Gwyn. She sat up and shivered in the chill air.

From inside the palace walls, a gong cut the night's silence and a man's melodious voice followed. He announced first in the common tongue, then in Yansk: "The stars shine above. A summer moon rises. The golden flowers sleep. Lokshin's empire grows. It is the Hour of the Fox." He repeated his chant twice which meant the Hour of the Fox was the second hour past middle night.

Halina stared into the dark and warred with herself. Gethen needed help. He was struggling to hold onto his humanity, but he didn't want her near him while he regained his power, and when she thought about what he might be doing to attain the souls he required, she shivered even more. "You're being a coward," she muttered, afraid of what she might see, afraid that it was far worse than what her imagination could conjure. She lay back, pulled the covers close and hugged his pillow to her chest. "Come back to me," she whispered into the dark.

A knock at the hut's outer door and the low rumble of the wolves met her plea.

She sat up and inhaled to call her husband's name again.

"Lady Rhyshis?"

Not Gethen. Disappointed, Halina grabbed the Chonyn sword and balanced it across her knees. "Yes?"

"I apologize for the lateness of my arrival, but I have a message from our emperor."

"Wait." Halina clambered from bed and shoved her feet into her boots. She opened the hut's front door, keeping the sword out of sight. Qadan waited several feet back from the doorway, a battle mage beside her.

She bowed and nodded to the man. He stepped forward and extended a long-handled paddle with a fold of parchment balanced on it. So, they knew about Gethen's ward. The way Qadan's gaze slid away from Halina's told her everything. Lokshin had rejected their request for a meeting. Halina read the note.

Teleyansk does not involve itself in family squabbles. I encourage you to return home to Tatlis and find peace with King Ilker. He will need your strength, Red Blade. There's no greater ally than family.

"Thank you." She refolded the parchment. "I'll discuss this with the Sun Mage."

The Third Empress bowed again and turned away from the guest house, leaving the battle mage on guard.

Halina returned to bed and slowly slumped over onto her side. Somehow she had to convince Lokshin to see her. Teleyansk's army was her last hope. She reread the message.

"There's no greater ally than family." She rubbed her brow. "No worse enemy, too."

A terrified shriek broke the peace. Halina was off the bed

and out the door before she'd fully drawn the Chonyn sword from its scabbard. Duesh and Gwyn charged past her. "Semele's blood," she hissed as she came to a sudden stop in the courtyard.

Chaos reigned, chaos and two creatures that stole her breath.

Wraiths. Inky blackness that moved fast, serpent-like and unnaturally silent. Within the living shadows, mangled faces snarled and screamed but made no sound. Clawed hands reached, sharp teeth gnashed, grotesque abominations writhed — souls suffering and the demons torturing them.

Halina staggered. She'd faced something like this in Kharayan Woods. Only one and it had come very close to killing her and Gethen.

Duesh and Gwyn slunk around her legs, rumbling low and dangerous, their teeth gnashing, tongues flicking forth in warning.

A scream snapped her from paralysis into action. Qadan cowered in the recessed corner of the closed palace gates as one of the wraiths loomed and two battle mages weaved shimmering golden shield spells to keep it at bay.

"Bollocks on you." Halina summoned her blood armor. If she was going to die this night, she'd die fighting. She strode to the middle of the courtyard as the blood-red armor formed around her.

"She's not the one you want! I am!" she shouted and brandished the foreign sword. "Come get me, you cunny whores!"

Gethen emerged in the midst of madness at the edge of Lokshin's royal compound. Clad in blood armor, Halina battled shrieking black wraiths side-by-side with yellow-clad mages. The Third Empress crouched in the barbican, the gates to her back, a wall of mages and Halina standing between her and the monsters.

Outside the flower perimeter, citizens watched, their faces filled with terror, their bodies rigid and their feet rooted as the wraiths drew power from their souls.

Gethen strode toward the gateway but was repelled by it, thrown to his back and nearly knocked senseless. He cursed and scrambled up. "Lower the ward!"

Halina spotted him. "You're late!" she shouted as she dodged twisting tentacles. Duesh and Gwyn snarled and snapped at the nebulous beasts, tearing away bits of the wraiths' bodies when they took corporeal form to strike at the soldiers.

A battle mage went down beneath the assault, his body bent in ways no mortal should. Gethen reached out and captured the man's soul, taking much of its power and flinging the core of it across the Voidline. "Dammit, let me cross the ward!"

Halina cursed as a wraith flung the dead mage and the body sent her crashing through one of the posts supporting the guest-house's porch awning. The roof groaned and settled but held. She was slow to rise, kept momentarily safe by two battle mages and the wolves.

Gethen roared, reaching deep to summon his power. Like a cleaver, he found the ties connecting the wraiths to the innocent citizens and halved them with a sharp spell. Freed from the demonic grips, the men and women collapsed, groaning and crying.

"Go!" he shouted. Other residents emerged to help the victims. "Get them out of here!"

As the mortals fled, the wraiths shrieked at him, distracted from their assault on Halina by the sudden lessening of their power. But they weren't distracted long. They found new strength in the mages they'd injured, jerking the men and women across the ground and stealing their souls.

"Enough of this!" Gethen drew up his power to create a glowing shield and focused a rending spell on the golden flower ward. He tore a hole in it large enough to step through. It sucked at him, stole his breath and stopped his heart for a painfully long moment, but no spell would stop him from reaching Halina. With a sound like the sky tearing, the ward yielded to him, snapping back with a thunderous crack as he released it. His ears popped and his hands tingled, but Gethen's only concern was his wife. He'd seen her nearly killed by a wraith once before. He'd be damned if he'd stand by and watch her be pummeled again.

Wraiths feared few things, but mage fire was among them. Lokshin's sorcerers were employing it in golden shields, protecting first the empress then themselves and Halina. But their flames lacked the power that a sun mage wielded.

Gethen drew flames from the lanterns in the imperial palace, the Court of Guests, and the nearby homes. He spun it into two columns of amber mage fire and wrapped it around the wraiths, enmeshing them as he had Yisun. He tightened the flaming nets, ignoring the monsters' shrieks and struggles, ignoring their ghostly tentacles as they lashed out at him, striking bits of armor from his body.

Halina came forward and batted aside their assaults. She'd drawn up a sword, a long blood-red weapon formed from her blood magic. She was a quick study, powerful and sure in her use of weaponry. And anything could be a weapon in Halina's hands.

"Help us!" she snarled at the mages. A group peeled off from the corps protecting Qadan. They flung spells at the wraiths, keeping them contained as Gethen tightened the flaming net.

Still, the wraiths battled back. One snapped out a deadly dagger of shadow, struck the head from one mage's shoulders and impaled another. It lifted the struggling, screaming man and hurled his body at Gethen. Halina rushed into the path and knocked the body away. But the force took her down. The wraiths' inky shadow arms reached for her. She didn't raise her sword, didn't stand. Duesh and Gwyn lunged between her and the threat.

"No!" Gethen sent a surge of power into his mage fire nets and followed it with a mass spell. White light filled the wraiths, illuminating the demonic faces churning inside their dark depths, like lighting flashing inside a black storm's heavy clouds. His incantation swelled the wraiths, pushing against the nets. The magic squealed. The wraiths howled then exploded in a blinding flash and a thunderous crack. Gethen was flung off his feet. He landed hard, the wind knocked from him, the shock searing his spine and brain.

For a moment all was dark and silent. Then the torches and lanterns sputtered to life throughout the palace and the Court of Guests. Around him, mages groaned and got to their knees. In the shadows of the barbican, Qadan peeked around her remaining protectors.

Ignoring all others, Gethen scrambled to Halina as she slowly rolled onto her back. A long groan escaped her. She sat up. "Blood and bones," she hissed and touched her shoulder. Her hand came away bloody.

"The armor splintered." He lifted her hair away from her eyes.

"Not unbreakable, I see," she said, her voice tight from pain. "Is the empress safe?"

"I am, thanks to your bravery, our battle mages' skillful magic, and your husband's swift arrival," Qadan replied as she reached them. She snapped her fingers at the guards who'd finally opened the white gates and emerged with swords and pikes drawn. "Your cowardice will not go unrewarded," she told the captain as he stopped before her and bowed. "Help our guests. Lady Rhyshis is injured."

Gethen surged to his feet. "No. I will tend my wife."

The captain blanched for the second time in as many minutes.

Qadan nodded. "Our master healer will provide you with any herbs or medicinals you require, Lord Rhyshis."

Gethen helped Halina to her feet, murmuring, "I'm sorry," as she hissed and cursed beneath her breath.

"Duesh and Gwyn. Where are they?" she asked. As if on cue, the wolves emerged from the beneath the guesthouse eaves. Blood marred Duesh's black muzzle and Gwyn favored her right hind leg.

"Come," Gethen said as he kicked the guesthouse door open. He had healing to do and he didn't give a rat's arse what Lokshin's people did or didn't do as long as they stayed out of his way.

TWENTY

"Stop squirming."

"I will when it stops hurting," Halina snarled through clenched teeth as Gethen extracted fine shards of blood armor from her upper arm and shoulder. "You didn't tell me this could happen."

"No armor's perfect. Just like no soldier."

"Don't you have something you can use to numb the pain?" She struggled not to flinch as his tweezers dug into her flesh.

"No." He sounded weary. "Not until I get all the shards out of the wound. They're too hard to see otherwise." Something rattled and he handed his belt to her. "Bite."

Halina didn't hesitate. She shoved the leather between her teeth and bit down hard as he dug for more blood-red armor. She groaned and fisted the blanket on the bed. Gethen sat beside her, focused on cleaning and treating her wound. Considering every other inch of her was bruised and scratched, coming away from that fight with only a shoulder wound wasn't bad.

Pain spiked down her arm and she drooled as she cursed. He

handed her a rag. She wiped her chin. There was no shame in it. What he was doing hurt, a lot.

Finally, the tweezers splashed in the rinse water as he finished torturing her and dropped them into the bowl. "I think that's all of them."

Halina's jaw ached as she eased off the belt and pulled it from her teeth. She rotated her neck to loosen the muscles. Cool liquid ran over her shoulder and down her arm and back. Her pain eased and she sighed gratefully. "Despite this bitch of a wound, that armor was more effective than anything I've worn before. My old plate wouldn't have withstood most of those hits."

He grunted.

"You should see to the wolves," she said.

"I will once this is stitched. Stay still so I can make quick work of it."

He smeared unguent on the wound, deadening her pain further. She relaxed and let him focus, ignoring the tug of the stitches. It was a sensation as familiar to her as breathing.

True to her word, Qadan had sent unguents and potions from the emperor's healer, each with an explanation of its use and a list of ingredients.

"Provided I got all the shards, this wound should heal quickly."

"Really?" She flexed her arm and shoulder, wincing at the movement. "Feels like my arm is coming off."

"That's the necromancy burning your nerves."

"Fantastic."

He turned to Duesh and Gwyn, assessing their wounds. Duesh's were superficial and Gwyn's ministrations had gone far in cleaning and treating them. But Gwyn's leg, though not broken, looked skinned from ankle to haunch. Gethen murmured incantations to settle her into slumber, then soaked the wound with the same wash he'd used on Halina's shoulder and followed it with a thick layer of unguent. He carefully bandaged the wolf's leg and stroked her neck as he slipped a few dried leaves into her cheek.

"Will she be all right?" Halina asked.

"Yes. She's worse off than you but handling it better."

Halina stuck her tongue out at her husband. He cleaned Duesh's face and chest and healed a wound on the wolf's neck. "This could've been much worse," he murmured.

"You arrived just in time."

"I shouldn't have been away." The weariness in his voice had turned to bitterness.

Halina watched him. His hands weren't shaking anymore and the fatigue had left him. He'd found a soul or souls, powerful enough to allow him to obliterate those wraiths with terrifying ease. But there was something cold and aloof about him now, something that made her uneasy in a way that was strangely familiar.

"Where did you go?"

Gethen paused, bloody rag in hand, eyes downcast. "Do you really want to know?"

"I thought we weren't keeping secrets."

He sucked a deep breath, eyes closed and face drawn. "I went looking for animals. Instead I found an addict...and Yisun."

She inhaled sharply. "How? In the Void?"

He looked up at her. "In Yasan Khot."

"I don't understand."

"I don't either. But she lured me with the addict's desperation then tried to hold me back while you were attacked."

"Is that how your face got cut?"

He touched his cheek. "I forgot about that." He smeared unguent along the scabbed line. "The addict had a blade."

"And lost his life for it. Poor fool." She reached out to touch him.

He avoided her fingers. "Lost his soul for it."

"Why are you ashamed?"

"You know why." He went into the entryway and raised a ward. Amber and silver symbols hung on the air as he sent them into the guesthouse's upturned eaves and spread them across the floors and walls. He went to the door and did the same thing around the palace itself. The shimmering symbols arced over the curving hip roofs and conical towers, the walls and statues. He sent out waves of sorcery through the streets and fields of Yasan Khot, warding the entire city and its outlying fields.

When he returned, she expected him to be shaky and weak, but Gethen was unbowed by the draw on his energy.

"Yisun must have had a powerful soul," she said, watching him closely, trying to unfold all his layered emotions.

Gethen ran his fingers through his black hair. "I didn't want it," he said, the words coming out like they pained him. "It's cold and rotten and churning inside me like a mouldering black-apple eaten out of desperation." He sat heavily on the bed beside her. "Forgive me. I left you vulnerable. I let my weakness drive me, let our enemies use it against me. And people died because of it. You could've died because of it. Because of me."

She threaded her fingers with his. "I'm not the one who needs to forgive you, Gethen. You need that from yourself. And you need to decide what controls you. Is it really necromancy and Skiron? Or are you your own master?" She tugged his hand until he looked at her. She hated seeing pain in his eyes. He was such a strong man. If she could destroy the God of Death for any reason, it would be for making Gethen Rhysh doubt his own power and worth. "Is Skiron really as commanding as you think or is that control you're giving him?"

"Meaning?"

"When all the mythology of the Sun Mage is stripped away, what's your real source of power? Is it the gods and souls? I don't think so. I think it's you, just like my blood magic is a part of me. I don't know where it came from. I guess I was born with it. I think you must've been too, or Shemel and Skiron wouldn't have noticed you."

His brow furrowed, but he didn't protest, so Halina forged on.

"I've never seen any evidence that Skiron, Khotyr, and Semele actually exist beyond songs, stories, and rituals. They haven't saved my loved ones. They haven't prevented war or death. They haven't healed sick babies or saved mothers from dying in childbirth. They're symbols to me, Gethen. Of hope and fear. But they don't exist for me."

"I've seen Skiron. Spoken to him, had his heel on the back of my neck."

"Because you believe in his dominance over you."

He eyed her, a mixture of doubt, irritation, and hope at war in his expression. "You're saying I give Skiron his power?"

"I'm saying the gods are symbols for everyone but you." He shook his head, but she continued. "My father used to say, 'Our perceptions shape our reality.' What if you're stronger than the gods? What if they know it and fear you? So Skiron fosters your perception of his immense strength in order to control you. He feeds the things you fear the most about yourself — your addiction to souls, your ability to destroy with ease. Skiron ordered you to create chaos and bring death."

"To fulfill his agenda and keep the mortal world's need for the gods alive."

"And he did that knowing you'd hate yourself for it. Skiron is a liar. He wants you to think you're at his mercy."

Gethen looked at their hands, lost in thought. "What difference does it make? The addiction is still there. The need for souls to fuel my sorcery is no less consuming and shameful."

She squeezed his fingers until he looked at her again. "Your magic is yours to command and summon, with or without souls to empower it. It was there when you were a young boy and I'm sure you weren't stealing souls then. Do you remember when you first noticed it?"

He nodded. "At the bee tree when I was five." He fell silent, his gaze distant as he recalled a long-lost incident.

"Tell me."

"My poor governess nearly dropped dead from fright." He gave a little laugh. "There was a dead tree in Ystwyth's Blue Garden. Halved and hollowed after being split by lightning decades ago, it was wide enough for three boys to stand inside and was one of my favorite hiding spots." He smiled and added, "A fact every royal governess knew, though they always pretended not to." He rubbed a line of dirt from her palm with his thumb. "A queen honeybee found that tree one summer morning and erected her hive inside. The garden was cleared so its new residents could build undisturbed. But their buzzing mesmerized me." He touched his chest. "It thrummed through me and I was certain the queen and her workers wanted to meet me." Gethen extracted his hand from her grip and retrieved the metheglin he'd brought from Ranith. He offered her a glass and raised his own to the flickering firelight. The golden wine shimmered inside. "So I escaped my governess and made a beeline to that hive, unconcerned about the possibility of death by a thousand stings." He met Halina's surprised gaze. "I was determined."

"But they didn't sting you?"

He snorted. "Oh, yes they did. I reached right into that hive, looking for the queen, and her workers did exactly as they'd been charged." Gethen glanced at his hand, his brow furrowing as if he was re-experiencing the pain. "They chased me across the garden and trapped me in Khotyr's White Pool. Kept me there and my governess and guards at bay until the queen bee thought I'd learned my lesson."

"Did you?"

He grinned at her. "Clearly not. I still like the strong ones with the sharpest sting and fiercest temper."

She smiled back, wrinkling her nose at him. "Where does the magic come in?"

"That buzzing in my body never stopped. Those stings healed almost as quickly as they were delivered. And I knew the hive's intentions." He downed his mead. "I still do."

"And you've learned respect for them."

"Definitely." He refilled his glass. "That hive awakened the magic inside me. It's always there, humming like ten thousand bees, as sharp and quick and powerful as their collective sting."

"But did you need to draw power from the bees to tap into your magic that first day?"

"No." He watched the flickering fire dance on the hearth. "I did not. They awakened my awareness to it, but it's always been there." He looked at her. "You're right. I've always had that foundation of magic humming inside me. Even transitioning from being the Shadow Mage to the Sun Mage didn't require taking a soul. Your strength buoyed me and hurried the transition, but I didn't *need* your blood magic to make that change. It was already part of my nature."

She nodded, encouraging him. "Which means what about Skiron?"

"He wants me addicted."

"I think so too."

He made a face like a dog that knows its enemy is close, a silent snarl, bared teeth. "The gods know it weakens me."

"You've been misled."

214

"I blindly followed." He downed his drink again and clunked the glass on the table. "Blood and bones, Halina, why couldn't we have met a decade ago?"

She laughed. "You wouldn't have liked me much then. I was arrogant and foolish, too full of my own bravado and still believing the stories being exaggerated about me."

"Then we weren't so different." He nodded. "You're right about my magic. I had it before I ever took that first soul. Why shouldn't I be able to find it now and use its full strength without leaving death in my wake?"

"That well resides within you. Just like my blood magic." She pressed her fist to his chest then thumped him gently. "You taught me that."

He captured her fingers and pressed them to his lips, then he nodded for her to get under the covers. "You've given me a lot to contemplate, wife."

Halina settled into the pillows. "Good. You can do that while I sleep. And, husband?"

"Hmm?"

"Be kinder to yourself."

Halina stared around the Court of Guests the next morning when she and Gethen emerged from the guesthouse. The transformation of the courtyard was breathtaking. Not a flower was blemished. Not a stone upturned, not a single furrow gouged in the gardens. The destruction of the previous night had disappeared and the palace's outer courtyard looked as pristine as when they'd arrived.

"It's like nothing ever happened," she murmured.

Gethen nodded. "Impressive."

They'd found clean clothing laid out with their breakfast, as well as fresh bath water and new towels. They'd decided to make one last appeal to Lokshin. If the emperor turned them down again they would depart immediately for Besera.

One of the yellow-clad battle mages approached and bowed. "The wards are your doing, Lord Rhyshis?"

"Yes. I needed sleep and the threat that visited your palace last night hasn't abated. We wish to appeal one last time to your emperor and request an immediate audience. If he refuses, we'll depart at once and take our enemy's attention with us."

The mage bowed and offered a folded parchment. "A message from His Imperial Highness."

Halina accepted it. Reading aloud, she couldn't help but feel a mixture of trepidation and relief. "His Imperial Highness Lokshin requests your immediate presence in his receiving room in the Hall of Wisdom." She refolded the sheet. "Is this for an audience or an execution?"

The man blanched. "If his Imperial Highness wanted you dead, Your Ladyship, you would have felt our assassins' blades already."

She nodded. "Lead the way."

Gethen frowned, but she took his arm. They'd weathered the test and then some. She knew very little of Teleyansk's emperor, but he had a reputation for being a principled man. "Come, Mage, let's convince an emperor to help us kill a king."

TWENTY-ONE

Three sets of massive gates stood between the Courtyard of the Guests and the House of the Golden Flower, Emperor Lokshin's private residence. Between those gates were successive courtyards with increasingly impressive displays of beauty and artistry.

The first courtyard contained gardens surrounding a neat white building, extraordinary in its lack of adornment.

"The Temple of the One God," their escort said. "Neg Burkhan Sum."

Statuary stood throughout the gardens, all depictions of the soft-featured One God. Neither male nor female, the god seemed almost child-like with a bald head, flat chest, wasp waist, and delicate features. All bore the circle-and-crescent symbol on their forehead.

The gardens were laid out in straight lines and sharp angles. The flowers were all golden yellow blooms or pure white. White-clad servants moved shoulder-to-shoulder along the paths, clipping the grass blade-by-blade with small shears. They bore white bags into which they deposited the clippings.

"Neatness and order are essential to the One God's existence," the battle mage remarked.

"I see that," Gethen replied. "Doesn't Ilker follow the One God's teachings?" he asked Halina.

She nodded. "Strange that he would embrace Waldram's chaos."

"Very. And more proof that his mind is no longer his own."

"Or at least his will."

The next set of gates was also white with the golden seal of the One God, but when they passed through them and Gethen glanced back, he saw they were red on their reverse.

"The Ministry of Teleyansk occupies these buildings," the yellow-clad mage said. "Mergen Ukhan Baishin — the House of Wisdom."

While gold and white flowers also dominated these gardens, fountains and meandering paths softened the vast space. Two smaller buildings flanked the larger palace. Its scalloped, purple roofline imitated the frills of the golden flower blooms scattered throughout the garden.

"There's more whimsy here," Halina remarked as Gethen admired a creek burbling through the courtyard. Large rainbow-hued fish darted among its stones and white blossoms floated atop.

The final gates surprised him. They were black iron and the inlaid golden seal of the One God flashed brilliantly in the sunlight. Three buildings stood beyond them, an enormous black, red, and gold palace, flanked by two smaller palaces.

"Welcome to Shin Gurn Ezen Khan Ordon — the Imperial Palace of the Shin Dynasty, the home of Teleyansk's ancient Shin Empire."

Qadan waited at this gate. She took over the tour, sending the mage back to the Courtyard of the Guests. "Sarn Ger Baishin — the House of the Moon — where the empresses and their children dwell," she said, gesturing to the small white-and-silver building to the right of the monumental palace. She indicated its white-and-gold twin. "Narn Ger Baishin — the House of the Sun — home to the emperor's consorts and their children." She indicated the black, red, and gold palace dominating the scene. "Altan Tsetseg Ordon — the Palace of the Golden Flower."

"The emperor's private residence?" Halina asked.

"Yes, and where he welcomes his most honored guests."

They crossed the broad courtyard, their steps echoing off the surrounding buildings.

Unlike the flowered courtyards, only tiles covered the innermost bailey of the Imperial Palace complex. Made of white and gold marble, they formed a pattern of circles and crescents with the One God's symbol at their center.

The palaces sat high above the courtyard and wide stairs led to their columned entrances. A towering marble statue of the One God stood atop the Palace of the Golden Flower, arms outstretched and gaze benign.

Sixty-six steps in all, Gethen counted as they climbed toward the dwelling of Teleyansk's revered leader. As they entered, a low gong reverberated from somewhere within the building. Gethen couldn't help but marvel. Judging from Halina's wide-eyed, roaming gaze, she was just as impressed.

Where the tiled courtyard was regimented and austere, entering the palace was like stepping into a thousand jewels.

As a child, Gethen had one treasured toy, a kaleidoscope. Now, walking through the gold and glass of Teleyansk's palace, he knew what living inside that toy would've been like. Red-and-gold silk carpeting muted their steps and led the way through halls lined with wide columns. Overhead, swaying candelabras hung within blue-and-green glass globes. Carved animals cavorted across the wooden bases of the walls and columns, gold foiled to reflect the light. Rainbow-hued panels stood as the palace's walls and doors, the geometric symbols of the One God cut into their wooden frames. Songbirds warbled and flitted among the rafters, but no feathers or droppings marred the pristine floors. Lokshin's army of caretakers kept every inch of his impressive palace spotless.

Gethen had forgotten about his kaleidoscope. Shemel forbade him to bring it to Ranith when he left Ystwyth as a nine-year-old boy.

Another gong cut the quiet, followed by the hourly pronouncements.

"The breeze blows gently. The rivers run clear. The harvest is bountiful. Lokshin's empire grows. It is the Hour of the Horse." The caller repeated his chant eleven times.

Three men in tall black hats and red robes joined their party. They bowed silently then turned and led the procession through the bejeweled hallways, twisting and turning through halls and interior gardens.

"Lord Rhyshis and Lady Rhyshis have arrived," one of the men leading the procession announced as they stopped before a pair of black-and-gold doors. Once again the gong sounded, louder and closer this time.

The doors swung open.

The members of the procession moved forward, carrying Gethen and Halina along with them.

They entered the emperor's throne room, its carpet an elaborate pattern of gold and blue blossoms. A white rug led to a gold throne resting on a low dais. Seated upon that was Lokshin, dressed in black, red, and gold.

The emperor's thick, black hair brushed his shoulders, its movement arrested by the elaborate gold-and-fur crown he wore. Encrusted with pearls and firestones, it arched across his head like a rising sun nested in a cap of white fur. Peering out from the fur were six black wolves with firestone eyes, their faces made from glittering black gems. Perched above the wolves, the One God's symbol decorated the crown's center, formed from a faceted, orange firestone that flashed in the lantern lights, as large as a baby's fist and more valuable than Khara itself. More firestones blazed on Lokshin's ears, from chains around his neck, and set into the rings he wore on all his fingers. He had dark, keen eyes and the stacks of gold and bejeweled cuffs on his wrists clinked as he stood and spread his arms.

"Welcome, most honored guests." Youthful in appearance though older than Gethen, Teleyansk's handsome emperor descended the dais and waved them to straighten as they bowed. "No. No-no, you will not bow before me like servants." He clapped his hands and said, "Leave us," to the mages and ministers occupying the fringes of the room. After they'd all shuffled out, only Qadan remained, still kneeling before her husband.

"Welcome, Empress," he said and touched her cheek.

She stood. "Your servant, Qadan, Third Empress, thanks you, most honored Emperor."

"Don't thank *me*," he said. "We've brought our friends from Quoregna here to thank *them*." He gestured for her to stand at his side then turned back to Gethen and Halina. "I expect my servants and soldiers to battle to the death to protect my family. I don't expect such devotion from strangers at my gates. But Qadan told me of your bravery and efforts. Such kindness deserves repayment. How can I thank you for protecting my beloved Third Empress?"

Halina said, "We didn't defend Her Highness to curry favor with your Imperial Majesty. The wraiths were sent to kill me. I couldn't allow them to injure and murder innocent victims in their efforts to reach me."

"And I couldn't permit that either. Protecting my wife is my priority," Gethen said, "but I believe in the sanctity of life."

"Even though you're a necromancer?" Lokshin asked, his gaze calculated.

Gethen gave him a pained smile. "Especially because I'm a necromancer, though few believe that."

"Few see with their eyes, Sun Mage," Lokshin said. "Your reputations precede you both." The emperor gestured for them to follow as he crossed the throne room. "I want to show you the might of Teleyansk."

They passed through another door and followed another rainbow hallway.

"Lady Rhyshis, I understand you are friends with Essendra's new margrave, Magod Osten. Have you any news of him? When I last saw him, he was on a mission to find your glorious younger sister, Princess Arevik. Did he succeed?"

Halina smiled. "He did, indeed, Your Eminence. They were wed in the early summer."

"And expect their first child this fall," Gethen added.

Halina's head jerked around. "What? Who told you that?"

Lokshin laughed as Gethen grinned and said, "I'm a healer." He shrugged, sheepish under her intense scrutiny. "I know the signs."

"And you didn't tell me?"

He felt even more sheepish as he mumbled, "I forgot?"

Lokshin clapped Gethen on the shoulder. "I think you've been a busy man, indeed, if you failed to share that secret with the Red Blade." He winked at Halina and added, "Perhaps your husband can be forgiven the slip, Your Ladyship. After all, he's been battling wraiths and demons at your side."

Gethen added, "And nearly drowning, and traveling the Northern Wastes, and healing you."

She did not look mollified as they exited onto a balcony at the western flank of the palace. But the view it afforded distracted both of them from her ire.

The entire bay they'd only glimpsed as they'd arrived in Yasan Khot spread out below them, occupied by a fleet of ships that was breathtaking in its size and variety. Filling the bay were small corvettes and larger frigates, two-masted junks, and enormous six- and seven-masted schooners, their hulls deep and wide enough to host an entire army. A sea of yellow sails spread out below them, more ships than Gethen knew existed in one navy, some larger than he thought seaworthy.

"You see half my fleet and a fraction of my army."

Gethen took in the view of hundreds of ships, their segmented sails unfurling to catch the wind.

Halina gazed from one end to the other, then turned and considered Yasan Khot. "Now I see that Quoregna is an island surrounded by an empire." She met Lokshin's gaze and added, "I never realized the extent of your reach and power."

He nodded. His expression wasn't one of gloating but of acceptance. "It's a vast and ancient empire. Sometimes overreaching her bounds."

"That's the only reason Quoregna remains independent," she said.

"Though I've been greatly tempted by Nalvika's steel, I've also learned from studying my predecessors' successes and mistakes. Patience usually rewards me with what I want. I prefer to let matters unfold gradually rather than by force. One must value life, especially when lives are entrusted to you."

Halina and Gethen nodded. "Power and responsibility cannot be separated," she said.

"No matter how we wish they could be at times," the emperor added. "I understand you, Lady Rhyshis. And you, Lord Rhyshis. We all share the burden of responsibility and the battles of ambition."

"I wish all our peers saw the wisdom of patience and the follies of greed," Gethen remarked.

Ships tacked to and fro, cutting through the green waves with speed and ease. The massive tall-masted ships plowed forward, behemoths unbothered by the smaller frigates surrounding them. Archers stood in formation upon the decks, their golden shields and steel swords glinting like the jewels on the empresses' gowns.

Teleyansk's combined army and navy was a vast and terrible force. If Lokshin chose, he could crush Quoregna and brush aside the kings and their armies like so many gnats. "Who could stop you if you wanted to make Quoregna your own?" Gethen mused.

"You, Sun Mage," the emperor replied. "Only you." He smiled and added, "Which is why I prefer to keep you as an ally. I would not wish to make you my enemy."

Gethen wasn't so sure he had the power Lokshin imagined, but he nodded nonetheless. Better to let Teleyansk's emperor believe the exaggerations about his sorcery than offer the truth to a conqueror and invite opportunity. "Nor do I wish to be anything but your friend."

Lokshin smiled. "You requested an alliance with Teleyansk. I refused. However, I'm a man of principles and when my guests are attacked upon my doorstep, it's an insult to me. When they suffer wounds in the defense of my family, they have done me a great favor. What do you offer in exchange for an alliance against King Waldram and King Ilker, Lady Rhyshis?"

"Nalvik steel, Your Eminence. We'll remove Nalvika's mad king from power and place his daughter, Princess Federika, on the throne. Then Teleyansk's requests for fair negotiations for fine Nalvik steel will be met with honorable intentions rather than insulting trade terms and unfulfilled contracts."

Lokshin nodded. "You've thought this through. Is the girl ready to rule?"

"She's only twelve years old, but I've begun her training in politics and war. And we'll place a chancellor at her side who can be trusted and is known to the other kings of Quoregna. Someone fair-minded and even-handed. Someone I trust with my life."

He looked at Gethen. "You?"

"Definitely not," he replied. "Someone agreed upon by Quoregna's Council of Kings."

Lokshin faced his navy, his eyes focused on the future. "Steel isn't worth blood, but security is. An enemy who would attack a guest within my own citadel is someone who has no honor and gives no respect. Such a foe must be stopped. Though the One God advocates peace and order, I will aid you in this quest." He nodded slowly. "Quoregna's stability benefits Teleyansk. And I like the thought of decent steel." He smiled and turned his gaze on Gethen and Halina. "We'll bring peace and order back to the four southern kingdoms and make Nalvika's young queen very rich."

TWENTY-TWO

Teleyansk committed thirty thousand soldiers and sailors to support Halina. It took six days for Lokshin's chosen generals and admirals to organize the troops and supplies.

She stood on the emperor's balcony watching the systematic loading of ships — one hundred all told, including ten of the enormous schooners. Towering wooden cranes lifted pallets of grain, hay bales, cages of chickens, and crates of fruits and vegetables aboard the supply ships from dozens of wharves stretching across miles of waterfront. Line after line of pickets held horses waiting to be led aboard. Soldiers marched up the loading ramps, orderly and disciplined, shining pikes with yellow banners over their shoulders. Swords rattled and leather creaked, so numerous that the sound carried all the way up to the palace.

"Gods, Gethen," she murmured as he leaned his arms on the balustrade beside her. "This could work."

"It's an intimidating force, but the battle mages are staying behind and I think that's a mistake."

"Do you?" Lokshin said as he came through the doorway behind them.

"Yes," Gethen replied. "Your troops are facing a powerful necromancer, trained by the same pillock who taught me, and who's recruited other mages and witches to his cause."

The emperor shrugged. "We have Quoregna's Sun Mage. I'm not concerned."

Gethen squinted at the gathering force. "I'm that Sun Mage and I *am* concerned. Waldram shouldn't be underestimated, especially if he's being advised by my dead master."

Lokshin considered the ships and troops. "I'm bringing my personal sorcerer." His gaze slid back to consider Gethen and he added, "After all, I'm traveling with a powerful necromancer. Better to keep my own mage at my side, just in case. Eh?"

Halina said, "Because there are no allies?"

He nodded. "Only family. And my personal mage is my Fifth Son."

The hourly gong sounded and the caller announced the time.

"The army prepares. The ships set sail. Lokshin's empire readies for war. The Empire of the Golden Flower cannot be defeated. The Hour of Steel is upon us."

It was immediately followed by another, higher gong and a call to prayer. Below them in the shipyards, aboard the ships, and among the fields and sprawling city, all the citizens turned, folded their hands, and bowed to the statue of the One God standing upon the Palace of the Golden Flower. A god of order. A god of peace.

Two temple priests dressed in flowing purple-and-gold robes appeared upon the balcony and knelt before Lokshin. Three more appeared, one carrying a golden water bowl, one a white silk cloth, one a golden platter. Lokshin washed his fingers, dried them, and left the cloth on the plate. A fourth priest laid a pillow at the emperor's feet and helped him kneel.

Gethen and Halina stood quietly as silence overcame Teleyansk. Prayer occurred morning, midday, and night, and all of the empire stopped. Wind whistled past Halina's ears. The banners on the palace pinnacles snapped in the breeze. Sea crows circled and cried.

After a few silent moments, the gong sounded again, echoing through the palace complex and carrying across the bay.

The emperor and his priests rose. The holy men bowed and left the balcony. Lokshin turned to Halina and Gethen. "The One God smiles upon Teleyansk and her allies."

"Even if they aren't family?" Halina asked.

The emperor laughed and left them overlooking the fraction of his army that would help them free Quoregna from the grasp of a madman.

Gethen watched the door close behind Lokshin then turned to his wife. "It's time I used some of this ill-gotten power to strengthen the protections around you."

She eyed him. "What's up your sleeve, sorcerer?"

"Duesh and Gwyn."

"What about them?"

"I've been thinking about Chono Khot and Kenbish's sons."

"I don't follow."

"The shrikers will be after you the moment we set foot on Quoregnan soil. Waldram is tracking you."

"Obviously," she said, needled by thoughts of her cousin. "But how?"

Gethen scowled. "I'm not certain, but I think the blood magic he stole plays a part."

Heat flushed her face and chest, irritation turning to anger.

She wished fervently for something to kick. "I will skewer that pillock. Skewer him and leave him to rot in the sun."

"A pleasant thought," he replied. "Meanwhile, I've devised a weapon he can't manipulate or use against you."

"The wolves?"

"Blaids."

"Whats?"

He chuckled. "Spirit wolves. I have their permission to transform them into their most powerful form."

Halina's jaw tensed. "Will that endanger them?"

"What do you mean? They're endangered anytime they fight."

"I mean changing their spirits." She hadn't realized she cared so much for Ranith's wolves, but she'd hated seeing them wounded. "They already give so much to keep us safe. I don't know if I can ask any more of them."

"They want to protect us. They didn't like losing to the wraiths and that's what was happening before I arrived with Yisun's spirit blazing. If I transform them into blaids, they'll have the power to call upon the souls of their dead pack."

That gave her goosebumps. "Really? How? That makes them like sorcerers. Doesn't it?"

"It's in the nature of wolves to work as a pack. They're connected in ways we can't understand. When I draw on one, I'm drawing on all the members of the pack because their spirits never really pass. Animals are that way. They don't have individual identities. Their souls are part of a collective that connects them to all the members of their pack, their species, and the world around them."

She followed him from the balcony as he returned to the palace and wound through the halls to their guest chambers. "Why are we different?"

"Because we choose to be."

229

Duesh and Gwyn waited in their room, resting comfortably after days of healing under Gethen's care and generous feeding from Qadan who'd insisted the wolves be treated as honored guests, too.

Her devotion had amused Lokshin. "She adores animals," he'd remarked when she'd insisted they be brought into the palace.

Gethen had already laid out herbs and potions, his copper pot, and a borrowed iron cauldron. Dried seed pods, roots, and ground antimony occupied a table beside the hearth.

Halina flopped onto the bed and watched him grind, pour, and mix. Duesh and Gwyn settled before the fire, their gazes following their master's movements.

Gethen whispered melodic words in an ancient tongue as he took fur and blood from both wolves, hair and blood from her and himself. He captured a handful of each animal's shadow, twisting his fingers around the darkness and coming away with a nebulous, living substance that defied gravity when he added it to the cauldron.

The room shimmered with amber sorcery. Incantations climbed the walls and crept into dark corners, setting them aglow before fading away like wolves' eyes at night, a secret teased then taken, a threat watching, waiting. Gethen worked without pause, sweat beading his brow and a ceaseless spell droning from his lips as he turned his companions into powerful guardians.

Halina shivered as her husband's magic slid across her skin, seductive and disquieting, mesmerizing her like it had aboard the *Banriona* the day that ship sank. She closed her eyes. Lulled by his deep euphonious voice, she drifted to sleep and dreamed of running through the woods, smelling the earthiness of fresh-turned soil, tasting the tang of blood, hearing the beat of war, the call of death, the cry of the wilderness. She awakened with a start and reached for her borrowed sword, certain danger was near.

What she saw made her stare.

Duesh and Gwyn sat before the fire, their heads bowed to Gethen, but they'd doubled in size and become intangible. Gwyn was white as smoke, her form shifting and curling like ground fog on a cold morning. Duesh was inky like shadows, his form creeping and curling back on itself, slippery as black algae sliding over rocks on a river's edge.

"Blaids?" Halina whispered. Both turned amber eyes on her, an internal glow flickering deep within them, the room glimpsed through their ethereal bodies.

Gethen rose. "Yes. And ready to fight any wraith or shriker to keep you safe."

"And you."

He smiled. "You're their responsibility."

"Will they return to their normal form?"

He shook his head. "They sacrificed all their power for the strength to prevent their pack from being decimated again."

She slipped from the bed and approached. "They remember the Rime Witch's attack?"

He nodded. "And they know she tried to destroy me again while the wraiths attacked you in the Court of Guests."

Halina reached out, wanting to thank the wolves for their sacrifice, but there was no flesh to touch. "Where are their bodies?" She looked around, expecting to find both wolves dead, but there was no sign of them.

"Gone. Transformed to aether to form their larger blaid forms."

"Oh." She lowered her arm and looked from one spirit wolf to the other. "Thank you," she whispered.

Gethen smiled. "I told you they think of you as one of our pack."

She considered the blaids and her husband, and murmured, "My pack."

The high gong rang, calling Teleyansk's people to evening prayer.

At the sound, Duesh and Gwyn faded into the shadows and the flickering firelight.

"That's where they hide?"

"They're always with us. She can emerge from any light. He can come from any darkness. There's nowhere enemies can hide that the blaids can't find them and attack."

Halina smiled. "I like that."

The gong faded.

She remarked, "I never knew the One God dominated Teleyansk so thoroughly. This level of organized worship rivals the strength of our gods."

Gethen collapsed on the low couch by the hearth. "It dwarves the Triumvirate, and Skiron, Khotyr, and Semele know it."

"That can't make them happy."

"Definitely not. They can't exist without the worship of their believers. Take away belief and you take away power. That's why Skiron needs this war. Why he wants me to cause chaos and suffering. I'm his mortal knife."

"And you refuse to cut."

"Indeed. He's decided I'm a very dull blade."

She laughed. "Well, he may find out just how sharp you and your blaids are."

The second gong sounded, releasing Teleyansk from worship. Footfalls resumed outside their room as the servants returned to their duties.

"A month. That's how long we've been away from Quoregna." Halina sat beside Gethen. "I hope Zelal is still safe. And Feddie and Elof. I hope Ambrosine and Ianthe have talked sense into my foolish brother and pulled him back from the brink of destruction." Her hands clenched, the knuckles white beneath her skin. She sighed. "No greater ally, no worse enemy."

"Who?"

"Family." She considered the colorful walls and the elaborate room. "Maybe Lokshin is right and I should've tried harder to bring Ilker over to my side."

"There was no winning that battle." Gethen rested his arm around her shoulders. "He has to break that spell himself."

"He really is under a spell. There's no other explanation for how Waldram could've convinced Ilker to join him. He's hated that prick for longer than I've been alive. There's no way my brother would willingly choose my rotten second cousin over me."

"If that's true, then he'll come back. Time will turn him."

"Time is something we've run out of. I fear for your brother. I fear for mine and our people." She swallowed a curse. "Marooned by Waldram's witches. Attacked by his wraiths. Skiron himself is working against us. We may not survive this war."

"I know." He brushed the hair back from her face and traced the healed scar marring her cheek, just one more scar marking a lifetime of battling monsters like Waldram. Gethen pulled her close and kissed her. "That's why we love each other today."

"Because we never know what tomorrow may bring." She pulled her husband closer and wanted nothing more than to feel his love and his body for the rest of the evening.

TWENTY-THREE

While Lokshin traveled with his personal mage and an army of servants and soldiers aboard the *Ayaruq*, Gethen and Halina occupied a cabin aboard the second largest ship of the navy, the *Jenisej*. With eight masts apiece and crews over one-thousand strong, both ships were far larger than anything seen in Quoregna, well-suited to traveling the rough waters of the Great Green Ocean and meant for long-distance sailing and carrying vast armies. The *Banriona* had seemed large and solid to Gethen, but Teleyansk's ships made her look like a toy in a tub. With flatter hulls but cross-bracing for strength and their uniquely segmented square sails, they cut through the green water, their prows barely disturbed by the pitching waves, their yellow sails billowing thunderously.

Two hundred sailors clambered across the decks and up the masts. The holds were bursting with food and livestock, warhorses and weaponry.

"A floating fortress," Halina said as she stood beside him on the massive forecastle, surveying the constant movement across the ship. "Waldram's witches will be hard-pressed to send these behemoths to the bottom of the ocean."

"Let's hope." He looked from the decks to the horizon. He'd been vigilant about the weather, watching the sky morning and night for any sign of trouble. But their ten days at sea had presented only blue skies and a steady wind carrying them closer to home, sea crows and silver gulls dipping and wheeling around the ships.

Admiral Masorin, Lokshin's Second Brother, joined them. He followed Gethen's gaze and said, "You don't trust our luck."

"Experience trumps luck," Gethen replied.

"And we experienced rotten luck on the voyage to Teleyansk," Halina added.

Masorin clasped his hands behind his back. "I understand you think our emperor should've brought more mages to this battle."

Gethen nodded. "We're facing a war in which magic will play a large part. King Waldram is utilizing dark sorcery — his own and that of other Quoregnan mages."

"The wraiths in Yasan Khot were his?"

"They were."

"I heard how bravely you both fought. It takes a great deal of skill to defeat one wraith, let alone two. Our own battle mages were hard-pressed to keep the Third Empress safe."

"I have first-hand experience with them," Halina said, "and I wouldn't let them harm the empress without going through me first."

The admiral considered her with a measured gaze. "Most soldiers would run."

"Halina isn't like most soldiers," Gethen remarked.

Masorin said, "But I understand it was your sorcery that routed the creatures, Sun Mage. If that's so, why do you fear Nalvika's sorcery? Surely it can't be greater than your own?"

"I'm only one man. And this war will be fought on many fronts. We also face shrikers."

"I don't think magic is required to stop your god's undead dogs. Just a sharp sword," the admiral said.

Halina surveyed the ships around them. "You have the confidence of a man who's always fought with the might of a tremendous navy and army at his back. We're not so fortunate."

He smiled. "You are now, Lady Rhyshis. The Yellow Guard is Teleyansk's elite force. They'll make quick work of Nalvika's army and bring your brother to his knees. Soon Nalvika's young queen will take the throne and you'll put Ursinum's affairs right. Besera will be free of invaders and Quoregna's plague of shrikers will be nothing but a pile of cursed bones." He smiled at them. "And Teleyansk will have new friends and the finest steel."

"Why risk Lokshin's forces for Nalvik steel?" Gethen asked. "I know it's renowned, but Teleyansk has expanded her reach for centuries without it."

Masorin stroked his trim beard. "Teleyansk is mighty, but we, too, have enemies. The Kalix Empire covets our wealth and violates our borders daily. No matter how powerful you become, someone always comes along to test your mettle."

Halina laughed. "There's the truth."

The admiral excused himself to speak with the ship's master, leaving Gethen and Halina to contemplate the endless green ocean.

He brushed a stray auburn lock from her face and tucked it behind her ear. "How's your shoulder?"

She rotated it. "A little stiff, but the discomfort is nothing. I was considering a practice session. I need the exercise and it's not a bad thing for our allies to see what we can do."

A slow smile spread across his face. "Is that a challenge, Militess?"

"Are you up for another fight, Mage?"

"If you think you can take it."

Her eyes narrowed. "Challenge accepted. Do your worst." She shed her cloak and summoned her armor.

Gethen summoned his and invoked his sword. He pointed it at her and said, "Let's see you conjure a weapon, Lady Rhyshis."

As her helmet formed to hide her face behind a blood-red mask, she raised her hand and called a wicked longsword to her palm, its sharp edge flashing like fire in the sun.

The murmur of the soldiers and sailors rose, a wave carrying over the wind. Shouts came from surrounding ships and the *Ayaruq* pulled near, the emperor and his generals moving to the rails to watch the spectacle unfold.

"Shall we give them a show?" Gethen asked.

Halina saluted him and lunged forward by way of answering. She pivoted and dodged, parried and attacked. He called upon the shadows to capture her, but she knew his tricks and had some of her own. Halina pushed her armor ambit to form nets and shields. She slashed his shadow bindings, seeming to realize that if she imagined a weapon, the ambit would produce it.

But Gethen still had heat and mass spells. He snapped a shadowy rope at her and she took to the rail. The sailors and soldiers cheered as she ran its length, pivoting around stays and leaping over blocks. But her position was vulnerable and Gethen proved it by blasting her with a mass spell. Halina anticipated it. She flipped her sword and hooked its hilt behind his left pauldron, pulling him to the rail with her weight as she fell back. Gethen was forced to grab her arm and the rail, stopping both of them from going into the water.

Face to face and breathing hard, she dispelled her helmet and smiled wickedly. "Look down, my love."

He did. She held a red misericord, its point poised to thrust between the joints of his chest plate and pauldron, a fatal blow.

"Point given," he said and pulled her back into the ship.

Halina kissed him and all around them soldiers and sailors cheered.

"You can't control everything and the more you try, the less you succeed. You're the one who told me that."

Gethen opened his eyes and considered his wife. "What made you bring that up?"

They lay in a tangle of sheets and limbs. After lovemaking, he'd dozed, the slow, rhythmic pitch and yaw of the ship lulling him, the sounds of sailing a regular part of their lives now. Halina lay awake, tracing his Beseran stripes with her fingertips.

"I know you want to control your magic and Skiron and the cravings and this war's outcome and my fate and the fate of the entire mortal realm and the shrikers and Lokshin's decisions and every other thing that may affect our futures. But you can't. *I* can't. We have to pick our battles based on the things that are truly within our control." She looked at him. "You were right when you told me I can't control everything. Neither can you. So what *can* you control?"

Geometric designs inlaid in gold and silver, including the One God's symbol, covered he cabin's low, coved ceiling. "My power." Gethen sat up, raised his hands, and summoned a ball of amber mage fire into his palms. It was cool and radiant, pulsing with power. His sorcery buzzed behind his sternum, buried deep and thrumming with vitality. It was the same magical power awakened by the arrival of the bees in Ystwyth's garden. And though it ebbed and flowed with his body's strength, it never completely abandoned him, no matter how he taxed it. "I swallowed so many lies fed to me by Shemel and Skiron that I don't know what the truth of my power tastes like. I've gagged on my own guilt, been driven by cravings created by a man and a god who wanted to control my strength. But that power has always been a part of me. I didn't need human souls to summon it when I was a child. So why should I need them now?"

He let the mage fire roll from hand to hand, a nebulous glowing ball of magic, proof of his ability so easily summoned he gave it no more thought than he did breathing. Until air was denied him, as Skiron had done. But no matter the games and trickery the God of Death subjected him to, Skiron couldn't strip Gethen's sorcery from him. Nor could Shemel.

"My power is the thing Shemel and Skiron sought to control. They fed me lies, tortured my mind and my body, threatened me and the woman I love, but they've never challenged me directly to a battle."

"Because you're stronger."

"Yes." He closed his hands around the mage fire and looked back at her. "I've known I'm stronger than Shemel for a long time. So did he. Even when I was a boy, it was obvious. It's why he belittled and tortured me so much, why he controlled me by threatening the animals of Kharayan Woods. He found the thing that mattered to me. He saw that I cared about others. I made it clear when I was so horrified by consuming that addict's soul in Besalee; the first he forced me to take." He shook his head. "I still feel that man's desperation and fear. It'll never leave me, Halina. It's a permanent part of me. And Shemel used it against me."

"Skiron too?"

"Yes. The night after I killed Shemel in the basilica, Skiron dragged me into the Void. He told me I was now the Keeper of the Voidline and I served him above all others. He bent me, physically, to his will. Showed me pain unlike anything Shemel had ever inflicted and told me there would be more if I failed him."

Gethen pulled her hand to his lips, kissed her fingers one at a time, and pressed her palm to his cheek. "Skiron told me you were made for me to use. That you were given blood magic and set in my path so my addiction would drive me to murder you and steal your blood magic. That was the height of his cruelty." He shook his head. "But I won't do it. I don't need your power. It's a lie that Shemel planted and Skiron fertilized. Now the gods wish to reap it, but I won't give them that satisfaction." He looked back at her. "I don't need your blood magic to be the most powerful mage in Quoregna."

"Because you already are, Sun Mage."

"Yes, I am." Gethen leaned over and kissed her.

Halina snaked her arms around his neck and deepened the kiss then pulled back and gazed into his eyes. "Trust me to defend myself. And use your power to defend the defenseless against those who would exploit and abuse them. You don't serve gods or kings, Gethen. You serve Quoregna."

He woke in the darkest part of the night. The ship's rigging creaked, her wood groaned. The slap of waves against her hull composed a tune for the slow dance she did with the sea. But he barely noticed because someone was close enough to his Ranith ward to trigger it and his bones and brain burned with the sudden blaze of sorcery.

Halina slept soundly, her breath slow and deep, her arm over his waist. Gethen tried to slip from the bed without disturbing her, but she murmured, "What's wrong?"

"Likely nothing. Go back to sleep."

She sat up. "You're a terrible liar."

He pulled his tunic over his head, followed by his hooded travel cloak. "I'm going to Ranith."

"I'll come with you."

She threw aside the covers to stand, but the amber magic of his travel incantation was already swirling around him, flapping the open front of his leather brigandine. "No. Stay with the ship. I'll return soon." Their small cabin disappeared, replaced a few heartbeats later by the dense blackness of Kharayan Woods at night. He stood on the path leading to his ward line.

A fire flickered between the trees. As Gethen approached the ward, the flames resolved into a campfire surrounded by a small squadron of soldiers. They wore Kharan blue-and-gold on their tabards, and Eugen sat among them.

"What brings Khara to my doorstep?" Gethen called from the edge of the woods.

The soldiers rose, hastily grabbing weapons and squinting into the darkness.

Eugen calmed them with a wave of his hand. "Loyalty, Lord Rhyshis."

"To whom?"

"Your good wife, sir."

"You deserted King Ilker's army?"

"We did." Eugen's voice and face were grim. "Besera saved Khara last winter. We won't repay their kindness with war."

Gethen crossed the ward line to offer his hand. "Fairly met, sir."

Eugen returned the handshake. "Thank you. We're grateful for all you've done for Lady Rhyshis." He peered past Gethen's shoulder. "She's not with you?"

"No." He scanned the unfamiliar faces of Eugen's troops. Two dozen Kharan soldiers shared several campfires. "Does Captain Thaksin know you're camped here?"

"I haven't seen the captain since he took a company north to hunt shrikers last spring."

"Well, you can come to Ranith with me and inform him of your status. He's at the citadel."

"Thaksin is staying with you?" Eugen's brows arched. He'd witnessed first-hand the animosity long brewing between Gethen and Halina's captain.

"War makes surprising bedfellows," Gethen remarked.

"Indeed."

They followed the path that wound through Kharayan Woods and led to the ancient outer walls of Ranith Citadel.

"Lady Rhyshis is well?" Eugen asked as their small band of soldiers came in sight of the barbican and its iron lattice gate. Beyond it stood an abandoned village, its residents driven away by the tower's necromantic masters many generations ago.

"Well and sailing south from Teleyansk with a force thirty thousand strong," Gethen replied as he raised the rattling gate with an incantation and a gesture. "The ships are twelve days from port in Ayestra. We'll put in there, strategize with those members of the Council of Kings who are available and sound of mind, then we'll pursue King Waldram and King Ilker, force them out of Besera and Or-Halee, and place a sane leader on Nalvika's throne."

"Thirty thousand?" Eugen asked as a soldier beside him whistled. "That's impressive. How'd Her Ladyship convince Teleyansk to give her such a force?"

Gethen lowered the gate as the last soldier passed through the barbican. "She battled two wraiths to protect the life of the Third Empress."

The soldiers nodded and Eugen said, "Sounds like something she'd do."

As they approached Ranith's gates, Thaksin emerged from the dark-gray citadel, his sword in hand and expression grim. But his eyes widened when he saw the source of the voices echoing off the tower's walls and he raised his hand in greeting.

"This is a better surprise than I expected when I heard the racket of your approach." He and Eugen clasped hands. "Found your bollocks and left our king's idiocy behind, I see."

"Sadly, yes," Halina's former steward replied. "Though I hate to admit it, our young king follows a monster's folly." He gestured to his companions and added, "We chose not to be party to the destruction of an ally."

Gethen invited the soldiers to camp in the village. There was no sign of Federika or Elof in the bailey. He pulled the captain and Eugen aside. "Keep the princess inside the tower. I don't want anyone to know Waldram's daughter is in Ranith." They nodded. Spying Odruna standing in the wicket door of the main entrance, Gethen told her the same. "Where's Queen Cerys?" he asked.

"Haven't seen her since this morning." She squinted at the sky. The sun was well past zenith. "She's grown quieter since Ursinum attacked Besalee Portcity."

Gethen cursed beneath his breath. "I didn't know they'd gotten that far."

"Where've you been?"

"Teleyansk. Halina's sailing toward Ayestra with thirty thousand ally soldiers."

Her chin lifted at that. "The queen will want to hear that."

"Exactly." He looked around the small bailey. "Did you check the basilica for her?"

Odruna nodded. "No sign. She may have gone to the bee yards."

"I'll search there." He strode around the tower's perimeter, passed through the squealing postern gate, and struck out along the path through the woods that led to his bee yards. He'd warned Cerys to remain on the tower's grounds, but after more than a month of waiting, he wasn't surprised she'd grown restless.

She wasn't among the towers of wooden bee boxes and tall lavender edging the bee yard and Gethen grew concerned. Kharayan's forest was dark and dense, its paths rarely straight. It was easy to grow confused and lose the way back to the tower, especially deeper into the woods where the dense canopy obscured the view of the broken citadel.

On a hunch, he took the path leading to the one other large clearing found in the woods. As he exited the forest into the grassy area, he spied the queen sitting beneath the marble portico of a white, octagonal mausoleum. Gerezel toddled around the foot of its steps, smacking the heads off dandelions with a wooden sword.

"Strange playground you've chosen, Your Highness," Gethen called.

She turned toward him with a gasp as the princeling grinned and ran to him, shouting, "Unca Gedden, look at my sord!"

Gethen crouched to examine the toy. "That's a fine weapon and I see you're putting it to good use. How many dandelions have you conquered?"

"A dousand million!"

"So many? You are a fierce warrior, indeed, nephew." He stood, lifting the boy into his arms, and strode to Cerys.

"What news?" she asked, standing and brushing grit from her skirts.

Gethen released his struggling nephew to rout more flowers then offered his arm to his sister-in-law. "We've secured an alliance with Teleyansk and soon Halina will arrive with an army to rival the combined forces of Nalvika and Ursinum."

She came off the steps and followed him along the path he'd taken. "That's good news. Finally." She looked around and called, "Gerezel, come with Mummin." The boy galloped after them, his sword raised in triumph.

Gethen glanced back at the mausoleum. "What brought you to this place?"

"It offers a view of the Beseran coast all the way to Or-Halee."

"You've been watching troop movements."

"Yes." Her grip tightened on his arm. "And contemplating joining the fight."

He sensed she had more to add as they walked beneath the trees. Gerezel turned back and raised his arms to Gethen, who obliged the boy with a shoulder ride.

Cerys continued. "But your wife made a compelling argument against foolhardiness and I took her words to heart." She reached up and tousled her son's hair. "This is my battlefront. My part in this war is clear." She met Gethen's gaze. "I'll kill or die to keep the Rhysh line alive."

"My brother chose his queen well."

"I've had a lot of time to think, brother. I've realized what's important, and it's not riches and status. It's people and duty and hope and family. As long as we stand together, we can restore peace to Quoregna."

"I agree. And my hope grows stronger with each passing day."

"It must. You and the Red Blade have procured an alliance I never thought possible. I've watched from afar as day after day Beseran, Dargani, and Or-Haleean forces keep the larger Ursinian army at bay. The gods are on our side. Even the One God." She smiled up at her son. "And now you've arrived to tell me of this approaching force from Teleyansk." She squeezed Gethen's arm again. "We cannot possibly lose."

TWENTY-FOUR

The storm came up as sudden and inexplicably fierce as the one that sank the *Banriona*. Rain lashed the decks, horizontal and stinging, combining with crashing waves that dwarfed and sank the smaller frigates and supply junks.

Sailors shouted and directed the soldiers. They scrambled up the huge masts, battled the snapping, whipsaw sails and the wild pitch of the *Jenisej*.

"Get below!" Masorin shouted to Halina as she clung to the stern's taffrail and cursed the unnatural gale. Gwyn and Duesh slunk around her, their rumbling deeper than even the thunder. They knew magic when they sensed it, and she watched them, certain their reaction meant Waldram's weather witches were behind the tempest.

"Where's Lord Rhyshis?" the ship's master shouted, his words ripped from his mouth and replaced by salt spray.

She blinked stinging water from her eyes. "Ranith!"

The man forgot the storm for a second to gape at her. "Ranith? How?"

"Magic, you fool!" the admiral shouted back. "Go to your

cabin, Your Ladyship!"

Halina shook her head. She'd rather stay on deck and be ready to escape again than be trapped below should the ship capsize. "Tie me off!"

"Are you mad?" the master shouted.

"Maybe, but I lived through the last storm King Waldram sent to drown me. I intend to survive this one as well."

"Will the Sun Mage return?" Masorin called over the gale.

"Yes. But will there be a fleet for him to return to?"

The admiral scoffed. "Teleyansk's navy has seen worse, Lady Rhyshis. We've sailed the Kholdolson Sea north of Kalix. This is a mere shower compared to the ice storms we've survived!"

As if hearing his boast, a tremendous wave swelled around the *Jenisej*. The ship climbed its face, nearly vertical as smaller ships around them capsized and disappeared beneath the storm-tossed sea. The emperor's ship was lost to their sight as their schooner plummeted down the other face of the wave, her prow plunging beneath the foaming black water and emerging again minus half her crew.

Masts and yards groaned. Stays twanged, snapped, struck more sailors and soldiers off the deck. They split men and ship into pieces, bathing the deck in blood.

The master disappeared from their side. Halina didn't know if he'd gone overboard or down to encourage his sailors to keep the ship afloat.

Beside her, Masorin looped a rope and tied her to the mizzen mast and himself to the ship's wheel. "You've made some powerful enemies, Red Blade!" he shouted, his words barely reaching her over the screaming gale.

She nodded, not bothering to test her voice. She didn't care to drink more of the Great Green Ocean. She'd had enough of that to last a lifetime.

The sudden appearance of amber magic announced Gethen's return and Halina reached out to capture his arm as the wind threatened to throw him overboard.

"Blood and bones!" he shouted and planted his feet wide.

Around them, ships floundered, came apart and sank. The wind shrieked, louder than the sound of ten thousand soldiers clashing upon a battlefield. The main masts groaned, the hull creaked. The sails were tatters and the foremast was gone.

Halina tied her husband to her side as he raised his arms and began a susurrus counter curse to the madness unleashed by Waldram's witches.

Ever so slowly the storm eased, the waves were tamed, the rain stopped lashing, hail stopped crashing through the sails and splintering wood, glass, flesh and bone.

He raised an arc of amber fire, illuminating the darkness and pushing the weather outward. It was as if they now sailed in the eye of a hurricane. Walls of waves, rain, and clouds whorled around them, demonic in their violence but unable to reach the *Jenisej*. The ship still pitched and heaved as the waves crashed against her, but they no longer attained their monstrous proportions, ready to swallow even the largest of Teleyansk's ships.

"I need a dozen volunteers!" he shouted to the admiral who nodded and pointed at sailors on the decks below.

The men and women immediately obeyed, all nursing bruises, cuts, and gashes. Halina sent away a sailor whose eye had been split. She was astonished by the man's resolve to serve his shipmates.

Gethen spun the ward spell's anchors around the sailors. "You're the incantation's strength," he said. "Your lives empower it. You protect your ship, your crew mates and soldiers. The weather witches can't sink the *Jenisej* as long as you stay strong and defy them."

The men and women showed no fear of Gethen's dark

sorcery, and Masorin clapped each on the shoulder, thanking and assuring them in Yansk.

Gethen staggered as he released the ward to its anchors. They staggered, too, but revealed only determination even as the power of the storm beat against them and the ward pulled from them, sending some of them to their knees.

The admiral stepped up. "Let me lend my strength to this anchor," he said.

Gethen nodded and wove another sorcerous link to connect the admiral to the ward, the sailors and soldiers. "Go below deck," he rasped. "Stay warm and tend your wounds. Remain rested. You'll be taxed by this spell for as long as King Waldram's witches continue their assault."

Halina looked around. "Where's the ship's master?"

"Drowned," a sailor replied. He wore the uniform and insignias of a chief's mate.

Admiral Masorin said, "You're now the acting master, Senya."

The man bowed smartly and wasted no time organizing repairs and rescue parties. They checked the sides of the ship for sailors clinging to stays and found two. One alive, the other drowned.

Lookouts scrambled up the masts and searched for other ships. Within the calm circle of magic, a dozen smaller vessels limped along. All the ships came together. One was too damaged, her hull breached and water pouring into her holds faster than the sailors could make repairs. Her crew salvaged what supplies they could before scuttling her and boarding the *Jenisej*.

The wall of storm churned beyond Gethen's protective ward, blocking the fleet, the ocean, the sky and the world from view.

"Ahoy!" lookouts shouted from the masts, hoping to hear from ships outside the ward's perimeter. No answers came and with every passing hour, hopes dimmed that the fleet remained nearby or even afloat.

As night approached Master Senya summoned all aboard to the deck. "We are safe and sound. If the *Jenisej* survived this madness and she was the target of the sorcerous storm, we have every reason to believe His Imperial Majesty lives and sails onward, determined to reach the nearing shores of Quoregna."

Masorin spoke next. "This monstrous storm, sent to drown our allies and punish us, proves only what cowards and weaklings we face as we go to war with Nalvika's dark king. He so fears Teleyansk's forces that he sent his witches to destroy us. But look at the power sailing with us! See how the Sun Mage has tamed them with his sorcery. We will prevail in this war and bring order to Quoregna. We will open up new trade opportunities to benefit Teleyansk and our new allies in Ursinum and Besera, Or-Halee and Ayestra. And even Nalvika when its new young queen takes the throne, a friend to those who sail with us."

Senya added, "Will Teleyansk's bravery be dimmed by a few witches and their paltry attempts to sink our might?"

"No!" thundered the sailors and soldiers.

"Will we stand by our allies and bring order to Quoregna? Will we follow the way of the One God to help our allies attain the peace and harmony their lands and people crave?"

"Yes!"

"Then fear not for yourselves, your fallen brethren, and our glorious emperor. The One God guides us. The One God brought the Sun Mage back to our deck. The One God will show us the shining path to peace, prosperity, and order."

"Hail His Imperial Highness Lokshin! Praise the One God!"

The master dismissed the crew and produced a compass as Halina, Gethen, and the admiral gathered in his storm-tossed cabin. The ships were tied together but adrift, sails furled and repairs underway.

They stared at the compass as its point circled wildly, unable to find a bearing.

"How will we sail if we can't see the stars or the shore to get a bearing?" Halina asked.

Gethen folded his arms and glared out the wavy glass ports at the churning storm and the shimmering amber magic. His hands shook. As much as he'd benefited from taking the Rime Witch's soul, he'd finally burned through her power. "I can solve this," he muttered.

The admiral and master looked at him then Halina.

"What do you need?" she asked.

Gethen rested his hands upon the table, no longer trying to hide his fatigue. "How many horses survived the storm in our hold?"

"We only lost eight," Senya replied. "Why do you need horses?"

"To borrow the strength of their souls," he replied.

The men exchanged glances and Halina said, "They won't be harmed. Gethen does no harm to animals."

The men nodded, understanding dawning in their gazes. His refusal to eat meat had been the subject of a great deal of interest among the crew. Now they saw a clearer picture of the unusual necromancer in their midst.

Halina and Gethen had been surprised by the acceptance he'd found among Teleyansk's troops. It seemed they saw battle mages as weapons and viewed Gethen as a powerful one. Halina had worried they viewed him as something other than human, but it didn't seem to detract from their willingness to work with him.

Master Senya ordered a sailor to take Gethen into the live-stock hold. Halina followed.

Over two hundred horses occupied narrow stalls. They had enough room to turn and lie down, fodder and water, and clean straw for slumbering.

As Gethen entered the hold, the horses, cattle, sheep, pigs, and chickens started such a racket their keepers moved among the stalls searching for the cause.

He raised his hand and said, "I'm pleased to see all of you are well, too," and the animals calmed.

The keepers and sailor gawked as he rested a shaking hand on the muzzle of the nearest horse and murmured to the bay stallion. The horse nickered gently and tickled his palm with its velvet lips. Gethen smiled. "Thank you, my friend." He slid his hand up to the horse's jaw and silver mage light shimmered beneath his fingers. Gethen and the horse closed their eyes. He rested his forehead against the stallion's nose and sighed with relief. He released the courser after only a few seconds and the animal shook his head and snorted.

"No. There are many friends here. I only require a little aid from each of you. Keep your strength. We'll need your strong back in the coming battles."

He moved from stall to stall, greeting each horse, drawing only a little soul magic, and leaving with appreciative words and reassurance. Every horse offered more and was told to save its strength. And with each animal, Gethen's back straightened, his stride lengthened. The shaking ceased and his voice gained strength.

He visited all two hundred horses and when he was finished, the power of them glowed beneath his skin and behind his eyelids when he blinked.

"Now we'll show Waldram and his weather hags what happens when you threaten a Sun Mage and his allies." He raised Halina's hand to his lips and kissed her knuckles. "We'll show Nalvika's idiot king the error of his ways and take his magical force down a few pegs with one decisive blow."

She followed him back to the stern. "What are you planning?"

"The witches' magic flows from them into this storm. I'll follow its threads back to the source. It's like lightning. It feeds from the clouds and also reaches up from the ground to meet in the middle." He stood at the rail and gazed into the churning tempest. "It's time to send a clear message to the witches and sorcerers who've sided with Nalvika's necromantic king." He looked back at her. "None will be spared." A question hung in his gaze. "This is war, Halina."

He wanted her permission and was offering a warning. Gethen was overstepping a boundary he'd set for himself and entering the fray as more than just her protector. She touched his arm. They'd not had a moment to speak since he'd returned from checking on his ward. "What did you see at Ranith?" she asked, fearing the answer.

"Ursinum has devastated my homeland and now breaks against Besalee's defenses. Eugen and Khara's forces have deserted their king."

She closed her eyes. "They may hang for that."

He brushed her cheek, heat following his fingers. "Ranith remains secure, but my brother's fate is uncertain, and Besalee Portcity may fall."

She squeezed his hand. "I'm sorry about your homeland."

"So am I. But its destruction proved nothing is permanent. That's why I'm not counting on my ward around this ship to last us until port in Ayestra. It's why I'm employing this option, though mages and witches will die."

She squared her shoulders and put steel in her voice. "Do it."

He nodded slowly, deliberately. "Step back and don't touch me. And...don't be afraid."

Halina swallowed. Gethen had never said that to her before. It made her nervous, but she said, "I trust you," and moved to the other side of the stern. It wasn't a lie. She trusted Gethen more than she'd ever trusted another person — family, servant, or soldier.

"You wanted to see all that I am, Halina." He raised his hands outward, palms facing the storm. He spoke ancient words, his voice taking on a pitch like the darkest depths of a tomb, something dead and long desiccated. He intoned spells that raised the hairs on her arms and made her shiver. Few things frightened Halina Persinna Rhysh, but this was more terrifying than even Waldram had been as he'd drained her blood magic and her life.

As Gethen intoned, the storm roiled and lashed at the ward. Churning faces appeared in the clouds. The howling wind took on near-human voices, some female, some male. They came and went and their expressions were agonized, their screams turning from threats to pleas. The silver light he'd drawn from the horses' souls lit him from within, making his eyelids glow, shining out from behind his lips as he continued his necromantic incantation.

His voice deepened. It took on the sepulchral tones of the Void, the words carrying death, disease, and damnation. He opened his eyes and the whites had been replaced by a flat blackness that threatened to suck Halina in. She looked away and locked her hands behind her back. This time his magic wasn't seductive, it was terrifying.

Gethen exhaled a thin, black brume, spewing it into the churning storm. Ropy and rotten, hissing louder than the screaming, pleading winds, it was snakelike and sinewy, filled with death and decay and the promise of suffering. It held a hatred that made Halina's guts twist and she stepped back again, truly terrified of her husband and beyond thankful that he wasn't her enemy. They'd fought side by side many times, but she'd never seen him like this. She'd never feared him.

Until now.

All light followed the vaporous cloud and it wrapped around and around the storm, choking it off, dragging it into the sea, strangling the faces she'd seen in the clouds until the entire storm collapsed into the Great Green Ocean with a wheeze like the last gasp of a dying man, the hiss and scream of a cornered animal. Waves rolled outward and the amber of Gethen's powerful ward flashed and shimmered across the water like oil resting upon its surface.

His incantation faded. He grasped the taffrail and closed his eyes, breathing heavily.

Halina stepped forward, forcing her feet to unstick, her knees to bend, her brain to let go of the paralyzing fear that had driven her back from Gethen.

She'd looked into the face of death and it was her husband's handsome visage.

When he opened his eyes, they were the familiar gray she'd always known and loved. He turned slowly. "You didn't run."

"I considered it." Her voice trembled. She reached out her hand. He took it and the gratitude in those gray eyes almost made her cry. "But I love you, Gethen Rhysh, even if you scare the piss out of me sometimes."

TWENTY-FIVE

Alarm bells pealed across the Bay of Ayestra and back to Gethen's ears as a massive Teleyansk warship and ten frigates and junks in various states of disarray creaked into port. He stood with Halina at the *Jenisej's* taffrail. She turned to Masorin and said, "I doubt Ayestra has a wharf large enough to accommodate this ship."

The admiral nodded. After conferring with Master Senya, they dropped anchor in the bay and lowered a rowboat. Masorin, Halina, Gethen, and two sailors descended a rope ladder and set off toward the quay.

The journey had taken nine days longer than planned and there'd been no sign of the rest of Lokshin's fleet. Whether they trailed, had sunk, or turned back was unknown, but Masorin and Senya remained true to their orders. "We are committed to following our emperor's directives, Lady Rhyshis, until we receive different commands from his Imperial Highness or the One God."

Troops awaited them when they climbed the nearest wharf. A single Teleyansk trade ship was unusual but not unknown to Ayestra. Traders came and went through their port from all parts of the world. But warships of their fleet's size hadn't been seen before and word quickly traveled to King Danas's patrols and beyond.

A captain stepped forward, the white ship of Ayestra emblazoned on his dark blue tabard, his gaze jumping from face to face as he took in their strange party. "State your names and the business of Teleyansk warships in our port."

Halina gestured to Masorin. "This is Admiral Masorin of the Imperial Navy of Teleyansk. I'm Princess Halina Persinna Rhysh and this is my husband, Gethen Rhysh, Duke of Rhyshis in absentia. We've come to stop Nalvika and Ursinum from destroying Quoregna. These warships sail into Ayestran waters in the name of peace with the full support of His Imperial Highness Lokshin and an invitation from King Danas."

The captain's chin lifted and he looked down his nose at her. "Produce it."

Halina's head jerked. "Produce what?"

"The king's invitation. Prove that—"

"I don't have to prove a damn thing to *you*, captain." She stepped toward the Ayestran man. He held his ground as she got in his face. "You will send word of our arrival to King Danas. Now."

"No. Will come with me to the castle," called a familiar voice and Magod shouldered his way through the crowd forming around them.

Gethen grasped his old friend's hand. "You're a welcome sight," he said.

Halina's belligerence collapsed as Magod took her hands. She smiled and murmured, "Most welcome, indeed, Lord Essendra."

Magod laughed. "Magod to you, Your Ladyship." He tucked her arm through his and offered a welcoming handshake to Masorin. He nodded toward the *Jenisej* and her company. "A fine sight, Teleyansk's ships. Good of you to endanger yourselves on Quoregna's behalf, Admiral."

"Emperor Lokshin speaks of you with great affection, Margrave Essendra," Masorin replied. "His Imperial Highness always comes to his friends' aid."

"Is generous with his strength," Magod replied.

"He was more generous than these few ships imply," Gethen said. "A storm separated us from much of the fleet during the passage."

"Storm?"

"Yes, and not the first unnatural one we've faced," Halina replied.

Magod shook his head. He noticed the captain and soldiers standing awkwardly at attention and waved them off. "Can attest to the identities and motives of these people. Will take them to the king myself."

The captain protested. "They can't produce papers of—"

"I. Vouched. For. Them. Captain." Magod bit off each word like he was biting off the man's head.

The captain swallowed the rest of his sentence and turned to his men, busying himself with orders. The soldiers dispersed the crowd and one ran ahead to announce the visitors to King Danas. Magod led their small group to the main road that would take them to Tanaw Castle.

As they walked, Gethen and Halina told of their misfortunes and the turn of events that eventually led them back to Ayestra with a diminished fleet.

"How is my sister?" Halina asked as they passed into the pale castle's inner bailey.

"Well." Magod smiled. "Arevik is well." But some hesitation in his manner made Halina frown. Gethen thought his friend meant to say more, but the king's chamberlain appeared at the wicket door and ushered them inside.

"Rooms await you," the man said as he led them up Tanaw's winding North Tower stairs to the guest wing. Arrow slits offered glimpses of blue sea and blinding sunlight. Sea crows wheeled past, flickers of shadow gone in a flash.

A beehive of activity filled the main hallway. Servants bustled between the rooms. Some trundled buckets of steaming water. Others bore towels, bedding, and clean clothing. All directed by the chamberlain's sharp tongue and sharper gaze.

Magod followed Gethen and Halina into their quarters rather than heading to his own. "Have something for you, Halina," he said pulling a small bundle of black silk from his coin purse. He rarely used her given name and her gaze sharpened upon hearing it. He considered the cloth for a moment then sighed and held it out to her. "Is my misfortune to bear the worst news to you."

"Arevik?" She took the small bundle.

He shook his head. "Is safe at home in Essen Citadel, thank the gods." He closed her fingers around the fabric. "Found this at Gwyncardarnlei three weeks ago." Regret clogged his voice. He winced. "I'm sorry."

She slowly unfolded the cloth. It shrouded a round, silver brooch featuring a gold bear with garnet eyes surrounded by ivory nightingales. Embroidered on the silk, a large, red bear gazed down upon five red cubs. "Why do you have this?" she whispered.

Magod looked helplessly at Gethen who put his arm around his wife's shoulders and said, "Halina, sit."

She shook him off. "No. I want to hear why Magod has this." The sharp edge of grief stabbed through her words. When Magod hesitated, she bared her teeth. "Say it!"

He swallowed. "Lady Ianthe and Prince Vernard are dead. No one has found Queen Ambrosine's body."

She went still as a statue. "How?"

Magod wet his lips. "Shrikers."

Halina clutched the cloth and brooch in one hand and rubbed her chest with the other. Her eyes closed. Her head lowered. "Thank you for telling me." She handed the items to Gethen then retrieved the kirtle and surcoat left on the sofa for her and went into the bathing room.

Brow furrowed, Magod met his gaze. "Woe to Waldram when she meets him on the battlefield," he murmured.

Gethen pressed his lips together and shook his head as Essendra's margrave took his leave. Halina had destroyed her own study in Kharaton Castle over a much lesser injury, so her silent acceptance of this tragic news worried him. He sighed, retrieved his own clean clothes, and went after his wife, leaving the evidence of murder on a table beside the bed.

She was already in the tub. "Scrub my back?"

He took the soap cake from her, dipped it in the water, and ran it across her scarred, muscular shoulders. "Halina—"

She stopped him with a sharp shake of her head. "Don't."

"You can't keep it inside."

"I can for now." Folding her arms on the tub's edge, she rested her chin. "This isn't the time for tears."

"When is?"

"After the fight is over. After Waldram is dead."

He leaned down and kissed her temple. "Just remember I'm here for you."

She turned her face toward him, captured his lips in a slow, mournful kiss, and murmured, "I never forget that."

"I no longer have the luxury of neutrality, Red Blade," King Danas said as he considered the map of Quoregna they'd spread across a table in his throne room. "Ilker has decimated Besera and pushed Zelal back to Besalee. Besera's soldiers stand with the Dargani and Or-Haleean troops while Nalvik reinforcements cross the Silver Sea daily. It's only a matter of time before Waldram's gaze turns to Ayestra."

Halina nodded. "What of Ursinum?" Ianthe's brooch flashed in the late evening sunlight. Pinned to her copper surcoat's breast, it held the fallen prince's handkerchief beneath her kirtle and over her heart.

He shook his head and Magod answered, "No word, Your Ladyship. Last message from your spy placed Nalvika in Valmer, but that was twenty days ago."

"Bollocks," she muttered. "They could be in Tatlis by now." She placed a red marker on the map to indicate the occupation of her father's kingdom.

"Do you have troop counts?" Masorin asked.

"Six thousand Nalviks and fifteen thousand Ursinian archers and foot soldiers in Besera and heading for Besalee," Danas said.

"Eight thousand Nalvik soldiers in Ursinum," Magod added.

"Is Khara occupied?" Gethen asked. "It wasn't ten days ago when I returned to Ranith."

"We believe it's fallen to Nalvika. They're crossing at Iania to circumvent the Valmerian Mountains. They made Sokos a point of blockade and are crossing the Silver Sea from there," King Danas replied. "I'm sorry to bear so much bad news, Lady Rhyshis."

"Thank you, but the whole of the four kingdoms occupies my mind, Your Majesty. We must end this fighting and restore order before all of our lands become nothing but ash."

Everyone standing around the table nodded.

She placed a finger on Sokos. "Nalvika's blockade sits here." She ran her finger southeast across the sea to Besalee Portcity. "Heavy fighting here."

Danas indicated a narrowing of the South Selga River where the Silver Sea turned toward the Great Green Ocean. "Eskis and Or-Halee have chained the South Selga between Emelin and Fayet. All indications are they've succeeded in stopping movement north and south."

Halina moved her finger north to the Choker, a series of narrow fingerling rivers that connected the North Selga to Ayestra Bay. "Where are Nalvika's boats entering the Selga to move troops and supplies?"

King Danas pointed at a place where the North Selga intersected Lake Jera's outlet. "They're crossing the Selga at the Jera Delta, though it's difficult to know the exact location with the fog."

"Fog?" Gethen asked. "Still?"

"It's hung over the delta for weeks."

Gethen folded his arms. "To hide their movement and numbers."

"Hmm," Halina murmured. "Two can play that game."

He nodded. "Sneak our force past them on the Selga."

She slid her finger to Ursinum's westernmost holding. "What about Floria?"

"Unoccupied according to most recent accounts," Magod replied.

"Good," she said. "We'll row the smallest ships north toward Lake Boorsook then turn south past Floria, picking up their forces on our way, and sail into Lake Tatlis."

Admiral Masorin considered the map. "Take Master Senya and the smallest ships to navigate the Choker's rivers, Your Ladyship." He traced the southeastern and southern shores of Or-Halee. "Which leaves the largest and fastest ships to hug the coast and head south around the bottom of Or-Halee. We'll enter the South Selga and row hard for Kharaton."

Danas asked, "Do you have Vala's and Eskis's support, Your Ladyship?"

"If those lords still draw breath, I have their swords, Your Majesty," she replied. She touched the marker on Besalee. "What about Besera, Or-Halee, and the Dargani?"

Danas offered a grim smile. "I'd worry more about your brother's foolishness in pursuing them, Your Ladyship. He's mired in the desert's sand and heat with Nalvika coming up behind him. I don't expect that alliance to hold much longer, since I've dispatched word to Ilker of Waldram's betrayal."

"Let's watch that closely," she said. "If I can bring my brother back to my side, I will. His mind has long been compromised by our second cousin's sorcery."

Ayestra's king sighed. "I didn't want to believe Waldram is using necromancy, but the evidence only grows to support your accusations."

Halina nodded and Gethen muttered, "I wish it wasn't true."

Masorin slapped the table and straightened. "Then we are settled on a plan."

"We are," Danas replied and the rest of them nodded.

War was at hand.

"Is it fog or is it smoke?" Master Senya asked as he peered into the brownish haze enveloping their two ships.

Ultimately, they'd chosen fifty-three sailors and soldiers to take the two smallest ships up the Choker's central river. They'd snuck past Nalvika's southern border, the dip of their oars and the ships' creaking wood silenced by Gethen's incantations. The unnatural brume wrapped them in its thick cloak. At the Jera Delta, they'd waited until early morning before they set their oars into the water and rowed slowly past Iania.

Gethen stood at the prow, his focus on the tumult of air and water against the shoreline where the lake emptied into the river. Swirling eddies and violent currents threatened the ships as surely as Nalvika's patrols did.

And that was the other thing he scanned for. Choosing to make their passage in the dark, Gethen had assured Senya he'd get them safely through the hazards but now wished he hadn't made that promise. The fog was enough to hide them from prying eyes, but the continuous patrols and transports of supplies and soldiers from Nalvika to Iania made finding a gap in traffic nearly impossible during daylight hours.

So he maintained the silencing spell and stretched his senses thin feeling the movements of everything around them.

Though his spell hid the noise of their passage from any ears on shore or the river, it didn't block sound from reaching them. The eerie shrieks and screams of shrikers echoed back and forth across the river.

Wide-eyed, Senya murmured, "What is that?" to Halina who stood at Gethen's shoulder.

"Shrikers hunting for children's souls," she replied.

The ships were small enough that her words carried to the ears of the rowers below them on the main deck. Muttering rose from their ranks. A jerk of the master's head quieted them. They stared nervously into the fog, eyes as wide as startled deer, as if expecting the undead dogs to swim out to meet the ships.

"They're not a threat until we make landfall," Halina said louder. "And even then, a sharp sword and a lopped off head is all it takes to neutralize the beasts."

A flicker of movement crossed the water and surmounted the rail beside Gethen, the return of Gwyn and Duesh. He considered the eerie blaids then raised his right hand to indicate the ships should tack to the starboard side. "We're coming up on...something," he murmured. His head jerked up. "Stop. Stop!"

"Zogs!" Senya called in Yansk and the rowers reversed their oars. The anchors were dropped. The ships slowed, groaned, creaked.

"What is it?" Halina peered into the dark and fog.

"The wolves found something stretched across the river. A log, a rope, or..." Gethen focused on the blaids. "A chain."

"Semele's blood," she cursed.

He swept his hand from north to south. "Ox teams and drovers man each side."

"Clever," Senya said.

"Not clever enough," Halina replied. "How many drovers and guards?"

"Two drovers, each with three guards."

"And we're closer to the south shore?"

"Yes." Gethen knew her mind and turned with her. "I'll come along to maintain the silence."

She shook her head. "I'm sure our master has soldiers who specialize in stealth." She looked to Senya and he nodded and summoned four men.

She stripped off her boots, belt, and tunic, and gave Gethen Ianthe's brooch and the handkerchief for safekeeping. "We'll be back with blood on our hands."

"Tie them off," Senya ordered and ropes were tied around the waist of each assassin, including Halina, lifelines back to the ship through the darkness and fog.

Gethen gave her a black look and received bared teeth in return. She itched for action, pacing the decks like a caged beast that smelled blood. He couldn't blame her for seizing the opportunity to strike. "Go slow," he said.

"Slow and steady wins the war." She slipped over the side of the ship, grasping the knots of the rope the crew had lowered into the water.

Silent as the dead, she and the Teleyansk soldiers slid into the cold Selga.

The blaids trailed Halina, and Gethen followed them, in turn, with his senses. The water rippled around her. She reached solid ground and crept ashore. "They've found the chain," he murmured to Senya who squinted into the darkness, his hands gripping the rail.

"Quietly," Gethen whispered to his wife knowing she couldn't hear him. "Keep the chain from splashing."

They did as he hoped. The souls' confusion enveloped Gethen as the drovers' and guards' throats were slit. The chain's movement vibrated through him as it was slowly lowered through the harness, link-by-link, and sank into the water, no sound betraying its passage.

He held his breath as the assassins and his wife returned to the water and followed the ropes back to the ship. He didn't relax until Halina climbed over the rail, dripping and grinning.

"Easy," she murmured.

Senya signaled the rowers to begin again. The ships moved forward, slicing through the water and passing over the place where the chain had been.

A shout went up from the shore: "Oy! Pull up the slack!"

Gethen cursed beneath his breath.

Senya cried, "Pull hard!"

The rowers put their backs to it.

Their ship passed the line.

A Nalvik called again. "Wake up, you lazy pillocks! You let the chain slip. If I have to come over there, I'll skin you and send your bollocks to King Waldram."

Halina went to the forecastle. Duesh and Gwyn trailed her,

rumbling deep in their chests. "Carry my voice across," she told Gethen. Their second ship hadn't cleared the line yet.

He nodded and focused the sound with sorcery. "Go on."

"Bit meg, stihle uor!" she cursed back in Nalvik, sounding both sleepy and drunk.

The Nalvik guards and drovers laughed from the northern side of the river, while their leader started in with some colorful curses of his own. They mistook Halina for the dead female drover. The Nalviks threatened to row across and show her how real men yanked a chain. She told them they couldn't even yank their own cocks, so she doubted they could impress her with a chain. By that time, the second ship had cleared the sunken barrier and the rowers kept at it, the muscles standing out on their arms and backs, sweat breaking across their skin. Halina turned away and crossed the deck as she called, "I'm going to find a real man. I've heard the Ursinians are hung like horses. I'm tired of tiny Nalvik sheep cocks."

The drovers and guards kept shouting but none bothered to launch a boat and make good on their threats. Apparently, the Nalviks weren't compelled to navigate the river in the darkness, even if the insults were wicked.

She leaned against the rail beside Gethen and took the towel a sailor offered her.

"You enjoyed that whole foray too much, wife."

She grinned. "The Nalviks are pig lovers and not in a natural way. Any chance I get to kill and insult Waldram's army, I'll take it. They're on my lands now."

The Teleyansk sailors and soldiers laughed. They'd needed the release as much as she had. Gethen hadn't missed how they gave him a wide berth when he crossed the deck, their nervous glances when he summoned Gwyn and Duesh to move through the fog and be his eyes and ears.

"The crew understands the power of a battle mage," Senya

told him one night as they dined in the master's cabin, "but you bring a very different kind of sorcery to this fight, necromancer."

Halina had asked, "Is it the level of his power or is it the necromancy that makes them so nervous?"

"Both," Gethen replied. He considered his wife. "You're not even comfortable with the combination."

She looked down, then wiped her mouth with her napkin and reached for his hand. "My discomfort with your practice doesn't detract from my love."

Senya continued, "The way you transformed your wolves is uncomfortably close to Chonyn sorcery, which is forbidden in Teleyansk. You have power beyond anything we've ever encountered, Sun Mage. It's the kind of sorcery spoken of in legends. The kind that compelled our emperor's ancestors to create the Magistry and take control of mages."

"What's the Magistry?" Halina asked.

"The office that oversees all mages and witches in Teleyansk. Their practices and whereabouts are tracked."

"And controlled," Gethen said. "Because their power is considered a threat to the Shin Dynasty." He sipped the bracket Senya had served, a passable drink. He didn't like the implications of Teleyansk's Magistry. People who didn't understand sorcery shouldn't attempt to control it.

"Gethen uses his power to serve the mortal realm in Quoregna, Master Senya," Halina said. "It's why he's involved in this war, a position that's not traditionally taken by the necromancers who guard the Voidline."

Senya considered that. "Why become involved?"

"Because the God of Death commands it," Gethen replied.

"Your death god commands you to war?"

Gethen shrugged. "He commands me to do many things."

The ship's master grunted. "And we must obey our gods," he murmured.

"Must we?" Halina asked.

That earned a sharp look from the ship's master. "You don't follow your own religion's edicts, Red Blade?"

"I serve the people of Quoregna. If the gods' decisions benefit them, then I honor those demands. If they endanger my people, I reject them."

His bushy brows arched. "You consider your judgment to be equal to that of your gods?"

"I know what's best for the people who rely upon me to protect them, shelter them, provide them with sustenance and guidance," she replied. "I've seen plenty of evidence to convince me that the Triumvirate is weakening and makes decisions for their own benefit, not Quoregna's." She pushed her plate away and leaned forward, resting her arms on the table. "I doubt, Master Senya, more and more as my world comes apart because the God of Death encourages war and chaos to benefit himself and the goddesses, Semele and Khotyr."

He considered that. "Strange to hear of mortals questioning their gods' motives. Why do you say they work to benefit themselves?"

Gethen replied, "Because I've met Skiron many times. Our gods wish to provoke destruction and misery because it leads to need and prayer. Without our faith, the gods don't exist."

Halina sat back. She drained her cup, thunked it down on the table, and said, "I don't need those kinds of gods, Master Senya. Nor do my people."

The ship's master slowly shook his head. "Quoregna has a strange and frightening culture."

She laughed. "We could say the same about Teleyansk and your One God."

He smiled. "Ah, but some of your people worship our One God, too. Your own brother, for instance, yes?"

"Yes," she said. "And is still led by the nose by a king who serves Skiron's bloody dream. I'm afraid your One God isn't helping Quoregna much these days, either."

The master shrugged. "We all must take responsibility for our own actions."

"True," Gethen replied. "You can assure your sailors and soldiers that I won't act against their safety. If taking souls becomes necessary as we enter battle, I'm certain the Red Blade will usher enough Nalvik souls toward the Voidline to provide me with unlimited power."

Senya nodded slowly, but he didn't look very reassured. "You've given me much to ponder about the nature of gods and our relationship with them."

Gethen anchored the silencing spell to the rowers and retired to the tiny cabin he shared with Halina. She already slept in the hammock beside his, her arm lax where it hung over the side. He tucked it back beside her body and covered her with another blanket. The North Selga was cold, even in late summer.

They'd reached an inlet and anchored the ships at the northern shore, not too close to permit roaming shrikers aboard but out of the path of any boats that might emerge from the fog. As much as Gethen wished to remain alert and on deck, he couldn't go another hour without sleep. Three days of constant vigilance and sorcery had taken their toll and despite his reassurances to the ship's master, he couldn't ignore the seductive pull of the Teleyansk souls around him.

He climbed into his swaying hammock, checked the strength of the ward he'd set around the ships, and closed his eyes. Rest would go a long way to calming the cravings and easing the trembling that possessed his hands and scaled his spine.

He sighed. Why couldn't he find a way to tap the depths of

his power without needing souls? Why couldn't he shake that addiction? He was capable of magic without them. Halina had reminded him of that. Yet, he still felt the seductive pull of every human soul like an itch desperate to be scratched.

Tomorrow they'd enter Lake Boorsook. He'd go ashore and summon deer to lend their souls, if his need grew too great. He regretted not taking the drovers and guards Halina and the soldiers had dispatched at the river chain. But he also was relieved that he'd resisted. The crew wouldn't tolerate that, he was certain. It was best if they believed his control was absolute, his focus resolute.

He closed his eyes, lulled by the small ship's creak and sway, the gentle lapping of waves against the hull, and Halina's even breathing. Duesh and Gwyn prowled the decks, invisible to the crew. They'd summon him if anything threatened.

Gethen felt the tug and opened his eyes. A milky white river ran around his legs. Skiron stood opposite him, wearing a form he'd never seen on the god, one more chilling than any other.

"Do you like this appearance?" Skiron asked. He wore the One God's countenance, the sun-and-moon symbol emblazoned across his forehead, his head bald, his eyes blank, white orbs. "I think it suits my purposes."

Some instinct surged in Gethen, outrage mingling with fear and finality. "No. You will not take that form. You will not corrupt that practice!"

Skiron laughed and snapped his fingers.

Nothing happened.

He glared at his fingers as if they'd betrayed him.

The god's face warped between Halina's, Shemel's, Skiron's before settling again into the One God's sexless, youthful features. "You've gained some strength, Sun Mage," he said. "I respect that." His eerie, sightless gaze slid back to Gethen. "Respect it, but I won't be troubled by it." He winked out of existence.

Gethen snarled a curse. He closed his eyes and reopened them to the gray light of a foggy morning.

Halina's empty hammock swung to and fro. Her boots were gone.

Calls carried down from the decks above.

"Watch the eddies," Master Senya shouted.

Gethen rolled over and peered through their cabin's only portal. The fog had thinned. Murky shapes defined a distant shoreline.

"Ships! Ships ahead!"

Gethen tumbled from the hammock at that cry. He jerked upright and smacked his skull on the low wooden ceiling as the next cry went up:

"It's the *Ayaruq*! The One God is merciful!"

"And the fleet!"

"Praise to His Imperial Highness Lokshin!"

TWENTY-SIX

While the *Jenisej's* crew cheered and waved at their comrades in the flotilla waiting at the mouth of Lake Boorsook, northern Ursinum's charred landscape mocked Halina for as far as she could see.

Gethen reached her side. He took in Lokshin's mass of ships then the destruction of Halina's homeland. "It's like Besera," he murmured, wrapping his arm around her shoulders.

She leaned into him. Even during the War of the Winds, Ursinum had been spared the worst of the fighting. She'd never seen such utter destruction, as if one of the swirling cyclone storms of the southern Beseran Plains had wreaked havoc all across Northern Ursinum. Chaos someone chose to worsen by setting everything ablaze.

They'd smelled the smoke mingling with the fog for days, but she hadn't realized just how extensive the burn area was. The Nalvik shore of Lake Boorsook was verdant and lush. The opposite shore was a black-and-gray wasteland. No trees remained, no buildings, no crops. There'd been a large fishing community all along the southern shore of the lake and for more than a dozen miles following the Destri and Sinissi River forks. Now, even the island that split the two branches before they came together to become Lake Tatlis, was a ruin. Like a dog with mange, the land was scarred and denuded, scabby and showing only gray dust where once there'd been thriving villages and many acres of lush fields growing red rye and berries, sweet peas, summer beans, and early squashes.

"The people will starve," she whispered.

"If they survived the assault."

"Lady and Lord Rhyshis, His Imperial Highness wishes you to come aboard the *Ayaruq*."

Halina turned, her gaze reluctant to abandon her scarred homeland. But Master Senya had relayed the emperor's orders. She nodded slowly, still stunned by the absolute destruction of Ursinum and wondering how far south the wound extended.

Gethen took her elbow. "We'll come immediately." His tight grip drew her attention back to him and Senya.

She exhaled despair that she could ill afford to indulge. "Yes, of course."

The master led them to a small wooden boat. The crew swung it over the side and lowered it into the water, then Gethen, Halina, two sailors, two soldiers, and Senya climbed down and set out for Lokshin's ship.

She studied the *Ayaruq* as the men rowed. "Her sails are undamaged."

Senya said, "They must have put in at a port somewhere."

"Not Ayestra," she replied. "We'd have known if they'd arrived there before us."

The ships looked almost untouched.

"Seventeen are missing," Senya said, "but those that survived came through remarkably well."

"A testament to Teleyansk maritime skill and construction,"

Gethen murmured. But his tone and the stiffness in his posture set off alarms in Halina. She rested her hand upon his. He turned his palm up and threaded his fingers with hers. Something wasn't right. He sensed it too.

As they approached the Teleyansk ships, Halina saw they were anchored. "They were waiting for us."

Gethen nodded.

"How fortunate," Master Senya said and his fellow soldiers and sailors nodded, all smiles and laughter.

"They sailed the Ballard," she realized. "It's the only explanation." And it meant they'd navigated through the heart of Nalvika and past the long northern river border that separated Schorvala from Waldram's kingdom. "They evaded detection at the Fist and the Thumb?" The chances of such an impressive fleet not being spotted were zero.

Gethen only frowned, doubtless thinking the same thing she was — Lokshin had encountered Nalviks. The question was whether they'd battled or befriended Halina's enemy.

The boat bumped against the hull of the emperor's massive warship and was tied off. Their group climbed the tall side of the ship.

Awaiting their arrival on deck, Lokshin perched upon a gold-encrusted throne, his entire crew prostrate around him. He smiled and rose, spreading his arms and welcoming them and Senya. Sunlight flashed off his gold and jewels.

Halina eyed the display of fealty. None of his soldiers or servants had displayed this much subjugation back in Yasan Khot or at any time as they'd sailed.

After she and Gethen bowed, and Senya scraped and groveled, Lokshin asked, "So few ships came through the storm?"

Master Senya answered, "We are twelve strong ships, Your Imperial Highness, but only two came across the Choker from

Ayestra. The remainder travel south around the coast of Or-Halee and will reach the Silver Sea by the South Selga River."

"Ah, you split the small fleet. Wise. A brave crew accompanied you through the heart of enemy territory and past many Nalvik ships and troops to reach this place."

Senya puffed up at the praise of his inherited crew and small ships.

Lokshin gestured for Halina and Gethen to join him as he strode across the deck, making for the stairs to the imperial cabins. His guards and attendants followed, but he waved them off. "Only our honored guests may accompany us," he said and the uniformed men and women fell back.

They reached the wooden door to his apartment. A boy slid it open. Lokshin entered and crossed to the ship's open portals. He surveyed the destruction of Ursinum beyond the glass. "It's a terrible thing to see such waste. The people of Ursinum and Besera are suffering. But we can avoid worse."

Halina waited. The emperor had something to say; the weight of it hung between them. Gethen watched the man, his gaze a sharp blade, as if trying to peel back the emperor's skin to deduce what was hiding beneath.

Lokshin surveyed the flotilla. "Our route carried us through the heart of Nalvika, Lady Rhyshis. And you know we could not remain undiscovered, as you apparently have. The Fifth Son does not possess the Sun Mage's knack for stealth." He turned from the window. "Lokshin met with King Waldram in Nalvika's Fist."

Gethen clasped Halina's hand. "What did Waldram offer?" Caution tempered his voice, he too had noticed the strange distancing that had crept into the emperor's self reference.

"He matched your offer and sweetened it with the rule of Ursinum, the prospect of swift peace and order for Quoregna."

Halina whispered, "Of course he did." She met Lokshin's bright gaze. "And you accepted it."

"We did." He glanced back at the charred countryside. "Though we didn't consider how extensively the land was damaged. We might have asked for more had we known how much his forces had abused your homeland."

"What of King Ilker?" Gethen asked, his voice admirably calm. He'd conquered the tremor that had begun to creep into his hands again.

"Alive, ignorant, and routed from Besalee Portcity. The coward's forces retreat across the Silver Sea." Lokshin settled upon a wide chair, his face in shadow as the filtered daylight coming through the portals backlit him. "We were also offered Besera if we deliver both of you to King Waldram's forces."

"Will you?" she asked.

His demeanor morphed from calm to chaos. "No," he snarled and shook his head violently, grimacing and gripping the arms of his chair.

"Are you unwell, Your Eminence?" Gethen asked.

Shadow and light flickered as Duesh and Gwyn slunk around the cabin, disturbed by the strangeness of the emperor. They paused by something on the floor beside the emperor's bed. Halina squinted and spied the golden robes of Lokshin's Fifth Son. Teleyansk's most powerful mage lay on his back, a dagger jutting from his chest, his eyes staring sightless and surprised. Gethen's hand tightened on hers. He'd seen the body too.

"We had an agreement," Lokshin snarled through bared teeth. "You've negotiated with honor, while King Waldram sent wraiths to Yasan Khot and sank our ships." He shook his head again, eyes closed, teeth clenched, nails digging into the chair's armrests. "Don't trust us," he whispered. "The opportunity he offered was a lie. The other one took hold."

"We had an alliance, Your Imperial Majesty," Halina said.

"And I warned you, Red Blade. There are no alliances, there is only family." He opened his eyes and his pupils were gone, replaced with white. He leaned forward, struggling against some unseen force. "Your freedom is my gift and my only hope. Flee, hide, if you want to survive." Lokshin slowly stood and a phantasm, shimmering and white, emerged from his skin, part of him but separate. It took the form of the One God, the glowing sun-moon symbol writhing snake-like on its chest and forehead.

"Shemel," Gethen snarled and invoked a magical shield as his former master, in wraith form, exhaled a poisonous brown brume.

Halina jerked her husband out of the cabin and toward the stairs, summoning her blood armor as she pulled him behind her. "Come on!" she shouted while Gethen maintained a litany of incantations punctuated by curses that would've made her proud had she the time to stop and consider the creativity behind them.

They emerged to startled faces as the still-prostrate crew raised their heads.

Ignoring them, Gethen pushed Halina behind him. The blaids circled, their snarls eerie and low.

The god-like figure followed, leading Lokshin's senseless body, feeding off his soul and surviving inside his skin, a master inside his own marionette.

The crew called out in awe. Prayers filled the air as their One God appeared in possession of their emperor, the Shin Dynasty's divine birthright sanctified before their eyes.

Shemel's voice emerged from Lokshin's mouth, parroted by the nebulous god-like figure he'd adopted to fool Teleyansk's masses. "Servant of Death, would you summon the power of the grave to destroy a peaceful god?"

"I take no issue with the One God," Gethen replied, "but I won't ignore an imposter, Shemel Ebbe. Go back to the Void where you belong."

"Your lies and deceit will only end with your death, Sun Mage," Shemel replied. "You cannot be permitted to harm the Emperor of Smiles."

As if that statement was a catalyst to the prostrate troops and sailors, all the people surrounding them scrambled to their feet and brandished their weapons.

"Surrender," Shemel murmured, a perfect picture of false humility and benevolence for the believers around him. "Surrender and be spared."

"Like you spared Lokshin's Fifth Son?" Halina threw back at him.

With a voice like the grave, Gethen snarled an incantation that knocked back the surrounding forces. Soldiers and sailors tumbled over each other, across the deck, over the rails and into the water. He redoubled his spell, his voice gaining in volume even as it pitched lower.

The deck trembled and heaved beneath their feet. Wood groaned, twisted, cracked. Troops shouted and panicked. But not all. The twang of bowstrings brought Halina's focus to the stern a moment too late as two archers loosed arrows. She jerked Gethen aside and hit the heaving deck with a curse. He went down, but never stopped his spell. Rolling over, Halina wished for a shield and didn't have time to be thankful when her blood armor conjured one. She blocked the next volley of arrows.

Above them the ship's masts shivered and torqued. Stays snapped. Sails tore. The wooden deck heaved, bulged, exploded. Massive splinters shot up, gutting soldiers and sailors, tearing through flesh and breaking bones.

Soldiers ushered their godly emperor to safety as Gethen's

incantation tore apart the ship beneath their feet and he drew on the power of dead men's fleeing souls.

More arrows flew as the archers shifted to get around Halina's shield. Untroubled by the flying bolts, Duesh and Gwyn charged the men, tearing souls from flesh and scattering enemies.

"Gethen!" Halina grabbed his arm, but when his gaze found hers, his eyes were black orbs, dark as the Void's sky. He was using necromancy, drawing souls in and powering his sorcery with their energy, and she shuddered at the sound of death coming from his mouth, the look of it in his empty eyes. Still, she didn't pull away. Instead, she shook him and shouted, "We have to go!"

He blinked and the incantation died on his lips. His pupils returned to their normal size as he cursed and wrapped his arms around her. His travel incantation followed and amber magic lifted water from the splintered deck to create a shimmering vortex around them.

Shemel's mocking laughter and the Teleyansk crew's shouts and prayers thundered in Halina's ears as the scene dissolved.

The incantation dispelled to reveal Ranith's gray tower and walled bailey. Silver clouds diffused the midday sun. Sea crows rode updrafts, diving and soaring above the citadel. Their voices vied with the crash of distant surf below the tor.

Two slight figures emerged from the kitchen calling their names in greeting.

"Your Ladyship!" Feddie dashed across the grassy bailey, scattering chickens and forgetting all formality as she threw her arms around Halina.

Smiling, Halina returned the princess's embrace. Her world looked darker, her hope had dimmed, but seeing Feddie and being embraced next by Elof restored some of her resolve.

Remembering herself, the princess stepped back. "Lady Rhyshis," she said and curtsied.

"Very pretty manners, Your Highness," Halina replied, bowing in return. "But I'm more interested in seeing your sword skills. Diplomacy is dead."

Gethen added, "Murdered by a madman and a god."

"I don't like the sound of that," Thaksin said as he followed the two Nalvik children.

"Honor and loyalty are in short supply," Halina said and grasped his hand. "You taught me the value of both."

"Your bid to win over Teleyansk failed?" Odruna asked.

Halina shook her head. "The alliance was stolen from us."

"This war won't be won with partnerships between strangers," Gethen said. "Even the gods are our enemies now."

Eugen scratched the back of his bald head. "Come into the tower. You're soaked and look like you could use a stiff drink."

Thak nodded. "You can tell us what happened with the emperor of Teleyansk and we'll plot a way toward victory after you're dry and drunk."

Gethen and Halina sat shoulder to shoulder in Ranith's library, sipping mead with Thak, Eugen, Odruna, Marja, and Cerys.

"How long before Teleyansk and Nalvika turn their eyes toward Ranith?" Thaksin asked, his voice gravelly, his words slurred.

Halina peered into her cup, sighed, and finished the drink, welcoming a night of muzziness. She'd more than earned it.

"Sooner than we'd like," Gethen replied. "But it's pointless worrying about their timetable. There's a plan to be devised and a mystery to solve."

She looked up. "What mystery?"

"How Shemel and Waldram are tracking us." His gaze roamed the library before settling on something near the hearth. He reached out his palms and a moment later, Duesh and Gwyn pressed their insubstantial noses against his hands. "Hello, friends," he murmured. "I'm glad you found your way home."

Halina shivered as the blaids considered her with glowing eyes. They exhaled cold breaths and settled at Gethen's feet.

"Could they be tracking your magic?" Cerys asked him.

"Probably Halina's blood magic." Gethen considered the mead in his cup.

"You could be wrong," Halina mumbled as she reached for his drink. "I haven't been in many battles since we left for Teleyansk." She frowned at the meager amount of liquid in the cup. She was not as drunk as she wanted to be.

Gethen's gaze swung to her. "No, but you've used blood armor," he muttered.

"Wha?" She squinted at him.

"Your blood armor." He took the cup back and drained it. "Waldram stole your blood magic. Your armor demands a tremendous expenditure of it. He must feel the surge and get a sense of where you are. And if he knows, Shemel does too."

She shook her head, a futile attempt to clear the drunken fog. "Can you use it to cripple him? Like you did the weather witches?"

Gethen grimaced. "If it worked that way, he would've incapacitated you already."

"Right." Halina rested her elbows on her knees and sighed. "I really, really need to cut off King Jigglestick's head."

Odruna, Marja, and Thaksin laughed. Cerys looked aghast and Eugen remained stolid as ever.

Gethen put the cup on a nearby table and stood, pulling Halina up beside him. "Let's sleep. Drinking and thinking won't bring us any closer to a solution, and our enemies won't go away overnight."

It was late and the tower was quiet. Duesh and Gwyn glided beside them, their forms shifting and changing with the flicker of Gethen's mage fire as he lit the stairwell's braziers on the way to his bedchamber.

They reached the room and the blaids patrolled its perimeter before settling before the hearth. Gethen set its wood ablaze with a flick of his fingers.

Halina sank onto the bed. She ran her hands over its familiar furs and blankets and sighed. The knowledge that Waldram was using her greatest strength against her was sobering. "The gods want me dead."

Gethen crouched before her. "We all reach the Void someday."

She studied his face. "I still like the look of you, Lord Rhyshis," she said, tracing the strong line of his jaw.

"I like the look of you, Lady Rhyshis." He captured her hand, kissed her palm. "I won't let the gods have you. Not for many years."

He unlaced her boots and tossed them close to the hearth. He pulled her close, kissed her gently. "We won't let our enemies take away our love. They'll never have that." He added his boots to hers and crawled under the blankets and furs, pulling her down with him.

Halina snuggled against him. She loved how he smelled, like honey and wax, maluk and brimstone. And she loved the feel of his strong arms around her, the brush of his warm breath on her neck and cheek. "I love you."

"I know." He brushed his lips across her forehead. "I love you too." He closed his eyes. "Now go to sleep."

"And don't dream?"

"Dream of Waldram's head on a stake, Shemel ceasing to exist, and peace coming to Quoregna."

"Dream of the Voidline closing and Skiron doing his own dirty work."

Gethen chuckled, his muscles shifting against her. "That's a good dream."

Her eyes closed. "Dream of being together."

His arms tightened around her. "Forever."

TWENTY-SEVEN

Halina stood on the slope of Kharayan Tor at the edge of Gethen's ward circle, its black stones beneath her feet. Overhead the forest's lush canopy swayed and a breeze lifted her hair around her face in a ghostly dance of dark auburn strands. Sun and shadows flickered around her as the leaves and branches shivered in the wind. Soldiers surrounded her and spread out across the tor, a vast army stretching toward the shores of the Silver Sea. Their focus remained on her as she considered something in the distance. Gethen peered in that direction, squinting through a haze that obscured distant Besera's purple mountains and even the closer towers of Kharaton Castle, but he couldn't see what held her attention.

A cloud passed over the sun. Shadows swallowed the gathering. When light returned, the soldiers at the edges of the army had become insubstantial, shadows standing among the living. Halina didn't notice. Her focus remained on some distant target. The group shifted, a ripple of uneasiness slowly unfurling around her as shadows took over the clearing again and more warriors joined the ranks of the incorporeal.

"Halina." Gethen approached his wife, but she didn't acknowledge him. He tried to push through the crowd, but his hands passed *through the soldiers as, singly and in groups, they lost substance and turned into shadows. He seemed rooted in place, incapable of forward motion. "Halina!"*

Finally, she looked away from her target and found him, her figure muted by the incorporeal army standing between them, her gaze direct, voice heavy. "You know this has to happen." She reached for him.

Gethen went cold. She, too, was becoming a shadow. "No. No! I won't lose you." He tried to grab her hand but his fingers passed through hers. "Halina, don't!"

Gethen jerked awake, his heart pounding, his breathing quick. Beside him, Halina slept soundly. Too disturbed by the nightmare to go back to sleep, he slipped from their bed and donned his trouzes, brigandine, and boots.

"Come," he murmured to Duesh and Gwyn as the ghostly blaids appeared at his heels. Leaving his wife behind with her dreams and the security of his warm bed, he descended the dark stairs, heading for his stillroom.

A summer wind howled around the tower. The wooden shutters clattered against the window when he entered the room. Clouds swept the sky. The stars and a crescent moon winked. He captured and secured the errant shutters.

Odruna and Marja slept in the adjoining infirmary and the door opened. "What's wrong?" the Schorvalan militess asked, her sword drawn halfway from its scabbard, her trouzes loose on her hips.

"Nothing immediate, but I'm moving Cerys, Gerezel, Feddie, and Elof. You'll both go with them."

"Now?"

"Yes, now."

Marja appeared behind Odruna, fastening the front of her gambeson. "I'll rouse them." She headed for the guest quarters.

"Tell them to dress warmly," he said. "It's cold in the Northern Wastes."

"I'll tell Thak and Eugen," Odruna said.

"No. No one else should know where you're going. Not even Halina."

Her brows rose. "You don't trust her?" Displeasure rumbled behind her words.

He scowled. "Don't be daft. I trust her with my life. But I don't trust that Waldram can't worm information out of her mind against her formidable will."

Odruna bared her teeth. "Someone needs to skin that snake."

"It's on my list of things to do."

Polite but suspicious, the Schorvalan militess trusted him only because Halina did and not nearly as readily. But she was a fierce fighter and she'd protect the queen and the children with her life. Halina considered her loyalty absolute, which was why he was sending her and Marja with the blaids to a distant land. It was a risk, but he had to take it. Waldram would track Halina to Ranith, which meant Feddie wasn't safe there. Chono Khot was the one place where she hadn't employed her blood armor, and neither Waldram, Shemel, nor Lokshin knew about the village.

Odruna pivoted on her heel and gathered the few belongings she and Marja had brought. They traveled light, just like every member of the Order of the Red Blades.

Gethen descended to the kitchen and unbanked the fire on the hearth. He warmed gruel and made tea. Both were waiting when the children and militesses appeared on the servants' stairs. Cerys arrived behind them, her servants on her heels and a very sleepy Gerezel in her arms.

Thaksin and Eugen entered. "What's going on?" Khara's steward asked.

Gethen gestured for them to eat. "I'm moving my charges. Odruna, Marja, Duesh, and Gwyn will go with them."

"To where?" Thak asked.

"You're not to know," Marja said as she spooned gruel into bowls for the children.

"Eat quickly," Gethen said. "I want all of you gone before the sun rises."

Elof yawned. He dropped his haversack on the floor, sat, and shoveled food into his mouth. Cerys sat beside him and the boy offered a spoonful of gruel to Gerezel. The crown prince rubbed his eyes and opened his mouth. Elof continued to share his food with the toddler.

"Where are we going?" Cerys asked, her dark eyes keen.

"You'll find out when you get there," Gethen replied.

Feddie spied the pacing blaids. "Are the wolves coming with us?"

"Yes."

"Why?" Marja asked. She blew steam from her tea and tracked the nebulous blaids. Odruna considered him through narrowed eyes and poured Schorvalan soma into her own cup.

Gethen touched the wolves, their fur like a cold fog against his fingers. "Because they're known and respected where you're going."

"Is that necessary?" the militess asked.

"Yes."

Thak crossed his arms. "I don't like this."

"I didn't ask for your opinion," Gethen growled. He raised his hands to stop the questions and defuse the anger that flared in Thak's eyes. "If Waldram can track Halina across the Great Green Ocean, he can certainly find her in Ranith. That means none of you are safe. But you will be where I'm sending you."

Odruna said, "But Halina's not to know."

"Why?" Cerys asked.

Eugen deduced, "Because Waldram may be able to pry that information from her mind."

"Correct." Gethen faced the men. "When she awakens to find we've left, she'll want to follow. Do not let her."

"She can do that?" Feddie asked, her spoon poised between her mouth and her bowl.

Gethen nodded. "I've given her the means."

Eugen and Thaksin exchanged a knowing look. "Alright," Thak said. "Though stopping that woman from doing anything is like facing down a phalanx of shrikers."

Gethen nodded. "No doubt you can handle the task."

"Your faith may be misplaced," the captain muttered.

Eugen gripped his shoulder. "We'll manage her. We always have."

"You have." Thak grabbed Odruna's flask and took a long pull from it. He wiped his mouth and added, "I usually receive her fist with my face."

Kenbish welcomed all of them without hesitation. "You'll be safe here, Your Highness," she assured Cerys. "Enemies of the Red Blade of Or-Halee are enemies of the Chonyn. Friends of the blaids and the Sun Mage are friends to us." She tickled Gerezel under the chin and laughed when he did.

Terbish happily led Feddie and Elof into the main lodge. "I'll teach you how to play Chonyn yas."

Arban showed Odruna and Marja to the large tent they'd share with the children. He smiled widely for both soldiers, his ego not the least bit bruised by his encounter with their leader. "Have you ever tasted gonsu? I make the finest brew; best you'll find in all Chono Khot. The Red Blade and Sun Mage can attest to its quality."

Gethen bowed to Kenbish. "Thank you, Kuchin Shulam. Halina and I are grateful for your generosity."

She waved that away. "Bah. You'll always have our support, Kuchin Togoldor."

He pressed a kiss to Cerys's forehead. "You're among friends here. These people hosted Halina and me when we had little reason to hope. Your stay will pass quickly."

"Thank you, brother." She squeezed his hand. "Be safe and protect Halina. Quoregna needs you both."

Kenbish took her to the tent he and Halina had shared.

This is the right decision, Gethen thought as he took in the bustling Chonyn camp — the people focused on their morning tasks, the tents like hulking beasts, the wind-swept Chono Steppes.

The wolf warriors offered safety, but they couldn't solve all his problems. His late-night dream was a signpost pointing in the direction he should travel. He'd rejected it many months ago and met with ever-growing catastrophe. But perhaps that way lay the solution.

He sighed. He'd settle for an army, right now.

Gethen turned his back to the wind and invoked his travel incantation. Afternoon sunshine slanted across the bailey's green grass when the swirling, amber magic dispersed around him.

He considered the tall, dark-gray tower with its ruined upper floors and small, circular bailey. Motion at an upper window drew his eye. Halina stood there, glaring down at him, her mouth a grim line. He faced a lashing from her sharp tongue. He raised his hand. She responded with a universally unfriendly gesture.

He chuckled and started toward the extraction room. The beehives were sorely neglected. Honey and wax wanted harvesting. The splits hadn't been made. It meant a lean winter and empty coffers. "If I live to see next winter," he muttered and stopped on the worn path. The smell of smoke lingered on the breeze, a reminder of Ystwyth's destruction. The pale-gray stone beneath his feet was as hard as his untenable position.

Halina needed an army and every avenue was closed to them...save one. One he swore he'd never travel. One that offered the death, chaos, and suffering Skiron wanted but that also might end the war.

He turned. A squat, stone building and a crooked overgrown graveyard abutted the citadel.

The basilica was the oldest part of Ranith. Predating the tower by ages, it served purposes long forgotten by the citadel's string of necromantic occupants. His predecessors had made it a charnel house for torturing the souls out of innocent people. The Rime Witch made it a crematorium for all the animals of Kharayan Tor. Gethen demolished one wall and made it a shelter for the animals slowly repopulating his forest.

He strode across the bailey and through a narrow gate to the cemetery. He rounded the long wall of the basilica — half buried by time and the rambling vines of ebonberry bushes — and moved among the graves.

Every shadow mage had taken an apprentice. Every apprentice had murdered their master and buried their body here.

Including Gethen.

Stone cairns, crumbling wooden stakes, or nothing at all marked the graves — generations of mages rotted and ruined in service to Skiron, thrown into holes and forgotten by time. "So much wasted mastery," he muttered.

He stopped at the stake he'd driven into Shemel's grave, right where he'd guessed his master's heart would've been had the man possessed one. He'd carved the name into the wood, splinters sliding beneath his skin — Shemel's vengeance hurting him even after he'd stabbed the man to death and dumped his carcass in a hole.

He bared his teeth then spat on the weeds beneath his feet. "Still plaguing me, Pudding Prick?"

Shadows flitted around him. They hissed his name and willed Gethen to join them in the cold of their misery. They were power shackled, awaiting a commander, an unstoppable, immortal army anchored to the tor beneath Ranith's foundation.

Why had the Shadow Army been formed? Which mad mage had deigned to lead such a terrible force? Which one had the power to leash it?

With an army of undead shadow mages and their wraiths at her command, Halina could crush Waldram's forces. She could free Lokshin from Shemel's grip and send Teleyansk's army home. She could ensure Princess Federika Janne Boorsook became the legitimate ruler of Nalvika. She could free Besera, banish the shrikers, and restore her brother's senses. Halina could restore peace to Quoregna.

But that army shouldn't leave the tor no matter how much the shadow mages wished it. The anchor chaining the shades to Kharayan existed for the protection of all four kingdoms.

Many months ago Gethen had wondered if the Sun Mage could release the army. The Rime Witch had proven it was possible. Doubtless Shemel would harness their power as soon as he had enough of his own to overcome Gethen's wards.

"I don't think so, you rotting pillock," he said. "If anyone is going to wield this army, it will be me."

"No, Sun Mage."

He looked toward the basilica. A golden glow emanated from within its depths, the source of the voice.

"Sulwen." He crossed the graveyard and entered the columned space. Stopping on the square where an altar once stood, he considered the glow surrounding him, the spirit of the only other Sun Mage to have existed before him. "Why not?" he demanded.

"Because that army is not for you or any other mage to command."

"Then whose is it? Who formed that force?"

"You do not want to take that path." Steel crept into the former Sun Mage's disembodied voice, a dangerous tone Gethen had never heard before. *"That power will destroy you and everything you love."*

"Why?"

"They were not chained for you."

"Who then?" Silence. "Answer me, Sulwen!"

As if struck by lightning, a shock shot from his feet to his brain and Gethen hit the floor. The wind burst from his lungs. Gasping and struggling to regain his breath, he opened his eyes to the colorless nightmare of the Void.

"Me." A woman's hand reached out to him. A scarred hand with halved fingers. Gethen refused it and stood on his own. Skiron wore Halina's appearance again. "They were chained for me," the god said, "just as you are."

Gethen crossed his arms. "You don't control me."

"Don't I?" The god raised Halina's hand and considered her halved fingers. "Did your woman convince you of that?"

"You fear my power."

"Fool!" Skiron seized Gethen's throat and lifted him off the ground, shook him like a rag doll, and threw him a dozen feet to land in a heap. Immediately hovering over him as he started to rise, the God of Death pressed a booted foot against Gethen's chest, slamming him back into the Void's dust. "Don't you see? The evidence of your failure comes right from her lying mouth. Even your own woman diminishes our existence. To you no less!" Skiron's form morphed into something black, bloody, hideous, a mass of rotting flesh, scrabbling claws, gnashing teeth. The god pressed Gethen into the Void's grave-dust ground and breathed into his face, the putrescence of death and decay. "Lies. Deceit. Atheism meant to discredit us, ruin us, relegate us to insignificance. She would make us no more than superstition, fables, and engravings upon the oldest tombs!"

Gethen's ribs cracked. Pain knifed him and air refused to fill his lungs. He struggled to escape Skiron's boot, but the god yanked him to his feet, once more wearing Halina's visage. "If you do not restore the mortal world's fear and respect for the gods, I will slaughter Halina Persinna Rhyshis, and I will use your hands to do it."

"No!"

Changing form again, Skiron's skull elongated and grew a wide rack of antlers. Gone was Halina's armored figure. Instead, the god's white flesh sloughed off in chunks and strips, splattering the ground with viscous fluid, raising puffs of dust with each splat. His fingers became long and bony. Skiron spoke, revealing bleached bone and jagged teeth in an all-too-familiar stag skull. "Yes. You. Will." Blood frothed from the god's mouth and nostrils.

"You cannot force me to do this."

With a gesture, Skiron's fingers transformed into vapor. They wormed up Gethen's nose.

He roared as the vapor filled his throat and lungs. His brain turned from love to bloodlust. He immediately grasped the power available to him if only he ended Halina's life. He could easily take her blood magic, summon the Shadow Army, and march across Quoregna, leaving death and suffering in his wake. All souls would empower him. He would be Skiron's Sword, death incarnate. He would bring the straying flock back to their shepherds, send them scurrying to Khotyr for protection, Semele for succor. The world would burn, bleed, bow before him, and break beneath his feet.

"And the Shadow Army? I like this idea," a seductive voice whispered in his mind. "Use that force, Sun Mage, and I will allow your woman's soul to exist separate from you. She will be your general, a puppet obeying her master and her gods. Eternally enslaved by you, fulfilling your every desire, yours to bend and break."

The god released him and Gethen fell to his knees. His mind cleared, leaving only despair over a cursed fate he never wanted.

Skiron had adopted Halina's form again. The god pulled him up, pressed her body against him and purred, "I look forward to the carnage."

"Spare Halina and I will do this for you."

"Oh, you will do it." Skiron stepped back and turned in profile to him, hands behind Halina's back. "I have no doubt. After all, your power only exists to conquer Quoregna."

"She doesn't have to die."

"Of course she does. She's mortal. Just. Like. You." Skiron turned further away but peered at him, Halina's head twisting at an unnatural angle. "Don't disappoint me, Gethen of Ranith." He pivoted back to face Gethen and bared Halina's teeth. "Or I'll burn your heart out. Burn it and keep you alive to suffer."

Skiron raised Halina's hand and snapped her fingers.

Gethen was sprawled on the basilica's floor. Struggling for breath again, he peered into darkness. The sun had set. Sulwen's light was gone. And he would be too, if he failed his mad god.

He rolled onto his back and stared. He wasn't alone.

Halina stood over him, encased in her blood armor, sword in hand. She was guarding his body, just as she'd promised to all those months ago. And she looked mad enough to chew anvils and spit nails.

TWENTY-EIGHT

Halina had awakened to find Gethen gone, and a quick search of the tower had proven he'd left Ranith with Odruna, Marja, the children, and the blaids. Before she could use the ambit to reach him, Thak and Eugen had intercepted her.

"You can't leave," Thaksin had said.

"Of course I can."

"No, Your Ladyship, please don't." Eugen had touched her arm, something he rarely did. "Your husband asks you to remain here, for the safety of the children."

Then she'd remembered Gethen's suspicions. As much as his distrust hurt, she didn't hate him for it. He was right. Waldram had tracked her. Who knew how much her mad second cousin could glean from her mind without her being aware of the intrusion? The thought chilled her.

When Gethen had returned hours later, she was relieved and newly angry.

She'd gone in search of him, snapping and snarling, until she found him lying flat in the basilica. Had Waldram and

Shemel reached him through her? Grief and horror had rushed through her, leaving cold sweat in their wake.

Then Gethen had twitched and groaned, revealing he was in the Void.

So she'd stood guard over him as the sun set and the basilica darkened.

Deer and birds, squirrels, and rodents arrived and bedded down for the night, undisturbed by their presence.

Pain and rage crossed his face. His teeth gnashed and ground. His fists clenched. He suffered and struggled for hours.

Halina could only watch and wait, an agonizing vigil.

Finally, Gethen drew a ragged, wheezing breath, rolled over, and opened his eyes to meet her gaze.

"Are the children safe?" Her voice echoed from the marble walls and ceiling. It sounded as hard and cold as they were.

"Yes," he rasped.

She pursed her lips. "I was beginning to think you weren't coming back."

He blinked and wiped sweat from his face. "Relieved to be wrong?"

She squatted. Face-to-face with her husband and filled with an anger spawned by fear and helplessness, she replied, "If you ever skulk off like that again, I'll gut you, Lord Rhyshis."

He sat up and spat blood. "I believe you, Lady Rhyshis. But I had to get them away from you."

She bit back an angry reply. There was nothing to say to that painful truth.

Standing, swaying, he pulled her into his arms and buried his face in her hair. He was shaking.

All her anger left her, worry taking its place. "What's wrong?" This wasn't like him.

"Skiron has made me such a threat to you." He shook his

head and tightened his grip. "Gods, Halina, I can't lose you. And I can't see a way out of this disaster."

"We discussed this, picked apart Skiron's manipulation."

He rambled on as if he hadn't heard her. "Skiron's Sword. That's what he wants me to be. An apocalypse to drive the populace into Khotyr and Semele's arms, power fueled by the blood magic I'll tear out of you." He groaned, pressed his fists to his eyes. "Ah, gods, Halina! You don't know how seductive that vision was." His voice dropped to a pained whisper, "The power of it. The beautiful madness in all that destruction!"

"Gethen?" She shook him, frightened by the haunted, hungry look in his eyes when he met her gaze. "Why are you giving him power over you?"

"Giving?" He laughed, a wild edge to it, and paced away from her, running his hands through his hair. "You don't understand. There's no giving, only taking. The stag, the Rime Witch, the wraith in the woods. Shemel's survival, Yisun's attack. All of this has been Skiron's doing! It was all designed to drive us together and put my hands around your throat." He clenched his fists.

"You're not making sense."

"Yes, I am." He faced her. "And that's the worst part. It all makes perfect, horrible sense." He strode from the basilica into the graveyard. She followed. Gethen kicked a rock. It skittered and bounced across the darkened ground, pinged off a stone grave marker and spun into the ebonberry bushes. "I came here to ask Sulwen about the Shadow Army. Instead, Skiron dragged me into the Void."

She didn't understand what had swayed him back to his belief in the gods' power over him. "So you spoke with the god again. So what?"

"So what?" He stalked back to her and seized her shoulders. "So your very existence is meant to push me into a frenzy!" His mouth pressed into a thin line before he finished, "Disbelief, yours and the rest of Quoregna's, is the reason for all of this."

"I'm to blame?"

He looked stunned then contrite and shook his head. "Atheism is to blame. The growing belief in the One God is to blame. You're just a beautiful, seductive tool."

She crossed her arms and stared at him, trying to understand his sudden mania. Weeds grew between the rocks at her feet, obscuring the grave of some long-dead necromancer. "I need an army, and you thought to summon the Shadow Army?"

"Yes. An army that can end this conflict quickly and decisively."

"But Skiron...blocked you?"

"No." He laughed bitterly. "Oh, no. He encouraged me to use them. He showed me what will happen if I do." Gethen closed his eyes, but the horror of it showed on his face. He opened them and held her gaze, his eyes no less haunted. "You'll die."

"You don't know that."

"Yes, I do," he said. "Skiron drove you into my arms because your blood magic is powerful. Your death at my hands is inevitable. Once I summon the Shadow Army, the desire for necromantic power will drive me mad. I'll take souls, Halina. So many...yours, my brother's, Magod's, anyone's and everyone's to fuel my addiction to power. Harnessing that army means releasing my worst impulses. I'll make Waldram look like a blessing." He leaned heavily against a crooked tree. "But if I don't summon the Shadow Army, Waldram and Shemel will do it instead. They'll enslave Quoregna and destroy everyone and everything I love." Gethen scrubbed his hands over his face. "Gods! I need a way out of this!"

Halina was silent for a long moment. "Quoregna doesn't need gods who exist only if we destroy ourselves to preserve them."

"They fear irrelevancy."

Her gaze fell on him. "They fear *you*. You keep forgetting that."

Gethen opened his mouth to reply then winced and looked toward the forest.

"What's wrong?" she asked.

"Something just slammed against my ward." He strode into the basilica, pushed through its interior doors, and jogged up the narrow hallway that led into the citadel's tower. She followed, trepidation souring her gut like spoiled milk. He climbed the wide, winding staircase, taking the steps two at a time. They passed his still room, passed the guest quarters, and his own fourth-floor chamber.

He stopped before a door leading to the fifth and sixth floors, areas of the citadel long disused, cursed and destroyed by one of his overly ambitious predecessors. Another gesture and a murmured incantation opened the door to reveal a narrow, dark stairwell. Lighting the way with mage fire, they passed the fifth floor landing, gaps in the walls letting in cold air and making cobwebs sway.

They reached the top floor. There was no roof, only the skeleton of one made from shattered wooden beams. Gethen's arm blocked her from crossing the threshold.

"The floor is unstable and missing in large sections." He edged around the perimeter of the round tower until he reached the remains of a window, its ledge long gone. Gethen sent up a large sphere of mage fire to illuminate the forest and beyond. He scanned the distance.

Halina chafed beside him, unable to see past his broad back. "Well?"

He ushered her toward the doorway and stairs. "Waldram and your dear brother stand at the edge of Kharayan's wards.

Their armies are setting up camp between the tor and the Silver Sea, a force stretching as far as I could see."

"How? How could they have reached Ranith so soon?"

With a bitter smile, he replied, "The same way we did."

Their footsteps echoed in the narrow stairwell. "Waldram moved two full armies using a travel incantation?" She couldn't believe he'd gained that much skill.

At the fourth floor landing, Gethen leaned heavily against the closed stairwell door. "Our enemy has grown more powerful with the addition of countless innocent souls."

"Bollocks! Great big bollocky bollocks!"

"Indeed. Your second cousin has grown quite a pair."

Halina would've laughed if she wasn't torn between rage and despair. She exhaled a slow breath. "What does it take to lead the Shadow Army?"

His gaze sharpened. "What? No. I won't even consider it."

"Not you. Me. What do I need to do?"

"Forget it. I won't do that, Halina." He slashed the air with his hand. "Don't ask me to."

She lifted her chin. "I have experience leading thousands of soldiers into battle."

"I don't care. What you're considering is suicide. Even yoked by your blood magic, that army will burn through you. You can't control that much power."

"How long?"

"Until what?"

"Until I'm used up."

He stared at her like she'd lost her sanity. "Have I not made this clear? The only way you can hold the reins of that army is with your blood magic, but they will strip every last trace of it from your body and you will die." He grabbed her arm. "I won't let you do this."

"You have no choice. I need an army, Gethen, and I need it now."

He shook his head, his breath heavy and fast.

"Our only possible ally was corrupted and now sides with Waldram. No one else is coming. No. One. We can't hold out forever. We can't keep running and we can't hide behind Ranith's wards while Quoregna burns. I *won't*. The battle comes to a head here where it began. If Skiron wants a war, I'll give it to him. But once Waldram's and Ilker's forces are routed, I'll relinquish that power. That's something you can't promise. That's what Skiron showed you. Right?"

"You'll die before you can finish the fight. Halina, you're asking me to sacrifice you just like Skiron predicted."

"No, not like he predicted. By your own admission, you can't be the one to control the Shadow Army. But I can. I'll pay a price either way. At least their frenzy will be short-lived under my command. We both know that won't be the case if you lead them." She grabbed his arm. "Summon the army, Gethen, and let's finish this war."

"No. This is reckless. You're being reckless because you're afraid to fail."

The words stood between them, a wall of truth, tall and wide, as slippery as Kharaton Castle's ancient, mossy taluses.

Rage burned up her spine and set her mind afire. But it smothered as quickly as it had flared and left a cold nausea in its wake. Gethen saw through her. Of course he did. Just like he had the night they'd met, when he conquered her hubris with the simplest spell, a twist of her mind that had unveiled the thing driving her — fear of failure.

But she had no more hubris, no more secrets. Of course he knew her greatest fear. She wouldn't let that stop her. She couldn't. The Rime Witch had summoned the Shadow Army and nearly taken control of it. She'd shown it could be done.

"You're right. I *am* afraid to fail. Because if I do, the whole world will fail with me. Everyone and everything I love will suffer and die or worse." She pulled him closer. "You can't stand to lose me? Well, I can't stand to lose you either. And I can't do nothing when there's even the slightest hope in this suicidal plan. I would rather die knowing you'll live than live only to watch you and everyone else suffer and die."

Gethen stared into her eyes. His head lowered, jaw clenched. But when he met her gaze again, there was steel in his eyes. "*I* will summon them and *I* will control them. Not you."

Halina followed him back into the basilica. "But can you control yourself?" She caught his arm and pushed him against Ranith's stone wall. She stared into her husband's haunted eyes and asked, "Can you let all that power go once you've harnessed it?"

"I'll have to."

She searched his gaze and found his certainty lacking. But Halina held her tongue.

Once more they returned to the basilica. Once more Gethen made his way to the rectangle of golden marble that marked where an altar had stood long ago.

The sounds of soldiers and steeds joined the cries of sea crows, a distant cacophony rising up the cliffs and filtering through the woods.

He lit the space with a dozen drifting balls of mage fire. They hung in midair, defying nature and testifying to his command. He met her gaze. "I want you to leave, but I know you won't."

"My place is beside you and between my friends and my foes."

He sighed and walked a circle around her, twice following the path of the clock and moving once against it to lock the spell. "Don't speak and don't move. Do nothing to draw the shadows' attention to you." He stepped into the center of the altar square and closed his eyes. He stretched his arms out to his sides and began a low incantation in the oldest of Quoregna's tongues.

A susurrus spell, Gethen's words beckoned the shadows that flickered and danced upon the distant walls. They surged forward to surround him and Halina. Black vapor oozed through cracks in the marble flooring and coalesced into forms — generals and officers armed with black swords, long-dead shadow mages chained to Kharayan Tor for just this purpose.

Gethen's black armor formed to his body, fashioned from magic and the shadows that had so long haunted him. The ranks of soldiers increased with each word, writhing, demonic shadows clamoring to be freed from their bonds.

Halina had seen this army before, summoned by the Rime Witch with malevolent intent and banished into the ether by Gethen's sun sorcery. She never thought she'd see her husband call them to his side. The sepulchral tones of his voice, the black-death stare of his eyes chilled her more surely than time spent in the Void had.

He'd warned her not to attract the shadows. But if she stood by and allowed him to take control of this army, he would lose himself to necromancy's seductive power, and she would lose him forever.

The shadowy ranks grew and Gethen's voice deepened, his expression changed as desire crept into it. His focus locked onto her, predatory and deadly. She shivered. She'd seen that hungry look before and her husband had warned her away then. He'd said he was the greatest danger to her.

Now she truly felt it.

And Skiron wanted this. The God of Death craved this very outcome, Herra Tomruma harnessing the Shadow Army, killing her, and conquering the world.

Halina swallowed. She couldn't let Gethen command this

force, even if stopping him meant forfeiting her life. Praying her blood magic would be an enticement too great to resist, she stepped from the protective circle, raised her misericord, and sliced her palm.

"Follow me," she said, putting all her years of command into those words. "I am your marshal. Follow me and I will give you my blood magic."

"Blood and bones, Halina!" Gethen snarled, but it was too late. He couldn't undo her offering. Shock replaced the hunger on his face.

The shadows surrounded her. Their strength beat through her, amplified her heartbeat and the power of her own wild magic. The Shadow Army faced her, their numbers growing as they surged through the gaps in the basilica's ancient floor. They spilled into the dark graveyard, surrounded the citadel, and spread into the village and forest.

Foremost were the souls of dead shadow mages, skeletal wisps wrapped in gloom. They reached for her hand. Their nebulous fingers passed through her flesh and pulled ethereal red wisps of magic from the blood pooling in her palm. As they absorbed the magic, they gained solidity and became corporeal once again. Smiling bony, rictus grins, they raised their hands and marveled at their solid, gray flesh. Drawing swords and armor from the shadows, each saluted her.

This was the power Waldram desired most — an undead army answering to him alone, loyal to him by the fact of their very existence. It was the power Shemel sought, to become flesh once more, marshal an army of his peers, and rule over the mortal realm as a demigod empowered by the souls of dead innocents. And it was the power Gethen never asked for and didn't want, the power he feared to wield and feared would destroy her.

The marble floor and walls shivered as the army moved in

formation. Halina led them through the opening of the building, into the graveyard, the army she so desperately needed.

She looked back. Gethen stood upon the marble square, his shoulders bowed, eyes no longer blackened by necromantic magic but, instead, haunted by sadness.

Halina reached out to him. "Help me."

He shook his head. "To kill yourself? No."

She'd been right. Her blood magic was more compelling to the Shadow Army than Gethen's sun magic was. He needed necromancy and death to control them. Or he needed her blood magic. Skiron knew that. The god counted on it. Either way, the God of Death would reap the chaos his servant would sow. Like Shemel and Waldram, Gethen could maintain the army indefinitely by drawing upon the power of innocent souls. That was Waldram's plan. It's why he'd used shrikers to capture children's souls. And he'd almost succeeded.

"I can't let you be Skiron's monster," she said. "Please understand."

"I do, Halina. I understand you'll kill yourself to protect the world from me." Gethen's shoulders slumped. His chin slowly sank to his chest and he gave a sad little nod. "I'm sorry."

There was nothing more to say.

She swallowed a lump and turned away. Her chest felt heavy and her gut knotted as she followed the path to the bailey. She was leaving Gethen behind, and he was letting her go. She slowed and looked over her shoulder. He was there, watching, his gaze unflinching. She wanted to turn, go back to him. She wanted to tell him it was a mistake, that they'd find another way. But...she couldn't. And he let her leave.

Shadow riders appeared in the woods, mounted on black horses, animals made of shadows and bones, death made substantial. One brought such a horse to her. Halina mounted. With a last look at her husband, she wheeled the horse around and kicked it to a gallop. She led her army of dead sorcerers and shadowy wraiths through Ranith Village and down the ancient path into the woods that surrounded Gethen's citadel.

She didn't ride out to face her brother and cousin with thoughts of glory. She rode with hopes for peace and with a heavy heart, resigned to her own death and the death of her marriage.

TWENTY-NINE

"**I** can't let you be Skiron's monster."

Gethen followed Halina and her dead army through Kharayan Woods, wracking his brain for a solution to their problem. He paced their fringes as black night turned to pale morning. His throat was dry, but his palms were sweaty and he rubbed them on his trouzes. He couldn't accept her decision to lead the Shadow Army. Her death wasn't an inescapable fate, not if he had any say in the matter.

She could control the shadow mages only for as long as she remained alive, and with them draining her blood magic, her life was a dwindling resource. Her army wouldn't obey anyone but her and they'd protect her from all threats. Including Gethen because he was powerful enough to sever the bond she'd created.

Unfortunately, so were Waldram and Shemel.

If his adversaries reached her before this battle ended, they'd tear the Shadow Army from her control, then no amount of sun magic would stop Shemel from destroying the world.

Gethen cloaked himself in the forest's shadows and lurked at the ward's edge, surveying the invading force and watching his wife as she awaited King Ilker and King Waldram. Duesh and Gwyn circled him, agitated by the shifting powers and threats. "Stay with her," he said. They obeyed, disappearing into shadows and light.

Sunlight sparkled upon the Silver Sea's waves and a strong breeze fought the tents as Nalvika's and Ursinum's soldiers erected a sprawling camp. Thin clouds scudded across the light-blue sky, their bellies aglow with the rising sun's amber light. That same hue colored the wet shoreline as blue-gray waves rolled in. Gethen inhaled. Crisp salt air and the astringent sweetness of pine mingled with the stench of unwashed bodies, the pungent tang of cook fires, the stink of anxiety and excitement.

Once before an army had camped upon these scrubby, windswept hillsides and rocky shores. That had been King Vernard's force, and it had ushered Halina into his life. Now he fervently hoped another army wouldn't take her away.

Ilker and Waldram thought to lay siege to Kharayan Tor, which meant Waldram couldn't break Gethen's wards.

"Of course not," he murmured. Waldram's plan had been to come to Ranith with Shemel to expel Gethen from the citadel and take the Shadow Army, but Shemel had abandoned him for Lokshin. "Why settle for being a king when you can be a god?"

The army continued to march into view, the clang and stomp of their armored feet carried on the shifting wind. Horses whinnied. Wagons creaked. The kings' banners snapped at the wind like dogs chasing bees. The clonk of mallets on wooden stakes and shouts of soldiers vied with the groans of the trees around Gethen and the sharp cries of circling sea crows. Already the encamping army was ten thousand strong and many thousands more crawled over the hills and roads toward Ranith Citadel like ants marching resolutely toward some promised morsel.

On the path below, Waldram and Ilker halted their destriers

before Halina. Nalvika's murderous king scanned the dark forest behind her as his horse fought the bit, pawing the ground and flattening its ears.

"Where's your sorcerous husband, cousin? Drowned in some distant lake?"

"I told him to stay out of this," she said.

"Why?" Ilker asked, surprise and suspicion at war in his expression.

"Because Skiron was too keen on Gethen's participation and that's an ill omen," Halina replied. "I prefer not to have the God of Death lurking too close to a battlefield when I'm upon it."

She'd dispelled her blood armor before clearing the forest. The wind lifted her unbound hair in a capricious dance, and the shriker scar on her left cheek stood out, as red, jagged, and angry as its owner.

"Sister, lay down your sword and shield. You stand alone against thirty thousand."

She bared her teeth, looking like a rabid fox in search of a coney. "I'm not alone, Ilker. The soldiers and mages under my command have allegiance to me alone. They fight for no king or kingdom, and they kill only for the power of death." She glanced at Waldram and added, "Something our cousin will appreciate before he dies."

Waldram's gaze went from her to the darkened forest and his eyes narrowed as they searched. He returned his attention to her and sneered. "Her mind is broken."

"Open your eyes, Halina!" Ilker pleaded. "You have no armor, no warhorse, and no army behind you."

"And there's a stolen kingdom behind you," she snapped back. "Are you ignorant or are you so spellbound that you haven't noticed your ally has taken Tatlis, brother?"

"You've been fed lies." He thrust his gloved hand forward. "Surrender now and I will guarantee your safety."

She laughed and the sound carried across the trampled hillside, rolled through the spreading camp, and floated out to sea. "Ilker, you idiot. Don't make promises Waldram won't let you keep."

Gethen scanned the camp, picking out the first threat to his wife and her shadowy force; hedge witches and necromancers, made obvious by the wide berth the soldiers gave their tents. Among the hundred or so stood a handful of weather witches, their flowing robes and blue-painted faces calling them out. "So some survived." Seven altogether. "Not for long." More than any of the other mages, they endangered Halina's success. Once they realized she'd marshaled the Shadow Army, they'd summon clouds to block the sun. Without sunlight to define them, the shadows would be swallowed by darkness and her army would lose strength and cohesion.

His first task was to kill the witches. He recognized two of the women, Birgitta and her adult daughter, Enna. He'd sold them unguents and metheglin and had shared a bed with both. He liked them, but they'd made themselves a threat. Perhaps they'd bartered their knowledge and skills for their lives. Regrettable that they now had to die. "You should've come to me," he muttered. "We could've helped each other."

He closed his eyes and felt for the currents of warm and cool air swirling around the tor. Yes, the power was there for the taking, and this time Gethen Rhysh would tap the magic that had lived in him since birth. This time he'd do it without souls and without Halina's blood magic.

This time he had no other options.

Halina stood in her stirrups and called to the gathering army, her voice carrying down the long slope and across the trampled field. "Soldiers of Ursinum! Conscripts of Nalvika! Surrender your weapons and turn away from the battlefield. You have only one chance to save your souls. I offer it to you now!"

Ursinum's soldiers shifted among their ranks and a murmur spread, but their commanders called them to order. A few broke rank, men and women who'd served Halina in Khara and during the War of the Winds.

Thaksin and Eugen appeared at the edge of the forest. Spying their captains siding with their former margrave, a group of militairs spurred their horses forward, breaking formation and taking a line of infantry with them. More of Khara's troops followed, moving away from the main force, but not enough. Too many were loyal to their king. Halina didn't blame them, though she was gratified to see any take her side. Few Nalviks fled. Drunk with their victories in Besera and northern Ursinum, the career soldiers laughed, jeered, and offered her rude gestures. A handful of conscripts tried to defect and were gutted by their commanders. Their grisly deaths dissuaded others from believing her nebulous threat.

Ilker urged his horse forward, but she drew her sword and pointed it at him. "I hate that I can't trust you," she said, "but Waldram has blinded you to reason and reality."

"Stop this," he commanded. "You're tearing Quoregna apart."

"Impossible. You've already done that." Her voice's edge was as sharp as her blade's. "Ilker, please do as I ask. Leave while you still can." She lowered the weapon, wheeled her horse, and galloped back toward the forest as he called after her.

"Don't be a fool, Halina! You have no chance!"

Nalvika's laughter filled the air. The army clattered their swords and axes against their shields, a clangor meant to scare their lone enemy.

Idiots, she thought. As if the sounds of battle could scare the

Red Blade away from her target. Nothing would stop her from killing Waldram. Nothing but her own death.

She turned the black horse at the stone ward line to face the sea of soldiers. A seething mass of steel and flesh stared up at her, awaiting their chance to kill her, led astray by a madman and a fool.

"Gveed, enaith, a cysgud, amdivin vi ad vy engilenion." Her voice rang out as she prepared for the most important battle of her life. Shadows swirled around her and blood magic flared, turning the world dark red for a heartbeat.

Recognizing the spell, Waldram cursed and spurred his horse toward the camp. Ilker stared at Halina, his mouth hanging open. "Blasphemy!" he cried, his face ashen. He sat deep in his saddle, backed his horse, then turned the gelding and followed Nalvika's king without a backwards glance.

A wave of astonished cries replaced the jeers and clatter of weapons. It spread through the camp and hillside as Ursinum's and Nalvika's soldiers witnessed Halina's blood armor forming around her, ribbons of blood-red shadow encasing her body. As the crimson armor settled, Halina raised her hand and called forth her forces. "Shadows, take my blood magic and kill anyone who raises a weapon against me. Spare any who surrender."

Howls rent the air. The forest's darkness came to life and streamed outward, an army of wraiths followed by their commanders, undead necromancers eager for souls.

More enemy soldiers broke rank. Some Ursinians followed Khara's defectors. Others fled along the pebbled shore.

A rush of greedy desire overwhelmed Halina. She looked out at the field and saw through the dead eyes of a thousand necromancers. Souls for the taking, souls to enslave. With that many souls, she could obliterate any army, rule any kingdom. With all the spirits in the world at her disposal, she could be a god.

Halina shook her head to clear that savage vision. Godhood

wasn't why she'd taken the Shadow Army from Gethen. She wasn't a necromancer. She couldn't actually wield her own blood magic and she had no means of replenishing it. Once the army burned through her, she would die. Her husband had made that crystal clear.

The undead army swirled around her, pulsing with power as they siphoned away her magic. She spurred the shadow horse forward and the Shadow Army surged. Halina saw darkness, madness, and the wide-eyed fear of the soldiers on the slopes below her.

The ground shook with the feet of thousands of men charging toward, and running from, her army. The thunder of hooves, clank of metal, and creak of leather were lost to the howls and screeches of a thousand wraiths. Mortal horses shied, terrified of their nebulous shifting forms, the claws, jaws, and screaming demon faces that made up the monstrosities.

Weapons passed through the wraiths, leaving no damage. Yet the ghostly creatures gained solid form when they struck back, cutting off screams, spraying blood, crunching bones. The massive monsters flowed across the battlefield, undeterred by the puny weapons of men. As mortal soldiers fell, dead necromancers swept down the hill behind the wraiths, pulling souls from dying bodies, the whole mad army tethered to Halina, directed through the reins of her blood magic.

Gethen watched his wife as she kept to the slope's higher ground, her destrier pacing as she oversaw her force's attack. Her expression remained impassive, but she had first-hand experience with the murderous strength of a necromancer's wraith. It had been one of Gethen's forest guards and he saw her shoulders twitch as the monsters bashed their way through

Ursinum's and Nalvika's forces. Gethen wondered if she felt each blow and mourned the loss of each life as it passed from flesh into the grasp of a soul-sucking necromancer.

He didn't want to remember his wife broken and bleeding on that horrible day. A cloud passed over the sun, and he looked up. Storm clouds gathered, an unnatural vortex directly over the battlefield. He found the black tents clustered together at the bottom of the hill, housing the weather witches, hedge witches, and mages recruited by Waldram. They'd blot out the sun and weaken the Shadow Army.

"Unwise to take shelter," he murmured.

The maelstrom of volatile air the weather witches believed was their weapon offered an opportunity for Gethen to strike a killing blow. He closed his eyes and reached toward the clouds, felt for the currents within them, the wild air crashing together in the sky. Potential sparked there, the buzz of power building. He'd have only one chance at this. But Waldram had been a fool to let his sorcerers cluster together, an easy target.

He reached for the buzzing currents, twisted them together, and directed a bolt of lightning down toward the black tents. It struck with a deafening crack. Horses threw their riders. Men and beasts dropped dead, victims of lightning that spread like a lethal web of heat and light. Others survived, but lay dazed, burned, and bruised. Waldram's witch tents blazed. Screams erupted from them as witches burned beneath the flaming canvas.

Taking that as her unspoken cue, Halina charged down the hill and entered the fray, her weapon swinging, her black horse crushing soldiers beneath its heavy hooves. She'd traded her sword for a war hammer and crushed skulls as efficiently as the wraiths did, the sound like melons hitting the ground from a great height. She rode down soldiers, spurring her steed to keep charging, never slowing enough for her enemies to grab hold of her. Blows glanced off her armor and that armor strengthened as it pulled blood from her dying foes. Like a queen's cape, the blood flowed up from the fallen bodies and encased her, a cloak of death and gore.

But while the blood energized the armor's underlying ambit, it did nothing to strengthen Halina. The Shadow Army drew out her blood magic, straining her tenuous control and draining her. Her magic was inextricably tied to her soul. As one was depleted, so too was the other.

Two cavaliers charged her just as Halina planted the pick end of her hammer into the helmeted skull of a Nalvik captain. Her horse pivoted and reared, snapping its teeth and striking out at the attacking militars. Gethen's heart lodged in his throat as he watched his wife counter her attackers. The hammer tore from her grasp, remaining embedded in the dying man's skull as he collapsed, but she summoned her sword and countered the blows with ease. She ducked one man's swing and stuck her sword through the other attacker's open visor as her horse reared again, pawing at their enemy.

She spurred the animal forward and escaped being caught by another pair of Nalvik militars, charging the field without concern for the men and women falling beneath her dead beast's hooves. This was war. They'd had their chance to flee. They'd made their choice and would die for it.

The Nalvik and Ursinian armies were in disarray as most soldiers tried to flee the army of wraiths and their necromantic commanders. Caught between the Silver Sea, the attacking force, and the rest of their arriving army, many soldiers threw down their weapons and ran north along the rocky shoreline. Some were cut down by their own commanders. Others clustered together, trying to repel the wraiths with weapons that were ineffective against creatures made of nightmares and suffering.

Gethen searched the field for his wife, her brother, and their insane cousin.

Ilker was in the midst of the fray on a small rise, more a hindrance than a help to his militairs. Halina rode straight for him, determination on her face.

And Waldram was nowhere to be found.

Halina met her brother mid-field. Their horses circled. She held her weapon ready, but it trembled in her grip. The Shadow Army was draining her faster than the battle was being decided. If she hoped to survive, she needed to score a decisive blow to dishearten the Nalviks and Ursinians and force their surrender or their retreat. She prayed that blow wouldn't be taking her brother's life.

"The day is lost to you, Ilker," she proclaimed, the strength of her voice defying the weakness of her body.

He removed his helm and stared. "You can't be my sister. She's not a gore-soaked witch, clad in armor made from blood and magic."

"Please, Ilker, leave the field. Don't make me kill you," she pleaded. "You're the only brother I have left."

He slowly shook his head, but he didn't raise his sword. "I won't fight you, Halina. Queen Ambrosine doesn't want us to fight. And I never wanted it to come to this. Why couldn't you just return to Tatlis and meet with the queen and me? We could've avoided all this needless suffering and chaos!"

She swallowed. "Ambrosine, Ianthe, and Prince Vernard are dead, Ilker. Waldram's shrikers murdered them at Gwyncardarnlei."

He blanched. "More lies from your mage?"

"Nalvika burned Tatlis while you were doing Waldram's

bidding in Besera like a slavering lapdog. He brought the war to Emelin. Tatlis, Khara, Floria, they're all ash!"

Ilker bared his teeth at her. "The Sun Mage burned Tatlis. I have that on authority—"

"Whose? Waldram's?"

Shouts rose above the fray. They drew her attention and Ilker's followed.

Waldram spurred his horse across the field toward Ursinum's only surviving rulers, a snarl on his lips, the white stag on his tabard stained red. Nalvik militairs surrounded him. Outrage followed in his wake and Halina forgot her brother, stunned by the sight of Queen Ambrosine in the saddle before Nalvika's king.

She looked back at Ilker. "You brought the queen into battle? Are you insane?"

"I don't...I didn't!" He shook his head, his astonishment no less than hers.

Waldram halted on the other side of Ilker's destrier. He smiled at Halina. "I have a proposition, cousin."

Her sword hand steadied. "I didn't come here to bargain with you, pillock. I've heard enough of the dog's drivel that spills from your mouth. Release Her Highness and withdraw from Ursinum's borders."

Ignoring her demands, Waldram said, "A queen for a princess. Give me Federika and I'll release Ambrosine."

The queen's gaze was steady, her chin held high. "I won't be a pawn, you insolent puke." She looked from Halina to Ilker and added, "Do not agree to his terms."

"Release Her Highness, Waldram," Ilker commanded.

"Don't think you can hide Federika in Teleyansk, Halina." Waldram grinned like a mad dog. "I'll have my daughter's soul. She's mine to use as I please!"

Cold crawled up Halina's spine. Did he know where Feddie

was? She shook her head. No, he was bluffing. *She* didn't even know the girl's location.

Behind them, confusion spread as Ursinum's soldiers spied their queen on the field. They moved toward her en masse, abandoning their Nalvik allies. Chaos spread among the Nalvik troops as the attacking Shadow Army surged into the gap created by the shift of the Ursinian forces.

Halina looked down her nose at her second cousin. "There'll be no trade."

"I hoped you'd say that." Waldram shoved Ambrosine from the saddle and drew his sword. Ilker was off his horse in an instant, but Ambrosine was no helpless old woman. She dodged Waldram's blade and brandished his own dagger, stolen from its sheath at his waist.

"End this," she said to her son then thrust the dagger under Waldram's tasset and into his hip. He roared and his backswing slammed into her skull with a sickening crunch.

"No!" Ilker and Halina shouted. Queen Ambrosine gasped and collapsed as her son bellowed.

Ilker lunged toward his mother. Waldram snarled and thrust his sword at Ursinum's king. Ilker jerked sideways, but the blade sliced across his eyes. He screamed and grabbed his face. Blood erupted between his fingers.

"Pathetic!" Waldram snarled. "Your weakness was crippling me!" He brought his sword back to finish Ilker, but Halina's longsword intercepted the blow.

Ilker's militairs moved to his defense even as Ursinum's own troops came for their king and queen. With a curse for Halina, Waldram yanked the dagger from his hip and spurred his horse away.

Ilker pitched forward. Halina dismounted and grabbed her brother. She looked to the edge of Kharayan Woods. "Gethen!"

From his vantage above the fray, Gethen had witnessed Waldram's attack. He reached Halina's side in a whirl of magic. "I'm here."

"Save the queen," Ilker pleaded.

Gethen was already leaning over Ambrosine, but it was too late. Her hair was crimson and slick with her own blood. Her skull had caved into her brain. Her spirit circled him as he closed her sightless jade-green eyes. He stood and met Halina's anguished gaze. "I'm sorry."

"No, no, no," Ilker moaned and clung to his sister.

"Can you save his eyes?" she asked.

"No, but I'll try to save his life."

"Do it." She pulled her brother to his feet. Two Ursinian militairs took the king's weight from her as another helped her mount her undead horse. "Waldram is a dead man," she said, her voice colder than he'd ever heard.

Gethen grabbed her reins. "Halina, your strength. You can't keep going like this. Waldram will win."

"Not without Shemel's power. Not without his witches and mages. I'm a better swordsman than he is."

"You're losing your life to control that army!"

"Then I'd better kill him quickly, and you'd better save my brother in case I fail."

"Halina." Gethen reached for her, but she kicked her mount to a gallop and charged back into the battle, her course straight for Waldram at its center, her will set to a singular, deadly task.

Beside him, Ambrosine's spirit surged, its power like lightning crackling between clouds. She didn't like Halina's recklessness either.

Gethen turned back to King Ilker and caught his arm. "You've been a blind idiot, Your Majesty."

Ilker groaned. "I should've listened to Halina. She begged me to see the truth right in front of my face. Why didn't I listen?" He grabbed blindly, capturing the front of Gethen's brigandine. "Forget me, Sun Mage. Save Halina. Ursinum needs her more than they do a blind excuse for a king. You have to keep my sister alive."

"I'm trying," Gethen snapped. "But first I need to save your idiot arse."

Her time was running out. Her limbs were growing heavier, a cold emptiness was spreading deep. She'd felt that emptiness before, as Waldram stole her blood magic. "Khotyr, help me," she begged. "Just a little longer." She had to end Waldram. If it was her last act, so be it. She'd die peacefully knowing that cock-swallow had paid for his crimes.

Chaos reigned around her. Nalvika continued to push the assault. But as news of Waldram's betrayal spread, Ursinum's soldiers turned against their Nalvik allies. And the Shadow Army continued its attack on both forces.

An ear-piercing, gut-curdling shriek rent the air. Halina knew that sound and ran her hand over the dead horse's bony neck, trying not to shudder at the feel of its sinewy muscles and papery hide. "Steady," she said as the animal tossed its skeletal head. Even dead creatures feared shrikers.

A shout went up, and another. The first of terror, the second of triumph. She followed the sounds. A mass of shrikers charged into the fray, killing soldiers from all sides and taking down shadowy necromancers and their wraiths.

So.

Waldram had a counter for her weapon.

"Well, he won't counter my sword gutting him like a pig."

She spotted her cousin. Grinning like a madman he cut down Ursinians at the center of the melee. But the view beyond him chilled her to the bones.

Ships were dropping anchor off Khara's shores, ships with billowing yellow sails. Teleyansk had arrived, impossible but true.

Her gaze dragged back to Waldram. He laughed as he killed soldiers, indiscriminate with his aim. With a shout and a kick, she sent her mount plunging into the midst of the chaos, intent on the maniac at its middle.

Halina scattered Nalvik soldiers — peasants with little armor and less skill. She had no time for regret as weakness and chill crept into her limbs, the inescapable drain of the Shadow Army. She had to slaughter her insane cousin and stop his death march.

With her focus split between the foot soldiers around her, Waldram ahead, and two Nalvik militairs rushing toward her, Halina missed the shriker until her horse shied and the monstrous stinking beast knocked her from the saddle.

She rolled and came up armed and facing Waldram's undead dog. It charged, maggoty jaws snapping and rheumy gaze fixed on her. It was a massive thing, half the height of her warhorse and near the bulk of a cart dray. A pallid glow emanated from beneath its desiccated skin and mangy fur, the spells Waldram had used to animate it. She blocked out its terror-inducing screech and parried its claws as the beast swiped at her. There was power in the monster's blows and Halina nearly lost her sword, stumbling back and cursing with each strike.

Battle boiled around her as soldiers, wraiths, and shrikers clashed and heaved, a fury of sound and violence. The ground was mud- and blood-slicked, trampled grass and trampled bodies. With the next blow, Halina lost her footing and went to her knees. The shriker screamed and lunged. She invoked her shield to knock it aside, but the monster tore it from her grip, breaking her left middle finger. The creature snapped at her face, its breath a horror. Halina's sword struck its muzzle, sending brown teeth flying. But the monstrosity got past her defenses and seized her left arm as she raised it to fend off another strike. Her blood armor squealed and cracked as the beast's jaws crushed it, forcing sorcerous shards into her flesh.

The monster shrieked. Halina screamed back. She slammed her sword into its skull as the monstrosity shook her like a child's doll. She gripped the sword with all her strength, gritting her teeth against another scream. Her shoulder throbbed. The armor compressed. It sliced deeper.

Suddenly she hit the ground, her arm still in the shriker's jaws but the monster's head no longer attached to its body. Thaksin stood over her, sword in hand. He wedged the weapon into the beast's mouth and pried its jaws open, freeing her.

Halina accepted his hand and got to her feet. Her arm was on fire. Her shoulder and neck too. "My thanks," she said and yanked her sword from the monstrous skull.

No time for pain. No place for fear.

Thak nodded and turned back into the melee as Halina whirled in search of Waldram.

The battle raged on, a clamor of screams, shouts, shriker cries and the howls of the wraiths. It was impossible to tell friend from foe anymore.

"There, Your Ladyship!" Eugen joined Thaksin and pointed toward the shoreline where Waldram was being dragged back from the emperor's ship. The *Ayaruq* sat in shallow water and Lokshin stood at her rail, staring down at the battlefield with glowing, white eyes and a delighted smile.

"You promised me!" Waldram screamed. "You promised I would be the one! Me! Not some foreign lickspittle!"

The Teleyansk soldiers threw him face down into the blood and muck at the water's edge and turned away, heading back to their dinghy.

"Shemel, you bastard!" Waldram got to his feet and cursed them. Horseless, he limped across the mud and rocks, wild and ranting. "I don't need you!" He unsheathed his sword and waved it at the raging battle behind him. "I did this! All of this! I did it without you!"

"Waldram!" Halina ran at her cousin.

His head jerked her way and a feral smile curved his lips. "Yes! The last of the Persinna shits!"

The world fell away as Waldram became her only focus.

"This is the final battle, bitch," he sneered a she drew near.

"For you."

Her cousin's attack on Ambrosine and Ilker proved that nothing but stinking evil and madness filled the spaces between his bones. But Nalvika's mad king was a fine swordsman and Halina couldn't underestimate him, even with his injury. Fatigued by the Shadow Army's drain, she wouldn't last long against him. This fight had to end swiftly.

He favored his bloodied left leg and had been abandoned by his mentor; weapons she'd use against him. But they'd also drive him harder toward desperation and make him more dangerous.

She gloated. "Tossed on the kitchen midden by your dead uncle? Discarded like so many stinking table scraps. After all you sacrificed for him? I bet that stings more than being stabbed by an old queen."

Snarling, Waldram took the bait and lunged at her.

She turned aside his blade. They pivoted to face off again. Halina pressed the attack, slashing, thrusting, pushing him back. He cursed and parried, tripped on a body. She pursued him, ignoring her throbbing shoulder, her broken finger, the weakness plaguing her. She'd have his blood on her blade or she'd die.

But Halina misstepped and overshot her target as he recovered and turned aside her blade. Waldram came around fast, his longsword jabbing at her like an asp. Only the black band on her ring finger saved her as she raised her sword arm. The blade glanced off its ensorcelled metal. Pain flashed across her knuckles as the sword sliced through the top of her hand.

Waldram howled at the sight of her blood on his blade. He dodged, pivoted away from her sword, caught himself and came at her in a fury, snarling and enraged. Sloppy. Vulnerable. Like a child in the practice arena.

Sidestepping, Halina deflected her cousin's blade to her left, caught its cross-guard and used it to yank Waldram forward, putting her own longsword through his gut.

King Waldram Boorsook's light-gray eyes widened. He made a small, surprised sound that ended with a grunt. Pain and disappointment crossed his face. She twisted his sword from his grasp and tossed it aside. His breath rasped, hot on her face.

He pawed at the misericord sheathed on her sword belt.

"No," she said and lifted the dagger free. "You don't get that satisfaction." She twisted her sword in his gut. He went to his knees, his face a rictus of pain, his voice hoarse, panting. She leaned close. "That's for my mother, my queen, and the infant prince." Holding him skewered in place, she slammed her misericord through his eyes from temple to temple. He made a strange keening, an animal suffering sound. "That's for my brother, whom you blinded months ago." She yanked out the dagger and slit Waldram's throat with it. "And that's for King Vernard, whose death you orchestrated but were too craven to carry out with your own blade." Halina planted her boot on Waldram's chest and pushed him off her sword. She stood over him. "I'm glad my face was the last thing you saw before you died." She spat on him. "Cousin."

His mouth gaped open and closed, a sallow fish dying in the mud on a foreign beach. Blood gurgled from the gash in his throat. He twisted and arched. Death wasn't swift. Halina was glad when his chest stopped rising, gladder still when his body went slack. The moment his soul left his body she hoped fervently that one of his own beastly shrikers chewed it up and shat it out. Even if it reached the Void, Gethen would see to its torment. The thought greatly pleased her.

Halina turned away from King Waldram the Dead.

The clash and cacophony of battle suddenly returned, like bells pealing into a once-silent night.

Mud and guts marred the field.

Blood stained the Silver Sea.

THIRTY

Appearing beside Halina, Thaksin wiped his face, leaving red streaks behind. "Whose side are they on?" He jerked his thumb toward the water where Teleyansk's soldiers rowed toward shore.

"Not ours," she said, regret alighting heavily on her shoulders.

Eugen appeared beside her on horseback, her wraith horse's reins in hand. "We must fall back, Your Ladyship."

"He's right," Thak called above screams of desperation and dying. Halina gained the saddle as he added, "Pull back to the citadel. Ursinum's forces will follow you."

Eugen said, "Regain your strength, Your Ladyship. We can't win like this against Nalvika and Teleyansk."

Slashing aside weapons, she scanned the field as she followed her men through the fray. They were right. Waldram was dead, but Shemel was just getting started. They had to change their approach now that he'd gained corporeal form and joined the battle with Teleyansk's zealous force at his beck and call. Her strength was waning. If she lost control of the Shadow Army, he would seize it and doom Quoregna.

"Do it," she said.

Eugen sounded the retreat on his battle horn.

Thaksin called to the forces, "Fall back! Soldiers of Ursinum, fall back to Ranith Citadel!"

The shout was taken up and echoed across the hillside and beach, out to the sea and into the forest.

Halina spied Gethen at the top of the hill, standing at his ward line. She raced to her husband's side, Thaksin and Eugen with her. "Will you shelter our allies in the woods?"

He nodded, raised his hands, and dispelled the wards with a sweeping gesture.

Halina forced steel into her spine as the soldiers and mounted militairs passed into the forest. Some hesitated at the line, then spied Eugen and Thaksin already across the stones that marked Ranith's ward. They followed their captains into the shade. The howling army at their back surely compelled them too.

"Hold this line," she ordered the Shadow Army. Its wraiths and necromancers took positions at the outside edge of the ward line as the last mortal stragglers entered the safety of Kharayan Woods.

When Halina was satisfied that all who could join her had, she nodded to Gethen. He raised the ward, its amber energy shot through with nebulous red sigils, the incantations that made them deadly now made visible. They warned all who stood outside their limits to stay back or die a gruesome death.

Teleyansk and Nalvika gathered around the perimeter, a seething mass of steel and snarling, unable to pass the Shadow Army or break Gethen's ward.

By her count only a few thousand fought for her now. Ursinum's army was decimated, but so too was Nalvika's. Only the arrival of Teleyansk had robbed her of victory.

"Bollocks." She cradled her injured arm. Her agony surged

and she vented a string of curses long and colorful enough to make a dock trollop blush and some of the soldiers around her chuckle.

"You're wounded," Gethen said, fury smoldering behind his eyes as he glared at the invading army roaming just beyond his woods.

"There's a war. That happens. How's King Ilker?"

"Alive." He swung up behind her onto the black destrier's back. "Let's ensure you remain that way too."

She shook her head. "I need to see to the queen and the troops. There are wounded to treat and food and shelter must be organized. And the dead—"

"Are in the Void. Their bodies will feed the forest."

Thaksin said, "I'll manage the soldiers."

Eugen added, "And I'll take charge of the queen's remains."

Gethen's tone brooked no argument as he said, "Your wellness is my priority, wife. Ilker's in no condition to command and a Persinna must lead Ursinum." He pressed his lips to her ear and murmured, "Like it or not, right now you must be queen."

Halina sighed. Kings and queens commanded from the rear. They remained safe, rallied their troops, and directed their movements. They were too valuable to lose in melee combat. Waldram and Ilker knew that and ignored it. Now she was picking up the pieces of Ursinum's shattered army and burned kingdom. And Nalvika was leaderless.

"He's right," Thak said. "You need healing." He nodded at Eugen. "We'll manage the survivors."

"Is there food for the troops?" Thaksin asked.

"Not enough for all. They'll have to forage," Gethen replied. "But the wells in Ranith Village are safe. They can draw clean water and shelter in the buildings." He turned to Eugen. "Bring the queen's body to Ranith Citadel."

"See to the wounded while I attend our king," Halina

ordered. She wanted to see that her brother still survived, in no small part because she wanted to kill him herself.

"King Ilker was injured?" a nearby soldier asked. She was supporting a wounded comrade whose right shin sported an arrow all the way through it. Absently, Halina wondered if the bones were shattered. If the man would walk normally again. If he'd die from infection.

A man behind them snarled, "Blinded trying to defend Queen Ambrosine from that traitor Waldram. Saw it with my own eyes."

"Why would Nalvika do that, Your Ladyship?" a young woman nursing a bloodied arm asked.

So many wounded, so much death.

"His Majesty was blinded by Waldram's deceit long ago," Halina replied. Her voice sounded distant to her own ears. "Nalvika was never your ally." She straightened in the saddle, lifted her chin, and squared her screaming shoulders. She would be the picture of regal command that her troops needed, though she wanted to collapse against Gethen. She was drained and in pain, the steel in her spine rusty and close to crumbling.

"You all fought valiantly for Ursinum. Your loyalty to the kingdom won't be forgotten," she called to the mass of wounded and bloodied troops around her. "Queen Ambrosine will be avenged. I promise."

Gethen whispered to the horse. It broke into a gallop, heading for Ranith Citadel.

Halina didn't know if the war was lost, but her first goal was won. She'd freed the world from Waldram's tyranny. She'd kept Feddie safe. Nalvika would have its first queen.

But the price paid by all of Quoregna was steep, steepest for the Persinna family. She remembered Ambrosine's broken body and wondered if too much had been lost in the doing and how they would defeat Shemel and his fanatical stolen army.

Halina trembled and cursed. She wore clean trouzes but only a chemise to cover her chest. The pain of her wounds and the draw of the Shadow Army were overwhelming, distracting her from the needs of her soldiers, her brother's agony, their terrible losses. Now she was the one battling withdrawal and she didn't much like the feeling. This was why she'd never tolerated nocoli use among her troops. She pressed her thumb against the stitches closing her wounded knuckles and hissed between gritted teeth as pain surged.

"This is becoming an unfortunate habit, wife," Gethen muttered. Using tweezers, he picked shards of blood armor from her shoulder, his hands steady, his brow furrowed with concentration.

Sounds of suffering drifted through the open infirmary window.

"I always think, if I just keep fighting the gods will see my need and grant me victory." She scowled at her jagged fingernails. Dried blood discolored them. "But what have I done for these people?" Her gaze drifted to the bed where Ilker lay, the blankets and floor stained with his blood. "Brought death and suffering."

Thaksin had rejoined Halina and Gethen. His right arm was bandaged and he winced when he gestured, but it took a greater wound than that to lay him out. "You're wrong, Halina," he said. "You've brought them hope."

She shook her head. "I don't think so."

Ilker said, "We'll speak to Ursinum's troops together, so they know you're now my eyes and my sword. Given the opportunity, they'll choose a militess and a mage over Nalvika's mad king."

"Waldram's dead," she replied.

He paused. "Is he? Good. That's good. You killed him?"

"Yes."

"Who's leading Nalvika?" he asked.

"Teleyansk," Gethen replied. "Shemel's taken possession of Emperor Lokshin. He's impersonating the One God."

Ilker's fists clenched. "That's blasphemy."

"Yes," Halina repeated and sighed. "How do you know Ursinum's troops will trust me, Ilk? Waldram worked hard to assassinate my good character."

Gethen dropped the tweezers into a metal bowl. "And I've done little to prove mine."

Ilker was slow to answer. "He burned us. Tore us limb from limb. I'll tell them the truth. I'll ask them to see what I couldn't: The Red Blade's loyalty is beyond doubt."

"The troops saw Waldram's attack, Halina," Thak added. "They haven't forgotten what it's like to fight beside you. You go on even when victory seems hopeless. That gives a soldier heart."

A man appeared in the doorway, scratching absently at a line of stitches across his forehead, the silver-and-red of Eskis barely recognizable through the mud covering his tabard. "Excuse me, Captain Thaksin. The hunting parties have returned mostly empty-handed. Said they've never seen a forest with so little wildlife."

"I warned the animals to leave or go to ground," Gethen replied as he washed Halina's shoulder. "There are plenty of root vegetables, mushrooms, and berries, plus honey from the bee yards and grubs if you turn the soil. Pull supplies from Ranith's dry stores — grain and potatoes. There's hard white cheese, nuts, pickled vegetables, and dried fruit in the extraction room."

"Grubs?" The man looked aghast.

"Roast them," Gethen said.

"I thought you didn't eat living things," King Ilker remarked.

"I also don't starve when food is scarce."

Thak snorted then changed the subject. "I sent scouts to assess enemy strength and movement. We're vulnerable up here."

"They'll try to burn us out," Halina said.

"Of course," he agreed. "It's what you'd do in their position."

"Yes, it is," she replied.

"I won't let that happen." Gethen straightened and set aside his washrag. "I can't sit by and watch the world fall into Shemel's hands."

"Why do you keep saying your old master is behind this?" Ilker asked.

"Because he is with Skiron's backing."

"Wait." The soldier at the door gaped at Gethen. "The God of Death created this disaster?"

"Don't sound so surprised," Halina muttered. She winced as Gethen stitched.

"Sorry," he mouthed, then replied to the soldier, "To benefit the Triumvirate."

"That makes no sense," Ilker said from his bed.

Gethen glanced at Halina's brother. "Belief in the One God is spreading and worship of the Triumvirate is waning. Nothing makes gods relevant like suffering, misery, and death."

"But—"

"When death holds a knife to your throat, who do you pray to for solace and strength?" Gethen asked.

Thaksin replied, "Khotyr and Semele."

"Exactly."

"Bollocks," the Eskis soldier muttered. "How do you win a war when even the gods are against you?"

Halina replied, "With blood and sweat and steel."

"And no small amount of sorcery," Gethen added. He finished stitching and snipped the thread free.

Silence followed as they all pondered the coming battle.

Herra Tomruma had never taken sides in the kingdoms' disputes. None of them knew what to expect, not even Gethen.

Ilker grimaced, doubt and hope at war on his face.

Thak pushed away from the wall. "Medicinals. You make the best, Lord Rhyshis. Have you any to spare?"

Gethen nodded and led the captain into the stillroom. The soldier from Eskis followed.

Halina settled on the edge of her brother's bed. "That must've been hard to hear."

He grimaced. "There's room enough for all the gods in Quoregna."

She laughed. "Tell that to the gods."

"Perhaps your husband can."

"I'm sure he has. Skiron doesn't appreciate being questioned or dismissed."

"So this is my punishment for embracing the One God's philosophy of peace and order?"

"Ironic." She smoothed the blanket over his chest.

"Are you badly injured?" he asked.

She shrugged, winced, and regretted the old habit. "Just my left shoulder. Shrikers have mighty jaws. Hard to get them to let go once they've gotten hold of you."

"That fancy magical armor didn't do its job?"

"Ha! If not for the blood armor, I'd be missing my arm."

He was quiet for a moment then, hesitantly, he asked, "What happened at Gwyncardarnlei and Tatlis?"

She swallowed. Those wounds remained raw. Ambrosine's death only salted them. But he deserved to know and she wouldn't soften the blow. "Waldram's shrikers and soldiers did the killing and the burning. Gethen and I were in Teleyansk seeking an alliance with Emperor Lokshin." She laughed bitterly and added, "An alliance Shemel corrupted before it bore fruit. We returned to find slaughter in Gwyncardarnlei and Tatlis in ashes."

"Gods," Ilker muttered. "I'm such a fool."

"Yes, you are."

He reached out and she caught his trembling hands. "I had an understanding with Waldram. I told him Persinnas didn't murder each other," he said. "We agreed that you'd be spared. We had an agreement on that." He swallowed but his voice cracked as he added, "I knew nothing of his duplicity. I should have, Halina." He shook his head. "How could I be so ignorant?"

"He was a sorcerer, Ilk. And not one with an ounce of goodness inside his black heart."

"So is the Sun Mage, but all the treason I accused him of was carried out by Ursinum's so-called ally." There was no hiding the desolation in her brother's voice. "This is a painful lesson and all of Quoregna is paying the high price for it. Our mothers and our innocent brother paid the price for my stupidity."

"Don't lessen the queen's bravery with self-pity. She'd slap you for it."

Ilker laughed bitterly. "You're right." He pulled her fingers to his cheek. Tears dampened them. "I am sorry, Halina."

She sighed. "I know, Ilk." She pulled her fingers free, stood, and kissed his bandaged face. "Rest. You can speak to the troops at dawn."

When she entered the stillroom, Gethen stood at the window, his spine straight and shoulders tight. But his voice was even as he said, "Kharaton Castle and the village are burning." The acrid smell of smoke hit her nose.

Halina balled her hands into fists. She wanted to break something, stab someone. Instead she drew a long, slow breath. "Can you stop the flames?"

He turned away from the window. "It's already done too much damage. The castle's east wing has collapsed into the sea and the village's Merchant Quarter, the Whores' Doors, and the Iron Quarter are raging."

"Shemel's first act?"

"Or Waldram's last order." He shrugged. "Does it matter?"

"No," she replied as Gethen retrieved a length of fabric from one of his cabinets and bandaged her shoulder. "What will you do?" she asked.

"About Shemel and Teleyansk?" He leaned back against the large table occupying the center of his workroom.

"You can't use the Shadow Army. I won't let you."

"No." He kissed her forehead. "I can't."

Someone cleared their throat in the doorway from the hall.

Halina turned. The soldier from Eskis stood with an armful of sheets. "We need more bandages," he said by way of explanation. "And Captain Eugen wants to distribute the mead and bracket that's stored in the extraction room. With Your Lordship's permission?"

Gethen nodded. "Of course. It was meant for Kharaton, but the castle and village are burning. No use letting it sit. The troops will appreciate it."

"Especially facing the queen's funeral," Halina said.

They headed out to the bailey and the extraction room. Gethen signaled Eugen and a handful of soldiers to help. He sorted barrels of mead and bracket and the troops rolled them into the bailey and toward the gates. A line formed and fit soldiers moved the barrels down the path from the citadel's inner keep into the village's makeshift camp. A cheer went up when Eugen tapped the first barrel.

"May the gods bless you, Red Blade!" someone called and others took up the refrain.

"Not me," Halina called above them. "Give your praise to my husband. That's the Sun Mage's brew and his decision to share it with all of you."

Tin mugs and wooden cups were raised in salute to Gethen. The praise grew heartier as the troops enjoyed their first sips of Ranith's finest distillates. Many had never enjoyed such quality and few would again.

Gethen nodded and remained silent, his arms crossed, his gaze keen as Halina moved among the soldiers, asking about their injuries, listening to tales of bravery that grew bolder with each telling.

"How do you know that's not poisoned?"

The strident voice rose above the masses and silenced the stories and praise.

A gruff, old soldier Halina recognized as a member of King Vernard's old guard stood in the center of the village square, hands on his sword belt and a frown on his craggy face.

"Why would it be poisoned?" she asked.

He jabbed a finger at Gethen. "That's no man. He's a monster and death shadows him. Skiron's servant," he sneered and spat on the ground. "You took a demon to bed and all of Ursinum's paid for it, Red Blade."

Halina drained her own cup. "If it's poisoned, then I shall die slaked and, after a few more cups, happily drunk. But we all know you're not whingeing about Herra Tomruma or Skiron. You're just another old man nosing around my sheets, another pismire who resents my choice not to be a tool for my father—"

"Or her brother," Ilker said from behind her.

Halina turned. The soldiers around them took a knee and bowed their heads.

"Your Majesty." She bowed.

"You shouldn't be out of bed," Gethen said. He did not bow. He didn't have to.

Ilker sat in a chair borne by three burly infantrymen. "I heard my soldiers were being served the finest mead in all of Quoregna and I'm thirsty."

Someone filled a cup and placed it in Ilker's hands. Ursinum's king drank every drop without slowing. When he finally lower the cup, he sighed and said, "Even better than I remembered. Thank you for sharing your brews, Lord Rhyshis."

"It's my privilege, Your Majesty."

Ilker held out his cup and it was refilled. He savored another sip. "I'm blind, but I'm not deaf or dumb," he told the old soldier. "You're mistaken about a great many things, misled by your king who was misled by his dead cousin's power. I lost my sight but regained clear vision. My sister wisely chose to marry the Sun Mage, and I am grateful for her husband's loyalty to her and his integrity in maintaining impartiality in most matters of the state. But what we face now transcends kingdom and fealty. It is by the order of the gods themselves that we suffer. The Sun Mage shelters you, feeds you, provides drink and medicine. He's chosen to defend us tomorrow in Ursinum's hour of need against a terrible enemy and without the support of the gods. I trust this man with my life and with my sister's future. More than that, I trust him with *your* lives."

Ilker paused for another long draft, lowered his cup and added, "And Lady Rhyshis is correct. Whom she beds is her business only. She's not a commodity to be bought, sold, or bargained away for a piece of land or an alliance. She is a soldier, the Red Blade of Or-Halee. She serves at her own leisure, and she has agreed to be your king's eyes and his sword. So, if you doubt, shut your stinking pie holes and drink up or have water and let the rest of us enjoy your portion of this very fine mead."

Cheering met those words and once again cups were raised, this time to King Ilker, as well as his sister and her husband.

The old fellow glowered into his mead cup and muttered about Captain Thaksin's opinions about the bloody Sun Mage.

Eugen stood nearby. He said, "The Sun Mage saved Captain

Thaksin's life, he saved King Ilker's life, and he saved Princess Halina's life."

"More times than you know," Halina added.

Thak's voice rose above the murmur of the crowd as he pushed through to the old soldier's side. "It's true I loath Lord Rhyshis. But it's truer that I respect the Sun Mage even more than I hate the mangy cur." He tapped his cup against the fellow's. "I trust him, old man. You should too."

Two women appeared at the edge of the crowd, breathing heavily. Thak's scouts. "Captain," one said and saluted. He returned it and gestured for the women to be given mead.

"We're being surrounded," she gasped out between gulps.

"Troops have circled around the woods to the west of here," the other reported.

"They've come to burn Kharayan Woods," Gethen said.

Murmurs turned to protests and anger.

The scouts nodded. "How do you know?" the first asked.

"The woods have eyes," he replied simply.

"And teeth," Halina added to which Gethen grinned, looking wolfish and dangerous.

"Fire won't touch Kharayan or Ranith. Not again. I'll make sure of it," he said.

Halina twined her fingers with his. She knew he was remembering how the basilica had burned with all the tor's animals inside. It still pained him. She tightened her grip.

"We can't stay here," Eugen said. "The citadel is strong but not supplied for a siege and certainly not for so many people."

Halina nodded. "At daylight, we face them again."

She'd have to stay at the back, directing and encouraging, but not in the fray. It made her itch. She never wanted to become queen. Halina liked being in the thick of battle, side-by-side and back-to-back with her soldiers. Queens and kings couldn't do that. They were too valuable to place on the battlefield. But Ilker was blind and as likely to succumb to his wound as survive it, despite his brave face. He was ashen and hunched, clearly sickened by infection despite Gethen's magic and medicinals. Getting out of bed was another foolish choice. Her brother was full of them lately.

"This time you'll fight with the Sun Mage bringing his full power to bear against the invading force," Gethen said.

Ilker raised his cup to that. The soldiers cheered and drank, doubtless daring to host a fragile kind of hope spun from desperation and the stories they'd grown up hearing about the powerful necromancers who dwelled in Ranith Citadel.

Ilker's aids bore him back to the tower. Gethen and Halina followed.

Once inside the bailey, he pulled her to a stop. "I've sat in my tower for too long and watched the world come apart, slowly at first, then faster, uglier. This is as much my fault for inattention as it is Waldram's. Shemel is my problem to solve and you can't win this war by sacrificing yourself, Halina. The Shadow Army will burn through you, then be free for Shemel to pick up and use as he wishes." He took her hands. They were shaking again. "Do you think I don't notice everything about you?"

She looked down and swallowed, tightened her fingers on his, but the tremor wouldn't stop. "Now I truly understand why you can't lead that army. Its power is seductive and dangerous. All those necromancers driven mad by their hunger for souls. All I saw when I looked on the battlefield were spirits to enslave. Thank the gods I couldn't capture that power."

"You wanted to, more than anything."

"Yes. I've never desired anything so much." She shuddered. "It's heady...and terrifying."

He pulled her closer. "I know."

"But, unlike you, I know I can release that force when we've won. And we haven't won yet. As long as Shemel threatens us, I'll wield the Shadow Army like a bludgeon."

They resumed walking toward the basilica.

"Then I must force Shemel to relinquish Lokshin. I don't want to harm Teleyansk's soldiers, they were our allies before my old master took hold, but I'll do what's necessary to end this war and destroy Shemel before the Shadow Army kills you."

"You're not in this alone. You have soldiers — flesh and shadow — at your disposal."

"No."

"Gethen, this is war. These are soldiers. We know what's at stake and we understand the value of our lives."

He ignored that. "Tomorrow I'll ward you and your commanders. Promise you'll remain in the ward circle, no matter what happens on the battlefield."

"If I'm needed—"

"Promise, Halina." He stopped, gripped her hands, and held her gaze. "I need to know you'll be safe, that Ursinum's greatest protector will be safe while I take on Shemel. I can't split my focus between my old master and you. I tried that before and you almost died. Promise you'll stay within the circle this time."

She grit her teeth. "Why do you need to remind me that Ilker's blindness falls heavily on my shoulders?"

"Because it's inescapable."

"Semele's blood," she muttered.

"Please."

Halina met her husband's gray gaze. "I promise to stay in the ward circle if you promise not to do anything foolish like sacrificing yourself."

He smiled. "I promise I have no intention of dying tomorrow." He pulled her against him. "I have too much to live for."

THIRTY-ONE

Soldiers surrounded their dead queen as she lay on her funeral pyre, cradled by kindling beneath a waxing moon. Her blind son slumped in a chair beside her head, feverish and trembling but unwilling to forego his beloved mother's last rites. At her feet stood her husband's daughter, chin high, eyes hard. Flowers surrounded the queen's body and Ursinum's soldiers paid their respects by placing mementos around her — rings and daggers, wooden carvings of the gods, cups of mead, coins, fruit and grain.

Gethen anointed Ambrosine's eyelids with ash mixed with ben oil as he droned her last rites. "Let go of the heart that no longer beats. Do not try to see through eyes that are blind. Step free of the flesh that no longer breathes. You, spirit, whose ties to this mortal body have been severed, rise and depart from the realm of the living. Your place is no longer with your family, your subjects, or your peers. Cross the Voidline and step onto the path that awaits you. Your journey through the Void begins and a new life awaits."

The soldiers echoed his words and six came forward to pour more ben oil over their fallen queen.

King Ilker leaned forward and kissed his mother's forehead then was moved back by his guards as Gethen lit a torch with mage fire and passed it to Halina. She thrust the flame into the pyre. It went up in a whoosh of sparks and quickly became a roaring inferno, dancing and throwing off embers and roiling wisps of whitish smoke, the queen's body lost to heat and fire.

But Ambrosine's spirit refused to leave. She dogged Gethen's steps, her demands clear: End the war and protect the last of the Persinna heirs. He hated when the nobles lingered after death to harass him.

Halina looked around the circle of men and women. "Queen Ambrosine died a wrongful death." Heads nodded. The soldiers murmured agreement. "I cut down that coward Waldram as he cut down our queen. I took his eyes as he took my brother's sight, cut his throat as he ordered my father's cut, gutted him as he gutted our kingdom." The soldiers approval grew louder. Halina's voice rose over theirs. "But Ursinum is not free of invaders. The army I brought to help free our kingdom was stolen from me by a monster more dangerous than Nalvika's king, more determined to see us grovel and die. Will we bow before a corrupted army?"

"No!"

"Will we let our kingdom fall?"

"No!"

"Then when the sun rises will you fight for your king? Fight for your fallen queen and a murdered infant prince and my own dead mother? Will you fight for your displaced families and friends, your burned villages, and slaughtered livestock? Will you fight for me and your own freedom, soldiers of Ursinum? Will you die to protect this kingdom?"

"Yes!"

"For the Red Blade!"

"For King Ilker!"

"For queen and kingdom!"

Determination showed in the hard set of Gethen's jaw, the fire flickering in his eyes as he stepped forward. "For Quoregna," he said. He too would fight to save Ursinum and Quoregna, and the soldiers' cheers rose with the ashes of their burning queen.

The early morning sun turned the sky peach and light blue as Gethen, Halina, and the remainder of Ursinum's army emerged from Kharayan Woods. Charred bodies lay all around the tor, from the ward's black stones to the edge of the churned battle-field. Gethen's wards and Halina's wraiths had decimated the men Shemel had sent to burn the forest. Beyond the field of death, an ocean of yellow canvas tents occupied the Silver Sea's rocky shore.

Sea crows circled, landed, hopped about and flapped their wings at each other, squabbling over the carrion corpses. More bodies burned in great pyres by the shore — men and horses smoldering together — Nalvik, Ursinian, Teleyansk — all the same in death. Teleyansk ships and frigates clogged the sea. The fires' acrid smoke drifted across the tor, a white, choking haze that made the early morning sunlight wan.

Gethen considered the muted sky. A tapestry had hung in his mother's parlor when he was a boy. It depicted the Silver Sea and distant Khara as seen from Besera's shores, Kharayan Tor and the thin, dark-gray tower of Ranith Citadel in the back-ground. Kharaton Castle's blue roof and white walls could be seen to the north. The colors were pastel and watery like this morning. Ships sat on the silvery water and black-and-white crows rode the air. Gethen had last seen that tapestry the day Shadow Mage Shemel had arrived at Ystwyth Citadel to take him as an apprentice.

The tapestry and the parlor housing it were nothing but rubble and ash now.

He squinted toward the camp and the emperor's large, purple tent at its center. Shemel was there, in possession of a good man and determined to move him toward monstrous acts.

Halina spurred her undead horse forward. She rode before the line of Ursinian soldiers and cavalry, her outstretched sword clashing against the upraised pikes of the infantry and the proffered swords of the mounted militairs. First to one side, then the other. Returning to the center, she faced her paltry army, stood in the saddle, and called out to the gathered force.

"I am responsible for what happens today, and I will do what I can, what I *must*, to end this conflict and better your lives. Together, we will drive our enemy into the sea and back to the Northern Wastes. Today we'll rid our land of the darkness that threatens the good and the innocent among us."

A gong sounded in the Teleyansk camp, strange and low as its note carried across the water and land. The hour was announced: "The army stands ready. The soldiers await the command. Lokshin's empire will restore peace and order. The Empire of the Golden Flower will be triumphant. The Hour of Blood is upon us."

The flaps of the emperor's tent drew back and Lokshin was borne out on his gilded throne. Shemel now appeared to Gethen as a shadow cloaking the eastern emperor, darkness behind his eyes and strangling his soul. Gethen would drive Shemel out of his victim. This time he would destroy his old master completely. No ambit would remain to be resurrected. He would wipe all evidence of Shadow Mage Shemel's existence from the world.

Halina called across the rutted battlefield. "Shemel Ebbe, you helped King Waldram murder my king, my queen, my mother, and my infant brother. You helped him destroy my lands and decimate my home and my kingdom. Did you think those losses would weaken me? They didn't, necromancer. My family's deaths only hardened my heart, my hide, and the edge of my blade!"

At those words, Eugen signaled the infantry. The clonk and whoosh of the trebuchets sounded in the early morning. Streams of black blood and clotted gore rained across the field as fifty heads — the skulls of Shemel's arsonists — thudded into the ranks of his army, sending horses plunging and soldiers ducking for cover.

Unperturbed, Lokshin sneered. "Still hiding behind a skirt, Sun Mage?"

Gethen moved past Halina to take point before her army. It surprised him that Shemel was no longer playing the part of the peaceful god. "You mean the champion who bested your puppet king?" He glanced over his shoulder at his wife and winked. Turning back he said, "Certainly I'll stand behind her. It's an honor to do so."

"Honor?" Shemel barked a laugh. "A woman with a paltry following and a bastard's weakness in her veins? Even her own brother rejected her." He waved a hand dismissively. "She's insignificant."

There was a lie in those words and Shemel knew it. "No," Gethen said, "she is the eldest princess of Ursinum, the Duchess of Rhyshis in absentia, the Red Blade of Or-Halee, and the commander of the Shadow Army. She is the leader who will drive you from my doorstep."

Shemel bared his teeth. "She is dead!"

Gethen's mass spell knocked him backwards and exploded the false throne into splinters. As Shemel looked out from behind Lokshin's surprised eyes, Gethen said, "Don't threaten my wife."

The possessed emperor slapped away help from the soldiers

who rushed to him. He rose, shook splinters from his robes, and wiped blood from his scratched face. He looked at his field marshal and nodded. "Take no prisoners. Bring me the Sun Mage's heart and his bitch woman's head."

The marshal's orders carried across the field, echoed by thirty thousand voices. The ground shook as the infantry thudded ten thousand pikes into the soil. The air trembled as they called with one voice, a battle cry to make their enemies piss their own trouzes and weep like children. Then silence. An opportunity gifted to their opponent to surrender before slaughter came for them.

Gethen cursed himself. Shemel had baited him and he'd risen to it too easily. But his master had given away a weakness too: He despised Halina. Gethen had forgotten how much the man hated women, especially powerful women.

"A strong woman is a plague," he was fond of telling his apprentice.

"Why?" Gethen had asked.

"Because, boy, there's nothing more spiteful, dangerous, and determined to ruin you than a powerful woman. I learned that firsthand from Shadow Mage Pythia. My master was a cunny whore."

"Is that how you learned to be such a pillock?"

Shemel's fist had been fast and hard that day, but Gethen had rarely scored an emotional hit on his monstrous master. Satisfaction had dulled the ache in his jaw.

Halina's voice filled the pause: "Shadows, take my blood magic and kill anyone who raises a weapon against me. Spare any who surrender."

While those words and the appearance and sounds of the wraiths and necromancers sent a tremor through Teleyansk's and Nalvika's forces, they elicited an entirely different response from Lokshin. Shemel's toothy grin split the emperor's face.

That grin widened and turned to glee as the Shadow Army pulled blood magic from Halina and spread out across the field, closing the gap between the invading army and Ursinum's only defense.

"Why are you smiling?" Gethen muttered. He knew not to trust Shemel's smiles.

Behind him, Halina called orders to her living troops. Enemy arrows whooshed overhead in great arcs. The Ursinian artillery locked shields to block the raining bolts.

As the two forces moved closer to colliding, Gethen watched Shemel's delight grow.

Was it glee driven by Skiron? Was the God of Death pulling Shemel's strings and drawing pleasure from the oncoming slaughter?

Gethen shook his head. That wasn't it. Skiron wouldn't need him if he could control Shemel. No, this excitement was driven by the unleashing of the Shadow Army. This was anticipation. Shemel saw the force coming toward him as a prize, not a threat. Gethen's former master reached out. Darkness spiraled outward from him, a seductive path leading the Shadow Army away from the Teleyansk and Nalvik forces and directly to him.

"No!" Gethen shouted, suddenly realizing their mistake. He turned. Halina's eyes were wide and glassy, the blood magic flowing out of her in waves of red mist. She was losing the army and her life force to Shemel.

His fears were coming true. As strong as she was, Halina's blood magic wasn't limitless.

As Gethen pivoted toward his wife, Ambrosine's soul surged across the field and slammed into Halina, knocking her from her horse. Like a knife, the queen's spirit severed Halina's connection to the Shadow Army and collapsed the waves of blood magic. An explosion of light and a thunderous crack marked the breaking of the powerful bond between commander and undead army. It also marked the obliteration of Queen Ambrosine's existence.

Halina gasped. Her undead horse collapsed into shadow and ash. Duesh and Gwyn closed ranks around her, ears flat and teeth bared as they moved to protect her. Like the blaids, Eugen and Thaksin went to her side, weapons drawn, protecting her from further assault.

Gethen raised a shimmering ball of mage fire and hurled it into the midst of the Shadow Army, setting a handful of necromancers ablaze.

Suddenly perceiving him as a threat, Halina's undead generals turned their wraiths against him. They reversed on the hill and charged toward their field marshal and the mage who stood between her and them, exactly as Gethen hoped they would.

He drew upon the power of the rising sun, then summoned rain-swollen clouds, dark and heavy. They blotted out the sunlight. Rain fell in sheets, a sudden heavy squall. Wind howled, tearing the voices of the oncoming wraiths from their throats. But without the light of the sun to define the shadows' edges, the undead army lost cohesion. As the sky darkened, the shadow mages roared over the wind and rain even as they melted into the darkness. And without the power of the souls their generals fed them, the wraiths' charge became a ramble as they unraveled and were carried away by the howling wind.

Halina stood and grabbed Gethen's arm. "Don't do this!" she shouted above the rain and wind. "Their numbers are too great." Mud covered her. Rain darkened her hair.

"I will because I must." He covered her hand with his own and squeezed her fingers. "You've given enough of your life to them; they'll get no more. And I won't permit Shemel to seize that force or steal your blood magic. Yesterday we were fortunate that our losses didn't include you or the Shadow Army. That luck just failed."

Her nails dug into his flesh. "You can't win this alone!"

"I won't be alone."

"But—"

"I didn't sever your connection to the Shadow Army. Ambrosine's spirit did that. The queen stayed to protect you. She saw the danger and saved your life."

She blinked rain from her eyes. "Queen Ambrosine saved me?"

"Yes, and destroyed her spirit in doing so. Don't squander her sacrifice." He gave his wife a little shake. "Yesterday was your battle. Today is mine." He cupped her face and held her gaze. "Please trust me, Halina. With your faith sustaining me, I cannot fail."

Tight-lipped, she hesitated, looking from him to the vast army arrayed below them. She turned back, held his gaze for a long moment, then finding steel in his certainty, nodded. "I do have faith in you." She tilted her head in Shemel's direction. "Avenge the queen. Destroy that pillock for good this time."

From the edge of the battlefield, the false god raged at being denied the Shadow Army and Halina's blood magic. Still in possession of Lokshin's body, Shemel came off his golden throne, fists clenched and teeth bared. Dropping all pretense of godliness, he snarled, "I will kill you, Sun Mage! I'll slaughter everyone who stands by you! Teleyansk will sow this battlefield with their bones and water it with their blood!"

Gethen kissed Halina hard then stepped away. He couldn't afford any distraction. His focus must be absolute. Shemel would test him unlike any foe ever had, and would be obliterated for the effort.

The wind calmed. The rain stopped and the clouds scattered. A breeze whistled past Gethen's ears, ruffling his thick, black hair and tickling his skin. It sang through his nerves, ballads of distant shores, vast oceans, clouds and birds using its invisible power to soar and scud. Every living thing pulsed with power, a vibration thrumming through him from the bees in their hives, the rodents beneath the grasses, the larger beasts with their thudding hearts and tense muscles.

The Teleyansk army spread out and marched toward him. Orders rose on the air. Nalvika's surviving soldiers joined the advancing ranks, their swords and axes hammering a discordant tune against their wooden shields.

"The world is a body and I'm part of it," Gethen murmured, Kenbish's lesson giving him direction. The power beneath his feet hummed, lines pulling him toward distant power centers deep underground. Roots moved inexorably there, too; powerful tree roots ready to push aside or through any obstacle, thin but innumerable plant roots wanting to wrap around whatever stood in their way, vines waiting to entwine anything they encountered.

Gethen summoned his shadow armor as all the world's magic poured into him, surrounded him, called to him. It wasn't seductive and greedy like death's power. This was living magic, giving magic, magic of growth and change, of light and heat and it connected the world to him and him to it. This magic swirled around him and offered itself to him, like Halina always had. It was the world's blood magic. It filled him and asked for nothing in return. He smiled. This was what he'd missed for so long, what he'd first recognized in Halina and feared he'd drain from her. But now he knew how wrong he was to fear that. The world had so much to give him. This was the magic he'd craved and it had been waiting for him all this time, waiting for him to invite it inside.

He didn't need the power of death.

He had the magic of life.

He closed his eyes, tilted his head back, and spread his arms. Gethen opened his mind, body, and soul to the world's magic. It filled him with power and scrubbed all doubt from his mind. He opened his eyes and found Lokshin across the field. He nodded once to his enemy then turned and held Halina's gaze.

"Remember your promise," he said then circled her and Eugen. He murmured a warding incantation as he walked the circuit three times, the last counterclockwise to lock the spell. When he was finished, he stepped back. To Eugen and the blaids he said, "Don't let her leave this circle, no matter what happens to me."

Halina's steward nodded. "You have my word, Your Lordship. I'll keep her safe."

She grabbed Gethen's arm. "Remember your promise, too."

He smiled. "I do, wife."

Gethen stepped forward. He needed to provoke Shemel and sow doubt among Teleyansk's soldiers and the Nalviks hoping to salvage their unjust war. "I thought the One God was a peaceful god." His voice carried strong and clear to the approaching army. His gesture swept the ruined field with its bloated bodies and carrion crows. "This doesn't look like peace to me." He pointed at Lokshin seething behind his generals. "He doesn't act like a peaceful leader."

Shemel shouted through Lokshin's mouth. "Do not stop until every man and woman before you is dead. Burn the forest. Slaughter the animals. Destroy Ranith Citadel. Those are your One God's commands!"

Gethen spread his fingers and reached out, testing the magic of the world's beasts. The buzzing presence of bees, wasps, and biting flies vibrated the air. "Fly to the invaders," he called as masses of the insects rose from the hills and forest. "Drive them from the tor. Defend the home they seek to destroy." In droning waves, they filled the air. Clouds of insects descended upon the invading army, flew into their helmets, into their eyes, noses, mouths, and ears. Soldiers shouted and swatted, they ran into the sea to escape Kharayan Tor's smallest defenders. But that was a mistake too, as Gethen pulled waves from the Silver Sea. They swept steel-clad soldiers off their feet and dragged them under. They swamped Lokshin's ships, washed sailors overboard, and pulled them into the watery depths.

Gethen planted his feet and felt for the deepest dwellers of Kharayan Tor. Beneath them all, roots shifted. The trees and plants of the forest and hillside stirred. The ground rumbled. Horses panicked, birds took flight from the forest, men stumbled and fell.

With a thought, a mere intention, he sent the roots smashing through black soil and gray rock. They emerged at the base of the hillside, splitting the earth like a great maw, teeth of stone, tongues of wood. The roots swept his enemies into the tor's hungry mouth, swallowing soldiers, tents, equipment. Horses bolted, leaving militairs in the path of the spreading rift, their armor clattering as they scrambled to escape.

Out on the heaving sea, came a lowing of horns, deep and sonorous, the traditional call to battle sounded by Beseran ships.

"Look!" someone cried from among Halina's troops. Shouts of recognition and delight joining the screams of Teleyansk's and Nalvika's dying troops.

Ships flying Beseran blue, Ayestran frigates painted cream and dark blue, and sleek Or-Haleean longships with their red-and-gold sails raced to block Teleyansk's floundering navy from retreating.

"Now," Gethen commanded and brought his hands together.

The roots responded, weaving together and closing the rifts, knitting the wounded ground like a healer suturing a gash. All lost to the maw were crushed and entombed.

He mounted the horse held for him and met Halina's intent gaze.

"Now?" she asked.

"Now!" He dug his heels into the gray stallion's flanks and sent the warhorse charging down the hillside on a collision course with a possessed emperor. Behind him, Halina called orders to her soldiers and the thunder of the ground came from above this time as three thousand Ursinian soldiers and militairs charged into the fray. Led by Captain Thaksin, they were intent on routing the remaining enemy soldiers as they staggered about the battlefield, nearly defeated by the land and the sea.

Teleyansk's soldiers turned to their godlike emperor and went to their knees. "Help us!" they cried. "Save us!"

Shemel sneered at their weakness but sent Lokshin striding forward through their ranks. He flung necromantic spells at Gethen and sent wraiths screaming toward Halina. They exploded against Gethen's shield and the ward he'd set around his wife.

But conducting the world's magic had taken its toll. Gethen's hands shook, his muscles ached. He couldn't hold shield, wards, and armor while countering Shemel's curses and flinging counter-curses. Something had to give and he'd be damned if it was Halina's life. Shemel would keep coming, keep fighting, unless Gethen forced him out of Lokshin and obliterated the remnants of his stinking, rotten soul. To do that would take all his power.

He had to make a choice.

He caught Halina's gaze and held it. "Keep your promise and trust me," he shouted.

Her eyes widened. She reached out. Eugen grabbed her arm.

Gethen dropped his shield and armor. He threw their power into the ward protecting her and took the full force of Shemel's incantations.

354

They knocked him off his feet, threw him back like Skiron's blows had and stopped his heart for one, two, three long beats.

Halina's scream echoed in his ears. So did Shemel's triumphant shout. Gethen waited and focused his will on his enemy and his stuttering heart.

Shemel struck him again. Gethen arched, the agony unlike anything he'd ever taken. The abuse sickeningly familiar, the rage it boiled inside him even more nauseating. Still he waited and let Shemel have his fun.

Choking on her own fury, Halina called his name, begged him. "Get up! Fight! You can't die like this!"

Eugen held her back. "No, Your Ladyship! You made a promise. Don't make his sacrifice pointless!"

Shemel cackled like the madman he'd always been and crossed the battlefield. "I told you I would win the war, boy!" he crowed. "Did you forget?"

Gethen gripped the soil.

Shemel reached him and kicked him in the gut. Pain spiked through him. Shemel summoned a dagger of shadows. "Look at me, weakling. I want to see the life leave your eyes when I kill you."

Gethen obeyed. He met Lokshin's dead gaze. He grinned. "Arse licker."

Roots exploded out of the ground and lassoed the possessed emperor, even as Shemel's shadow dagger shattered against Gethen's renewed shield. The roots tightened around the emperor's body, around his chest and throat. They covered his mouth, pinned his arms to his sides and held his legs tight.

Gethen stood slowly, his gut protesting, his muscles burning. He raised his fist and constricted the roots until Lokshin's eyes rolled back and his body went lax. He reached forward and flattened his palm against the emperor's forehead. He found the black iciness of Shemel's soul, hooked it with a spell only Herra

Tomruma could wield, and dragged his former master's malevolent spirit from the body of his victim, leaving the emperor's own soul in place. He released Lokshin from the roots. The man fell to his knees, gasping.

Gethen stared into the inky black vaporous thing that his former master had become and laughed. "You lose," he said, knelt, and carried Shemel across the Voidline and into the Void.

There, Shemel took form, skeletal, bent, rickety. They'd come to the white lake and the tree in the middle.

"This is where you'll remain for eternity," Gethen said. "Enjoy the view."

"I'll escape," Shemel hissed. "Skiron will free me."

"No you won't. And I forbid the god from releasing you."

Gethen chained Shemel's soul to the tree. His living spells were more powerful than anything the God of Death could conjure, unbreakable within the Void or without. "You're imprisoned by Herra Tomruma. You and I both know the gods can't violate the power of the Keeper of the Voidline. They can't interact with the mortal realm. I draw the power of this incantation from all that is living, and it cannot be broken by you or anything else compelled by death and destruction."

Gethen left Shemel up to his chin in white fluid, an eternal struggle to stay above the small waves that rippled across Skiron's featureless lake, the Tree of Death its only unique feature.

He returned to his body and sat up only to be slapped by Halina then pulled into her arms.

"You pillock!" she snarled. "How could you do that to me?"

He rubbed his jaw and held her trembling body tight. "He needed to believe he had the advantage."

"And my terror sold it?"

Gethen shrugged, feeling both contrite and triumphant. "Yes?"

She looked ready to gut him. Instead she kissed him, long and deep, clung to him and said, "Never again, Mage."

He tightened his arms. "No, Militess, never again."

Teleyansk's army retreated to the shoreline and milled about, confused by the chaos and the sudden release of their emperor's body from enslavement. Nalvika's army surrendered on their knees. Thaksin led Ursinum's forces through the ranks, tying hands and taking weapons.

Gethen saw the battlefield for what it was, a killing field. Roots, some as thick as his waist, twined and twisted over and through tents and carts. Dead soldiers lay where they'd fallen, their armor crimson and crushed.

He stood slowly, raised his hands, and bade the forest's fingers to retreat. As they pulled back, the ground shook, the rumbling gaining strength and volume. A terrible crack split the air. Gethen and all around him watched in silent shock as Ranith Citadel crumbled and collapsed, its windows shattering, its dark towers disappearing in a cloud of gray dust.

After the collapse stopped and the ground quieted. Gethen released a long, slow breath and muttered, "Bollocks."

"What happened?" Halina asked.

"The forest's roots go down for miles, finding the cracks in the tor's stone foundation and forcing through. Those roots are stronger than stone and bound the tor together." He sighed. "Destroying the invaders meant sacrificing Ranith's foundation. It was a risk I had to take."

"Oh, Gethen." She touched his cheek. "I'm sorry."

He shrugged. "I'll rebuild."

Eugen nodded. "We all will."

Lokshin stood slowly with his aides' help and said, "Teleyansk will help." He looked around the decimated field and tor. "We came here to restore order. We won't leave until we've helped Quoregna achieve that."

357

THIRTY-TWO

"It's been renamed the Council of Quoregna," Ilker said. He walked with Halina and Gethen through Drevya Linna's West Hall. Voices murmured along the walls and reverberated off the ceiling. The tall doors to the Throne Room loomed, thrown wide to invite Quoregna's peers to the coronation of Nalvika's first queen.

The north's famous dancing lights lit the fall sky, purple and green undulating across the horizon. Color shimmered through the hall's wide windows and reflected on the white marble floors and mirrored walls, the silver inlaid wood and crystal chandeliers. The Nalviks called it a good omen. Halina hoped they were right. The dancing lights were last seen on the night Waldram Boorsook slaughtered his royal family, save one — Princess Federika Janne Boorsook.

A long cerulean carpet replaced the red one that had once led visitors from the throne room's iron-hinged doors to Nalvika's white Skull Throne. The queen's new seat was white birch with a cushion that matched the blue runner. Its back resembled antlers fanning out. Halina thought it an appropriate choice, a nod to the ancient Nalvik stag that posed majestically on the kingdom's banners and stood watch above Drevya Linna's lintels and downspouts. New marble deer guarded the castle's gables, its walls, and its gardens, symbols of strength, nobility, and peace.

The Skull Throne had been anathema to the grace and majesty of the Nalvik Stag, but who was Halina to question the warrior kings of Nalvika? She suppressed a smile. She'd questioned them all right, and then some.

Ilker's hand rested on her arm as she guided her blind brother to their third cousin's coronation. "We've extended invitations to Ayestra and Schorvala to join the Council," he continued.

"Hence the name change," Gethen said. His gaze roamed the hall, assessing each intersecting corridor and every passing servant, lord, and lady. He didn't trust Nalvika's surviving royals to accept their young queen with grace.

Halina didn't share his paranoia. The Nalviks were war weary. They wanted their new queen to thrive and succeed, to return Nalvika to the glory of the First Rule, and bring peace. They had more to worry them than a girl on the throne. The peasantry had been devastated and fields lay fallow. Starvation pinched the bellies of the masses and would spread to the upper classes soon enough. They needed to work with their queen to placate their citizens and find ways of feeding and sheltering all Nalviks through the coming winter. None had the stomach for starting a civil war. Queen Federika was a symbol of change and it behooved everyone to guarantee her rule was a change for the better.

There remained the matter of shrikers. Hundreds still roamed Quoregna, many in Nalvika. Even before the crown rested on her head, Federika had deputized and organized parties of hunters to find and destroy the beasts. She'd boldly thrown off the fears of some wealthy citizens that arming peasants would lead to insurrection. "They've been pressed to fight for the wrong cause for too long," she'd replied. "Let them defend their families and their homes. Let them protect their villages and their kingdom for the right reason. Give them control and they'll give us loyalty. We must regain their trust."

Halina approved. And she didn't miss Eugen's influence in the girl's words and beliefs. He'd been the right choice for regent. He'd served Khara well and earned the right to influence the rebuilding of the northern kingdom. Not all had wanted an Ursinian sitting at the Nalvik queen's right hand, but Halina had pushed hard, arguing that the rest of Quoregna had a right to influence who spoke in the queen's ear and how her policies were shaped. For too long Nalvika was ignored and disaster after disaster resulted. "You don't put out a smoldering fire by throwing fuel on it and turning your back," she'd asserted.

Etherias argued against her when the Council of Kings agreed with Halina, but he had no voice on the council. Quoregna's surviving royals agreed that they had the right to influence Nalvik politics.

"Don't you trust your chosen queen?" he'd sneered.

"She's the last of the Boorsook line," Halina had replied.

"She's your puppet, Red Blade."

"At least she's not a blind fool," Ilker had snapped, putting an end to the debate by adding, "Lady Rhyshis saw the danger when none of us did. I'll take her eyes and words before I'll believe any of yours."

So here they were, entering Drevya Linna's high-ceilinged throne room. The last time Halina saw the vast space, it housed shrikers and death, was painted with blood and gore, the art of a madman. And she'd thought it would be her tomb.

Voices murmured, echoing around the room, quieting as the shifting crowd of lords and ladies noticed Ursinum's blind king, his sister, and her mage husband. Studied with open curiosity and thinly veiled suspicion, Halina didn't blame Gethen's animosity and distrust. Silks whispered and shoes tapped across the marble floor. Jewels of every hue winked from the throats and fingers of Quoregna's rich and powerful. They owed her. And they owed the Sun Mage even more. But they'd never admit it.

She sneered inwardly. *Cowards.*

"What do you think, Halina? Are we making the right choice?"

"About what?" She'd forgotten what Ilker was discussing.

"Changing the Council of Kings to the Council of Quoregna and including more voices."

"Oh, absolutely." She took his hand and helped him sit in the front row. "Ayestra and Schorvala have been silenced for too long and abused as a result. They deserve a seat at that table. So do the Dargani."

She sat beside her brother. Gethen settled on her other side. His hand found hers though his gaze still roamed.

Voices rose around them, a crescendo of words, snatches of conversation, musing about how the looters had taken so many things from the castle, how it was good to have a woman on Nalvika's throne, how they hoped Queen Federika would prove to be wiser than her forefathers.

Eugen left them and strode up the runner. He mounted the steps to the throne and took his place behind its right side.

"There are more changes coming," Ilker murmured in Halina's ear. He was unusually chatty, as if he needed to share information with her before they parted for a long time. He'd become fatalistic after the war, talking about death and the end of things.

Hush spread through the Throne Room as people hurried to their seats and others noticed Eugen, the Lord Regent, standing upon the dais.

"What kind of changes?" she murmured.

"Fundamental."

"What does that mean?" Her voice carried over the quieting crowd and she glowered at her brother.

"I can feel your glare," he whispered.

"Be glad it's not my dagger."

Ilker chuckled. At least he'd found a sense of humor. He'd lacked one for as long as she could remember.

"Who's planting nonsense in your head this time?" she whispered and poked him in the ribs.

He ignored her as a trumpet fanfare announced Princess Federika's arrival. All stood and bowed, except the few kings present.

Dressed in silver and white, Feddie strode up the runner, her head high, eyes focused on the throne, or maybe it was Eugen. He'd coached her for months. She moved with assurance, neither hurried nor dawdling.

Halina nodded. It was a show of confidence and strength. The peers would see past the girl to the queen beneath as Feddie brought out that queen in every step, every gesture, every word and decision. She bore the weight of a kingdom on her shoulders and the eyes of the world on her back. Halina didn't envy the girl. A crown's weight was an endless burden. Every mouth, every life, every choice rested upon it. Once you were the ruler, you ceased ruling over yourself. You belonged to everyone.

She sighed. It wasn't a fair obligation to place in Feddie's small hands. Maybe she should've let the girl exist in anonymity, die a peasant, free to do as she wished with few demands or expectations.

Gethen squeezed her fingers. She returned the pressure. He knew the burden of the crown and then some. He'd long been troubled with the fates of all the world's souls. Not even the kings and queens held the weight he managed.

"This is the right thing," he whispered in her ear.

Halina nodded. It was, but that didn't mean she had to like it or wouldn't regret it.

Eugen stepped forward as Princess Federika knelt one step below the throne. "Who are you and why have you come before Quoregna's peers?" he asked, his voice booming the traditional challenge into the corners of the high-ceilinged room.

"I am Princess Federika Janne Boorsook, only surviving member of the royal Boorsook line and first in line for the throne of Nalvika. I have come to serve my queendom. I have come to protect my subjects. I am here to wear the crown, lift the sword, and lead my peers. I am here to restore peace to Nalvika. I am here to feed her people, give her allies, and defend her against evil and tyranny. I am here to become Nalvika's first queen. I will rule by right and by the will of the people."

Only the first sentence had been the traditional response. Halina smiled and thought, *That's the way to shut them up.* Beside her Gethen nodded. Eugen had done his job well. He'd be a fine regent to the queen of Nalvika.

Heads nodded all around. The nobles murmured approval. She'd stirred their blood in the right way.

Eugen surveyed the gathered peers. "Are there any among us who present a credible claim to the Nalvik throne?"

"No," someone said behind Halina.

"No one," came another reply.

"No!" This more emphatic and taken up by many others until the room thundered with the word.

Eugen raised his hands and silence returned. "Rise and take your throne, Princess Federika Janne Boorsook."

Feddie stood, climbed the final step, turned and sat upon the new throne. She faced the room of peers, her gaze steady, her face stoic.

Eugen uncovered a hulking, age-worn sword and the Nalvik

crown — silver and gold antlers woven together with sapphires and diamonds. They sat upon a table behind the throne. He lifted the sword and placed its edge against Feddie's throat. She didn't blink, didn't flinch.

"Do you swear upon pain of death to lead your people to peace and prosperity?" he asked.

"I swear."

"Do you swear upon pain of death to rule with fairness for all your subjects, rich and poor, nobles and peasants?"

"I swear."

"Do you swear upon pain of death to be the voice and sword of Nalvika from this day forward?"

"I swear."

"Then take the Sword of the Boorsooks to wield as the protector of this queendom and all its people." Eugen placed the sword across Feddie's open palms. She raised it, her arms trembling from its weight. The weapon was longer than she was tall.

A ripple of approval ran through the throne room.

Feddie lowered the sword and rested it across her lap.

Eugen lifted Nalvika's crown and held it over her head. "Princess Federika Janne Boorsook, you are reborn today. Henceforth, you shall be named Queen Federika Janne Nalvik, First Queen of Nalvika. Today the Boorsook line ceases to exist. Today the rule of the Nalvik line begins." He lowered the crown upon her head and stepped back.

Federika stood and all the crowd rose and knelt as Eugen also took a knee and proclaimed, "All hail Queen Federika, First Queen of Nalvika!"

The throne room erupted in chants of "Hail, Queen Nalvika! Hail!"

The new queen faced Eugen. "Eugen Axelos, steward of Khara," she said, "you have been tasked with acting as regent to Nalvika and to its queen, but you are not a Nalvik, not a noble of the queendom's peerage. Do you swear to fulfill the duties of regent, to be true in your guidance, honorable in your actions, and fair in your judgment, even when circumstances place you at odds with your home kingdom?"

Eugen faced Queen Federika. "I swear to be true, honest, and honorable in all things and to help Her Majesty negotiate peaceful and equitable solutions for all parties, whether those involved are dear to me or foreign."

"And do you also swear to step aside and relinquish all power afforded to your position at the time of my twentieth birthday when I will be of age and deemed capable of ruling without a regent's guidance?"

"I swear that I will step aside, Your Majesty."

Feddie nodded. "Then rise and accept your duties as Regent Axelos of Nalvika."

He stood. "Thank you, Your Majesty."

Halina watched Elof fuss with the sleeves of his green tunic.

Sitting opposite her, Gethen eyed his apprentice and said, "Why are you so twitchy?"

They'd been invited to speak privately with Queen Federika after the coronation ceremony and now awaited her arrival in the small parlor behind the throne room.

"It feels funny to be wearing these fancy clothes," the boy replied. "When are we going home?"

He was helping Gethen rebuild Ranith. The tower had housed Gethen, but it had never been *home*. Inherited and haunted, the citadel was cursed in many ways. Its complete destruction was a gift from the gods, Gethen said. Rebuilding was an opportunity to create a haven for Halina and a future for Elof.

She considered them. Her husband looked only slightly more comfortable than his apprentice. It helped that they were away from the crowds of Nalviks with their jumpy gazes, guilt and suspicion, some resentment, and a very small hint of gratitude. Mostly suspicion hit Gethen. Snatches of whispered acrimony had floated around them as he'd moved through the crowd, parting the sea of nobles like a ship breaking ice.

"What's that one doing here?"

"I thought the kings decided no mages could be in the court."

"Someone said he murdered King Vernard."

"I heard it was King Hjalmer and Queen Ektrina he killed."

"He has no business being here. Is he trying to control another kingdom?"

Halina longed to smack the accusations off their lips. Instead, she held his arm and walked beside him, chin up, eyes challenging, hand on the misericord at her waist. *Say those things to my face. I dare you.*

None did. Nalvika bred noble cowards.

"Stop fussing," she snapped at Elof.

Trained to jump at the command in a noble's voice, the boy immediately dropped his hands to his lap and sat straight, face blank, eyes downcast.

She sighed, contrite. "Aren't you at least looking forward to the feast?"

He shot her a puzzled look. "Why would I, Your Ladyship?"

Halina pursed her lips. "Because the food was provided from holdings all over Quoregna. This is your chance to try dishes from as far away as Or-Halee."

Elof's eyes widened. "I'm going to the feast?"

Gethen rolled his eyes. "Of course. You're my apprentice. You need to learn social skills and etiquette."

"What's that?"

"How to eat in a formal setting without looking like you belong at a pig trough," Halina replied.

Elof grinned.

The door opened and Queen Federika entered with her Sword and her Shield — Odruna and Marja wearing ice-blue and white, Nalvika's new colors.

"Feddie!" Elof hopped up and took two steps then stopped and blushed. "I'm sorry. I mean, Your Majesty."

Feddie waved her hand as if to swat away his hesitation. "Bugger that, Elof. I'll always be Feddie to you. Now gimme a hug."

Grinning widely, the boy tackled his friend, almost knocking her off her feet. She was saved by her guards' hands on her shoulders.

She'd lost the stiff, heavy robes of state and moved more easily to sit beside Halina. "How did I do?" she asked.

"Very well, Your Majesty."

Feddie wrinkled her nose. "Are you going to call me that, too? Eugen does and I can't get him to stop. He won't even use Federika."

Eugen said, "Nor will I ever, Your Majesty."

"Would you prefer that we call you Federika?" Gethen asked.

"Feddie," she said. "I want you both to call me Feddie."

"Alright," Halina said, "but not in public. There you'll be Your Majesty."

Gethen added, "We already have enough detractors and suspicions following us."

Feddie's gaze rolled upward and she blew out a long breath. "They're dunderheads. Don't know who to trust and end up trusting the wrong people. They'd better wise up."

"Distrust follows the Sun Mage," Gethen said and shrugged. "I'd be worried if it didn't."

"Why?"

Odruna answered, "Because that would indicate complacency and that's how Quoregna got into this mess to begin with."

Feddie nodded. "True." She screwed up her mouth and brow then turned to Eugen. "Is that why the Council of Quoregna called for a meeting tomorrow?"

"They did?" Halina asked. Eugen made a sound, equal parts swallow and throat clearing and none of it happy. "Ilker mentioned something about changing fundamentals," she said. "What's he talking about?"

Eugen ran his hand over his bald scalp. He glanced at her then straightened and dug into his fathomless well of stoicism. "There are questions about your brother's fitness to rule."

Halina arched a brow. "A bit late to be wondering that."

Gethen's hand found hers. "There's no point in fretting about it tonight."

Eugen nodded. "Lord Rhyshis is correct."

Halina huffed. "Of course. Tonight we're celebrating a new queen and the rebirth of Nalvika. Elof, pour tokay for everyone."

The boy scrambled to obey. He knew when libations were in order to calm the madness that rode on the coattails of power and conflict.

Miraculously, Gethen had produced five casks of his Imperial tokay and he'd brought them to Nalvika for Feddie's celebration. Elof tapped one and they all savored the excellent brew. Liquid joy Halina called it and relished the fine mead on her tongue and the finer man by her side. She put away the skulking politics that kept turning her life into a dung heap.

"What's the queendom's state of affairs?" Gethen asked Eugen.

"Stable, Your Lordship. Steadiness is what Nalvika's surviving nobility crave. They're supportive of retaining a member of the established royal family, even if it's only a twelve-year-old girl. Her Majesty has comported herself admirably and won over quite a few doubters and detractors."

"With my regent's wise guidance," Feddie said.

Eugen bowed his head. "I want peace and prosperity for Nalvika, Your Majesty. That's the only way Quoregna will be harmonious. If we can't all have stability, none of us will."

"No truer words were ever spoken," Halina said and raised her glass to her former steward.

"What of Ursinum and Tatlis?" Feddie asked. "And Ranith? Is it true the citadel was destroyed?"

"Collapsed," Elof said, "but Master Gethen and I are rebuilding it."

"Just the two of you?" Feddie looked impressed.

"Nah, we have helpers."

Eugen asked, "Beseran?" and Halina wasn't certain if he was joking or serious.

Gethen peered up at him from beneath his brow and smirked, apparently deciding the man was funny. "Teleyansk."

Eugen nodded, but the faintest smile lifted his lips. It was good to see her husband and her former steward sharing a joke in their own subtle way.

Eugen touched Feddie's elbow. "We should join the feast, Your Majesty."

She nodded and sighed. "My time won't be my own anymore, will it?" She looked at Halina when she asked it.

"I'm sorry," Halina replied.

"Don't be. This is my father's doing, not yours. You've bled for me and the four kingdoms. Now I must make all that pain and sacrifice mean something. I need to undo some of the damage my father did."

"No, you don't," Halina replied. "Waldram was your father, not your responsibility, Feddie."

"Maybe not," she said, "but I'm making it mine. We all must

wear our scars," she gestured from Halina to herself and added, "some on our skin and some beneath."

Halina nodded. "But the wounds that made them toughen us, just like the scars do. They may feel tight and look ugly, but they make us stronger than we were before."

Feddie stood and held her gaze for a moment. "And they protect the brittle bones beneath." Her face settled into the stoic mask she'd worn for the coronation and she gathered her skirts. Eugen opened the door. The soldiers stationed outside it came to attention, the rattle of their plate and mail echoing across the hall. Laughter and music followed. Feddie lifted her chin and set her shoulders. The crown was safely stored and replaced with a smaller circlet encrusted with blue gems. Queen Federika Janne Nalvik strode serenely to her first celebration as the First Queen. Her regent followed a step behind and on her right shoulder, where he'd always be, an eye on Nalvika's troublemakers, a dagger behind his back for the queen's enemies, and an open palm for her allies. Behind him strode the queen's Sword and her Shield, two very real threats to Feddie's detractors.

"Go on, Elof," Gethen said. "Stay by the queen. Show them you're something and someone to her, no longer an invisible servant."

Elof grinned and scampered after his friend.

As Halina and Gethen trailed them, she murmured, "I will speak with my brother."

"I know you will." He directed her into an empty corridor. "And we'll manage whatever comes of it," he said.

"What's decided can be un-decided," she insisted.

"Not if it's what's best for Quoregna."

"If Ilker is removed from the throne, you know what that'll mean for me. For us." She pressed her palm to his chest. "I'll be queen, Gethen. And you're a mage. The Council won't care if we're husband and wife."

"We'll find a way around them."

"No, I'll make it clear that they can't foist their mistakes on me any longer. The crown will stay with Ilker, whether they like it or not."

"That's a lot of authority to defy."

She shrugged. "They don't scare me."

"Little does, wife. Please pick your battles wisely."

"I do." She cocked her head. "I picked you."

He cupped her face and kissed her. "And I'm grateful."

"Come out of hiding, you two," called a familiar feminine voice from the main hallway. Cerys and Zelal were there with Prince Gerezel.

Gethen pulled Halina with him as he reached for his brother's hand. "How are you healing?"

"Well," King Zelal replied and touched his empty left sleeve. "I'm a bit slower with a shield these days but making up for it with my sword." He flexed his right arm. The devastating wound hadn't slowed Besera's king or tarnished the brightness of his queen's smile as she gazed at him.

Gerezel emerged from behind his mother, one hand in his mouth, one on the hem of her velvet skirt.

Gethen crouched and held out his arms. "Come, nephew. I heard you've a new tooth pushing its way out of your skull. Let me see."

The boy grinned a mostly toothless, very drooly smile and tottered to his uncle.

Gethen swept the princeling up into his arms and kissed his mass of black curls. "I have something to ease those teeth through."

"Will it sooth his pain?" Cerys asked. "He doesn't sleep well." A hint of desperation lifted her voice.

"It will." Gethen passed the child to her and fished a small packet and a sugar spoon from his pocket. He rubbed a bit of amber paste from the packet onto the spoon and handed it to his nephew. Gerezel turned the spoon this way and that, smacked Gethen once on the chin with it, giggled, and shoved it into his mouth. He gummed the spoon, his expression intent.

Halina laughed and wiped her husband's chin. "Hit first, ask questions later. Are you certain he has no Persinna blood in his veins?"

"Regrettably, none whatsoever," Zelal replied and Cerys added, "It would be a fine thing if he did, Lady Rhyshis. I'd happily proclaim the connection to all within earshot."

The next morning, Halina lurked in a narrow hallway behind the throne room. It led to Drevya Linna's council chambers and she was awaiting her brother. Ilker finally emerged from the great hall, accompanied by four guards. She slipped from the shadows and intercepted him. "Ilker, a word."

"Lady Rhyshis, Your Majesty," one of the guards said.

Ilker snapped, "I'm not deaf, Vanix. I recognize my own sister's voice."

"Very good, sire."

Halina captured her brother's hand from Vanix and placed it on her arm. "Bring me into the meeting."

Ilker shook his head. "You know I can't."

"I know you can. As the King's Sword and Eyes, I'm entitled to stand at your shoulder and voice an opinion."

"But—"

"Ilker." Their father had used that reprimanding tone their whole lives.

He sighed. "All right. But the others won't like it."

"Since when have I given two shits for what they like or dislike?"

He laughed and squeezed her arm. "Since never. I'm fortunate to have such a fierce sister."

"Yes, you are." She tugged him toward the door to Queen Federika's council chamber. "Come, Your Majesty, let's show Quoregna's leaders just how much piss and vinegar still flows through the Persinna bloodline."

Ilker fell in step with her. "I think they know."

The soldiers stationed at the door eyed Halina but moved aside, and she and her brother entered the small room.

Silver and gilded, the council chamber's predominant feature was a round table with six chairs. Queen Federika, Arik-bohk, King Danas, King Zelal, and Schorvala's Chancellor, Samik Sklaar, sat around it, chatting and arguing, deciding Quoregna's fate. A handful of advisors and stewards sat nearby or stood at their shoulders, including Amma Xana, whose mouth twisted with wry amusement at the sight of Halina.

"King Ilker, I'm glad you've joined us and brought such laudable company." Feddie gestured at the empty seat to her right. Eugen stood at her shoulder, as always, and his brows rose at the sight of his former margrave guiding her brother.

Silence blanketed the small room as Or-Halee, Besera, Ayestra, and Schorvala noticed the arrival of Ursinum's king and his sister.

"Is the Red Blade your steward, Ilker?" Samik asked, her husky voice pitched carefully neutral.

"Halina is my Sword and my Eyes." He sat beside Feddie. "I trust her with my life, as well as my kingdom."

"That's new," Arik muttered.

Halina squinted at her long-time Or-Haleean friend and ran her finger down her scarred cheek, stopping it against her lips as if to say, "Hush, old man. You owe me."

He rolled his gaze to the ceiling and huffed a breath.

Once Ilker settled into his seat, Halina took up a wide-legged stance behind his chair, glaring at the assemblage.

Feddie rapped her misericord's hilt on the table. "This session of the Council of Quoregna will now come to order." She turned to Arik. "Arik-bohk, you requested this mid-quarter meeting. Please state your reasons."

Or-Halee's king, the elder statesman of all present, slowly surveyed his peers. "Quoregna needs powerful leadership." His gaze finally stopped on Ilker then rose to meet Halina's eyes. "Leaders who won't flinch from conflict, who won't roll over or stick their heads up their arses when the fighting breaks out."

"That's obvious," Danas said.

"That's why I offer a motion to remove Ursinum's crown from King Ilker and bestow the kingdom's rule upon his eldest sister, Princess Halina Avernia Sadiya Persinna Rhysh."

Zelal said, "I second the mo—"

"No!" Halina slammed her fist on the table.

Quoregna's leaders reacted, some jumping in their seats, others considering her with narrowed eyes.

"Bet you didn't see that coming," Ilker joked softly.

"I don't want the crown." She held Arik's gaze. "You know that."

"Then Princess Arevik will be queen," he said with a shrug, as if it was the simplest solution.

Halina straightened and folded her arms. "No, our sister is too young and about to become a mother. Don't shove this council's burden onto her shoulders or mine. You looked the other way while Waldram tore through his own family and kingdom. Ilker ignored my warnings after our prick cousin murdered our father and nearly me. Now Quoregna's gone to shit and you want me to fix it?"

Ilker sighed. "Be realistic, Halina. I'm blind and brainless. I couldn't see the sword coming when I did have eyes. I don't trust myself to fix this mess and neither does the Council. But they believe you can. You're the one the people support. You're the one the army follows. All I'd be is a figurehead and a burden, a body to trip you up."

"Fine. Be that figurehead. And you've yet to trip me. The crown stays on your head, Ilker. You will not yoke me to that burden."

Zelal protested. "But—"

"But nothing," she snapped. "This is Ilker's millstone to carry and the council's mess to clean up."

Ilker shook his head. "Besera and Ursinum burned because of me, Halina. Tens of thousands are dead or suffering because of me." His head lowered. "Our mothers and brother are dead because of me."

She gripped his shoulder. "I'll be here to help; you know I will. But I'm bone weary from fighting because the kings at this table have cocked up Quoregna so damned much."

Arik-bohk said, "You're the leader Ursinum needs, Halina. A strong queen."

"I was seventeen the first time I almost died for the men around this table. I'll never bear a child because of your wars." She rested her hand on the arm of Feddie's chair. "Nalvika's queen lost her entire family because of your apathy." The bones beneath her scars felt very brittle indeed. "Hundreds of innocent children and citizens died because of your inaction. And I struggled for months to end another war you could've prevented." She leaned over the table, her hands flat on its cool surface. "I've done more than enough to fix your cock-ups, Your Majesties. You don't get any more pieces of me."

"This council doesn't require your opinion on the subject, Halina," Arik said. "We command you."

She withdrew a dagger from her left vambrace and slammed it into the center of the table. It rocked to and fro as she leaned toward her old friend and replied, "Do you want to test that, Arik?"

He blinked.

Beside him, Zelal rubbed his own jaw. "I know what this means for you and Gethen."

"No, you don't," she snapped. "Keep your platitudes behind your teeth, Your Majesty. I don't need them because I'm not your slavering attack dog." She straightened, yanked the misericord free, and gripped her brother's shoulder. "I will support my king. I will not supplant him."

Beside her, Queen Federika rapped her hilt on the table. All eyes turned to Nalvika's young ruler. "I move to strike the motion from consideration."

"On what grounds?" Arik said, his voice rumbling with dissatisfaction.

"That replacing Ursinum's ruler with an uncooperative leader will destabilize an already fragile kingdom and threaten Quoregna's nascent peace."

Samik Sklaar rapped her knuckles on the table. "I second the motion."

"Thirded," Amma Xana said from her seat behind Arik.

Feddie tapped the table again. "The motion is carried. King Ilker Ambrose Persinna will remain Ursinum's monarch with the full support of his Sword and Eyes, Militess Halina Persinna Rhysh."

THIRTY-THREE

"Stop," Gethen called from the open second floor of the growing citadel tower. Elof stopped walking inside the enormous, wooden treadwheel they used for raising and lowering loads and set its brake.

"Set, Master Gethen," he called and remained inside the winch, waiting. Gethen pulled the swing arm's rope to bring the next stone block into position only a few inches above Ranith's growing wall. "Bring it down now. Slowly."

"All right." Elof released the brake and walked backwards.

The wheel creaked and the rope groaned then, with a scrape and a squish, the large piece of gray stone settled into place, guided by Gethen. He removed the rope holding it and swung the winch arm free, tossing the guide rope over the wall's edge. While he shoveled mortar into the gaps between the new block and its companion in the wall, Elof set the brake again and scrambled down the wooden scaffolding they'd erected around the growing new tower of Ranith Citadel.

The boy called up from the ground, "Another stone, Master?"

Gethen stood, brushed his hands on his filthy trouzes, and squinted at the lowering sun. "No, I think that's enough for today."

"We made good progress," Elof said as he squinted up at the tower and his master.

"You're a hard worker," Gethen replied and was thanked with a wide grin. "Get cleaned up and stoke the hearth fire."

"There's stew left, and some bread," the boy said and disappeared into the small kitchen that adjoined the tower.

They'd completed the kitchen and great hall with the help of men from Teleyansk — Masorin's lost crew, who'd rowed up the South Selga just in time to miss the final battles. Lokshin had happily left his forces behind to aid in rebuilding what he'd inadvertently helped destroy. Once the kitchen and hall were finished, Gethen had sent the workers to focus their efforts on rebuilding Kharaton Castle and its village. He and Elof had taken on the remaining tower build alone.

His gaze drifted north to the castle being rebuilt. Her ancient oak beams had burned for days. The roofs and floors had collapsed. What remained standing were blackened walls. All the stone had to be disassembled to the foundation.

He shook his head, climbed onto the scaffolding, and descended. His body ached from the hard work, but it was a good ache, the kind that felt like accomplishment. Pausing by the rain barrel beside the kitchen door, he washed his hands and face. His neck felt gritty. So did his mouth and nose. He'd probably snorted half a mountain of dust. He pulled off his filthy tunic and left it hanging beside Elof's on a peg by the door then kicked off his work boots and entered the kitchen.

The boy wore clean clothes and bustled around the hearth. His energy seemed boundless. Gethen didn't remember being so enthusiastic at that age.

He headed into the great hall where he and Elof slept, dined, and lived when they weren't up on the tower or out in the yard mixing mortar, chiseling blocks out of boulders, or planing logs into posts, rails, beams.

"Not enthusiastic," he muttered. No, he'd been apprenticed to Shemel and that had been a misery from sunrise to sunset. Those lessons in barbarism and cruelty weren't ones he'd teach his own apprentice.

Elof was learning construction, farming, beekeeping, and mead making. He was continuing his lessons in magery but only the healing arts. Gethen wouldn't create another necromancer, and certainly not another Voidline Keeper. He paused, looking around the barren hall. There was a confrontation coming and he couldn't put it off much longer.

Tonight, he thought. *If Halina can get away from the court.*

Refusing Skiron another mortal pawn was the right thing to do. Gethen couldn't see it otherwise. The gods had grown distant from their worshipers and that distance fostered indifference — on both sides of the Voidline. Quoegna didn't need gods who relished its people's suffering and failed to alleviate it. The souls of the dead could find new vessels without the gods' dubious help. The One God's worshipers proved the fallacy behind Herra Tomruma. A Keeper was Skiron's luxury, not the mortal realm's necessity.

Gethen shucked his dirty trouzes and pulled on a clean dark-blue pair, added a brown tunic, and warm house boots.

Returning to the kitchen, he found Elof spooning vegetable stew into a bowl from the pot over the hearth. Thick, brown bread already waited on the table with butter and the last of the summer sunfruits.

Gethen uncorked a bottle of mead and poured generously for both of them.

The boy served him first then dished up his own meal. They ate in companionable silence.

Gethen liked Elof, which had surprised him. He hadn't expected to replace Magod so easily, but like his predecessor, the boy spoke only when necessary, was a quick learner, and, perhaps from his years running around with a princess, didn't hold Gethen in too much reverence. He had some piss and vinegar in his veins, though he always cringed when he disagreed with his master. Still, he was smart and usually right to push back, and Gethen wasn't inclined toward punishment. So they got along well and he was happy to pass along his knowledge to Elof, happier still to have someone to help him with the daunting project of rebuilding Ranith. He could've kept the workers on, but with the hall and kitchen finished, they had shelter for the winter. He'd set up his work space in the hall, storage, too. They had everything they required to survive the snowy months.

Truth be told, Gethen didn't want more people around. Their distrust smothered him. Quoregna had judged him lacking and monstrous and no matter what Halina said, no matter how many times she reminded anyone who'd listen that he'd wielded the magic that had saved them from the worst tyrant, it didn't matter. No minds were changed. Suspicion cloaked him, heavy as a wet blanket, suffocating and chill.

He glanced at Elof. He'd tried to discourage the boy from pursuing sorcery, but it was in Elof's blood. Even now Gethen wondered if Lauma had been his mother, not his aunt, and if he might be Elof's father. The faint traces of discoloration forming patchy, swirling patterns on the boy's arms and wrapping his ribcage were a strong indication toward that truth. Still, she'd kept it to herself and the mystery had died with her in a dark village, bled out in the dirt beneath an old, wooden cart. It didn't matter. He'd taken the boy as his apprentice because Elof showed promise as a healer, he had no family and few prospects, and, honestly, Gethen wanted to pass on the better part of his knowledge.

"I'm going to Tatlis after supper. I may be gone for a few days. Work on cutting a few more stones and finish building that next stack of bee boxes while I'm gone."

Elof nodded and chewed. He was accustomed to Gethen's absences.

"If you need anything, take Pedran to the village."

Elof swallowed. "I'll make more candles, too."

"Is there enough wax?" Gethen asked. The boy nodded again, his mouth full of bread. "Good."

After supper, Gethen left his apprentice dipping candles at the hearth. He went into the bailey and stared up at the emerging stars. The sun had set, leaving a purple bruise on the horizon. Stars winked in a clear sky and a quarter moon rose, its weak silver light rippling like diamonds on the Silver Sea.

He should give Halina something sparkling and precious, a ring or a necklace. Not that she lacked precious gems. The Ursinum Crown Jewels had been recovered, anonymously returned in the night after Gethen had let it be known far and wide that he was looking for them, and anyone found in possession of them would have their bowels boiled.

Halina had remarked, "And you wonder why they fear you," when she'd heard about his threat.

He'd shrugged. "It worked."

Halina. He inhaled and could almost smell her — chingis spices and liminth flowers, horses and sweat and just a hint of lust. He smiled. A hint was all he needed. He loved his wife, loved her with every fiber of his being. And he hated sharing her with Ursinum, but he wouldn't give her up, no matter how many dirty looks he received in court. She was his. His wife, his inspiration, his conscience, his soul, his reason for existing.

She made life worth living, worth fighting for and worth dying for.

Besides, no one had the bollocks to challenge her defiance of the law blocking mages from the royal courts. Especially when she reminded the Council of Quoregna that it technically only applied to Nalvika's Boorsook court, which no longer existed.

He smiled. He wished he'd witnessed that meeting. The looks on the kings' faces must have been memorable.

With a gesture and a few ancient words, a swirl of amber magic and gray dust rose and pulled him into the maelstrom of a travel incantation, his destination the vast wooden lodge that had been erected on the grounds of Tatlis Castle, seat of the Persinnas and current home to his wife, Princess Halina Avernia Sadiya Persinna Rhysh, the Red Blade of Or-Halee, Duke of Valmer, Duchess of Rhyshis in absentia.

"Leave us," Halina said as the magic resolved around Gethen. He'd arrived in her sitting room at the rear quarter of Tatlis Lodge. Her tiny apartment was separated from King Ilker's quarters by an antechamber and a door. The temporary home of the Persinna royal family resembled Kenbish's great lodge and Quoregna's past, a time when kings weren't so far removed from their subjects.

Two court ladies sat across from Halina, embroidering and nattering about some nonsense that certainly didn't amuse her, judging by her sour expression. She stood. They didn't move fast enough, and she snapped, "I said get out."

The two women curtsied to her then scurried around Gethen and through an oak door, closing it with a thud behind them. "The King's Sword has a sharp tongue tonight," he said as he circled his wife.

"I've always had a sharp tongue," she replied, "for everyone but you, that is." She reached out and touched him, her fingers brushing down his cheek and jaw to rest on his chest.

She had little patience for the pretense of court life. That irritation only grew as winter approached, castle construction slowed, and cold, dark days brought the courtiers inside and into her path more frequently. Ilker had restored her lands and title and then some, making her the Duke of Valmer and placing all the lands east of the Valmerian Mountains and Lake Selt under her protection. In turn, she'd made Thaksin the steward of Khara and tasked him with rebuilding Kharaton Castle and restoring order to the march. Meanwhile she remained in Tatlis, overseeing the reconstruction of Tatlis Castle and reminding all visiting nobles that King Ilker was by no means vulnerable or alone.

Eventually she would return home to Kharaton, but not until Tatlis was complete and Ilker's advisors proved themselves loyal and reliable. And that would take a decade or more. She trusted no one; her brother perhaps least of all. Meanwhile, Gethen came and went, glowering at any nobles who dared meet his gaze, and whisking his wife away in a flurry of magic as he pleased.

Halina said, "I'm glad you're here."

"Why is that?" He captured her fingers, brought them to his lips, and pressed a kiss to each one.

She smiled, but it didn't quite reach her eyes. Her smiles rarely did these days. "I want to go to Essendra."

"Arevik had her baby?"

She shook her head. "Not that I've heard, but it's due any day now."

"All right. But there's something I need your help with first."

She twined her fingers with his. "The Void?"

383

"It's time I faced those pillocks and put them in their place. If Skiron wants the Voidline secured, he can do it himself."

"Are you scared?"

"Of Skiron? Maybe I should be, but no. He can't harm me, unless I give him that power." He tucked a stray lock of her hair behind her ear. "You taught me that." His fingers brushed back along her scarred cheek. "You reminded me that my power comes from life, not death, the world, not the gods."

"Good," Halina murmured. She turned her face to kiss his palm, then stepped away and shed her kirtle. "I'll guard you." She pulled on trouzes and a tunic then closed her eyes and summoned her blood armor. Once it was in place, she took a position in front of the door, and Gethen knelt on the thick wool rug in the middle of the floor. He closed his eyes and released his soul to cross the Voidline into the featureless, colorless nothing of the Void.

He opened his eyes. He stood at the edge of the milky lake that Skiron called home. In the distance, the Tree of Death still held the skeletal black soul that was the remainder of his former master. He ignored Shemel, who shouted gibbering curses and splashed madly. Instead, Gethen turned away and walked onto a vast plain. Nothing but gray dust stretched for as far as his eyes could see.

"Why have you come?" The voice was simultaneously inside his mind and all around him.

"To inform you that I'm the last Herra Tomruma."

"Really?" Skiron appeared before him, this time wearing Shemel's form.

Gethen waved dismissively. "If you think that will intimidate me, you're mistaken. I'm no longer impressed with you or your power."

Skiron eyed him, an empty gaze that would've had him

quaking in the past. But now he simply returned it and waited to see what the God of Death would do.

"Have we failed you?" This was not Skiron's voice. He turned at the feminine sound and his lips twitched with amusement. Two women stood behind him. One had white hair, bound in a warrior's braids, her clothing a warrior's leather and armor. The other had long black hair. She wore a gown that flowed around her body, its movement compelled by no wind.

Gethen bowed. "What an honor to meet Khotyr and Semele at last," he said. "Do you really need me to answer that question? You know the death and destruction I was ordered to bring. You know my objections to fulfilling those duties. You remained silent and complicit while the world burned and bled just to keep you alive."

Skiron suddenly appeared between his wife and daughter, arms folded across his chest and a black expression on his face. "Your objections are meaningless, Herra Tomruma. Your duty is all that matters. Our survival is all that matters. I told you if you did not fulfill your responsibilities, I would assure they were done by others. You did as you were told, we persist, and your world rebuilds. As for a new Keeper, we know you have taken an apprentice. Why lie to us? Do you think we can't see everything?"

"I don't care if you see it or not." Gethen folded his arms across his chest, mirroring the God of Death. "I'm not your puppet. If you want the Voidline guarded and chaos created, you'll do the dirty work yourselves. I'm finished with you."

Khotyr and Semele exchanged looks while Skiron sneered down at him, growing in size and turning to his demonic appearance. "You dare defy your gods?"

"Yes, I dare because you've only manipulated and lied to me. What kind of gods visit such horrors upon the people who worship them? Monsters, that's what kind. I won't facilitate your cruelty and selfishness any longer. I'm feared and loathed throughout Quoregna, not because I'm a monstrous person, but because I'm the symbol of monstrous gods. But the woman you placed in my path, the woman you thought would fuel my descent into cruelty and madness, did quite the opposite. She showed me that my heart is not black and empty. She reminded me that my magic was a gift from the world, not a gift from the gods."

Skiron snarled and raised his hand as if to strike Gethen a blow that would cleave him in two.

Gethen raised his hand, met the god's angry gaze, and said, "You're not my god."

Skiron's fist passed through him, a breeze that only ruffled his hair. Skiron stumbled. Khotyr and Semele gasped. Gethen stood his ground. The God of Death stared at him, his expression a mixture of astonishment, anger, and resignation.

"I no longer have faith in you. The Void is your domain. The souls within it are your responsibility. Guard the border yourselves." He turned then paused and faced them again. "Perhaps a different approach to existing with the mortal world is something you should contemplate." He smirked and added, "Unless you wish to become no more than superstition, fables, and engravings upon the oldest tombs."

Gethen turned his back on the Triumvirate and closed his eyes.

When he opened them again Halina still stood guard. She pushed away from the door and stretched her shoulders and neck. "I was about to fetch a chair."

"How long was I gone?" he asked as he stood. His back and knees protested with aches and twinges. The world was dark outside the two narrow windows of her chamber.

"Long enough to cramp my arse."

Gethen rubbed his aching shoulders, kneading the muscles

hard. "The King's Sword guarding a lowly mage. What's the world come to?"

"Madness," she replied. She took his hand. "Is it done?"

"Yes." He grinned feeling a tremendous weight lift from his shoulders. "And they couldn't touch me!" He swept her into his arms. "They couldn't touch me."

"You're free." This time her smile lit her whole face.

"Free." He laughed, swung her around, and kissed her until they were both breathless.

Halina's instincts were faster than Essendra's messengers. Arevik's son had been born two days prior. They were ushered into the margravine's bedchamber upon their arrival.

The sun was rising over Essen Citadel and Cerys was already there with Gerezel.

Gethen held out his arms and the sleepy toddler grinned and mirrored the gesture. "Let an evil uncle hug his nephew or I'll turn him into a toad to punish his parents."

Besera's queen laughed and passed her curly-haired son into his arms. Cerys and the crown prince were staying with Arevik and Magod while King Zelal oversaw the reconstruction of Ystwyth. Gethen blew raspberries against the child's cheeks and grinned to hear the boy laugh.

Halina crawled into her sister's bed and gently took her sleeping nephew into her arms. "What did you name him?"

"Halithen Rhian." Arevik squeezed Halina's hand. "We named him after the most important people in our lives."

Gethen smiled. "An honor."

Halina kissed her sister's cheek then gently fingered the boy's wispy chestnut locks. "You know, Halithen may be the first direct descendent of King Vernard not to have flaming red hair."

"But he'll retain the Persinna blue eyes," Gethen remarked. "He'll be handsome and formidable."

"Woe to the women of Ayestra," Cerys said and they all laughed.

Arevik smiled sadly and touched the scar splitting Halina's cheek. "You always bear the brunt of our family's mistakes."

"Nonsense. It makes me look fierce." Halina kissed her sleeping newborn nephew's forehead.

"Like you need any help there," Cerys remarked dryly.

Gethen laughed. His young sister-in-law had a sharp tongue and a sharper wit. He liked hearing her use them. Waldram's War had matured her. That may have been one of the few good things to come out of it.

Halina snuggled the sleeping infant.

Besera's queen said, "Don't let Lord Rhyshis near that child. He'll snatch him away and spoil him with affection. He's terrible that way."

Arevik's brows arched. "Really?"

Cerys laughed. "Oh, yes. Children soften his stone heart faster than sun does ice."

Arevik considered her brother-in-law and smiled sweetly. "I'll remember that when Halithen's fussing. Perhaps you can bewitch him then."

Gethen bowed his head. "I'll do my best, Your Ladyship." He put down Gerezel, who was squirming.

The boy grabbed his mother's skirts and whined, "Hungry."

Cerys picked him up. "Someone needs to break his fast," she said and left to find his nursemaid.

Magod appeared in the doorway, eating a blackapple. "Heard we had guests." He tossed an apple to Gethen. "From the orchard. Taste your handiwork."

Gethen caught it and took a bite. He nodded appreciatively

at its sharp snap and tart sweetness. It was a fine, crisp fruit with a surprising hint of honey and spice. "This is the new cultivar?"

Magod nodded.

Halina remarked, "We came here to admire *your* handiwork, Lord Essendra, not your orchard's."

Magod grinned wide enough to split his face. "Played only the smallest part in creating perfection. All credit belongs to your beautiful sister."

Arevik murmured her thanks.

Magod stuck the apple in his mouth and took his sleeping son from Halina. Settling on the sofa, he studied the babe's small face and quietly ate, his focus on the child's peaceful visage.

"Will you stay for a few days?" Arevik asked Halina and Gethen.

Halina nodded. "Two days, then I have business in Or-Halee."

"Good. I've missed my older sister." Grimacing, Arevik pushed up from her pillows and muttered, "Birthing babies is harder than you think when you're watching dogs and horses do it."

Halina plumped her sister's pillows. "Is there anything I can get you?"

Arevik eyed Gethen. "I don't suppose your husband has something for the lingering pain?"

He nodded. "I can brew a decoction that'll help you and won't affect the baby."

Magod stood and passed his son back to Arevik. "What tools and ingredients do you require?"

"Cramp-bark, yarrow, and motherwort. A clean copper pot and blackapple vinegar."

Arevik sighed. "You're a necromancer with a heart of gold."

He pursed his lips. "I don't know why your midwife didn't leave you with this tincture. It's a basic postpartum medicinal."

"Magod delivered the baby," she replied. "There was no time to summon a midwife."

Halina smirked at Gethen's surprised expression. "Persinna children come fast and furious, husband."

Arevik laughed. "And some never stop being that way, right, sister?"

Halina grinned. "Right."

EPILOGUE

Sun warmed Halina's bare shoulder. She lay in the same bed she and Gethen had first shared, a bed in a rocky chamber far away from Ursinum's struggles and Quoregna's politics.

Laughter and song drifted through the window's open shutters, accompaniment to the sun. A breeze stirred her hair. It brought the aroma of Amma Xana's kitchen fires, smoky and aromatic. Chingis spices and matad blooms drifted with it, a mixture of spicy and sweet. Leather soles slapped stone in the corridor outside their door as people hurriedly went about their day.

Appa Unegan's craggy voice rose from the stone square outside. He was leading his great-great grandchildren in a prayer song, thanking the sun for rising and the night for going to bed. There was a story in it, about jealousy and greed.

This quiet time with her husband was Halina's "business" in Or-Halee. Stealing away from the demands and restrictions of royal life was a monthly ritual they'd begun when she'd moved to Tatlis with Ilker. Sometimes they visited Gurvan-Sum, sometimes Chono Khot or the guest quarters in a loyal earl's castle in Sokos.

Someday they'd have a private bedchamber at Ranith.

Gethen's fingers traced the scars on her shoulder. His body warmed hers, naked and pressed against her from toe to chin, her back to his front. "What's that song?" he asked, as if reading her thoughts.

"It's the story of the sun and its shadow." Her eyes stayed closed. The sun warmed her face. His body against hers spread more heat through her. She smiled. The children's voices and laughter were filled with innocence and sweetness. "Everyone honored the sun, and the night noticed and grew jealous. It grew tired of lurking in the shadows, so it bribed the clouds to cover the sun's face. But that didn't bring the praise the night craved. Instead, fear grew and people remained in their homes and wept. Their crops withered and their cattle died. They cursed the darkness, lit candles and fires to emulate the sun and drive back the night. Finally, the sun grew tired of the night's jealousy. It grew hotter and hotter until the clouds fled its fire and the night's shadows dwindled. The people emerged from their homes, but the sun burned their skin and parched the land. The people cried out for the clouds to return and bring rain before they died of thirst. Realizing their pettiness was the cause of all the suffering, the sun cooled and the night accepted its cycle. The clouds crept back and brought rain. They washed away the misery and life returned."

"Huh," Gethen muttered. "Jealousy underlies a lot of the world's problems."

Halina opened her eyes and rolled over. "I don't want to ponder the world's problems right now."

"What do you want to do?"

"Lie beneath my husband and enjoy his body."

"Then I must find the will to fulfill my wife's demands." Gethen kissed her slowly, his lips caressing hers, his hands gliding over her skin.

A knock rattled their door.

Gethen paused mid-kiss.

"Ignore it," she said and squirmed against him.

The knocking continued and Baichu called, "Open up, layabouts. I've brought food. The morning's almost over."

"Go away," Halina said. She fished blindly over the edge of the bed, found a boot, and threw it at the door. It struck home with a resounding thud.

"What was that?" Baichu demanded.

"A warning," Halina replied as Gethen laughed. "I said, 'Go away.'"

"I will not. I carried this damnable tray all the way up from the kitchen. My shoulder aches and I haven't seen you in three months. Let me in."

Halina climbed from the bed and stalked across the room. She yanked open the door wearing nothing but a black ring and the sun's glory. "No, I'm not finished with my husband."

Baichu's cheeks reddened. She shoved the full tray into Halina's hands, pivoted, and hustled down the hallway. Lady Rhyshis's throaty laughter chased her around the bend.

Halina kicked the door shut and turned with the tray. Gethen sat up as she plunked it on the bed and settled beside him, pulling the sheet over her lap.

His stomach rumbled. She laughed and said, "Baichu did say morning is almost past."

He reached for bread and cheese. She poured bracket into two cups. "I needed the sleep," he said after swallowing. "I still don't sleep well when you're not in my bed."

Halina drained her cup. "Neither do I, but Ranith and Elof

need their master. King Ilker requires his Sword and Eyes. And you still scare the piss out of everyone in Tatlis."

He shrugged. "They'll get over it eventually."

"Well, they'd better hurry. Winter approaches and my bed is cold. My surliness will quadruple if the first snow falls and my husband remains at Ranith, kept at bay by their paranoia."

He dropped the food back on the tray and cupped her cheek. "I treasure every stolen moment with you. If my distance is what it takes to keep Tatlis and Quoregna peaceful, I'll make that sacrifice and accept my sleepless nights. The sun returns to me when you do."

She closed her eyes and turned her head, pressing a kiss to his palm.

"We're together, Halina."

She nodded and met his gaze. "I look for you in all the shadows."

"Sometimes I'm there," he murmured then smirked and added, "watching you undress."

She slapped his shoulder as he laughed. "You still have the morals of a pig's intestines."

"And you love me no less." Laughing, he caught her and pulled her close.

"It's true." Halina shoved her hands into his thick, black hair and held him so she could gaze into his gray eyes. "I love you more than life. You wormed your way under my skin and into the bones beneath."

He kissed her and murmured, "Where I intend to stay 'til the end of my days."

"Keeping me safe from myself?"

"Absolutely." His arms tightened around her. "Because you're nothing but trouble."

She laughed. "Then we're perfectly matched, Mage."

"Indeed we are, Militess. Indeed we are."

THE END

ABOUT THE AUTHOR

Monica Enderle Pierce and her characters have been kicking the crap out of evil since 2012. She writes fantasy and science fiction and her stories are filled with strong women, smart men, love, adventure, and magic. She has an English literature degree from the University of California, Los Angeles, and she lives in Seattle, Washington, with her husband, their daughter, a neurotic dog, and two crazy tomcats. When she's not sending characters into battle or off on an adventure, she's reading minds, seeing through walls, and reveling in the glorious Pacific Northwest rain.

How to reach me:
monicaenderlepierce.com
monicaenderlepierce@gmail.com

ALSO BY MONICA ENDERLE PIERCE

Militess & Mage Series

The Shadow and the Sun

A Castle to Keep

The Bones Beneath

To Give Her Heart (short)

Glass and Iron Series

Girl Under Glass

The Mother Element

A Sad Jar of Atoms (short)

Rust and Ruin (short)

The Apocalyptics Series

Famine

Short Stories

Love Lies Bleeding

Anthologies & Collections

The Dragon Chronicles

Prep For Doom

The Doomsday Chronicles

Once Upon a Time in Gravity City